Praise for
HALL OF SMOKE

"Long's writing is elegantly understated, filling out Hessa's complex world without ever stranding us – we are with her through every stumble and triumph. *Hall of Smoke* is ultimately a book about what it means to have your deepest illusions shattered and still scrape together the courage to begin again. A vivid and compelling debut."
Lucy Holland, author of *Sistersong*

"*Hall of Smoke* is a breath of fresh air. The world is unique, the fights are top-notch, and the cast is unforgettable. A dazzling, fast-paced story with clashing civilizations, squabbling gods, and an indomitable heroine caught in the center of it all, Hessa's is a tale that will grab you from the very first line and won't let you go. I can't wait to see what Long comes up with next."
Genevieve Cornichec, author of *The Witch's Heart*

"Hessa is a brilliantly written heroine, and I could easily have spent another 400 pages with her. The book's world-building is intricate and refreshingly original, and it all ramps up to a finale that is the dictionary definition of epic."
Allison Epstein, author of *A Tip for the Hangman*

"I have rarely read a fantasy novel that transported me like *Hall of Smoke* did. If you are a fan of myths and legends where gods and goddesses roam the earth and meddle with the poor mortals that serve them, you are in for an absolute treat with this book."
M. J. Kuhn, author of *Among Thieves*

Praise for
TEMPLE OF NO GOD

"I am obsessed with what H.M. Long has created—the clear, vivid prose, the captivating mythology, and the absolute force of nature that is Hessa. Utterly enthralling, and a world I loved getting lost in. I can't wait for the next book."
Claire Legrand, *New York Times*-bestselling author of *Furyborn*

"This standalone in the same world starts with a bang and doesn't let up, full of intrigue, betrayal, and action sequences that don't disappoint. Hessa is a heroine to be reckoned with."
Genevieve Gornichec, author of *The Witch's Heart*

"Once again, H.M. Long pulls us effortlessly into a landscape of warring gods, tribes and impulses... I can't wait to see what she does next."
Lucy Holland, author of *Sistersong*

"A poetic yet action-packed exploration of grief, longing, and obligation. Bold characters, shocking twists, and heart-pounding action will keep you turning pages long after lights out."
M. J. Kuhn, author of *Among Thieves*

"This book is a bonfire on a bleak winter night. Exciting and dangerous, brilliantly plotted and paced, this is the perfect followup to *Hall of Smoke*."
Joshua Johnson, author of *The Forever Sea*

"Fantasy readers who like their heroes battle-hardened yet thoughtful and tender – not in spite of war but because of it – will enjoy *Temple of No God*."
Suyi Davies Okungbowa, author of *Son of the Storm*

"A darkly realised world full of rich lore and characters that leap off the page."
Rob Hayes, author of The War Eternal trilogy, the Mortal Techniques series and more

PILLAR
OF
ASH

PILLAR OF ASH

H. M. LONG

TITAN BOOKS

Pillar of Ash
Print edition ISBN: 9781803360041
E-book edition ISBN: 9781803360058

Published by Titan Books
A division of Titan Publishing Group Ltd
144 Southwark Street, London SE1 0UP
www.titanbooks.com

First edition: January 2024
10 9 8 7 6 5 4 3 2 1

This is a work of fiction. All of the characters, organizations, and events
portrayed in this novel are either products of the author's imagination or are
used fictitiously. Any resemblance to actual persons, living or dead (except
for satirical purposes), is entirely coincidental.

A CIP catalogue record for this title is available from the British Library.

Printed and bound by CPI Group (UK) Ltd, Croydon, CR0 4YY

For Cheryl, my dear and infinitely creative friend, map-maker, and co-conspirator

ALGATT, EANGEN, AND THE NORTHERN TERRITORIES OF THE ARPA EMPIRE

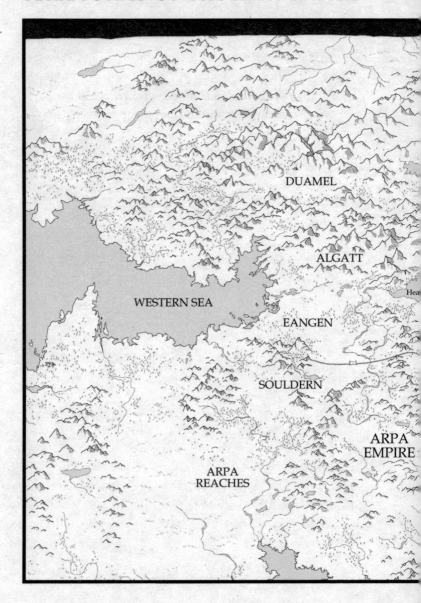

DUAMEL

ALGATT

WESTERN SEA

Hea

EANGEN

SOULDERN

ARPA
EMPIRE

ARPA
REACHES

NTERLANDS

EASTERN SEA

ARIUM

ARPA
REACHES

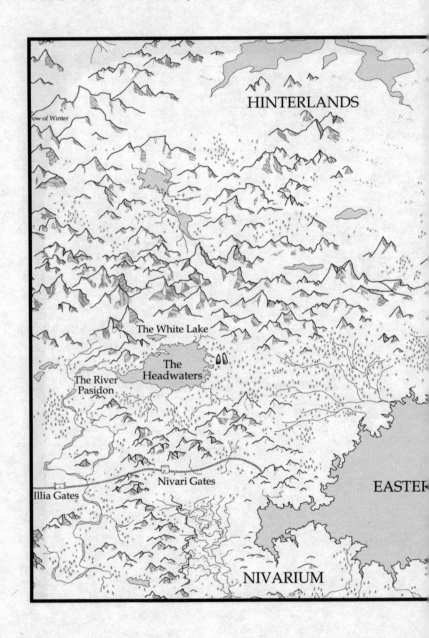

HINTERLANDS

ow-of Winter

The White Lake

The
Headwaters

The River
Pasidon

Nivari Gates

Illia Gates

EASTER

NIVARIUM

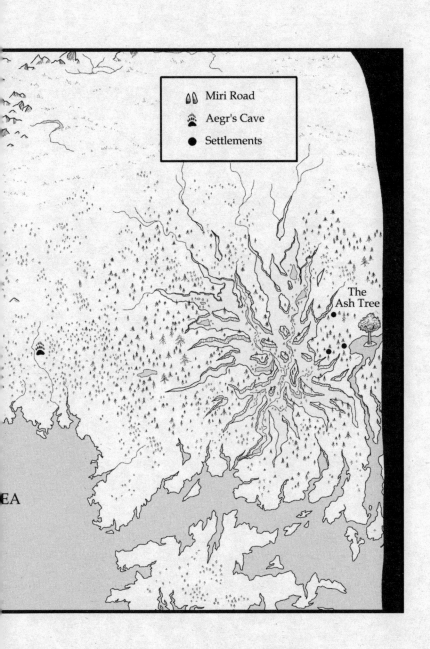

Miri Road

Aegr's Cave

Settlements

The
Ash Tree

EA

ONE

The knife was smooth and cool to the touch: simple, plain, but terribly sharp. Light glinted off the blade as my mother settled my small fingers around the hilt. When I tried to let go, her callused hand held mine in place.

"Do not come out until I call for you," she told me.

The wind picked up around us, heady with pending rain and violence. My gaze flicked past the arc of the shield on my mother's back, through the swaying trees and rustling undergrowth to the empty trail.

"Hessa!" a voice roared through the trees.

My mother clamped a hand over my mouth before I could whimper in fear. She hovered, perfectly still between the boughs of pale green needles.

They were looking for my mother. Whoever was out there in the forest was looking for her, and there was no gentleness, no forgiveness in their voice.

"Those are the Iskiri," my mother murmured, low and warning. "If they catch you, if they realize you're my daughter, they will kill you. Tell them you're Algatt, and pretend not to know me, even if I'm hurt. No matter what they do. Do you understand? Yske?"

I couldn't nod with her hand so firmly over my mouth, but I blinked a frantic, fluttering acknowledgment. Slowly, she let me go. I lifted the knife, clutching it with all the strength of my terror, and nodded.

Noting my clumsy grip, she grimaced and touched my cheek with a gentle hand. "I will teach you how to use that when we get home. Stay here. Stay silent."

I nodded again and she vanished into the forest.

Quiet settled around me. Nothing moved in the fir grove save the wind tugging the boughs and a few stray needles falling into my hair. Tentatively, I shifted to all fours and stared in the direction my mother had gone, but otherwise I did not move. I would be like a rabbit in the garden, I told myself, holding so still the dogs couldn't see me.

I heard a scream. It was a shocked sound, full of pain, but it belonged to a man. I bit my bottom lip and screwed my eyes shut.

Running. An outbreak of shouts and a husky, growling war-cry, fringed with bloodlust and ending in a cracking canine yip. My eyes flashed open as footsteps flitted past my fir grove, light and leaping. Their owner howled, then loosed a manic laugh.

I realized I was shaking, and that made the tremors worse. I sat down hard, dropped the knife, and covered my face. I prayed silently, a clumsy imitation of my mother's prayers—one prayer to Thvynder, god of my people, and another to Aita, the Great Healer, who made all things whole and well. When my prayers ran out I held myself tightly, wishing I was anywhere but here, and at the same time longing to be at my mother's side. At least if I could see her, I'd know she was alive.

It began to rain, hard and swift and cold. The trees swayed and the sky darkened, leaving me in a bewitching twilight. I squinted against the droplets and bowed my head, my misery and fear reaching a breaking point.

I didn't make a conscious decision to leave the grove, but my next clear memory was of hovering at its edge, watching a warrior with a blood-streaked face throw my mother against a tree. Her head cracked off a root. She rolled and tried to push up onto her hands and knees, but her whole body shuddered. Her head lolled, eyes blinking, squinting. Fluttering shut. Her axe lay on the forest floor, glistening in the rain, and a long knife toppled from her fumbling hand.

The rain did nothing to wash the blood from her attacker's face— multiple gashes bled freely, and as he snarled at my mother, I saw his teeth were filed to vicious points.

An Iskiri Devoted. I'd heard the stories many times in my eight years. Though the adults tried to protect us from the worst of those tales, other children gleefully whispered the details between themselves. Iskiri Devoted still served Eang, the Goddess of War, even though she was dead and hadn't really been a goddess at all but a Miri—a powerful being, almost immortal.

The Iskiri Devoted reveled in killing the priests and priestesses of new gods in the most brutal, bloody, and painful ways. But my mother wasn't just a priestess. She was the High Priestess.

She had killed Eang.

The Iskiri tore a hatchet embedded in a nearby tree and threw himself at my mother. My mother, already on the ground. My mother, who protected others, protected me. Loved me.

My fear flickered like a candle in the wind. That wind was a battering, righteous indignation, a refusal to accept the reality of the moment and the truth of what was to come. Then there was no thought in me, only rage that burst through my veins—hot, blinding and feral.

I shrieked. I threw myself from the trees and onto the Iskiri's back. My fingers clawed his face, his throat. They pried into his eyes.

He threw me to the earth and spun on me, spitting blood and roaring like a wounded bear. I rolled right back onto my hands and knees and weathered the force of his fury.

My mother's knife was in my hands. I darted forward and stabbed at his calf, down to the bone. The man stumbled and I went after him, still unthinking, carried on a wave of hate and the need to destroy the cause of my fear and my mother's pain. Another stab, this one to the thigh. He tried to grab me by the hair; I dodged and hacked at his ankle.

But rage couldn't change the fact that I was a child, and particularly small for my age. Another lunge—the Iskiri plucked me from the ground and threw me like a doll. I smashed back into the stand of firs, branches cracking and bending, tufts of needles painting blood across my skin.

I hit the ground and did not move again. I couldn't. The anger that had fueled me sputtered with the erratic beat of my heart. All I could do was stare through tear-filled eyes as the Iskiri picked up my mother's axe and advanced on her again.

I opened my mouth to scream, to try and save her with my tiny, torn voice. But Hessa moved. Wielding a fallen branch like a spear she staggered to her feet, smashed the axe aside and snapped the other end into the man's face. His head cracked back and she pressed—beating him again and again in the head, face and shoulders until he collapsed, choking on blood and shattered teeth.

My mother did not stop. She kicked him onto his back and straddled him, branch braced across his throat. He clawed and beat at her, but she was impervious—she didn't break his gaze until his hands fell limp and his fingers, creased with mud and blood, twitched on the sodden bed of needles.

Hessa unfolded slowly and stepped away from the corpse. Chest heaving, she spat blood and retrieved her axe, holding it loosely in both hands.

A new kind of dread gripped me then, twining through remnants of my ferocity and an incomprehension of what I'd done. That dread wasn't directed toward the blood on my lips, or worry that my mother was badly injured. It wasn't even because of the body, lying face-up in the rain. No, this new alarm came from the expression on my mother's face—cold, remorseless, and weary.

If my rage had been a fire, hers was a deep, drowning sea.

She saw me and her expression faltered. I didn't know if she'd seen everything I'd done, but I saw regret flicker through her eyes, the promise of a difficult truth. Then she brushed a tired hand over her face, slicking away blood and rain and black hair caked with dirt.

"Are you hurt?" she asked, composed now, her expression guarded.

I looked down at myself. I ached and was covered with cuts, but those pains were distant. "No," I said simply.

"Then stay there. Wait for me." She vanished into the trees again.

I stayed this time. I couldn't have moved if I'd wanted to, for as I sat beneath the fir boughs and watched rain drip on the face of the dead Iskiri, something within me fractured.

The days passed and we completed our journey to the northern settlement of Orthskar, but nothing my mother said or did could mend me. When I looked at her, I saw the cold weariness in her eyes, bloody rain on her cheeks, and how she'd held the Iskiri's gaze as she killed him. I remembered the heat in my blood, how I'd thrown myself on her attacker, and how I'd *wanted* to cause him pain.

It was my first true understanding of myself—of the potential for violence inside me, the nature of survival, and the fear that girded it on all sides.

My father and brother met us in Orthskar's great hall, full of light and warmth and laughter. I recalled little of the meeting, after—only that my father held me for a very long time, and my brother pestered me with questions about the attack. I didn't answer.

When the four of us retreated into a curtained chamber off the main hall, I noticed my mother limping. My brother fell asleep swiftly. My parents spoke for some time, then my father, too, grew still. From my pallet, I watched my mother massage her leg, wincing with each movement.

"Does it hurt?" I whispered.

Startled, she looked over at me and smiled consolingly. "Yes, but this one is an old wound, my love. It will stop hurting again, with rest."

"I wish I could make you better," I murmured.

Her face softened. "I wish that, too."

"Aita could heal you," I suggested with a child's innocent practicality.

Mother's smile slipped into the corner of her mouth. "Yes, I suppose she could. But Aita is a Miri, and I've no wish to owe her any more favors than I already do."

Miri. Eang had been a Miri too, before my mother killed her.

Memories of blood and violence swelled toward me again and I felt my muscles tighten, my tongue thicken in my mouth. Would I kill people someday? Would I hold their eyes as I choked the life from them, like my mother had?

My mother saw the change in me. She shifted closer, breaking me from my spiral, and brushed my blonde hair behind my ears—blonde like my Algatt father, not like her Eangen forebears. My mother and I looked little alike. "You did well, Yske. You're brave. So brave. I'll teach you how to properly protect yourself, and until you can, I'll always be there to guard you. What happened with the Iskiri will not happen again."

"No," I croaked.

My mother's brows drew together. "I will be there," she assured me, misunderstanding my protest.

"No," I repeated, more forcefully. "I don't want to hurt anyone."

"Want means nothing." She pulled back, her expression grave.

"I don't want to fight." I could feel myself starting to shake again and I tried to whisper, but I saw my father stir.

"That doesn't matter. Every child must learn how to protect themselves. Especially mine—you know that." She spoke firmly, but not unkindly. "You'll learn to do what you have to, just like I did."

"I don't want to be like you."

Silence dropped between us like a boulder into a stream. My mother's face blanked, but not before I saw a shot of hurt and indignation pass behind her dark eyes.

"I want to make people better," I said in a rush. "I want to be like Aita. Or Liv, who healed the Great Bear."

My mother eased back onto her pallet without a word.

"Mama," I leaned after her, desperate for her to understand. "I—"

"Go to sleep, child," she told me, her voice level and devoid of emotion. "Just… go to sleep."

Quiet regained its hold over our small chamber, but I could not rest. I tossed and turned, tugged my blankets, and covered my head.

A long time passed before I heard movement again. My father lay down beside me. He pulled me against his chest, sheltering me in the strength of his arms, and murmured into my hair.

"If you want to be like Aita, I'm sure she will be flattered," he said. "I'll speak to her."

I twisted to look up at his face, but all I found was scratchy beard. I wriggled away and peered at him through the darkness. "About me?"

"Yes," my father said decisively. "I know her very well. Would you like that? To learn from her?"

I felt a shock of hope and pure, childish excitement. But then I remembered my mother and how my words had hurt her, and my face fell. "Mama will be angry."

"Your mother wants you to be safe and happy," he told me, tugging me back into his chest. "She lives to protect you and everyone around her. She expects the same of you. But there is more than one way to protect. Berin will be a warrior. When he's injured, who will heal him? When he's being silly and reckless, who will protect him from himself?"

"I will," I said immediately, because this had always been my task. Now, though, the idea took new life in my mind, etching out a future not soaked in blood, but marked with solace and making broken things whole.

"Then tomorrow, I will speak to your mother," Father promised. "And after that, I will take you to the High Halls to meet the Great Healer."

TWO

There is always smoke in the Hall of the Gods. It drifts up from the ever-burning hearth, within the circle of thrones where the Miri once presided and gave the hall its name. It wafts between the carved pillars, where intricate runes merge with scenes from history and myth beneath garlands of holly. Sometimes the smoke is dense. Others, it lingers only in the corner of my vision. It does not harm the lungs, but it tricks the eye, here showing a previously unknown door, there concealing a path one has trodden a hundred times. And it rises from the bowls where Aita, the Great Healer, labors.

I stood at her side, watching as she crushed leaves between her hands and dropped them into a shallow iron bowl. Her simple gown was the palest green, bound above each broad hip with a trailing, braided belt. Her loose hair was wrapped in cloth that draped down her spine, and her face was beautiful and ageless, as only a Miri could be. If I'd been born in my mother's generation, I would have called her a goddess. Instead, I called her mistress—my mentor, my guardian, and my shelter from the blood and death of the Waking World.

The leaves were swallowed by clear, hot oil, and their bitter scent merged with that of the hall—smoke-laden cedar, beeswax, and lavender. It had been years since my mentorship under Aita ended, but I still knew the scent of each leaf, root, oil, and powder. I knew their properties and uses, their dangers and benefits, where they came from and how to prepare them. And I knew that, together, this particular creation could cure the deadliest fever.

Aita watched the leaves dampen and curl, and when a fresh tendril of smoke coiled from the surface of the oil, she lifted the bowl from its small brazier and turned to me. I set out a clay jar, its black glaze smooth and cool against my fingers, and she poured the mixture inside. We moved with thoughtless efficiency, a partnership honed by years. I needed no words to prompt me, just the barest glance, the lightest hum.

That silent competency, rather than satisfy me as it once did, now filled me with an aching nostalgia.

As the last drop fell and the clay warmed beneath my hand, I slipped waxed cloth over the top, wound it tightly with string, and set the little vessel aside as quietly as possible, reluctant to break the stillness. A soft tap of clay on wood. The shush of my sleeve. The brush of my fingers as I laced them over my soft belly.

"It is unwise for the living to linger in the High Halls of the Dead," a voice reverberated through the pillars, scattering smoke into eddies around a man in layered southern robes—burnt sumac red over earthen brown, embroidered with gold and white. His skin was pale as summer clouds and seemed to shift under my gaze, but his eyes were his most arresting feature: a deep bloody copper that once, my mother told me, had been the gentlest blue. "Go home, Yske."

As blunt as his command was, he delivered it with distraction rather than ire. He wasn't wrong. If the priesthood knew I still visited the High Halls as often as I did, they'd have said the same.

"Estavius." I gave a short bow and reached for my satchel, hanging from a peg on the nearest pillar. It was heavy, already full to bursting with the herbs and salves and tonics I'd come to gather from Aita's stores. I turned to conceal its weight, hoping the newcomer would not notice.

"What is it?" Aita tipped her head to one side, measuring the man as he approached. They both spoke in the Divine Tongue, the language of the Miri and the High Halls—a tongue no human could master, but which was universally understood.

Estavius, Miri and Emperor to the Arpa Empire in the south, remained quiet. I pulled the strap of the satchel over my head and settled it between my breasts, the hush thickening around me.

When Estavius had ascended to the throne of the Arpa Empire, drinking the blood of a true god and becoming that deity's vessel, the price had been simple—his heart. Where affection, love, and all the complexities of emotion once occupied his pale blue eyes, now there was only that sharp copper glow.

His eyes followed me now. Whatever had brought him here, he clearly had no intention of discussing it with me present.

I felt a flutter of irritation, but it had no teeth. I'd spent enough time in these Halls to know there was little point in openly resisting when the Miri decided to hide things from me. When I was a child, the secrets told in my hearing had been myriad. But now that I was a woman, keen-eyed and possessed of magics I shouldn't wield, the Miri were more inclined to guard their words.

I gave Aita and Estavius a lean smile and bowed. "Mistress, Lord."

The healer ducked her chin in farewell. "Bring me that sweet tear, whenever you may."

I nodded and, casting Estavius one last appraising glance, slipped off through the carved pillars.

The distance to the main doors was not what it should have been; to my eye, it was well over a dozen paces away, but the Hall brought me to it in little more than five. The Miri wanted me out, and the Hall, intrinsically bound to them, obeyed.

I pulled one of the great rings on the door, opening it just enough to slip into a cool summer night of churring insects and salt-laden breeze.

Before I pushed the door closed, I paused. I might be used to the Miri guarding their words, but that didn't mean I wasn't curious. Wood cool against my cheek and skirt brushing the dew-damp grasses, I put an ear to the crack between the doors and listened.

"...beyond the edge of the world, north of the rising sun," Estavius's voice confided. His words were quiet, but my senses had always been unexpectedly strong. "Movement, in the Unmade."

"A shadow in darkness?" Aita laughed and the direction of her voice shifted, as if she'd turned back to her work. "Human eyes are faulty. You place too much trust in your people."

Beneath my ear, the doors of the Hall of the Gods closed themselves with a soft, chiding tap. I stood back and stared up at them, every inch of the wood laden with knotwork and runes. Above them the steep roof of the hall swept out, the end of each beam carved in the likeness of animals and monsters, both of this world and the Waking one.

One of the creatures, a slit-eyed lynx, seemed to glower down at me for a moment, then returned her gaze to the looming sky. Sporadic stars trailed from horizon to horizon under her cool regard, the divided realms of the broadly termed High Halls united in a rare, uniform night.

I let out a shallow breath. *The edge of the world. North of the rising sun. The Unmade.* These were terms I'd heard the Miri use before, usually when they thought my child's mind immersed in bundling plants or grinding seeds in a mortar. In creation there existed the two realms of the Made: the High Halls, where the Miri and the souls of human dead resided, and the Waking World, where humans lived and the Miri meddled.

But there were edges to the Made, and beyond them was the Unmade. I knew no one who had seen that emptiness, nor anyone who had seen the place where the sun was born, each morning, at its edge. Yet it seemed that Estavius's people, the Arpa, had finally reached the boundary. And it had not been what they expected.

The thought was perturbing in a weightless, disconnected way. If I'd learned anything from my time in the High Halls, it was that the world was vast, and I was both small and irrelevant. I might turn an inquisitive ear to the Miri's conversations, but the secrets I gathered were pretty stones in a child's pocket. Novelties. Irrelevancies. What took place beyond the edges of creation was not my concern. What took place beyond the borders of my own village was not my concern.

Nor did I want it to be.

But then I saw the owls fly. They swept out from the slits of the hall's high windows, carrying messages to the north, south, east, and west, and my curiosity turned to a burning need.

Aita and Estavius were summoning the Miri to counsel.

I waited silently, in the shadow of the forest at the base of the hill, as time stretched. At last, runes pulsed in the night. Each heralded the arrival of another figure or two, stepping seemingly from nowhere in hazes of runelight. It was too dark to make out the identities of most, but the last one was undoubtedly my mother, small and muscular, striding through the door of the hall in a mist of lingering amber magic. The hall's double doors closed behind her with finality.

I hid my satchel in a tree and, gathering my skirts, slipped back up the hill.

By the time I convinced a side door to let me back inside—one carved with the face of a suspicious bear, who yielded to my pleading only after I sang him a whispered song—the council was deep in conversation. Voices drifted through the holly-wrapped pillars and the Hall's usual smoke had lightened, streaming only up from the distant hearth. There, firelight cast a circle of old thrones into varied silhouettes.

I closed the door with the barest breath of wind and brush of fabric, then moved into the shadow of a pillar.

"…myself," a deep female voice said from one of the thrones. Esach. She was the Miri who wove summer storms and birthed the yearly harvest. I saw her from the side, the slight curve of her pregnant belly visible above the arm of her chair. Her gray hair wound in a twist over one shoulder, stray hairs ignited by firelight. "Fate has said nothing of it."

"Perhaps whatever these Arpa merchants saw is already gone," Aita's calm voice put forward.

"They saw nothing," a male voice scoffed. I couldn't see him—he lounged in a throne with its back to me, one booted foot dangling over an arm of the chair. A burly shoulder and elbow protruded from the opposite side. This was undoubtedly Gadr, former god of the Algatt and Esach's temperamental lover.

I glanced around for their eldest son, but didn't see him yet.

Gadr went on, "There is nothing and can be nothing in the Unmade. It's *Unmade*. Why are you wasting my time?"

"Because what they saw may not be nothing," another younger man replied, tempering him. He stood beside the fire, clad in a tunic of gray and blue herringbone weave. This was Vistic, one of two physical representations of our true god, Thvynder. He was also my cousin, by bond if not by blood.

"Just because the Arpa are human does not mean they are foolhardy," Vistic reasoned, his golden eyes calm. His hair, dark and curling, was knotted at the back of his head.

The robed form of Estavius spoke from the other side of the circle, half visible through the rising hearthsmoke. "Agreed. They would not have come to me unless they were convinced what they saw was real."

An unfamiliar figure shifted, and my heart leapt into my throat. Her hair was white and her skin pale, her body clad in a light kaftan and her feet wrapped in shoes of pale leather. She was a Winterborn, from a half-Miri tribe in the far north, and she looked so like another of my cousins—there were few in this world to whom I could not trace some relation—that my heart ached. But Thray was still in exile.

"I've sent Windwalkers to the edge of the world in the far north," the Winterborn revealed. "They've yet to return."

"Fate has given no sign of a new threat in the mortal world," Esach put forward again.

Gadr threw in, "Go to her yourselves if you're unconvinced."

"I intend to," Estavius murmured. His patience for the meeting already seemed thin.

"Then that's good enough for me." Gadr's leg and shoulder vanished as he sat up straight. "Also, I feel I should point this out—Hessa's daughter is skulking over there. Is no one going to do anything about

27

that? Aita, if you're going to keep your pets in common spaces, you really need to take responsibility for them."

Every head turned and I pinned my spine to the pillar, biting the inside of my lips.

"Yske?" my mother's voice called from a shadowed throne.

I felt my cheeks flush. Steeling myself, I stepped out from behind the pillar and strode toward the circle.

No one stopped me as I drew up next to Aita's throne. Now that I had a clear view, I saw there were five Miri or half-Miri present: Aita, Esach, Gadr, Estavius, and the Winterborn woman. Then there was Vistic, standing by the fire. He couldn't be rightly called a Miri—he had been born to mortal parents and was mortal himself, though he carried a vestige of our god within him.

Another young man lingered at the edge of the circle, previously hidden from sight by Esach's throne. Isik, one of her sons by Gadr. He stood quietly at his mother's left, their resemblance clear in their wide-set eyes and calm posture. He was trying not to laugh at my embarrassment, his eyes crinkling and his chin raised as he suppressed a grin. The corner of my mouth tugged in response, despite my burning cheeks.

The last guest was my mother. She sat in the throne that had once belonged to Eang, her black braid heavy over one shoulder. She wore a simple slate-gray tunic and belt, hung with a hooded axe at one hip and a long knife, horizontal across the opposite thigh. Her face was young for her age, despite a few threads of graying hair—a gift, Aita had confided in me, from the forbidden honey and water of the High Halls. But I could still see every one of her hard years in the depths of her earthen brown eyes, flecked with gold.

She raised her brows at me. The high back of the chair framed her like a crown, its knotwork carved in the memory of blade-sharp feathers and an owl's watching eyes. "Daughter. Skulking?"

I smiled wanly. At least she didn't seem angry with me. I might be twenty-one, but my mother's disapproval still made my stomach curdle. "I was visiting Aita."

Aita made a faintly amused noise, though it was so soft, I wasn't sure anyone else heard.

Hessa watched me for another moment, then glanced back at the others. "What have we decided, then?"

"We do nothing, as my mother said," Isik put forward. The amusement had faded from his eyes. In this meeting, he was not just my friend; he was a Miri, and heir to the powers and responsibilities of his parents.

Isik turned to Vistic. "If Windwalkers have already gone to check the northern borders, I suggest we wait to see what they find. Then we can reconvene and reassess."

I felt my mother studying me and pulled my eyes from Esach's son.

Vistic glanced around the circle and caught Estavius's attention. The other man nodded, though barely, and Vistic concluded, "Very well. We wait."

After a few more closing pleasantries, the assembly dispersed. Gadr crooked a farewell smile at his son and sauntered off toward the doors. The Winterborn and Vistic departed too, the latter leaving a kiss on my mother's cheek before he followed Gadr out into the cricket-heavy hush of the night. Esach and Isik, however, fell into discussion and remained among the thrones as Aita and Estavius drifted away, wrapped in their own low conversation.

My mother put a hand on my back and prodded me out of the circle.

"I didn't mean to intrude," I said as we found a quiet spot among the pillars. "I only thought to visit Aita."

"There was nothing to intrude on—just Arpa murmurings of strange sights in the east, but I'm sure you gathered that." We were of a height and when my mother leaned in to speak in my ear, our foreheads brushed. "Have you spoken to your brother recently?"

"No." I glanced surreptitiously back toward the thrones. Esach and her son had begun to leave, and I suppressed an urge to call to my friend. "Why?"

"You should." Hessa sighed and followed my gaze, but she didn't seem to see the other pair. "I'll let him explain."

"Is something wrong?"

"Only that he's a grown man and his choices are his own, and I can no longer stop him from doing as he pleases." My mother paused, then took my arm in a gentle hold. "Speak some sense into him? Though please, tell him nothing of today. Speak of it to no one at all. This is a matter for the council, and there's no need to stir unrest."

I stilled, studying her face. "Of course," I vowed. "Though I wish you'd tell me what's wrong with Berin."

"He has one of his schemes, that's all." My mother gave me a tight smile and gestured off in the direction Aita had gone. "You came to speak to Aita, I won't keep you any longer. Goodnight, Yske."

THREE

I waited until my mother was gone, then traced her footsteps outside. The sea breeze stirred my hair and skirts as I descended the hill, thick with the scent of salt. In the Waking World, this was the western coast of Eangen, the land of my birth—two weeks' travel from home. But here in the High Halls, space and time were unpredictable forces. Day and night came without rhythm, and each quadrant of the sky might show a different time and season at once. A walk that one day took me an hour might pass in a handful of breaths the next, while a path I'd trodden for a dozen years might vanish overnight and never return. It was part of the magic of the High Halls, an overflow of the innate power that resided here in every leaf, every gust of wind, and every drop of water.

Head full of thoughts of Miri and the Unmade and my wayward brother, I retrieved my satchel.

"Yske," a voice called.

Isik hastened down the slope toward me, the slit sides of his knee-length tunic fluttering in a gust of wind. His deep-brown hair was black in the night, escaping its simple braid at the nape of his neck, and his beard was shorter than any Eangen man would keep it.

An answering smile spread across my lips. I glanced around, ensuring we were alone before I spoke. "Where's your mother?"

"Gone with Gadr," he replied. A large knife, nearly a short sword, hung horizontally across his thigh, and he touched the hilt as he approached—not in threat, but in pride.

"You don't have to carry that just for me," I chided.

"I carry it because I like it." Isik held out his hands in prompting and I stepped into his embrace, lacing my arms around his back as he barreled me close, his broad arms familiar and tight. "And it's still new. You know me... I enjoy new things."

"Mm," I replied happily, voice muffled by his shoulder.

"Though," he said over my head, "your father did remark on it recently. Who told him?"

I gave a grunting laugh. "Likely my mother. But she knows it's a gesture of friendship."

Isik shifted to hold me away from him, eyeing me critically.

I grinned, hard pressed to mute the affection in my eyes. Isik and I had dallied together when we were little more than children, my waist barely narrowed and his beard not yet grown. Those few years had been sweet, full of new experiences, laughter, and awkward exploration, all charged with the intensity and short-sightedness of youth. Their end had come gradually—a natural gentling of feeling as we aged and settled into our places in the world.

He was the son of two Miri, the first fullblood of their kind in a century. I was the daughter of the High Priestess and High Priest of our god—human, though with a little more magic in my veins than usual. In romance, we realized we were a match that could not last. In friendship, we remained forever bound.

I stepped back and glanced at the star-scattered sky, then south toward home over a spread of forest and the long, rocky shore of the sea. "I should go. It's been at least a day and a night since I left, and I shouldn't be here anymore without cause. My mother was distracted enough not to question me just now, but..."

Isik glanced at my heavy satchel. "That's not a cause?"

"No one can know about this, still," I reminded him in a low voice. The night was quiet and we seemed to be alone, but there were any number of creatures, seen and unseen, that might listen from the shadows—not least, the human dead.

Some of my friend's mirth ebbed. "Then stop taking the risk."

"There's no risk, not usually," I corrected. "I keep Aita's secrets, and she keeps mine. I trust you to do the same."

"Always," he returned with his habitual, tireless sincerity. But I saw the hesitation in his eyes. He glanced up the hill behind me toward the Hall of the Gods, then seemed to come to a decision. "Come spend the night in my hall. You're tired, and I'm sure you're hungry too. I haven't seen you in months."

The offer was tempting, particularly after all I'd heard tonight. My head was full, and there was no one more suited to discuss the council with than Isik. I wouldn't be descending the mountain tonight to talk with my brother, as my mother had requested. And Isik was right—we hadn't had an opportunity to talk for more than a few moments since winter, when a snowstorm had trapped me in my mountainside home and he'd come to keep me company.

"All right," I consented. "So long as your siblings aren't home?"

"Only Thvynder knows where they are." He offered me a hand, the other already tossing three runes into the air. They were different than Eangen ones, a blockier, older order I recognized but didn't know well.

The High Halls shifted at his command and a new path opened before our feet. The moon-bathed coast faded into a veil of fog as Isik strode forward. I trailed behind, and the fabric of the world folded in around us.

I'd only time to draw one breath before the landscape resettled into low mountains and open plains, divided by dozens of rivers and scattered woodland and wetland.

We stood partway up a mountain, near a longhouse with a single large door. The ridge of its thatched roof was carefully shaped, with a second layer of dried reed cut like arrowheads and pinned by intricate designs of woven willow.

Isik released my hand and preceded me through the door. A wash of warm firelight spilled across the worn earthen path between goat-shorn grasses, and I entered the house of Esach.

The familiar scent of smoke, pine resin, and beeswax surrounded us, joining that of roasting meat. Doorways at the back of the structure marked sleeping places, but there was no one else in sight. Three looms sat quiet, tucked along one wall, and baskets of carefully spun wool clustered around empty stools. A leg of deer hung from a hook over the fire, and as we entered a drop of fat made the fire spark.

Just as Isik had used runes to manipulate the distance between the Hall of the Gods and this place, his mother used runes to suspend her hall in time—a perpetual place of warmth, retreat, and plenty.

Isik took off his weapons belt and rolled it around his knife, setting it on a side table. "If any of my siblings do come home, it will be late. Until then you can eat and drink without fear."

I nodded and deposited my satchel on the table beside him. Eating and drinking in the High Halls was forbidden to living mortals like me. Common wisdom said it would kill us. But as the Miri and the High Priesthood had discovered long ago, it did quite the opposite—it blessed and changed, granting unpredictable power and, occasionally, long life. I'd learned of the effects of the High Hall's spoils in the same way I learned many other things—Aita's secrets, gifted to me with a wink, or stolen when I overheard something I should not.

In my case, eating and drinking in this realm had made my Sight particularly keen and allowed me to use runes with remarkable proficiency. It remained to be seen whether the length of my days would benefit or not.

I gazed at Isik's back as he nudged an iron pot from the coals of the fire. The disparity between our lifetimes had been a key factor in ending our romance, and though I was content with our friendship as it was, that did not stop old memories and possibilities from rearing up—every so often, in the closeness and quiet, and the privacy of moments like this.

Isik shoved a large wooden spoon into the pot, revealing a mixture of cooked grains and vegetables. I pulled bowls from a shelf on the wall and filled them for us while he cut thick slabs of venison, spearing them onto a shared plate on a nearby table.

We ate quietly for a time—I was too hungry to do much else, despite the thoughts crowding my mind. Isik filled our cups with sweet mead, a little watered down. Only when my cup was empty did I speak.

"What do you think of it?" I stabbed at a remaining chunk of venison with the tip of an eating knife and popped it into my mouth, chewing and swallowing before I added, "The Arpa reaching the edge of the world. The Unmade."

Isik lifted his head from a second heaped portion of food. "It's interesting. The mortal world is growing smaller."

"Humans are everywhere now," I nodded, as if I wasn't one of them. I tapped the tip of my knife absently on the venison plate, now holding only a pool of cooling juices.

Isik ate another few mouthfuls. "It was only a matter of time, I suppose. Stability breeds boredom among your kind."

I arched my brows. "Ah yes, and what does it breed in yours?"

He thought on this for a moment. "Ingenuity. Art. Creativity." He waved his knife at the ornate tapestries on the walls. "See."

"Tedium, vexation, and meddling in human affairs," I corrected.

"I don't meddle," Isik said, voice overly grave. "Though stopping my father from doing so is no small task."

I smiled back, but my thoughts drifted back to the Unmade. "What could it mean? Movement in the Unmade?"

"The explorers sniffed too much rotsnare," Isik suggested, fluttering the fingers of one hand at his temple. "Started seeing things."

I *tsk*ed. "I'm serious."

"So am I," he returned, but put aside some of his humor. "There is nothing in the Unmade to change or shift. What these Arpa claim to have seen is one of the few true impossibilities of our world."

I wanted to agree, but: "Then why call a council so quickly? And send me away? Estavius didn't want me there."

"Yet you snuck back in." Isik eyed me. My tendency to eavesdrop was a frequent source of contention between us.

"I'm curious, sometimes." I shrugged innocently and reached over to spear a chunk of carrot from his bowl. I sat back, popping it into my mouth.

"I wish you wouldn't be."

"Then keep me informed, and I won't have to skulk in the shadows."

His eyes met mine across the table, creased with warmth and an echo of something else, something older and nearly forgotten. "Of course. Anything for you, Yske."

FOUR

M y brother waited on the stone slab of my doorstep, shaded by the thatched roof of the circular house with its moss-and-clay-chinked walls and sprawl of lush garden. His meticulously braided hair was black like our mother's, thick, prone to curl, and shaved at the sides to reveal knotwork tattoos around each ear. His skin was a shade darker than mine, again taking after our mother's Eangen blood, where I followed our father's Algatt.

That was the way of us, my twin and I: his hair black to my blonde; his skin warm and freckled, mine cool and prone to flushing. His body was honed for violence, muscled and lean. My frame was soft, capable and sturdy but without a hard line in sight. The hooded axe at his hip was ever keen, while the knife at my own was dull from digging roots from the earth.

The warm sun cut across my face as I stepped from the trees. I didn't need to see my brother's eyes to know his mind was far away from my little house; his posture told me, elbows on his knees, fingers laced, and his gaze on the ground before his booted feet.

My mother's question drifted back to me. *Have you spoken to your brother?*

"Berin?" I called.

He looked up, unsurprised. "Where were you?"

I opened the garden gate and passed through, the satchel at my hip traitorously heavy. "The east side of the mountain, then the Halls to speak to Aita," I explained, patting the satchel as if it contained nothing but the usual array of mushrooms and cuttings I found in the forest.

My brother's focus sharpened, noting my long skirt and lack of weapons with disapproval. "I hate that you wander like that."

"Mother was in the Halls, too," I pointed out.

Mild interest passed over his face, but he'd never been one to think much on the Halls and the Miri. "I was thinking more of the mountain. It's dangerous to wander alone."

I gave him a long-suffering smile. "You'll be grateful for my foraging when Isa's time comes. Not everything she needs grows in a garden."

The clouds shifted, throwing me into shadow and Berin into a pool of sunlight. He squinted, dark lashes full of light. His wife Isa was often sickly, and now that she was pregnant with their first child, she'd barely left her bed in weeks. Hence my original visit to Aita—though neither Berin nor the priesthood would know where I found my ingredients.

"How is she? Isa?" I crossed the garden, back into the light, and stopped before him. The garden around us droned with bees and other insects, their wings light-filled blurs amid yarrow and wild rose.

Berin stood and opened the door of my little house, hiding his expression as he preceded me into the single room. "She's well. Today."

Narrow windows illuminated my home. The thatch of the conical roof gathered into a chimney above the central hearth. A triangular iron stand stood sentinel over the lifeless fire pit, where a flat iron cooking surface hung in southern, Soulderni style. My bed lay off to one side, neatly stacked with blankets, and the floors were layered with knotted rugs of reed and coarse fibers. The walls were heavy with orderly shelves of jars and dangling pouches, boxes and bundles, and every beam was strung with drying herbs. The air was thick with their smell, changing subtly as I made for one of the tables set beneath the windows—a cloud of sage, a drift of mint, a bitter spike of valerian.

I tucked my satchel behind a stack of folded clothing and turned back to Berin. "I'm glad she's well. But why are you here?"

Berin stared at the hearth. "Arpa merchants came to the hall a few weeks ago."

"And?" I paused to eye him, then pulled a basket of kindling from under the table. I set about making a fire, tucking bits of dried moss into a nest of birch bark and twigs. As I struck flint and tinder and he didn't speak, I prodded, "What of them? They come every year."

"They brought stories."

"They always do," I muttered. The tinder wouldn't catch, so I gave up and sat back to study my brother more critically. He looked distracted, but I saw uncertainty in the pinch of his lips, and a spark of something more dangerous in his eyes—excitement.

"Berin," I persisted. "What?"

He scowled but dropped into a crouch on the other side of the fire. "They brought stories from other Arpa merchants, in the east. Stories of people who worship the Great Bear. And stories of a dead tree, so huge it fills the sky. Do you remember Thray's story about that tree?"

I furrowed my brows. Our Winterborn cousin Thray was the daughter of our mother's best friend, and she'd been banished when Berin and I were children. She'd spoken once of visions, of a tree in the east, but my memory of that time was vague—strained by the threat of war and my sadness over her imminent departure.

"The Arpa saw the edge of the world and that tree was there. Against the blackness."

Estavius's words from the High Halls rang through my mind and my skin chilled, unnatural in the close warmth of the house. The timing of Estavius's and Berin's visits seemed an impossible coincidence, but Fate had never been gentle with my bloodline.

Berin went on: "There're people in the east who worship the Bear, Yske. And they have for centuries."

The Great Bear was Aegr, a creature of the High Halls who had escaped into the Waking World long before my brother and I were born. Combined with the tale of how he had saved my mother from a demon in her youth, it was the story of the Bear's healing by the ancient heroine Liv that had drawn first me to healing arts, and Aita.

"Our people must be connected," Berin said, leaning forward earnestly. "But how?"

I stared at him, my heart suddenly aching. I knew the look in his eyes, the light of curiosity, the urgency and excitement. He'd had the same look when, at fifteen, he'd declared he would be a mercenary and vanished into the Arpa Empire for two years, and last year, when he'd set off to winter in the northern kingdom of Duamel.

"Why does it matter?" I asked quietly.

His smile was easy and cajoling. "Because it's fascinating, Yske. A whole people live in the east, and we know nothing about them. But they know of *our* Great Bear?"

"He wanders," I said, trying to dismiss the topic. "Maybe there's a door to the High Halls in the east."

Berin shook his head. "No, no. Mother said there's no door. The eastern High Halls are inaccessible. They end just past their equivalent of the Headwaters of the Pasidon."

Gooseflesh crept up my arms. "The Miri never speak of that," I murmured.

Berin shrugged. "Speaking of it would mean admitting there's a place they can't go. Somewhere they don't have power."

I eyed him. "That's insightful, for you."

"I have my moments," he preened.

I bit the inside of my lip. Just because my mother said the eastern High Halls were inaccessible didn't mean it was true—I could name half a dozen world-changing secrets she kept and used daily. But Berin didn't know about those. And suggesting to him that our mother didn't always prioritize the truth had never gone well before.

I studied Berin's face. "You're not thinking of… going east, are you?"

"Of course I am," he replied. "The Arpa have, why shouldn't the Eangen?"

"Berin." I dropped my flint and tinder and stood so sharply I almost lost my balance. "That's ridiculous. You can't—"

"I can do as I please," he cut me off, unfolding to his full height. There was only one respect where he took after our father, and I our mother. He stood a head taller than her and me, and though he wasn't the tallest man in our village, it was enough to look down at me. "I'm not going alone, either. I've been gathering others who feel the same way. You know there are more than a few restless warriors in Eangen, and what are we to do? The Iskiri Devoted are all but whispers now. There's peace in the north and the south. I want to *live*, Yske, not farm and stare at the clouds to the end of my days. Peace is an opportunity to expand, to prove we're more than barbarians in the north. I want to see this great tree. I want to meet the people in its shadow."

"Merchants would hire you again," I protested, though I hated the idea of him leaving again in any capacity. "You could travel the Empire more. You could go back to Duamel."

"I've done that and I hated it," he retorted. "I'm no one's watchdog. My axe can't be bought."

I resisted the urge to roll my eyes. "Then volunteer."

He opened his mouth to say something scathing, but cut himself off. A moment of silence stretched between us, then he gathered himself and said, "I came to ask you to come with me."

I gaped. My eyes darted around my house, so orderly and familiar, so full of security and everything I could possibly need. I couldn't leave—panic flooded me at the very thought.

Berin carried on, "The journey will be long. Months. Longer. We have no way of knowing, except that the Arpa took four months from Nivarium, by boat and on foot—the forests are too thick for horses. We'll need a healer, and you're the best."

"You'd leave Isa?" I stuttered, horrified by the suggestion. No wonder my mother had asked me to talk sense into him. "You'd ask *me* to? She's ill, and pregnant. What about your child?"

A flicker of something, guilt or sadness, tugged at Berin's eyes, but he brushed past it. "She told me to go. She'll stay with her family, and Mother will be there to watch over her."

"Mother isn't a god, Berin," I hissed in frustration and started to pace, unable to keep still. "You should be there for your wife. I should, at the very least. You just said I'm the best healer in Albor."

"Isa will be fine," Berin said without a hint of emotion, and I turned to stare at him again, aghast at his denial. After spending the night with Isik, his thoughts always plain and his words genuine, Berin seemed particularly false. "We'll need you more than she will."

"She's not fine," I said, low and grim. "Your child wouldn't have survived the first weeks without my care."

Berin crooked a dry, amused smile. "They say I'm the arrogant one, you know."

I threw up my hands. "No. You're not going anywhere, and neither am I. If you wanted to throw your life away on a foolish journey, you should have done that before you married."

"She told me to go," Berin threw back.

"You're being—"

Berin stalked around the fire and glared at me. But the longer our eyes met, the more his façade began to crack. I saw something behind his anger, something raw and wounded. "She *told* me to go, Yske."

The meaning of his words sank in, so deep and so quickly that I lost my breath. "You mean…"

"She wants nothing to do with me." He smoothed his already perfect beard, trying to gather himself. "It's not… It's not over, but she needs time. Just time."

For a long moment, I couldn't find anything to say. I knew Berin wasn't an easy man to live with—he had his charms, but his temper and restlessness had always bothered Isa and led to unnecessary conflict and anxiety for the young woman. I didn't blame her for taking a stand now that their child was coming, but I also knew that beneath Berin's stalwart exterior, he hid as much emotion as I did. We'd just learned to manage it in different ways.

I swallowed. "I'm sorry."

He brushed my words aside and looked around my little house. "I

42

always thought you were mad, living out here alone, pushing away all the men who showed an interest in you. But maybe I understand it, now."

I almost managed a smile, but it immediately faltered into a sympathetic frown. "I understand why you want to leave, then. But why not go visit Father? You don't have to run to the edge of the world. And… I still can't leave. If you won't—can't—be there for her, I can."

He shook his head, jaw tight. "I've made up my mind. Come or not, I'm leaving. Soon. It would be best to find Aegr's worshipers before winter. We'll return next summer."

The blind simplicity in his plan chilled me. He had no way of knowing how long the journey would take, and it was already late summer. Did he expect to winter with strangers? How would he survive?

I knew my brother well enough, however, to realize I could not talk him out of this.

"I won't go," I repeated. I felt a tug of regret with the words, but walled it out. I'd no desire to leave, but the thought of being without Berin for so long made my chest ache. "I love you, but I can't."

Hurt sunk into his eyes. He let me see it for once, let me feel the weight of it, before he made for the door. "If you change your mind… I'll be in Albor."

I couldn't speak. I couldn't even nod as he went to the open door. He hovered there for an instant, as if debating whether to say something else, then passed though the shadow and sunlight of the garden and vanished beneath the summer trees.

FIVE

I trailed Aita through a field of wildflowers, pale blue and yellow blossoms bobbing under the weight of bees as I picked my way after my mistress. My feet were bare beneath the fall of my skirt and apron—I had a desperate aversion to shoes as a child, and Aita either did not notice or did not consider the summer-dry earth a threat to my small, dirty toes.

Aita paused and crouched beside a tuft of wiry-looking grasses, laden with closed blossoms. "This is duskflower."

I dropped into a child's unselfconscious squat and curled my fingers in my apron, careful not to touch the plant until Aita gave me leave. I'd been by her side for six months now, and I knew the rules.

"It discourages bleeding when its flowers are applied in a poultice," the Miri continued. "But they only open as the sun sets, which here in the High Halls is no predictable thing. If you should ever see duskflowers opening in the Waking World, fetch me some. But be careful not to crush them."

"I will," I promised solemnly.

Aita's eyes lingered on me, on my curled fingers and attentive expression, and her own gaze softened. "Come."

We wandered through the meadows and forest. Aita tested me on the names and uses of flowers and mushrooms, grasses and barks, mosses and saps. She pried spruce gum from a sticky tree and let me chew it as we walked, and for a time she was quiet, watching me out of the corner of her eye.

When we came to a creek, she unfastened a short-handled ladle from her belt and took a drink, then held it out to me.

I was thirsty, but my mother's warnings rang in my head. "I'm only supposed to drink the water Mama sent. It's dangerous."

Aita watched me, indecipherable thoughts behind her lavender-edged eyes. "Does your mother know more about the High Halls than I?"

I hesitated, trapped between my absent mother's will and Aita's pressing gaze. I decided it was safer not to speak.

Aita held the water out to me. "You already had the spruce sap, child. You didn't question me then."

I felt myself pale. I hadn't thought, hadn't realized what I was doing. Over six months of visiting the High Halls every other day, I'd never eaten or drunk a single thing that my mother hadn't sent with me. But today, without even knowing it, I'd broken a foundational rule. Never eat or drink of the High Halls.

My heart started to hammer in my chest. I stood back, petrified. "I'm going to die," I pawed at my mouth and stomach. "Mistress. Aita! Aita, I—"

"Hush, child," Aita came to hold my shoulders and stilled my panicked fluttering. When I tried to tug away, she took my chin in one hand. "Listen to me, and I will tell you a great secret. It is a Miri secret, a secret so big and so important that the only humans who know about it are your mother and father. But I've decided that you should know. Fate has a great destiny for you, I am sure. So you must be prepared."

I was afraid to move. My stomach puffed with my frightened breaths, up and down, up and down against my apron.

"Everything in the High Halls has magic inside it," my mistress told me. "Every rock and tree and flower and drop of water. And when you eat or drink those things, the magic becomes part of you. No, it's not a frightening thing, Yske. You already have some of that magic inside you. That's why your mother let you come here. Your mother and father lay together here, in the High Halls. This is where your brother and you were made."

At eight years old, I had only a vague notion of what that meant. But I'd seen animals rut and lived in a communal hall, where many families dwelled under the same roof. I understood that infants were created through strange acts, couplings under blankets and behind doors.

"Your life was sparked here," Aita went on. "Your mother and father drink and eat here as they please, and that magic is in their bodies. You are already part of the High Halls, and eating and drinking can only make you stronger. More powerful, like me."

"Will I be able to heal like you?" I gasped. I'd seen her heal my cuts and bruises with a casual word before, and the thought of having such power captivated me. "Like Liv?"

Aita released me at mention of Liv, the infamous healer of Eangen gone. She knelt on the soft moss beside the creek and gestured for me to kneel with her. I complied. "That kind of magic, I fear, is… not gone, but not something I can freely give. Liv, child, stole what was not hers. There is a cost to such magic—a cost to claim it, a cost to wield it, and a cost to replenish it. This is blood magic. Old magic. You are too young to bear such things."

The mention of blood magic quelled me. I knew of the three kinds of magic—the magic of the High Halls, the magic of life, and its cousin, the magic of blood. I'd heard the stories of blood magic from my parents and seen the sacrificial scars on their hands. But I was still a child and my disconnect between reality and experience too great.

Indignance churned inside me. I opened my mouth to protest, but Aita raised a hand and tilted her chin in a way that forbade further protests.

Still stewing, I swallowed my objections. Aita had not said no. She'd said I was too young. But I would grow, and I'd ask again.

And there was always the water, and the power it promised. The water flowing past us, glistening in the mottled forest light.

"Now," the Miri said, redirecting the conversation. "I cannot say what the magic of the Halls will give you, if you begin to drink and eat here. But do not fear it, whatever it will be. All is Fate."

"I want to be like you," I told her, brimming with hope and sincerity and only a little melancholy.

There was so much softness in Aita's face when she smiled that I thought she might embrace me. But she only lifted a finger and brushed it across my cheek. "Perhaps one day, little one. One day."

SIX

Exhausted as I was, I couldn't bring myself to sleep. I sat on a low stool beside the fire in my linen shift, with my thorn-scratched legs folded before me. An owl hooted in the forest outside, punctuating the steady hum of crickets and frogs with its low, steady calls.

I couldn't go with Berin, but I couldn't bear the thought of him going without me, either. I felt deep in my gut that he would not come home, not from a road so untested and a land so unknown. Nor would his companions. How long would it be before we finally burned empty pyres and marked empty graves?

How could I live with myself, knowing I could have saved him?

I couldn't do nothing. At the very least, I needed to learn as much as I could about the east and the path Berin was likely to tread, and arm him with knowledge. Aita had always been my source of wisdom, even the secrets my mother withheld.

I had to speak with her again.

The next morning, I rose in the deep twilight before dawn and stoked the fire just enough to bathe the house in ochre light. I pulled on a fresh overgown of mild blue, belted it, and sharpened my knife while my breakfast heated in the fire. I bound my hair in two long braids, threaded with a strip of cloth, and tied them around my head as the first rays of sunlight broke over the mountainside. The scent of the garden, earthen and damp with dew, swelled as I ate my breakfast on the stoop, set my pot inside the door, tugged on my satchel, and shut up the house.

I passed through my garden, past the wattle fence and down a winding trail on the forested mountainside. At its end a meadow opened, warm sunlight hit my face, and my skirt brushed through half-open poppies.

In the center of the meadow was an old shrine, little more than beams and roof tiles and sharp angles. This was once Eang's sacred place, where her priests and priestesses made pilgrimage and the most powerful passed freely into the High Halls of the Dead and the Gods.

My mother had come here as a young woman to beg Eang for absolution. Instead, the original village of Albor had been burned to the ground and my mother set on a path that had brought down the Old Gods and raised her to High Priestess of an older and truer deity: Thvynder, God of the Eangen and the Algatt, one of the Four Pillars of Creation.

I strode into the center of the meadow and touched my Sight. A slim golden rift appeared, stretching from the dew-heavy poppies to the height of my head. As I neared the tear broadened, adding a wash of deeper amber light to the rays of the rising sun. It smelled of honey, pine and dew, and for a moment I reveled in the scent and the solitude.

Then I stepped forward. The rift contracted and the world tilted, drowning me in a momentary rush of light and immaterial sensation.

When the world settled again, I stood in the High Halls' reflection of the meadow. Here, autumn reigned and the trees were a tapestry of red and yellow, brown and burgundy, shrouded in gentle, misty rain.

I wasted no time. Moisture prickled my skin as I sketched three runes in the air and strode into them. Again the world shifted, but this time I didn't slow or falter. I stepped out onto a windswept coastline before the Hall of the Gods.

"Child," Aita's voice drifted through a veil of smoke. I passed through an eddy into the rich herbal scent of Aita's workspace. Today it was tucked in a far corner of the hall. The braziers were unlit but several old candles burned on the tabletop, thick with dripping wax in a scattered sea of dried flowerheads.

She brushed a pile of lavender into one palm and looked up at me. "Tea?"

I shook my head. "I can't linger today, mistress. But I have questions I hope you might answer."

"I see." A frayed blonde curl escaped her headscarf and brushed her cheek as she strode to a small cooking pot. She ladled hot water into one of two ready cups and, setting her hips on the edge of the hearth wall, rubbed the lavender between her palms. Slowly, she let each crushed fragment fall onto the surface of the water and hummed under her breath. A golden glow suffused the mixture—the same magic that healed mortal wounds in my childhood stories.

"Are there any doors between the High Halls and the Waking World in the east?" I asked.

The Miri did not look up from her tea, watching the herbs saturate and sink. "There was, but it was cut off."

"Why? By whom?"

Aita shrugged a shoulder, still watching her tea. "It was long before I was born. The most eastern High Halls are untraversable, anyway. We had little reason to mourn their loss."

"Did the Gods of the Old World cut off the east?" I asked, citing the generation of Miri that had birthed her, Gadr, Esach, Estavius, and many others.

Aita looked up at me, her gaze slightly narrowed. "I suppose they must have. Why are you asking?"

"My brother is planning an expedition east," I admitted, easing myself down on the hearth wall. "To see what the Arpa saw. Not these… shadows in the Unmade, if they even exist. But a great tree, and a people who worship Aegr the Bear. Thray—our cousin—spoke of the tree once, and Berin's never forgotten it. She saw it in a vision."

"Ah." Aita nodded slowly. "Well, no living Miri has been so far east. We are powerful, but some of us are also lazy. Others must tend to duties, not gallivant across creation with no purpose. As to the half-bloods, the Winterborn may have strayed so far, but Esach's half-blood children are a boring lot, and they mostly enjoy their short lives among humanity."

"Not Isik."

"Isik's blood is pure." Aita's attention wandered for an instant, into memory, then she smirked. "Many… unexpected things happened after Thvynder came to power. Esach returning to Gadr's bed was one of the most surprising. But I suppose more of our kind must come from somewhere, and I'll not be parting my legs for that old goatherd."

"Isik will want a Miri companion someday," I pointed out, trying to sound pragmatic.

Aita sniffed. "Then he will have to plead with Thvynder to make him a wife. Or he can coax a Winterborn into his bed, or track down the woodmaidens. We are cousins to their kind; such a pairing would not be too impractical."

I eyed her, amused by her tone—though the thought of Isik wooing a white-haired Winterborn or bare-breasted woodmaiden discomfited me. "What about you? What if you bore a child by Estavius? He's handsome."

The Great Healer laughed outright. "What a perfunctory union that would be. No, it is not my place to bear children. Thvynder can create more Miri if it comes to that. I'll have no part."

As interesting as this conversation was, I returned to my earlier query: "So the eastern High Halls are truly inaccessible?"

"They are. Travel too far east in that realm, and you'll simply find yourself mired in fog and smoke and marsh that will not dissipate, no matter how powerful your runes." Aita's gaze sharpened, her tea forgotten. "But even if those lands were open, you would not be permitted to bring your brother and his companions through the High Halls."

She'd immediately seen my intentions. "Berin has as much of a right to be here as I do," I pointed out. "We share birth-blood."

"Yet his mind remains firmly bound to the grit of the earth, like any beast," the Miri returned. "Yske, I let you come here because you can be trusted with knowledge and secrets. I let you drink and eat of this realm, and in doing so gain its power, because you earned the right."

I looked behind us, momentarily terrified that someone—that my mother—might somehow overhear. The hall remained empty. But still, how could Aita speak so casually of secrets that might upend the balance of the world?

"Berin," Aita continued, "shows none of your quality."

Indignation scorched the back of my throat, and it was all I could do to keep my mouth closed. This was the double-edged blade of Aita's favor—she admired and praised me, but only at the expense of the rest of my kind.

"You show me too much grace, mistress." I bowed my head.

She made a considering sound and settled back, tea cupped between her hands. "It seems I will show you more today. You cannot shorten your brother's journey through the High Halls, but there is an old road east. It begins on the far side of the Headwaters of the Pasidon."

I blinked, catching myself before I could show too much shock. "An old road? How old?"

"Its age does not matter. It was built by the Miri, child, not humans." Aita puffed on her tea and took a sip. "The waymarkers will certainly still be there. Tell your brother to follow those, and his passage will be eased. But he is still unlikely to return."

"I know." The affirmation stuck to my tongue like sap. I wished I'd taken up her offer of tea, just to have something to wash it away with.

There was a knowledge growing inside me, one I couldn't push aside. What I'd overheard had shaped it; the look in Berin's eyes had given it an edge. Now, Aita's words turned it into a knife in my chest.

"I must go with him," I said. "I don't want to but… I must."

Aita stared at me, firelight turning her hair gold and her eyes piercing. "Why?"

"To keep him alive," I said, though I felt this must be obvious. "I can heal him. Protect him from himself. He asked me to join him already."

"You would go on a suicidal quest for a chance to save your brother," Aita said, slow and calculated. "Yet he doesn't hesitate to put your life at risk by asking you to come? Can you see the paradox, child?"

I shifted in discomfort. "That's not what he's doing. He doesn't realize how dangerous the way will be."

"So he'll kill you with his stupidity?"

Heat burned in my throat. "He's not… It doesn't matter. He's determined to go, and I'm determined to bring him home alive."

"What of his wife? The one with child?"

I hesitated. "She has her family, and mine. And your mercy, I hope."

Silence fell as Aita watched me for a long moment, her thoughts obscure. "I suppose. Then… go."

Her response unsettled me. Was her consent a challenge? A dare, to see if I'd balk?

I nodded slowly. An old question bubbled up through my thoughts, one I hadn't dared to ask since I was a child.

"Mistress…" I started to cut myself off, then found my courage again. "I have no right to ask anything more of you, I know. But you spoke once of a… another power. A power more like yours. You said I was too young and the cost too high. But the risks of this journey—"

Aita's expression closed like a shutter to the wind. She stood and the smoke swirled, thickening around us, not only cutting us off from the hall but dividing me from my former mentor.

"Go east with my blessing, child," Aita told me as the High Halls began to stretch the space between us, hiding her from my wide, pleading eyes. "And ask no more of me."

The goat-shorn path leading to Isik's hall was dry under my feet. A quick knock at the door found my friend standing before me, and his eyes immediately filled with concern. Chatter and voices came from within—the laughter of young women and a little boy. Isik's siblings.

Without a word my friend stepped outside, held out his hand, and I took it.

A few sketched runes later, and we walked a shady forest pathway. I regularly came to this region to forage, harvesting the myriad mushrooms that burst from decomposing logs and crept up their loftier companions' spines in orange, black, or white frills.

But something felt different about the forest tonight, though I saw nothing unusual—save foxfire tendrils on a rotting tree. It was white rather than the usual blue or green, and it illuminated the ranks of mushrooms on its barkless surface with pale light.

"We're alone," Isik assured me, mistaking my hesitancy. "What is it?"

"Why is that foxfire white?" I asked. "And why is it glowing when it hasn't rained?"

He followed my gaze, but was clearly unbothered. "Tell me what's wrong."

I pushed the strange observation aside and told him everything. I explained about Berin's journey and my growing understanding that I had to accompany him. I had to leave the warmth and security of the home that I'd made for myself and embark on a trek across the known world—into the unknown.

Isik did not take it well. "Aita's right. Risking himself is one thing, but risking you too? It's selfish. Unforgivable."

"But it *is*. This is the situation," I returned. The urge to defend my brother knotted in my gut, but it felt more like obligation than anything. "I cannot change it, or him."

"And if his legs were to be broken and he could not lead you to your death?" Isik asked, face dark with unabashed animosity.

"Isik," I shoved his arm. "Don't say things like that."

"You're human, Yske." My friend stepped closer and made to grab my hands, but I retreated from the intimacy. "You have one life. Sixty, seventy years at best. Do not throw them away for your brother."

I took a moment to respond, reading his face. Isik had never actually met Berin. All he knew of my brother was my stories, usually told in amusement or anger, and I pondered that I'd likely painted an unfair picture of my twin. But I saw more than anger in Isik's face—I saw frustration and fear and protectiveness. They softened my heart and hardened my resolve.

"Isik," I said, as gently as I could. "You can't hold on to me so tightly."

I saw a tremble pass through his lips, a boyish vulnerability masked by a man's stubbornness. "But I *can* come with you."

I almost laughed. "No! What would I say to Berin? 'Meet the Son of Gadr, who used to be my lover'? You know the way Berin is. He'll be hostile. He'll forbid you from coming."

"Forbid," Isik scoffed. "I'm—"

"A meddling Miri," I finished for him. I impulsively grabbed one of his hands and took it between both of mine, his long fingers and broad palm making mine look all the smaller. "I'm going east with Berin. He'll protect me with his life, just as I'll do for him, and we'll come back next summer whole and well and brimming with stories."

I smiled, convincing myself of the truth of my words as I spoke them. Adventure wasn't something I craved like Berin did, but I could conjure the impulse, if only for Isik's benefit, and let it glisten in my eyes.

Isik frowned, perhaps seeing through me. "I still don't want you to do this."

"I know. I hear you. But it won't change my mind."

His thumb trailed across my wrist for a moment, then he stepped back and nodded, rallying. "Then I wish you a safe journey, Yske."

"You're the first person I'll find when I come back," I promised.

"I'll be waiting."

SEVEN

I stepped through the open doors of the Morning Hall in Albor, eased my heavy pack from my shoulder and discreetly pried my sweat-soaked tunic from my spine. The building was high and broad, huge smoke-darkened beams supporting a vaulted ceiling and a partial upper floor, where the families of local Vynder priests and priestesses made their homes.

The main hall spread before me. Tables were pushed to the sides and the central hearth lay cool in the hot summer evening, while the open floor was full of movement. Children and dogs ran underfoot. Adults in festival clothing flowed past me with their arms full of benches and platters, bowls and pitchers. Some waved or cast me greetings, which I returned with distracted smiles and nods. I might be an unmarried recluse and frequently at odds with my family, but that didn't mean I wasn't well liked in Albor. Miracle cures and healthy babies could forgive a multitude of eccentricities.

"Ah, so you've come down from your mountain," a cool voice said.

I glanced back to find a young woman standing behind me, her short raven-black hair loose about her shoulders in windblown curls. Her eyes were rimmed with black paint, but unlike everyone else she wore a practical undyed tunic, loose brown leggings and tight legwraps to mid-calf. Her shoulders were sturdy and her arms lean with muscle, her straight waist laced with multiple belts, though she carried only a knife at the moment.

"Seera," I acknowledged, looking up the several inches between her dark eyes and my pale ones. The woman was a few years older than me, first daughter of Uspa—the next High Priestess—and Sillo, my uncle. She looked like her father and had inherited his height, but other than that her physique had always reminded me of my own mother—solid, strong, and capable of great violence.

Glancing over her clothes, I observed, "You're joining Berin?"

"I am." She looked over me in turn, taking in my flushed cheeks, long sweaty tunic, fitted trousers, and the pack at my feet. Surprise wormed into her eyes, easing her normal casual coldness. "He convinced you?"

I smiled wanly. "Well, if I'd known you'd have his back, I wouldn't have bothered."

The compliment was calculated, and it won a grin. Seera and I had never been close—in fact, she'd been quite cruel when we were children—but our progress into adulthood had smoothed the hard edges between us. Or so I hoped.

"Are you sure you can keep up?" she asked critically, and my hopes withered. She scanned me again, and this time her eyes lingered on my every curve and absent scar. "And carry your own weight?"

"I live alone on the mountain, Cousin," I reminded her, mirroring her coolness. "I hunt. I cut my own wood. I haul my own water. I'll be fine."

Seera watched my face for another moment, then nodded. Stooping, she grabbed my pack and took it on her own broader shoulder. "I'll put this with our gear, then. Go find Berin, before he drinks himself into a stupor because he thinks you're not coming. He's by the fire, north of the walls."

I started to protest—I didn't like the thought of anyone handling my supplies—but an offer of help from Seera was a rare gift. "Wait," I said, and fished my satchel from the top of the pack. "Is Isa at home?"

Seera nodded, her face inscrutable, and she wove away through the hall.

I stepped back outside and joined the flow of villagers out of the main settlement. But where they continued straight through the northern gate to an open section of field, I diverted into a side street.

Berin's house was small and neat, sharing a wall with a small shelter for livestock. The yard and garden were enclosed by an impeccably maintained fence, but the chickens and goats paid it no mind. Birds scattered from my path and a kid goat looked down at me from the roof, its slit eyes accusatory.

The stoop of the house was freshly swept, and when I knocked, it wasn't Isa's voice that bid me enter.

I found Berin's mother-in-law sewing beside the hearth. The room was small and cozy, with a ladder leading to a loft on one side and a storage area on the other, beams laden with bundles and chests. There was a second door beside the hearth to the livestock quarters, and the shutters on the windows were open to the fresh air.

Isa's mother gave me a tight smile and nodded toward the bed. Isa sat up at the same time, pushing her masses of black curls back from her face and keeping the blankets up over her rounded belly. I'd always considered her immeasurably pretty, her skin a rich dark brown thanks to her Soulderni father, her soul gentle, her delicate mouth always smiling. Berin had been besotted with her from childhood, along with every other boy in the village, and I'd been so proud the day they married. The day Isa had chosen my brother, our family, over any other.

Now her smiles were rarer.

"I brought you more medicines," I said, sitting on the edge of the bed and opening my satchel between us. I held up a jar of salve, then a large bag of mixed herbs and a tincture. "More salve, for the stretching. This tea will help you sleep, particularly as you enter the last months. This will balance your blood. Have you still been dizzy?"

Isa nodded and cleared her throat before she spoke. "Not today, but two days ago."

"She couldn't walk two days ago," her mother put in, eyes still on her sewing.

That worried me, but I tried not to show it. "Keep eating well, and keep this in your cup." I held out a knot of amber. It had been made in the High Halls and though I couldn't specify what benefit it would give, it wouldn't do any harm.

I pressed her with several more salves and remedies and preventatives, until Isa shook her head and patted my knee.

"Yske, I am glad you're going," she said sincerely. "Don't feel guilty for leaving me. You've already done so much."

I parted my lips to reply, but discovered my throat was clotted. "I can do more," I said, coughing a little to hide my emotion.

Isa gestured to the remedies stacked on the bed around her. "You will, even if you're not here. Keep…" The light was low, but I saw my sister-in-law's eyes glitter with unshed tears. "Keep him safe. I don't wish him harm. You know—"

"I know," I said. We embraced, long and tight. I felt the swell of her belly against my side and thought of the child within, the son or daughter that would be born while their father was on the other side of the world. My niece or nephew, whom I might never meet, and who might steal their mother's life in their coming.

On the way out, I crouched beside Isa's mother. Isa busied herself arranging her medicines on a shelf beside the bed, and I spoke in a low voice.

"If the birth goes badly, ask my mother to fetch Aita," I said to the older woman, whose eyes widened. For the first time since I'd entered, she paused at her stitching. "You will owe her nothing." I hardened my voice as I added, "I will pay the debt."

"Thank you," the woman whispered.

The fields outside Albor stretched toward the distant treeline in the deep gold of the setting sun, while a large flat space hosted a huge cook fire and hundreds of bustling, laughing, and chattering villagers. Long benches were settled far back from the fire and tables overflowed with bowls and platters. Pieces of what must have been a stag roasted while, off to one side, my brother lounged with its antlers balanced atop his head. Young men and women gathered around him, and one of our youngest cousins—Seera's brother Ulmen—sat in his lap, reaching for the dead beast's tines. The child nearly knocked a cup of mead from Berin's hand, and my brother hastily chugged the rest of it while his companions laughed uproariously.

My will to join Berin's expedition had already dulled, but the sight of my brother nearly dispelled the rest of it. The sun wasn't even down the night before our departure, and here he was, half-drunk. I almost turned back—to Isa or the hall, if not the mountain.

But at that moment, Berin saw me. He froze in the midst of a deep belly laugh and stared, some unintelligible emotion darting through his eyes. Then he lifted the antlers from his head, set them into the arms of one of his friends, and plucked Ulmen from his lap. Berin tossed the child over his shoulder and came to me, carrying him by his ankles as the child squealed in delight.

"Yske! Help me, Yske, Yske!" Ulmen shrieked into Berin's back, nearly choking on his own laughter.

I quickly snatched him away and set him on his feet. The boy's face was red and he staggered to find his balance, clutching my skirts. But still he grinned, his eyes dancing at Berin's attention.

"You came." Berin smothered me in a hug, his eyes liquid with gratitude and sincerity. Ulmen, squished between us, protested without a scrap of ire.

I let Berin hold me, first because I was too discomfited to move, and then because my heart had begun to melt painfully. Finally I returned his embrace, burying my head beneath his chin and laughing as Ulmen disentangled, scolding us all the while.

"Will you find the sunrise?" the boy asked, prodding Berin in the leg. "Will you?"

Cheek pressed into Berin's chest, I scrutinized the boy. "I suppose we might. How strange that will be."

Ulmen nodded sagely. "Very strange."

"We will tell you all about it," I assured him. "Now go find your parents, please."

"No."

"Go on," Berin affirmed, his chest rumbling beneath my ear. "I'll come find you later."

Ulmen scowled at the pair of us but sulked away, leaving my brother and I a fraction of privacy.

Slowly, I disentangled so I could look into Berin's face, and winced at the smell of ale and mead on his breath. Half a dozen warnings and cautions sat on my tongue, but instead I chose to smile, and reached up to scratch his beard. He turned his chin up like a dog for an instant, making a happy sound, then beamed down at me.

"I knew you'd come," he stated, but sounded as though he was still reassuring himself. "I knew it. Come, you need to meet our companions."

One by one, Berin introduced me to the men and women who would fill my days for the next year. There were seven in total, including Seera, who appeared not long after. I was familiar with all of them, to some extent—they'd been in my brother's circles for years, now plucked out as the bravest and finest Eangen, Algatt, and Souldern had to offer.

Ittrid was Soulderni, her skin dark, her black hair bound into a high braid and her frame tall and strong. Askir was a Vynder Priest of Algatt heritage, like my father—his skin pale, hair blond and his lithe body corded with muscle. He noted the yellow and blue Algatt paints I'd smudged into my hairline with faint approval, and bowed his head.

Bara and Sedi were a married pair from the far west of Eangen, she reserved and he quick to smile. Ovir and Esan were the last two, warriors Berin, Seera, and I had grown up alongside. They were Berin's closest friends and when they looked at me, I could still feel the ache of the bruises they'd given me during the days when my mother forced me to train and I refused to act. Fortunately the years had tempered those memories and bolstered them with more pleasant ones—dancing together at feasts, generous payments for wounds I'd healed, and even Esan's singular attempt to kiss me at seventeen.

I smiled at them. Esan nodded. As for Ovir, he gave a falsely shy wave, his black-lashed gray eyes crinkling.

The following hours passed in a whirl of greetings and conversation, food and drink and well-wishes. I'd expected more grim resignation from the people of Albor at the thought of Berin's expedition, but we were piled with blessings and unrequested advice, some more useful than the rest. Old warriors edged between us and told us of their own days in the forest, of the time when the Miri still ruled as gods, the Eangen and the Algatt warred, and rogue legionaries pillaged the southern borders. Others spoke to Berin and I of our parents, of fighting alongside them in the Arpa Empire—before the warring southern factions had been brought down and Estavius placed as their ruler.

They were stories Berin and I had heard a hundred times, growing up as children of the High Priest and Priestess. We bore them stoically for most of the night, but I could see Berin's guard rising and feel my patience fraying. To Berin, each story was a challenge to his own lack of glory and experience. To me, they were reminders of violence, of the life I desperately desired not to have.

It was near midnight when the songs began. Some were happy, sparking laughter and flirtation and cheers. Others were tales of battles. These earned raucous bellows and ululating war-cries, making the many hounds in the village howl and the babies cry.

A softer song came next, one of portent and promise. An elderly couple sang it alone, sitting across from one another on an open stretch of earth, beside the main fire. They echoed one another, harmonizing, weaving melodies like threads.

Their song was familiar. It told of the end of time, when our age would end in a rain of fire and ash, and the world would be born anew. The song suited my current mood, and I listened closely as my companions quietened and the last of the well-wishers filtered away.

Finally, a tall, dark-skinned figure approached us through the crowd: Nisien, our uncle, though not by blood. He, like Ittrid, was Soulderni, but had made his home in the North.

Nisien eased himself down between me and my twin, forcing us to shift aside for him.

Around the fire, a drum began to pound and more voices joined the old couple's. The tale of the end of the world faded, merging seamlessly into the next. This one was more forceful, a victory song that called on the blood of gods and the axes of their priests. Women interspersed it with yips and churrs, harmonies and echoes that made tension skitter up the back of my arms. All the while, the drum beat.

"Before you leave, you need to speak to your mother," Nisien told us in a low voice. "She hasn't slept in days. Did you even notice she's not here? I say this not to guilt you, but to warn you. If you leave without giving her your undivided attention, I will drag you both back by your braids."

Amusement crept into the corner of Berin's eyes. "As if you could drag me anywhere, old man."

Nisien cocked his head at him as, around the fire, the Eangen continued to sing, their mirrored lyrics harmonizing and separating. Our uncle's scalp was carefully shaved, but the shadow of beard on his chin was thick with gray. He wasn't young, but he was far from helpless, and we all knew it.

Nisien continued without acknowledging Berin's boast. "I've been past the Headwaters, in the direction you're heading. Not far, but far enough. The forest is wild, and there were more beasts there than should have rightly been. Estavius and I bound a demon there too, near the eastern shore. Be wary of it. Be wary of every step you take. Double your guards during night watch. Never let your fire burn low and stay in the camp at night."

I became aware that Berin and I were not the only ones listening to Nisien. Ittrid and Askir leaned in, too, and the muscular forms of Esan and Seera hovered between us and the firelight.

"There will be no help for you, not in those wilds. Askir can summon messenger owls, I'm sure." Nisien cast the young priest a glance. "But aid will not reach you quickly, if at all. You are all more than capable warriors, and Yske will be there to heal your wounds and cure your fevers. But remember, you are not immortal. You are not

Winterborn or Miri. You are flesh and blood, bound to families who love you, and will wake every day hoping you will return."

Silence settled over us. Glancing over at Berin, I saw his posture waver, his eyes tighten as he fought back frustration and, as much as he tried to hide it, anxiety. "We will return, Uncle. Safe and whole and full of stories. This is the beginning of something great, not something to be feared."

Nisien patted both of us on our thighs and stood up again, his shadow falling into the empty space between my twin and me. "I hope that's so. I'll be waiting for you too."

After our uncle left, Berin was quiet for a few heartbeats. Our companions respected that hush, murmuring among themselves or filtering off into the night.

"We should find her," I finally admitted.

Wordlessly, Berin rose, offered me a hand, and pulled me to my feet.

EIGHT

We set off together through the celebrations, Berin grinning and exchanging a few words here and there as we searched. But I stayed quiet, letting my eyes sift through the crowd for my mother's face.

As Nisien had said, she wasn't here. We made for the hall, passing through the eerie stillness of the houses and dirt paths, neatly fenced gardens and woodsheds. Leaves rustled in the warm breeze and a night dove mourned, nestled below the fringe of grasses and flowers that adorned every roof. We passed the open windows of a home, unlit, and caught the strains of a murmured lullaby—a father's deep voice soothing the whimpers of an infant.

I glanced at Berin's expressionless face as the voice faded and we neared the lording shadow of the Morning Hall. Did he think of himself when he heard that father's song? Did he think of the child whose birth he would miss, and the pain Isa would endure alone? Did it grieve him, or was there a part of him that was relieved his wife had cast him out?

My brother's face was inscrutable, and I did not ask.

We entered the hall to find the hearth still cold, though bowled oil lamps hung from pillars here and there, lending the space a passive glow. Up in the loft the sounds of sleepy humanity drifted, but there was no one in sight as we moved past the unused tables and toward the chambers where we'd grown up.

Berin knocked and our mother's muffled voice called us in.

The room beyond was not large, centered around a stone hearth along one wall. A door stood at the far end, leading to our mother's sleeping quarters—and our father's, when he was here. Berin's and my childhood beds were built into the walls, slim straw mattresses now neatly made for guests. Shelves stretched between painted runes, displayed weapons and a poor tapestry I'd woven as a girl. A battered shield with a stylized lynx hung over the hearth, every scratch and chip and crack left intact and unrepaired. My mother's old shield.

Hessa sat at the table next to the hearth with an empty cup before her. Berin bent to hug her, putting a kiss on her cheek and sinking into the next chair as he murmured some apology over not having come earlier. I came more slowly, my stomach a tempest of emotions. Would she be upset that I hadn't been able to convince Berin to stay? Perhaps. But I hoped she would also be proud of my bravery, in agreeing to go with him instead. We should be able to say our goodbyes with hopeful smiles.

But as her eyes drifted my way, my heart stopped. My mother was a guarded woman, her walls carefully formed over years of scrutiny from our people, our allies, and our enemies. She'd worn the same mask with Berin and me for most of our lives, only removing it here and there, at the most life-altering moments—the painful ones, the death of my aunt Sixnit, the banishing of Thray, and the joyful ones like Berin's betrothal, my ordination as a healer, my father's homecomings.

Seeing unfettered emotion in my mother's eyes was a sign of change. It meant that this moment was real and potent, and the impact of it could not be avoided, for good or ill.

Her eyes were glossy with tears as she rose to pull me into a tight embrace, one of her hands buried in my hair, holding my face to the side of her own.

When she released me, my vision was blurry. I blinked hard and forced a laugh, moving to sit next to Berin. "Don't make me cry, Mama."

"I'm sorry. In honesty, I've no desire to speak about your leaving," Mother said, looking at us both across the table. It was small and we all sat close, my knee against Berin's thigh, all six of our feet clustered on the reed mats. "Except for this. Tomorrow morning, I will take you and your companions through the High Halls to the White Lake. You can begin your journey from there."

Berin's eyes widened. "That will save us weeks."

My mother nodded. "Then you'll be back to me a few weeks earlier."

I hesitated, Aita's prohibition ringing in my ears. Living humans were only permitted in the High Halls for specific purposes and duties, and my mother herself was one of the loudest voices behind this law.

"That… that's forbidden," I pointed out. "Only Askir is a priest. The rest of them shouldn't be in the Halls, not for any reason."

Berin surveyed me, a spark of indignation in his eyes. "Us. You're not a priest either."

"Aita was my mentor," I placated. "It's different. I know how to move safely in the upper realms."

"What's there to know?" Berin rolled his eyes and reached for my mother's cup, then *tsk*ed when he found it empty. "Don't drink anything, don't eat anything, and don't bother the dead. There. I've revealed all your great secrets."

My mother broke in with a hard look. "I will personally see you to the White Lake. Your company will be in the Halls for no more than an hour, under my guidance."

"There will be questions," I warned. "The Miri will oppose it. Unless Thvynder is endorsing Berin's quest?"

I said the words carefully. One of the secrets I'd scoured from the Miri was that our god, Thvynder, hadn't spoken more than a handful of times since I was a child. Any direction "from" the god since then had come through two beings the deity had made—the Watchman Omaskat and the Vestige I'd seen at the counsel, Vistic.

Mother sat back in her chair, and, in the space of that small movement, the pieces of her mask slipped back into place. The sight of it was a fist in my chest.

"I am the High Priestess of the Eangen," Hessa said. "I guide and protect our people, as I will guide and protect my children. I need no permission for that. I will ask no permission for that, and if the Miri

67

protest, I will remind them they are no longer gods. Now, go back to your festivities. Enjoy the night and the glory—and in the morning, meet me at the foot of the mountain."

I did not let myself look down the path toward my cabin as we gathered in the meadow near the old shrine. The morning was already bright and my back slick with sweat from the climb, chafing beneath my pack. It would be so easy to walk away now, down that shaded path between the trees, back to my garden and the bees and the timbers of the roof, creaking in the rising heat of the day.

"Why do you live up here alone?" The question came from Askir, the priest. He stopped next to me, turning to glance down the path I would not look at.

"Solitude," I answered simply.

"You don't like people," he observed, not judgmental, but not understanding either.

"I don't like what people do," I corrected. If I'd been honest I would have added, *I don't like what I do,* but I barely knew Askir.

The priest glanced at me, blue eyes curious. His gaze traveled up to my blonde hair, where Algatt colors were still smudged into my hairline.

"I'll see my father today," I explained, though I wasn't sure why I felt the need to. "He gave me the paints."

"He's obviously the one you take after," the priest commented, no doubt taking in the Algatt-paleness of my skin, barely darkened by days in the sun, and my sun-bleached eyelashes and brows.

My mother's voice rose through the heat and sunlight on the meadow. "This way. Follow me, and do not stray. Askir? Guide them through the door."

I stepped aside to allow Askir ahead of me as the golden rift flared. Most of our companions did not react to the sudden light—only the Sighted, priests or those touched by the High Hall's magic, could see it.

Berin and I watched them go. My brother wore a fine sword along with his axe, one-handed and straight-bladed. He had his shield at his shoulder, painted with a leaping lynx to match our mother's old, battered one. He looked the picture of an Eangen warrior, his hair neatly braided and bound, sides shaved, his beard oiled and his skin clean. His armbands and torcs glinted in the sunlight, and I felt a pang of regret.

He was made for this. Those weapons. This moment. It encouraged me and filled me with dread in the same breath.

"A gift?" I asked, eyeing the sword askance.

Berin looked down the weapon and palmed the hilt. "Yes. From Uncle Sillo."

"He didn't give me anything," I muttered with feigned hurt.

Berin gave a huffing laugh and the tension of our departure eased.

I could resist no longer. I looked over my shoulder. The worn path I so often trod stretched out from my feet, a narrow line of dry, packed earth dividing the meadow and slipping away into the trees, where sunlight and shade shifted with the wind.

Berin smiled down at me, and I didn't think I was seeing things when I glimpsed a trace of shame in his eyes. "Thank you for coming," he said for the dozenth time since last night.

I let out a long sigh and grabbed his hand. "Let's go."

The world tilted and hushed as we stepped through the rift, and then opened again. We emerged in the same meadow to find early winter snow drifting from an obscured sky. It melted as soon as it touched the ground, but balanced lightly on the arcs of brown, papery grasses and the shriveling seedheads of poppies.

The wind was refreshing rather than cold and I drew a bracing breath. The rest of the company gathered around Hessa, taking in the High Halls with caution and reverence.

As they did, the snow began to thicken and mingle with a mist that wafted in over the tops of the trees. It came to cautiously swirl around us, and our companions muttered in unease.

"These are the realms of the Miri and our dead," my mother said, watching the company closely. Snow settled on her braids and the shoulders of her pale green tunic while, behind her, the forest disappeared. "But this is no time to seek out dead loved ones. If you stray from the path I carve for you, this realm will swallow you. Do you understand? You do not belong here, not yet. That is what this mist signifies. It protects you."

There were nods and murmurs. I noticed Askir step out to the periphery of the group, reaching a hand into the miasma. It licked at his skin like flames, then retreated. He was a priest, and the mist recognized the power in his blood. Just as it did Berin's and mine.

Berin, however, eyed the fog with grim caution from the heart of our company.

"Follow me." My mother set off. As she moved her fingers wove, the fog swirled, and runes flared.

A narrow path formed beneath our feet, damp and girded with snow-crusted grass. I brought up the rear, dividing my attention between the line of my companions, the path, and the quiet all around.

We were two hours on that path, or so it felt to me. We rested once while my mother scouted the way ahead, concerned by something I neither saw nor heard. The hush between the companions was marked as we waited. For my part I stood a little away from the group, passing my hand through the fog, watching how it danced around my familiar presence.

"I'll never understand how you spent so much time here as a child," Berin muttered, holding out his flask, which I took and sipped from. Moisture condensed on his beard and hair and beaded on the wool of his outer tunic, making his thick silver armbands glisten.

"It becomes familiar." I handed back his flask. "Without the fog, it's almost… It feels so close to the Waking World, I barely notice some days."

"Except for the lurking dead and gods know what else," he muttered wryly. "Do you ever see people you know?"

I nodded. "Thray's mother comes to me, sometimes. But most of the dead avoid me now. I think Father told them to. And it's not as though they wander aimlessly; they have patterns to their days, just as we do. At least until the pull of the Hidden Hearth grows too strong, and they begin their Long Sleep."

"You mean the dead eat and drink and tell tales?" Berin suggested, quoting the conventional Eangen wisdom.

"Food must be gathered and made, and mead and ale and wine do not flow in rivers," I pointed out.

"So I'll live a glorious life and die in battle and become a brewer?" My brother laughed. "So much to look forward to."

My mother returned, offering no explanation as to what had concerned her, and we carried on. Soon, our feet passed from dirt to stone, and a light bloomed through the mist—muffled and diminished, but present. It danced above us and reached high into the sky, like the northern lights, but without color.

Our company pooled on the edge of the High Hall's version of the White Lake, the lake sacred to Thvynder and the Vynder Priesthood. My mother sketched a few runes and the fog retreated, billowing back to reveal milky waters nestled between rocky shores. Wildflowers and grasses grew in tufts here and there, but none dared encroach on the lake itself.

A rift waited, a glistening golden crack between worlds. We passed through, emerging into the Waking World on a bright summer morning. The sun just peeked over the mountains to the east, barely higher than when we had entered in the meadow.

We'd crossed the length of Eangen and into Algatt in mere hours, just as my mother had promised.

A man waited on the shore for us, his gray hair in a topknot and his gray-blond beard oiled and braided, clasped by a thick leather band. His forearms were traced with tattoos and old ritual scars, and age had hardened rather than softened his frame. Blue paint was smudged into his hairline at the temples and he wore a simple brown tunic and undyed leggings, with plain wrapped leather shoes and no legwraps. He wasn't armed, but carried two warhorns at his belt. From the sleepy squint to his blue eyes, I suspected he'd recently awoken.

"Father!" Berin called with unashamed joy, unshouldering his pack and starting toward him.

Imnir, our father, gave his son a narrow grin. "Boy."

They embraced. At the same time a dog streaked across the rocks from the direction of a forest, huge and sleek and thick at the spine with boar-bristle fur. The creature made for Hessa in a blur of wagging tail and buffeting shoulders, knocking me aside with one distracted nuzzle before planting its paws on my mother's shoulders and licking her face.

Hessa staggered, laughing, and pushed the hound down. "Nui! I thought you'd decided Omaskat was your master now, you stinking dog."

Nui sat back with a lolling tongue and looked between my mother and me. On the rocks, her tail still thumped. She had been a fixture of my life for as long as I could remember, and had accompanied my mother to Arpa before I was conceived. Still, the years had done little to slow her, and only the graying fur around her mouth showed her age.

My father pulled me into an embrace and I buried my face in his neck. My heart had begun to ache, though I wasn't sure when, and the sound of Nui's paws clattering about on the rocks as she greeted Berin only made the pain worse.

When Imnir pulled away, he kept a grasp on my shoulders and peered into my eyes. "I see tears," he observed, thumbing one away.

I blinked and wrinkled my nose. "These? No, not tears. Though if we stay long, I'm sure I can find some."

He gave a soft huff of a laugh and reached down to his belt. He unfastened the two horns and handed me one. The other, he held out to Berin. "So you can always hear one another," he said.

I met Berin's gaze and saw his lips waver at the corners. Then he nodded, a short, perfunctory nod, and fastened his new horn to his belt.

I took longer to look at mine. It was mottled gray and white, smooth and carved with runes and scenes of hunt, both ends capped with embossed silver. It was beautiful, twin to Berin's as we were twin to one another.

I lifted the horn to my lips and, drawing a deep breath into my belly, blew. The sound filled the valley, reverberating and repeating in a rich, strident call. It ended in a twisting crack, Algatt-style, and I smiled at my father as I lowered it.

"Thank you," I said, fastening the instrument to my belt as Berin had.

Imnir nodded and gestured toward the end of the valley, where the mountains folded into a pass that led down to a larger, glistening lake below. The Headwaters of the Pasidon River—and beyond it, the vague line of green that was the eastern shore. "Your boats are waiting. Walk with me, Daughter?"

I slipped my arm through his and began the long descent to the Headwaters, the boats, and that distant eastern shore.

NINE

"Where's Hessa's son?" A large boy sauntered into the ring of pounded earth. His wolfish eyes scanned the crowd and his body was honed by labor and training, but his cheeks were still soft and wore only the first hint of a beard. He couldn't have been older than fifteen—four years older than Berin and I were on this hot, dusty festival day. Those lupine eyes, however, were too old for his face. They were sharp and guarded, hiding a ravenous hollow beneath.

A boy with much to prove, my mother would say.

Every muscle in my body tensed. There were many strangers in Albor, gathered for the summer festival that had brought celebrants, warriors, and priests from across Eangen to the Morning Hall. A gathering like this naturally led to games and rivalry, and, as befit a people still named after the dead Goddess of War, martial contest.

Crowds gathered all around Albor's walls, backed by lines of tents and wagons and tethered horses. The air smelled of dust, sweat, and cooking food. Faces from every Eangen clan pressed in, marked out by slight variations in their hair and clothing. Pale-skinned Algatt and dark-skinned Soulderni were almost as numerous, and ale flowed under the hot sun.

"I'm here." Berin shouldered through the throng and stopped with his toes at the edge of the ring—to step over the rope barrier would be to accept a challenge and commit to a fight.

At eleven my brother was already tall, with broadening shoulders and a deceptive thinness to his face that tricked the eye into thinking him much older. Still, he was a child, and murmurs rippled through the assembly.

Seera shoved up to my side, followed closely by Ovir and Esan.

"Who's that?" Seera asked me in a low voice.

"I've no idea," I whispered back, shuffling to the side to give her more room. She didn't really need it—where the approach of womanhood had gifted me round cheeks and broadening hips, it had made her lean and willowy. But her posture demanded space, and I was in no mood to rile her.

"Do you live up to your mother's legacy, boy?" the young man in the ring asked, pacing and eyeing my brother in a way that made my skin crawl.

Seera snorted and exchanged a toothy grin with Ovir and Esan.

"What an assling," Esan muttered. At fourteen he was as gangly as Seera, though taller, and bore the disproportionately large hands, feet, and nose of many boys his age. Ovir was stockier, inching closer to the muscular frame and heavy strength that would mark him in adulthood.

Berin stepped over the rope line. Some older figures in the crowd laughed at his brazenness, amused by the spectacle, but Berin didn't seem to catch that. His chest puffed. "Don't waste my time. Face me and find out."

I lunged and grabbed the back of his shirt. My own toes stuttered, almost over the line of the fighting ground.

"Berin, don't listen to him," I hissed. "This is stupid!"

The challenger's eyes flicked to me. "Aw, your little sweetheart's afraid for you, Son of Hessa. He's already in the ring, love. No turning back now. Unless he's a coward?"

Berin's body stiffened and he tugged from my grasp. "I'm no coward, and that is my sister," he said coolly. "Her *name* is Yske."

"Oh, the twin!" The challenger grinned and spun back on the crowd, beckoning someone else. A young woman parted from the press, a few years his junior and carrying her own battered practice sword. Without a moment's hesitation, she stepped over the rope line. "I've a sister too. Doubles, then?"

"No," Berin snapped and stepped in front of me, blocking his opponent's view. "She doesn't fight."

The challenger gestured to his sister's feet, already in the ring. "Pity, she's already here. Looks like you'll have to fight both of us alone."

Hands pressed into my back. I squawked and twisted to find Seera trying to shove me into the ring. "Seera!"

"You can't let him fight alone!" she scolded, appalled by my apparent stupidity. But I saw the fear in her, too. Berin would, at the least, be humiliated today.

"You go!" I swatted at her, a strike she easily batted aside.

"I wasn't challenged!"

"Yske's not good enough," Esan interjected, and I was almost grateful, even if shame burned on my cheeks.

"At least she can distract one of them, give Berin space to breathe," Seera hissed.

Hurt gouged deeper than fear. My cousin was suggesting I let myself be beaten like a pell.

Ovir looked uncertain. "That's—"

All at once Seera shoved me. I stumbled into the ring and Berin turned, staring from my feet to my face with wide eyes. I stared right back. For the first beat of my heart, I was too petrified to move. With the second beat came anger, hot and blazing. I spun back on Seera, but she only smirked, hiding her former appalled expression with an arrogant turn of her lips.

"It's your own fault you're terrible," she reminded me, as she so often did. "Learn or get hurt."

Ovir leaned out and offered me his own wooden sword, urgency in his eyes. "Focus on protecting yourself."

My heart pounded. I scanned the crowd, looking for an adult who might intervene, but everyone here either respected the rope boundary and the customs of the ring or was too cowardly to speak up.

If I'd been a few years older, I would have simply walked away. I might have talked Berin out of this foolishness and broken tradition.

But in that moment, there was no going against expectation. I was a child—the rules of the world were still black and white, and the crowd might as well have been a stone wall.

"Find Thray," I hissed to Ovir, accepting the sword. Someone else passed me a shield. I didn't see who—I wasn't paying attention, and nearly dropped it on my foot.

"Your mother—" he started to say as I fumbled.

"Not her! Find Thray." I turned to stand next to Berin. I was shaking, the shield heavy in my left hand and the sword firm in my right, but my quaking was more from anger than fear now. I hated Seera. I hated this arrogant challenger who had goaded my brother into the ring.

And I hated myself, because Seera was right. I started to heft the shield, felt my shoulder already begin to burn, and braced my elbow on my hip.

Berin glanced down at me. He looked how I felt, his expression a mixture of fear and anger. "Stay behind me and out of the way."

I couldn't figure out how to talk, so I just made a bitter sound. Trying not to get bloodied was something I'd had a fair amount of practice in. And from the way our opponents watched us, with overexaggerated patience, enjoying our scrambling, I certainly wouldn't be leaving this ring without pain today.

I risked one glance back at the crowd. Seera still watched, arms laced over her flat chest, with Esan beside her. Ovir was nowhere to be seen. Had he gone to find Thray, like I'd asked?

I turned back to our challengers, raised my shield into a low guard, and pressed my sword into its rim. My shield arm continued to quake, but I gritted my teeth.

Berin followed suit, half a pace ahead of me with his sword behind him, hidden from our opponents' view.

They took up their own shields, found their stances, and a horn blew.

Our opponents immediately began to move and I fixed my gaze on the sister, expecting her to come at me. But she didn't. She charged Berin, and the brother sprinted for me.

What happened next was a blur. I threw up my shield just in time to block a thrust to the face. The sword deflected but the rim of his shield slammed into mine so hard, my shield cracked off my head. Blackness burst across my vision.

Before I could fall a second hit took me in the stomach, then my eyes were full of sunlight and my mouth with blood and grit. I twisted in pain, uselessly trying to protect myself.

The light cut off as someone stepped over me, then resumed its blinding burn.

I blinked, caught an agonized breath, and rolled. Berin. Where was he? Was he all right?

There. Through a flutter of dusty lashes I saw my brother beating back his challengers with his sword alone. His shield was gone, toppled into the crowd and out of play, and blood ran from burst skin around his eye. I'd spent enough time with Aita to recognize how he favored his side, and he kept his left foot forward instead of his usual right. He was hurt, and the match would be over in moments.

Rage welled up, high in my chest. It pressed into my throat, on the edge of eruption, and for the space of two rattling breaths I had a choice—subdue it or let it free.

The challenger feinted toward Berin, thrusting out his shield to catch my brother's sword. Meanwhile, he stabbed at Berin's belly—nearly the same move he'd used on me. But before either strike landed, he twisted away, throwing up his shield to protect his head.

Berin fell for the ploy. He lunged, throwing himself into a thrust for his opponent's exposed torso. As he did, the sister darted in, slamming her sword across the back of Berin's head. Berin staggered.

I didn't see if he fell. My rage erupted—rage for Berin, rage at Seera, rage at my own inability and the injustice of this stupid, stupid contest.

I howled and launched myself off the blood-splattered dust. The sister and I went down in a heap, all bones and fists, clumsy weapons and feral shrieks.

I slammed my fist into her face. I tore out one of her small braids and ground it into her mouth. I felt my knuckles shred on her teeth but there was no pain to it—her howl of startled agony alleviated mine.

A hand grabbed my hair. My victim's brother dragged me off her and tossed me away. I hit the ground and rolled twice, then scrambled up and threw myself at his legs. He went down too and I climbed him, ignoring a smashing sword hilt, struggling against flesh and muscle until I felt his throat. I slammed all my weight down on his windpipe.

Hands clawed at me from behind—the sister again. I smashed my elbow into her face, but lost grip on the brother at the same time. My fingers raked skin like claws.

We rolled. My back hit the earth and a fist struck my face. Once, twice.

Nothing. Blackness. Then a face rimmed in white hair, full of sunshine. I blinked dust from my eyes and started to cry. I didn't sob, or make a sound. Everything hurt too much for that. But tears cut down the sides of my face, one trailing into my ear in a hot, unpleasant droplet.

"Hush. Don't move," Thray, my cousin, soothed. She was tall and strong, with an oarsman's muscled shoulders, and broad hips and thighs that gave her the solidity of an oak beneath her light linen tunic. Her skin held a rich Eangen undertone, cast with freckles, and her smile was double-edged—kind for me, furious at the situation.

The fight rushed back to me as Thray straightened and looked around the ring. People immediately slunk back and I saw Berin sitting close to me, one leg bent before him and the other extended as an older man felt at his foot. He met my gaze over cheeks streaked with blood and dirt, but I saw bright tears hidden in the corners of his eyes. He looked shocked. Boyish. Vulnerable. And it made my heart twist.

Our opponents were on the other side of the ring, surrounded by a handful of their own friends or kin. Both had numerous injuries, but it was the claw-marks on the young man's face that caught my eye, and the fact that his sister was missing two teeth. Blood streamed down her chin and she glared at me with murder in her eyes.

I looked down at my bloody knuckles and nails. I felt no satisfaction. My temper was depleted now, leaving only an empty kind of humiliation—and dawning horror at what I'd done.

Thray, daughter of Sixnit and the fallen immortal Ogam, spoke. "I hope you feel shame," she said, returning her eyes to our opponents and letting them drag to Seera, who scowled more fiercely to hide her embarrassment.

"Did you think it would be glorious, beating children?" Thray asked the brother and sister who'd so unfairly challenged Berin. "I see you're barely more than children yourselves, but that is no excuse. You are pathetic, attention-hungry cowards, and you are no longer welcome here. Go home to lick your wounds, and know you've disgraced your kin in the sight of Albor and the Priesthood."

My heart swelled, full of justice and the fire of righteous indignation. The pair started to leave, half dragged by those around them, but they looked back as they went. The looks they cast Berin and me reignited my anger, offering a blistering, ecstatic relief.

This time, I swallowed it down. This time, I pushed it away, stowing it back into the iron lock-box of my chest.

But my shame now refused to be contained. My own wildness, my savage disregard for other human beings, disturbed me. What if I'd had a real blade? What if I'd been stronger, been better? What if I'd had the skills to truly do harm?

I squeezed my eyes shut and covered my ears as the murmuring of the crowd returned to a full, riotous clash of voices—laughter, chatter, shouts and mutters.

I had no answer to those questions. Because I would never, ever let myself find out.

TEN

The Headwaters of the Pasidon stretched before us in a vast, shallow inland sea. The prows of our boats parted water as smooth as poured glass, and the slosh and drip of our oars was the only sound—until, every so often, the surface of the lake erupted into a series of frothing springs. The pristine reflection of blue sky and drifting clouds shattered and the boats rocked, but my companions plied their oars without falter.

We'd left Hessa and Imnir on the western shore, along with a handful of priests and priestesses who dwelled around the White Lake. Goodbyes had not been easy, but by unspoken agreement they'd been brief. We'd exchanged crushing embraces, then pushed off from shore. My parents were, to their core, forged by loss—they didn't turn to empty words and impossible pledges of safe returns.

Instead, they'd sent Nui. Or rather, Nui had charged out through the shallow water after us, leapt into my boat and refused to leave again. So now the dripping mass of hound sat behind me, resting her head on my shoulder. She had become our tenth companion.

Late afternoon, we dropped our packs on the eastern shore and began to pull the boats into a thick stand of cedars. I set my pack on a rock and made to grab the prow of one of the vessels, only to find Seera's hand already there.

"Let us," she nudged me aside and hefted the dripping craft. "And don't wander off alone. This isn't Mount Thyr."

"Of course it's not—" I cut off my retort as Esan hefted the other end of the craft.

He glanced between my cousin and me. "You two are going to make this miserable, aren't you?"

Seera swore at him, but kept hold of her end of the craft. They bore it up into the safety of the trees and left me to stew.

I busied myself ensuring each pouch was fastened to my pack and nothing had gotten damp in the crossing. I shouldn't let Seera's disdain under my skin. Yes, I was no warrior. I was a pacifist in a people whose legacy was bloodshed and martial prowess, who still carried a fallen Goddess of War in their name. In the eyes of everyone here, I was a liability, someone who had to be guarded and couldn't be trusted to guard them in return.

But I was not here to fight. I was here to heal.

Nui trotted up and nosed under one of my wrists, sniffing at my hand for food. I bent and took her head between my hands, peering into the creature's eyes. She looked back at me plaintively, and I cracked a smile.

"Well, it won't be long before Seera cuts herself open or catches a fever," I muttered, low enough that only the hound could hear. The urge to rage swelled, crested, and passed. "Then who will she come to?"

Once a campfire was blazing, I turned to gathering the night's wood, trudging through the forest as Nui darted around me, overjoyed to be in a world of new sights, sounds, and smells.

The forest itself was calm. Demure. It showed no signs of being any different than the woods in which I lived, save that this one was a little less rocky. Perhaps the years since Nisien's visit had softened this wilderness. Or, perhaps, we were simply not deep enough to see its true threat.

I stared upward at the canopy, where dark cedar bows met the brighter green of an oak and the myriad fluttering coins of a birch. A small bird darted from branch to branch, and the blue of the sky beyond had only just begun to seep into the deeper hues of a delayed northern dusk.

A branch cracked. All my calm dissolved and I spun, snatching my knife and horn from my belt. I could blow it as I ran, praying that Berin heard me. The knife—it wouldn't do much good against anything bigger than a rabbit, but if I went for the beast's eyes—

"Yske. Yske! It's me," Berin laughed. Seeing my petrified expression only broadened his grin. "Gods below, you're skittish. We're barely out of sight of the shore."

My cheeks burned. Nui trotted up to nose at the dead grouse in my brother's hand, and, holding it out of her reach, he said, "Come back to camp with me if you're so nervous. Someone else can gather wood."

"Nisien said he'd bound a demon near here," I reminded him, eager to legitimize my reaction.

"So? We brought a priest." He nodded at the dangling grouse, its head limp on a broken neck. "Come on, you can pluck this for me. I'm terrible at it."

I frowned at him. "No, you're just lazy. I'll finish my own task, thank you."

He shrugged and vanished into the trees with the grouse still held high, Nui trotting behind him.

I found a dead pine and took my frustration out on its branches. Finally, hair dusted with crumbled bark and arms laden with more wood than I could comfortably carry, I went back to camp. I met no unbound demons on the way, nor saw the Binding Tree where Nisien and Estavius had imprisoned theirs. No strange beasts stalked me—to my knowledge—and no poisonous vines crept out to snare my ankles. I was almost disappointed by the time I deposited the wood near the fire and stretched my sore arms.

"What's it like out there?" Ittrid glanced up as she plunged Berin's grouse in and out of a pot of boiling water. My brother himself was, predictably, nowhere to be seen. "You're covered in… something."

"Just like home." I offered her a small smile, brushed off my hair and held out my hands for the grouse. "Here, I'll help pluck. Then if you've an extra pot, I'll make us some tea."

That night I lay my oilskin and blankets next to Berin under the shelter of the cedars, between knots of gnarled roots. The earth here was soft and the canopy thick, blotting out the stars. But through the shadowed pillars of the tree trunks, the light of a sickle moon bathed the Headwaters in the barest, murky illumination. There was no movement on the water now, no whisper of a breeze or distant bubbling of springs. The shallow lake slept. The forest slept. But I lay awake for long while, listening to my brother breathe.

Eventually I dreamed of a woman, standing between me and the silent water. I could see only the shape of her—aging and lean, clad in a long tunic with her legs bare, her hair falling in waves past her shoulders. She did not look at the lake or the trees, or any of our sleeping companions. She saw only me and Berin, side by side.

In the next breath, the woman crouched over me on all fours— knees at my waist, hands beside my head. Though I still could not see her face, light awoke behind her, soft glows of white and green hidden among the branches of the cedars. Foxfire. But these trees were alive, and that made no sense. *Just part of the dream*, I thought.

I could smell the stranger now—the scent of old, dry wood and a muddy freshwater shoreline, half dank, half sweet. She was close enough that I felt her breath, but I was unafraid. I was simply an observer of the moment, watching her without comprehension or feeling.

Leaning down, she inhaled the scent of my skin. I felt the brush of her tongue across my lips in a slow, calculated gesture—chin to nose, rough and damp and burning like nettle.

I awoke with a gasp, raking the stink of musk and damp fur into my nose. Instinct made me freeze, my mind blank and breath lodged in my throat.

Darkness loomed over me, but it was too thick for the shadows beneath the trees. Slowly, a shape came into focus—a monstrous, furry head. I felt the brush of fur across my temples and the nudge of an animal's nose against my chest, sniffing and licking me like Nui might a pup.

This was not Nui's scent. No, this smell was deeper, sharper. I heard a snuffling grunt—a sound I'd heard at the base of my door enough times to know what it was.

A bear. I was lying, helpless, beneath a bear. It nudged me again, this time nearly lifting my arm with its casual searching. A huge paw landed beside my ear, and I felt the vibration in my bones.

"Berin," I started to whisper, but bit my lips closed as the bear paused in its snuffling. My mind raced. Where was Nui? Who was on watch? And why had none of them sounded a warning?

Abruptly, the bear turned away. Its footfalls were deafening, and I thought my teeth might shudder out of my jaw. But after a few hammering heartbeats, the steps began to fade. There were no growls, no screams. Just the sound of the beast wandering off into the forest.

Finally, Nui let out a startled bark and launched out of the shadows. As if a spell had been broken, my companions jerked into wakefulness. Berin rolled over in an instant, seizing his sword and blinking in half-conscious confusion.

"What is it?" he demanded. "Ittrid, the fire! Who's on watch? Yske, calm that dog!"

Our companions clamored, voices clashing and accusations flying. In the midst of it I sat up, testing each muscle and limb, stunned to find myself unharmed. The memory of the dream, the tongue, and the bear still clung to my skin with the prickling intensity of a summer storm, but I managed to shout, "Nui, here!"

The dog came, buffeting me as I fumbled onto my knees and wrapped an arm around her chest. She quivered, letting out several more barks before she whined and eased back into me. As big as she was, when she perched on my knees her head was well above my own.

"Hush," I chided, stroking her chest and scratching beneath her pricked, vigilant ears. "It's gone, you lazy hound. You could have warned us earlier."

"Warned us of what?" The question came from Seera, stalking out of the shadows with the wordless form of Askir. She glared from me to Sedi and Bara, who looked trapped between ashamed and horrified.

Light washed over us as Ittrid turned the lifeless coals of our fire and fed it a wispy nest of birch bark, then began to add twigs. She looked drawn, and an axe lay close at her side.

"There was a bear," I said. "It licked my face and wandered off."

Berin stared at me, aghast. "It… What? Why didn't you wake me?"

"There wasn't time," I said. My voice didn't shake, but I hoped no one would notice how tightly I held Nui. "It was right above me, Berin. If I'd startled it, I'd be dead."

"How big was it?" Askir asked, more curious than concerned. I was almost offended.

I thought of how the beast's head had filled my vision, and its questing nose had pressed into my flesh. "Very, very big."

Berin sheathed his sword with a frustrated thrust. "Askir, Seera, make sure it's gone."

The pair faded without a word, and my brother turned to glare at Sedi and Bara. "You fell asleep," he accused.

Bara's stricken expression was answer enough. Sedi turned and walked away, hiding her face in the darkness, and compassion tugged at me.

"It's our first night," I soothed. "We lowered our guard, but now we know better. No one was hurt and all is well."

Berin ignored me. "Sedi, don't walk away from me. You realize what could have happened? This is our first night. *Our first night*, and you can't even manage to stay awake for a few hours? My sister could have been killed!"

"Berin—" I tried again, stepping between him and our faulty watchmen.

My brother pushed me aside and advanced on Sedi and her husband. "I should send you back across the lake."

"I wasn't asleep," Sedi broke in, turning around. "Bara was, and I didn't have the heart to wake him. But I was awake, Berin. The whole time. I saw nothing. I heard nothing. I don't know how it happened."

Berin scoffed, his temper rising. "You think lying to me will make this better?"

Suspicion, unformed and vague, drifted through my mind. Leaving Berin and the others to fight, I moved to pluck a birch branch from the stack of firewood, lit it in the flames as Ittrid watched curiously, and went carefully back over to my bedroll. As oily birch bark curled and warm light flooded over earth, I made out the shape of the bear's tracks—the puncture marks of huge claws and the curve of footpads. Nui trotted up, distorting the markings, but not before I'd seen what I needed to. A little disappointment trickled through me.

Berin and the others continued to debate.

"What is it?" Ittrid asked me, voice low.

I glanced over at her. "Is it… is it possible the bear was Aegr? We are looking for his people, after all, and if Sedi was awake… Aegr is a creature of the High Halls. It might explain why she and Nui didn't sense anything."

Ittrid shrugged, eyes wide and cautious at once. "I don't know. Have you seen him before?"

"No." I stared at the paw print. It was huge, but perhaps not huge enough. "But my mother did, when she was a girl. He saved her from an unbound demon."

"He does that," Ittrid agreed with a distracted nod. "Perhaps he saved us from something?"

My thoughts drifted to the dream, of the woman and the burn of nettle. It had been a dream, of course, but…

I let the thought go as Ittrid's gaze drifted to where Bara and Sedi stood shoulder to shoulder, watching with dread as Berin conferred with Ovir and Esan. There were tears in Sedi's eyes, and I caught the threads of Berin's conversation. They were still discussing sending Bara and Sedi home.

Sedi met my gaze and I saw a flicker of pleading. My stomach dropped. If she thought I might be able to persuade Berin because he was my twin, she'd already been proven wrong. I was the one who'd been in danger, and Berin would not back down. But what else could I do?

Words came to my tongue without bidding. They burned there for a moment, flush with pending shame. But I still spoke up. "It was the tea."

They all turned to look at me, and Berin furrowed his brows. "What?"

"I put sweet tear in the tea to help us sleep," I lied. "I didn't think about how it would affect those on watch. Or I added too much, I don't know."

Bara cut me a startled look. "But I didn't dri—"

Sedi elbowed him discreetly, her gaze fastened on me.

"Sweet tear soothes the nerves and encourages deep sleep," I explained, speaking over him. "Like I said, I didn't think about it, and I must have added too much."

Berin's expression rapidly shifted through anger and disbelief to uncertainty, and finally settled in a cold mask I'd no doubt he'd learned from our mother. "That was stupid of you."

"I didn't think," I repeated a third time. The disapproval and incredulity of my companions made my stomach knot in discomfort. But there was relief in Sedi and Bara's eyes, and it gave me the strength to go on. I might not be able to persuade Berin to have mercy on them, but he would be merciful to me. "I've never done this before. I drink it nearly every night at home and—"

"Enough," Berin cut me off. He grabbed the burning birch stick from my hand and tossed it back into the fire with a whoosh of sparks. "Go back to sleep, all of you. Askir and Seera can take watch when they return; I trust *them* to have the discipline to stay awake. There are only a few hours 'til dawn anyway."

I felt ill as I settled back onto my bedroll, avoiding the gazes of the others and the mutters passing through them. Even Sedi joined in, her relief fading into faux indignance. But just before I lay down, Bara crouched beside me.

"I didn't drink your tea," he murmured, lending me the impression of a smile. Gratitude etched around his tired eyes. "And I doubt you gave any to the hound. We owe you a debt, Yske."

I gave a wan, secret smile in return, and he slipped away.

ELEVEN

A ita's road lay hidden among the trees, marked by two moss-covered milestones. One stood half-buried in a patch of ferns spilling out onto the broad shoreline in the shade of ancient oaks. The other had fallen, pushed from the earth like a splinter from flesh as roots vied for space.

I crouched beside the displaced stone, moving carefully under the weight of my pack. Runes were carved into the waystone's face, just visible under moss and lichen. Their shape was familiar, square and measured. They were part of a Miri system I'd seen many times in the High Halls, but couldn't entirely read.

"This must be it," I said, putting a hand on the stone to help myself back to my feet. My tired legs immediately protested, though the sun wasn't even halfway high in the sky.

"I don't see a path." Seera looked from the stones to the treeline, nose wrinkled. She was as sweaty as I was under the late-summer sun, but the glisten on her forehead and the way her tunic clung to her flat, muscled stomach just made her look more intimidating.

Feeling puffy and overripe, I scraped damp hair back from my forehead and hoisted my pack a little higher. The rest of the company spread out around us, in various stages of sitting, staring, and blinking sweat from their eyes.

"This must be it," I repeated calmly.

Berin drew up beside me and scrutinized the supposed road. The forest looked no different between the milestones than it did on either side.

It was thick and overgrown, a wilderness that had never been picked over by humans or tamed by wandering livestock. The trees were old, girded by the decomposing remnants of their comrades, twined with vines and interjected with boulders, shallow ravines and gouges in the earth.

It was the latter three that the road lacked. The forest might have grown over the smooth surface of the ancient road, but it had been well-built beneath. It was level and unbroken, stretching off into verdant shadows.

"This is it," Berin agreed. He glanced back the way we'd come, to where Nui nosed about the shallow edges of the Headwaters, and whistled. "Let's go."

The forest seemed to hold its breath as we entered, Nui bursting ahead of us in ecstatic leaps. Songbirds trilled in the distance, swooping and rising with the rush of wind in the leaves. Despite the thickness of the forest there was still enough breeze here, near the edge, to chase away the humidity, leaving us in a sanctuary of mottled sunlight.

For those first few paces, my heart rose. I thought that, perhaps, this journey would not be so challenging as I'd expected. Then the trees closed in, the canopy clotted, and the wind choked out. The warning drone of mosquitoes rose from the forest floor on a wave of moisture, and the heat wrapped around us like a sodden blanket.

I sighed—short and brusque, so as not to inhale the insects—and reached into a pouch on my pack. I pulled out nine bundles of herbs on leather cords and held one out to Ovir, the closest of the companions.

"Here," I said as he flattened a mosquito against his bare, muscled forearm and tugged his sleeve down. "This will keep them away."

"Thank you?" the man said, looking confused, and sniffed the bundle. He made a face. "Gods, this smells terrible."

"To you and the insects," I said with a smile and put my own around my neck, then picked up my pace to pass them to the others.

In a few moments, the buzzing of mosquitoes retreated to a threatening hum. The sickly-sweet smell of the herbs followed us in a cloud, mingling with the sharp musk of sweat and damp earth.

I caught Seera glancing at me, hard eyes hiding a begrudging gratitude. I suppressed a satisfied smile.

Bara offered me a steaming cup of tea and sat beside me in the entrance to one of our three tents. Around us our companions slept soundly, their breathing interrupted by occasional snores. The forest itself was restless, rife with the repetitive call of a night whirl, the distant brush of wind against the canopy and the drip of moisture.

A misty rain had come and gone during the late hours of the day, leaving the forest even more damp and humid than it had been in the daylight. Mosquitoes continued to assault us in whining clouds, but I'd set a bowl of more herbs in the edge of the fire. Between the scent and the smoke, I hoped we would not be exsanguinated in our sleep.

"I promise it's only a little chicory and dandelion in the tea." Bara nudged me good-naturedly with his shoulder. He spoke low so as not to wake the others. "No sweet tear."

I suppressed a wry smile and took the cup. Settling back against my pack and Nui's sleeping bulk, I said, "Your wife hasn't spoken to me today."

Bara shrugged, puffing steam from the surface of his own tea. "Berin's threat to send us back terrified her. She's grateful to you, but she won't admit her failure. She's too proud. And she believes in this venture too much."

I cradled my cup between my hands and watched his expression. The company had dismissed my pondering that the bear had been Aegr, though Ittrid and I still had our doubts.

"What does she believe about it?" I asked.

"That opening up the east can only benefit our people," Bara replied. "We're all too young to remember what life was like before peace with the south, but we know the stories. Our people are healthier now. We live longer and the world is unfolding around us, full of new stories and new traditions, new skills and languages. Gods below, even the color of our skin is changing." He held out a hand, showing off the light brown of his skin, bronze in the light of the fire. His mother had been Soulderni, and his father half Algatt, half Eangen. "We're becoming a new people, in a way, and we—Sedi and I—want to be part of that change. It's a new age. We'd like to be remembered in the next."

"What if you don't come home?" I pried gently, trying to find the edges of his resolve. "Do you have children?"

"No. And we've made our peace with that. All of us here know that we might die. But it's worth the risk. The adventure." He looked at me across the space between us and searched my face. "Why are you here?"

"Berin," I said simply. I raised my cup to take a sip and, finding it still too hot, set it aside—out of the reach of Nui's dream-twitching paws.

Bara looked genuinely startled. "That's all? Not even a little curiosity?"

A great tree. Shadows in the black. Movement in the Unmade, beyond the edge of the world.

"I am curious," I admitted. "But I'm more determined to get Berin home alive. I'll do the same for all of you."

Bara gave a small smile. "I appreciate that. Perhaps you could start by recommending a tea that keeps sleepy husbands awake."

"I suppose I could do that," I smiled, a little smugly, and glanced out at the night. "I need to find a bush."

"Scream if something tries to eat you. I'll do what I can."

"That's all I ask."

I disentangled from Nui and slipped out of the camp into the night. Moss cushioned my feet as I searched for a spot close enough to see the firelight but far enough to claim some solitude, and saw to my needs.

I tied my trousers and resettled my tunic, along with the horn my father had given me. Other than my movements, all I heard was the occasional drip of drying leaves.

I relished the solitude. It wasn't that I was uncomfortable sitting watch with Bara. He was kind and his company pleasant. But I was used to a life alone and undisturbed; the constant interaction with others drained me, and the tension of the day and the group's overall disapproval had yet to fade. I needed to be alone for longer than a moment in the bushes, but doubted I'd have the opportunity for months to come.

As my eyes adjusted to the darkness I picked out more detail—twigs bobbing with lingering moisture, a patch of ferns glistening with damp, and a vine of pale flowers lacing up a tree patterned with soft white light.

That light was growing stronger, and with it many more sources appeared among the trees. They clung to roots and branches and laced up trunks like veins. It was white foxfire like I'd glimpsed with Isik in the High Halls, though here it was interspersed with more normal shades of blue and green. The longer I looked the more I saw, until the entire forest around me seemed to glow. It reminded me of my dream of the woman by the Headwaters, how the foxfire had entwined the living trees around her head.

But the former had been a dream, and Isik had been unconcerned in the High Halls. Yet there was something uncanny about this moment. And there seemed to be a pattern to the light: a direction. It flowed, ever so slowly, toward a singular source.

That source, I discovered when I crept forward, was a dead tree. Here the light condensed, tracing each crack and crevice of the ancient, peeling bark in fine lines. It pooled in carvings, outlining runes I instinctively understood. They were Soulderni and Arpa. I knew neither well, but these specific ones were etched into my stifled mind— runes for binding and suppression, warning and protection. They and the foxfire laced almost the entire tree, right up to its lofty branches and down to the tangled roots that tripped my feet.

A Binding Tree. My heart labored in my chest, struggling for each beat. This was Nisien's Binding Tree. It looked whole, unbroken, so there should be no need to fear an unbound demon. But why hadn't Askir noticed it?

"Yske?"

I whirled. A shadow moved, then a familiar face materialized, barely illuminated by the foxfire—a handsome face with a short beard, tanned skin, and eyes like Esach, Miri of Storms.

"Isik?" I stared at him, stunned. My nerves still sang from the presence of the tree, and the sight of my friend failed to calm them. "What are you doing here?"

Isik approached, unfastening a pouch from his belt as he did. The short sword I'd given him was at his thigh and he looked as travelworn as I did.

"Did you follow us?" My words were more accusation than question.

"I suppose?" He held out the pouch, his eyes traveling over my shoulder to the tree. "Aita sent me with a gift... Is that a Binding Tree?"

"Yes, I just found it. But it looks whole." The thought of Aita sending me a gift was just enough to distract me from the tree, and even from Isik's unexpected arrival. I took the pouch slowly. It was so light, it felt empty. "What is this?"

He shrugged, still looking at the tree. I pressed up onto my toes and leaned into his line of sight. "Isik, what's in here?"

His eyes tracked to my face. Whatever expression I wore made him crack a smile, fondness filling his eyes. My earlier disgruntlement couldn't withstand that look. I dropped back down into my heels and relaxed.

"It's a leaf," he said, unhelpfully.

"There are a lot of leaves in this world." I gave him a flat look and opened the pouch. Inside was a fold of cloth, smelling strongly of beeswax. Inside that was a single leaf, as Isik as said, stained dark with something I couldn't identify.

He peered with equal curiosity. "Aita said to tell you it's the same gift she gave Liv to heal the Great Bear, and she wanted you to have it."

Excitement was my first reaction, swift and bright. But: "Aita didn't give Liv a gift." I lifted the leaf so I could look at it more closely. "Liv stole it."

Isik startled. "I didn't know that."

I shrugged, maintaining a calm exterior, but my heart pounded. "That just makes this a greater honor, I suppose?" An understatement if there ever was one.

Uncertainty entered Isik's eyes now, but he wasn't used to Aita forcing him to consume mysterious concoctions, placating him with vagaries. I was. Aita would always explain eventually, guiding me through the properties of a given thing as it affected my body—usually as I threw up or stared at my tingling hands, or watched non-existent butterflies cavort around my cot.

I picked up the leaf and put it on my tongue, as I knew Aita would intend. It tasted acrid and I was tempted to spit it out, but resisted. I swallowed the leaf and bore the bitter aftertaste on my tongue.

Isik grimaced, and I laughed.

"Don't be so worried," I chided, trying not to screw up my nose at the taste. "I trust Aita with my life."

He frowned at me. "Perhaps I'm more concerned that you just ate a mysterious medicine, given to you by a man in a dark forest, in the shadow of a Binding Tree. What if I'd come out of that tree to trick you?"

I snorted. "You don't look like a demon. Demons are hideous and desiccated. You are…" I reached out to poke at his bicep, then squeezed it. It was soft at first, beneath the damp fabric of his tunic, then he flexed and my fingers found themselves stretched over a knot of hard, lean muscle. I met his eyes, pretending there wasn't a flush creeping across my cheeks. "Well, you are not."

"Thank you," he said graciously. I dropped my hand and we watched one another for a moment, then a thought seemed to distract him. "I thought you had a priest with you. Why didn't he warn you about the tree?"

I brushed a hand across my face, half to clear it of sweaty hair and half to erase the feeling of Isik's muscle beneath my palm. That was a good question. It was Askir's job to manage threats of a more spiritual nature, but he hadn't found the Binding Tree. It was moments from our camp and he hadn't even sensed it was here.

First Sedi and Bara had fallen asleep on watch, then our priest hadn't sensed a bound demon.

"We're going to die out here," I muttered.

That alarmed him. "Don't say that."

I waved him off with a hand. "It's all right. Aita gave me a leaf." I grinned. "We'll be safe now."

He stared down at me, incredulous, until I laughed and he sighed. "All right. You should go back to your fire."

"No, wait," I protested. "What else did Aita say?"

He shrugged and looked toward the camp, but I could tell that his nonchalance was forced. Isik was too easily read. "She said it was the same one she gave to Liv, and that you'd know how it worked. That's all. Why haven't your companions come looking for you yet? I don't like this, Yske."

I pushed thoughts of Aita and Liv aside for now, though I continued to worry at them in the back of my mind. "Our company of heroes isn't as sharp as they could be, I'm realizing. Come sit by our fire?"

Isik slowly shook his head. "I need to catch up to the rain if I'm to get home in good time. And I… I realize there would be questions about me if I showed up in your camp."

He was right, I knew. He could summon rain and control the wind under most circumstances, but his power also came from those elements. Once the earlier rain got too far away, his power would go with it, and he could be stranded in his physical form.

Besides, a Miri would cause a stir in our camp, and there would be questions I couldn't or didn't wish to answer.

"I understand," I said, disappointed.

Isik took a step back, mirroring my change in mood. His low voice was a rumble in the dark as he added, "I do wish I could stay. This is… unwise. Humans, traveling alone in a place like this."

In his words, I heard an echo of long-held Miri sentiments. Miri's long lives and great power often led to abuses, but in some it overflowed into a sense of duty to weaker beings. Esach was one of these, lofty and removed and yet pouring out her strength into the harvest each autumn. Estavius was another, giving up his very self to protect and stabilize the Arpa.

This Miri mentality didn't precisely chafe me—there was a practicality and usefulness to it that I couldn't deny, not after so long at Aita's side. But when it came from Isik, it made the distance between us feel too broad. It made me feel not like a friend, but a duty. It reminded me why our romance had died, and it tainted the warmth in my heart.

Thankfully, Isik didn't dwell on the topic. He said, "Whatever Aita's gift was, she was discreet. Perhaps it's something your mother and the priesthood would not approve of. I would not mention it to the others."

I nodded slowly. I could feel his departure looming and it made my throat tighten. "Thank you, Isik. Please send my thanks to Aita, and my regards to your mother."

He watched me for a long moment, thoughts hidden behind his eyes, then stepped forward and embraced me. I let myself be enveloped in him, in the scent of wind and sweat and rain, in the press of muscle and the solid warmth of his frame.

Then he let go, stepped back, and vanished into the forest night.

TWELVE

The following weeks passed with little interruption, save for a pack of wolves pressing too close to camp and Esan nearly being gored by an angry boar. The wolves fled when we banked our fire and the boar we butchered, the night's watches smoking the meat to preserve it for the hot days to come. I tended Esan's wounds, and he healed with remarkable speed.

The heat was intense. We sweated through our clothing, but didn't dare shed it in the clouds of mosquitoes. I ran out of herbs and couldn't find opportunities to replenish them, so we soon became mottled with welts.

Still, we forged ahead, uncovering mossy milestones, skirting swaths of marsh, and fording murky rivers.

I did not speak of the Binding Tree Askir had missed, though I feared that might be a grave error. Covering for a sleeping watchman was one thing, but ignoring a deficiency in our priest might be even more deadly. Yet the further we trekked, the less relevant it felt—Askir proved his capabilities several times, warning us off an ancient burial mound and a seemingly natural spring that turned out to be rune-cursed. So I added the missed Binding Tree to my cache of secrets, and plodded on.

Most of my thoughts were occupied by the unknown potential of the gift Aita had given me. Would my wounds heal faster now? Could I heal with a touch? I considered experimenting on my companions when they brought me their ailments, but that seemed unwise. I could cut myself, but the memory of the scars on my mother's hands and arms stopped me. Shedding blood to test Aita's gift felt far too much like a sacrifice to a Miri, and that I could not stomach. I would simply wait and see.

The month waned and the weather became more consistently overcast. The rain never fell hard, but its frequency ensured both us and the forest remained in a constant, miserable state of damp. I pulled burrowing insects from my companions' flesh, treated a passing fever and made salves for Ittrid, whose skin broke out in a terrible rash.

I did not complain, no matter how difficult the foraging became, how terribly my back ached, or how badly the veins burst across my shoulders from the straps of my pack. I grumbled only to Nui and the trees as I gathered firewood, seeking the consolation and solitude of the forest before dusk. I hunted for wild carrots, berries, and mushrooms, and filled my folded tunic with burdock and lily roots. I replenished my herbs whenever I could, and hung them to dry beside my sweat-soaked tunic each night.

Finally, we topped a ridge to see a clear, bright river, toppling over shoulders of rock smoothed by time and plunging into shallow pools. The trees gave way, permitting the river and falls to sparkle in the light of the sun.

"Gods below, I'm having a proper bath," Seera declared, already starting down the hill with a skidding, balancing step. "Leave me behind if you have to!"

Berin glanced at the sun overhead, but there was a smile on his sweaty face. "We'll stop for the day," he decided, though Seera was already out of earshot, dumping her pack on a sunny expanse of rock and pulling her tunics over her head.

Cheers and laughter accompanied the rest of the party down the hill and onto the rocks. Nui bounded after them, knocking a half-naked Ovir into the pool before joining him with a great splash.

Berin and I descended more slowly, he holding out his hand to steady me as I skidded through last year's deadfall and emerged from the shade of the trees. On the sides of my pack, bundles of herbs and wild carrots swung.

"You look like a bush," he told me fondly. "And you smell like a sickbed."

"It's a sacrifice," I informed him with a weary grin.

We shrugged off our packs a little away from the others. All our companions save Askir were in the water already. I watched the priest leap a narrow arm of the river and vanish back into the trees to scout.

"What's wrong?" Berin watched me set my pack against a boulder.

I winced—I was so sore by now that it was hard to move, and with just Berin nearby, my guard slipped. "Nothing. I just... Everything hurts. But this is good. The river. The rest."

He pulled his tunic off. I noted the welts of insect bites across his chest and started to *tsk*, but he waved me off. "Back, witch. At least the mosquitoes are dying off. It means summer is ending, but I'll gladly take a cold autumn over heat and insects."

I thought nervously ahead to the colder months and the certainty of snow. "What if the Easterners won't let us winter with them?" I prodded, not for the first time.

"Yske, we've discussed this. They welcomed the Arpa, why wouldn't they welcome us?"

"But we're not Arpa." Bending down, I removed the small circular pin from my legwraps and began to unwind them, relishing the cool breeze on the sweat-soaked fabric of my trousers. "We're the barbarians the Arpa didn't even bother to conquer."

"Don't worry so much," Berin chided, scratching at the bites on his chest and eyeing the water. He started forward, then glanced back at me. "Coming?"

"Go on," I told him, waving at the river. "I'll find a quieter pool to bathe in."

Berin glanced from me to our swimming, laughing companions. "We've all seen your skin before, Yske."

"All the same."

"Don't go far, then." He left me, shed the rest of his clothing into a pile and made for the others.

I watched him go for a moment, suppressing a sudden surge of loneliness. Esan and Ovir hurled sodden pinecones at one another and Nui raced between them, leaving trails of dripping water on the warm rock. Berin joined with a splash that nearly washed Ovir out of his pool and down into the next. Seera laughed freely at them from where she, Ittrid, Bara and Sedi floated, sharing a pot of soap between them.

They were happy. Harmonious.

I gathered my sweat-soaked clothes and strode to an empty pool behind a stretch of bushes. I fetched a knot of dried widow soap leaves and lavender from my pack and set to grinding the leaves on the smooth rock ledge. I splashed a little water into the mixture, then left it to bubble as I slipped into the pool.

The water was cool but shallow, and the rock bowl it lay in was warmed by the sun. I scrubbed dirt and sweat from my stiff hair and flushed skin, letting the water wash the pungent suds over a ledge and downstream. Then I scooped up what remained of the soap with my clothes and scrubbed them as best I could.

I tossed them over the bushes to dry in the sun and breeze and drifted, belly up and eyes half-closed. I could hear the chatter of the others all around, but with my ears just below the water I could almost fool myself into thinking I was alone, back at my favorite bathing spot on the slopes of Mount Thyr. I heard Nui barking and saw her frolic through the shadow of the trees, chasing a churring squirrel. I smiled, my sore muscles eased, and my lingering tension did too.

"Do you have more widow soap?"

I raised my head and cracked an eye to see Askir standing at the side of my pool, naked and lean. I watched him for a moment, pulling myself out of my imaginings of home, then floated my feet down to the bottom of the pool and stood.

"In the side of my pack," I pointed. "The third pouch, with the bone fastening."

He vanished without a word of thanks. Disgruntled, I turned away and began to work the tangles from my hair, wishing I'd thought to bring my comb over.

Askir reappeared without a single scuff or murmur of warning, widow root leaves in hand. "May I?" He gestured at my pool.

I was too startled to resent the invasion of privacy. "Of course."

He slipped into the water and, spying the rock I'd used to crush my own soap, began to do the same. I eyed his back, the nape of his neck caked with dirt and blond hair in a knotted tuft atop his head.

"Nothing worrying in the forest?" I asked.

"I wouldn't be naked if there was," he informed me, scooping water into the crushed leaves with one hand. While it began to bubble he looked back at me. "I've been meaning to ask you something."

Ah. So there *was* a reason he was here.

"You have an aura about you, like the Miri," Askir informed me. His gaze was unsettlingly direct, but I was coming to recognize this as one of the priest's defining traits. "You and Berin both, but you a little more."

I settled deeper in the water, leaving only my head above the surface. Water licked at my chin and my hair drifted in clumps. "You can see that with your Sight," I observed. Every Vynder priest was gifted with the ability to see magic in its various forms, some stronger than others.

He nodded.

"Hessa is our mother and Imnir is our father," I pointed out. "Both of their blood is more gold than scarlet."

"Then why is your aura stronger than Berin's?"

"I'm blessed."

Askir didn't reply immediately. He untangled his hair from its leather tie and ducked under the water to wet it, leaving me in a stretch of bubbling quiet. Then he resurfaced, puffed water from his lips and set to scrubbing his hair with soap. He hadn't added lavender, and the bitter smell of the leaves wafted over to me.

"Your aura has grown stronger in the last few days," he informed me. He kept his eyes closed as he clawed his scalp. "It seems to me that the farther we get from home, the stronger it becomes."

I froze, taken aback. He chose that moment to duck under the water again and held there, rummaging his fingers through his hair to loose the dirt and soap. Brown suds floated away on the gentle current and vanished over the ledge.

Aita's gift had increased my aura. My Sight was strong, but I hadn't thought to examine myself since Isik's visit.

"You must be mistaken," I told him when he resurfaced a second time, shaking his head like a dog and blinking water from his eyes. Whatever was happening, I didn't like that Askir had noticed, or was questioning me about it. I'd sworn to Aita that I would keep her secrets and those of the High Halls. "That doesn't make any sense."

Askir watched my face, water still dripping from his blond beard and hair. "You don't know why it's happening," he observed.

"No," I said, with enough honesty to believe it myself. "You're our priest. This is why you're here."

He wiped the water from his beard and nodded slowly, unaffected. "I'll think on it."

He set to washing the rest of his body, and I left the pool. Padding back to my pack, I let my skin dry in the sun while I dug out my spare linen undertunic and my comb, and set to untangling my hair. But as warm as the sun was, and as calming the routine, Askir's words stayed with me.

What was Aita's gift doing to me, and how long would it last? When I returned home, would my mother notice it too?

"Berin!" Ittrid's voice cut through the air. "Everyone! Come see this!"

Comb still in my hand, I hastened to the nearest ledge, bare feet curling on the warm rock. Several tiers below I spied the Soulderni woman, dressed and damp-haired, waving from a place where the river veered back into the forest. Between us the rest of our companions swam or lay in various stages of dress, but at Ittrid's words they stirred.

"What is it?" Seera called, hopping on one foot to pull on her trousers.

"A cave," Ittrid replied, tone caught between excitement and awe. "And a Great Bear."

The rush of water and the pad of our bare feet were the only sounds in the cave. Light chased us through the yawning mouth and peered through gouges in the rock above, where tree roots stretched toward a central pool with tangled, crooked fingers. They formed a living veil between Berin and me as our party spread out.

The light from the holes in the ceiling reflected off the water, casting patterns across the stone walls. I eyed the latter, noting several varieties of lichen, moss, and mushroom as I trailed Ittrid deeper into the cave.

"There's something in the water," Sedi's voice echoed around us.

I turned to see Berin leap to a boulder out in the pool. He grasped a dangling root for support, earning a rain of dirt and deadfall from above, and peered straight down into the water. Furrowing his brows, he crouched and slipped a hand beneath the surface.

The pool was not deep. Before his shoulder touched the water he pulled back and held an object beneath a beam of light.

It was a golden spearhead, as long as my forearm and evidently dulled with age, given how casually Berin turned it about in his palm.

"There's more," Askir said. He slipped into the pool and bent, both arms submerged. When he straightened, his palms were full of dull arrowheads of various material and sizes, from stone to green-tainted bronze. "These must be offerings. Though there's no power here."

Berin nodded, still poised on the boulder. "Offerings to who?"

"The Bear," Ittrid replied.

I followed her pointing finger across the walls, tracking the lichen and water stains. Deeper into the grotto they gave way to stronger lines and more unnatural patterns. Runes. Images.

Almost unconsciously, I moved toward them. A pleasant coolness wafted across my naked legs—I hadn't had time to fully dress—and I slowed, waiting for my eyes to adjust. I trailed my fingers across the cool stone. Lichen flaked beneath my fingers, dusty and the palest green.

"What is it?" Berin's voice called to me. Beyond him I saw Nui poised in the mouth of the hollow, head cocked curiously.

"There are markings on the walls," Seera answered before I could. She materialized at my shoulder, her damp hair pulled back into a quick, efficient knot. She had her long knife bare in one hand, though she hadn't taken the time to put on her belt, and the remnants of black paint were smudged around her eyes. She pointed along the wall. "I see a woman."

"And a bear," Ittrid added, gesturing at the space before us. And above us. "Look up."

There on the walls of the cave, the lichen gathered into carvings in the shape of a huge bear. It stood on its hind legs, its huge clawed back paws originating just before Ittrid, Seera, and me, its head watching from above. Its jaw was closed, its eyes unseeing.

In the center of its body was the life-size profile of a woman, her generous breasts and hips reminding me distantly of Aita, and in passing, myself. But this was not Aita. There was only one woman in our stories associated with a Great Bear. A Great Bear who had been wounded by a spear.

I became aware of the others crowding in around me, craning to see the Bear or edging in to scrutinize the woman in its protection.

"Aegr and Liv," I observed, voice edged with awe. "This is where the Great Bear was healed."

THIRTEEN

INTERLUDE

Aita surveyed an expanse of bare rock, unbroken save for a few patches of reedy marsh where the rock bellied and rain gathered, and lines of stalwart sumac grew. A river meandered to the south, close enough that I could see its glinting water and hear its rush.

Creases of moss and frail purple flowers gathered in smaller seams in the rock. I walked along these, enjoying the cool squish beneath my bare toes.

"Why are we here?" I asked Aita absently. The seam of moss I was following ended, and I jumped to the dry warmth of stone.

"We're waiting to see if a rumor is true," Aita replied. She looked away from the barren landscape and up to the sky, to the divisions between the four quadrants of the High Halls: the twilit dusk to the west, the snow-diffused daylight of the south, warm summer from the east and a dark night to the north, rippling with blue and white lights, like a swirl of skirts in a festival dance. It made the light around us strange and prone to unpredictable shifts. But I was used to it by now and had learned to enjoy each turn of season, weather, and sun as they came.

"What rumor?" I wanted to know, poking at the moss again with my foot.

"We will see," Aita returned.

Curious, I returned to my mistress and hovered beside her skirts.

Eventually, a distant sound drew our gaze south. I saw a man standing on the riverbank—or, at least, the shape of a man.

"Stay behind me, and do not ask him any questions," Aita told me in a voice that brooked no disobedience.

I opened my mouth anyway. "Why—"

"Otherwise he will eat your flesh," she told me flatly, "and craft himself a new pet from your bones."

I clamped my lips shut as Aita took my hand and led me toward the man beside the water, always keeping me one step behind her.

As we drew closer, I saw that the man was not a man. He was male in shape, but his skin was woven reeds and each of his eyes held riverstones, smooth and sparkling orbs of jade. Those strange eyes turned to Aita, then to me, partially hidden behind her skirts.

He smiled, reed lips turning up to reveal rows of fine fish teeth. His hair was the only thing human about him, thick and black—even at nine years old, I realized that it likely did not belong to him.

A riverman. I knew of these creatures from stories, usually the frightening kind that Berin loved and I avoided. I understood then why Aita had forbidden me to ask any questions—rivermen hated being questioned on any topic, and were dangerous and unpredictable.

"Your kind are not welcome in these halls," Aita said coolly.

The riverman looked at me, water pooling about his woven feet. "Hello, little shadow. Aita, have you finally spawned? Who is her father? Pity I couldn't serve the role."

At the last, his grin curled lasciviously, showing every one of his fish teeth and the bulge of a lithe black tongue. Human men might not have such teeth or tongues, but that smile was one I had already learned to be wary of, and I edged a little further behind my mistress.

Aita ignored him. "Thvynder could destroy you for this trespass."

The riverman slowly turned his jade eyes to Aita. "If they were here, perhaps. But their journey stretches long. Very long."

I was captivated by the riverman's strange eyes, but the implications of his words still struck me. "Thvynder is everywhere," I said, every inch an indignant daughter of the High Priesthood. Being indignant felt better than being afraid. "They're not on a journey."

Aita shot me a silencing look, but it wasn't the command in her expression that quieted me. It was the tightness around her eyes. Worry.

"Ah," the riverman said, looking from me to the Miri. "Your shadow doesn't know that her protector god is gone? Do any of the humans, I wonder? The priests?"

"You are here," Aita observed, ignoring the riverman's words again. In her effort not to ask questions, her words seemed stilted. "Many of your kind may be as well."

The man shrugged. "I wouldn't know. I'm not as sociable as some."

"You will all leave." Aita stepped forward, slipping her hand from mine. I felt a moment's fear for her—she was a Miri but she carried no weapons, and she wasn't a warrior like my mother. The riverman, with his teeth, each one so fine and pointed, glistening in the sun...

"This is not your realm," Aita stated.

"There is no realm for us," the man returned, a note of true lament in his harsh words. "We are born of the same creator, you and I, but my kind have languished in the human world while *you* Miri feasted here, drank these waters. You made yourselves gods. We became nightmares for children." At the last, he looked to me and smiled again, needle teeth straight and sharp. "No more. Not with so few of your kind remaining. Not with your god a year gone, with no sign of return."

I thought of the water Aita had given me to drink, the honey and the berries. I'd understood, on some level, that these things made Aita strong and helped her magic, and they'd do the same for me. But even young as I was, the riverman's words sparked a deeper, more dangerous understanding.

We were born of the same creator.

You made yourselves gods.

"I will assemble the council," Aita declared, her voice as hard and unyielding as the stone beneath our feet. "You and all your kind will be driven out of the High Halls. You may have passed a few moons in these waters, but our power is still vastly beyond yours. Go back to whatever den you've been hiding in, and never return."

The riverman's lips curled in anger, reeds splitting and cracking in fine lines. "Try, cousin."

With that, the riverman slipped back into the water. His eyes lingered on me as he left, and I swore that I heard his voice once more, his lips twisting as he farewelled me: "Little shadow."

Aita led me away from the riverbank. I was slow to comply, eyes still pinned on the place where the riverman had vanished beneath the shining water.

"Is Thvynder really gone?" I asked, because it was easier to talk about my god than the monster.

Aita looked over her shoulder at me, thought for a long moment, then nodded. "Yes. But you must never speak of it again. Thvynder is searching for their sister, Imilidese. The last Pillar. She left creation long ago and still has not returned."

That made perfect sense to my child's mind—if Berin was missing, I would search for him too. "Will Thvynder come back?"

Aita stood, nodding firmly. "They will."

"How do you know?"

"Fate ordained it." Aita squeezed my hand and cast her eyes north, looking toward something far out of sight. She started to walk across the rocks, and I dutifully followed, running to keep up. "Just like she ordained you be here, by my side."

"She talked about me? When?" I pestered, intrigued. "What did she say?"

"Fate does not speak, not in the sense that you mean. And I will tell you no more."

"Please!"

"No."

I accepted that, frustrated though it made me. "When will Thvynder come back?"

"I cannot say exactly," Aita told me. "But all will be well—so long as you keep all the secrets I've entrusted to you, especially this. Do you promise?"

"I promise," I said without hesitation. I grabbed her hand and leaned my head into her arm. "Mistress."

She smiled at the title, but her expression turned grim as she added, "And if you should ever encounter a riverman when you are alone, Yske, you must never ask it any questions. You must never let it touch you. You *must* run. Promise me."

"I promise, mistress."

FOURTEEN

I sat on my bedroll and watched orange light spill over the carving of Aegr and Liv as the last of the daylight faded. The tumbling river outside was slowly sapped of color, and Nui abandoned her post on the cooling rock to settle at my side with a canine sigh.

We'd laid our bedrolls in the cave that night, building our fire on a broad ledge and claiming sleeping spaces around it.

"The story of Liv isn't so well known in Souldern," Ittrid commented during a lull in the evening's conversation. She sat against a boulder, cleaning and oiling a stack of our boots and shoes. She directed her words to Askir, who stretched out on his back under the carved bear's lording head.

His hands laced behind his head and eyes fixed on the bear's, the priest replied, "Are you asking me to tell it? It's better sung, and I'm not much of a singer."

"Yske is," Berin said from next to the fire. We'd strung ropes between the dangling roots, and behind him our drying clothing ruffled in a breeze from outside.

I asked him, "Who says that?"

"I do," my twin replied, raking out his chest-length hair with crooked fingers and beginning to pry at it with a comb. "Sing it for us."

The others glanced at me, some prompting, some curious. Seera, checking the blades of her hatchets in the firelight, prodded, "Go on, Cousin."

Seera's prompt almost made me refuse, but I bit back the childish impulse. Instead I went over to Berin and took the comb from him.

"All right," I said as I went to work untangling his hair, combing it back from the shaved, tattooed sides of his head. "I'll sing."

If the heart of our people had once been war, stories and songs were the blood that kept it beating. Liv's tale was a rare one, a story that celebrated mercy and healing instead of violence and martial ability. And regardless of how Liv had actually acquired the herbs to heal the Great Bear, my love for the tale remained.

So when the soft melody fell from my lips that night, it was with honesty and intent. There was power in kindness and a gentle hand, and in a sacrifice to staunch another's pain—particularly in a world of falling axes and bloody vengeance.

My voice was low for a woman's, like my mother's. But mine was smoother than hers, gentled by solitary mornings in my garden and honed by myriad festivals in the Morning Hall, where the people of Albor sang and danced for days on end. I'd never sung a song in desperate worship of a war-mongering Miri, not like she had. I sang only for the power of the words and the beauty of their sound.

I told the traditional tale, of how Liv had grown among her many sisters, all daughters of the hero Risix and his love of a woodmaiden. Liv had happened upon Aegr one day in the forest and seen the great wound bleeding in his side. She'd gone to a mortal healer to beg for herbs to heal the bear, only to learn that the wound was eternal, and delivered to the Bear by none other than her father. Determined to right her father's wrong, Liv had gone to the High Halls and begged Aita to help her. Aita had gifted her magical herbs, Aegr had been healed, and in thanks he'd protected her to the end of her days.

When the last low note of the song reverberated around the chamber, I looked up. Every eye was on me, even those of Esan and Sedi, who sat watch in the cave mouth. Beyond them was a wall of darkness, but I saw another figure there, listening with a startled gentleness to his posture.

Isik? No, a trick of the eye. I blinked, and the figure was gone—if he'd been there at all.

"See?" Berin prompted into the quiet, obvious pride in his voice.

"Do you know the story of Liv's conception?" The question, to my surprise, came from Askir. He'd sat up on his bedroll and watched me with interest.

I found my heart was beating a little too quickly in my chest—though whether that was from attention of my companions or the sight of Isik, I couldn't decide. Surely, I'd been mistaken. He wouldn't have followed me. He'd long returned to the Hall and his mother and siblings.

I shrugged, refocusing on the company. "Risix and the woodmaiden fell in love."

"What was the woodmaiden's name?" Sedi asked.

"Woodmaidens have no names," Berin told her. "They're trees."

"They do," I corrected. "And they're… not quite trees. They're connected to the forest, yes, but they're not trees themselves, or even spirits of trees. They're women, and can look precisely the same as human women, if they choose to. I've met several. Some were permitted into the High Halls like the Miri, and they care for the forests there."

Berin, unhappy at being corrected, shot me the barest frown, and some of the pride ebbed from his expression. Askir, too, was studying me with something deeper than curiosity or admiration. His interest in my connection to the High Halls clearly hadn't faded.

"Perhaps all that is a story for another night," I suggested. I was growing discomfited by the attention and my gaze kept straying back to the spot where I thought I'd seen Isik. "We should rest."

"What's more restful than being sung to?" Bara asked no one in particular. "I feel better already."

"Sing!" Ittrid prodded. "Please."

I pried my eyes from the cave mouth and conjured a distracted smile. "All right. The story of Risix and the woodmaiden, but that's all."

It wasn't all. When that tale ended, Berin had another request, and then Ittrid. By the time I'd finished my fifth tale I made my excuses and slipped out into the night, padding across the smooth rock, still warm from the sun. The firelight made my shadow stretch long ahead of me toward the forest, and out of the corner of my eye, I saw the faceless silhouettes that were Esan and Sedi watching me go.

Once I was safely shrouded in the forest, I searched for any sign of Esach's son. Firelight played across the rock and the river rushed under a curtain of thin starlight, while around me the trees breathed in the warm night.

"Isik?" I called. When there was no response, I dared to raise my voice a little more. "Isik?"

Still no reply. The aching fatigue of my muscles reasserted itself and I brushed a tired hand over my face. We'd be off again at daybreak, and I was wasting time.

I saw to my needs and returned to camp as an owl hooted in the distance. I cast it a distracted glance, nodded to Sedi and Esan, and slipped back into the cave.

I dreamed of owls winging through the darkness and a shattering, rotting tree, so huge it filled the sky. I tasted the leaf on my tongue again, and scented lavender and pine in the air. I opened my eyes, only to find myself surrounded by a thick, clotting ash fall.

I jarred into true wakefulness as Nui leapt over me, barking wildly. Her claws clattered on the stone as she charged out of the cave, past the still-smoldering fire and the shape of two figures, weapons bared. Seera and Berin.

I couldn't see a threat but I felt it, thick and foreboding in the night air. A startled croak escaped my lips but I couldn't form words, my vision still blurred with sleep.

My companions lurched into motion, some faster than others. One staggered—Seera, with something else, something wrong, clinging to her back. A beast? No, a man. A man with claws who emitted a chattering, shrieking howl and prepared to bury a fan of fine teeth in my cousin's neck.

Berin parted from the gloom in a dusting of his bruised amber magic, clad in shadows and absolute silence. This was the gift our parents' magic had passed to him, and it was nearly as eerie as the sight of the chittering monster. Shadow Walking.

My brother was shirtless, armorless, and the armbands on his wrists and biceps flashed in the dim light. He seized the creature's head and stabbed a knife into its throat. Then he was blocked from sight, Seera crumpled, and monsters surrounded us.

One chattered at my feet, so close I felt its sounds rattle in my chest. I screamed right back, half hysteria, half vengeance, and kicked out.

My assailant toppled into the fire. Blazing coals scattered and I threw up an arm to shield my face as the creature shrieked. I'd heard the sound earlier, but now I was awake, my mind livid with sight and sensation. There was nothing human about the creature's cry—it was the rush of rivers and the rasp of reed, and yet it was also the grating, crackling squeal of trees tossed by the wind.

Time stretched, elongating and thinning like pine sap in the sun. The firelight dimmed and sparks plumed, filling the scene with fading needles of illumination. I saw my attacker contorted in the coals—a wild eye, a twisting body made of reed and mud and moss.

A riverman? My thoughts snared on the memory of Aita and me at the river when I was a child. But this couldn't be a riverman. He'd died so easily and I'd seen human bone beneath his woven muscles, which had been thick with sap and packed with leaves. This was a thing constructed, a man made of river and forest and salvaged bone.

An arm locked over my throat, thick with reed-rough muscle. Then I was being dragged—not toward the mouth of the cave, but into the pool.

Cold liquid wrapped around my shoulders, then my back. I kicked and fought, legs beating uselessly against the rock. Still the creature dragged me in deeper, frigid water sloshing across my shuddering belly and into my screaming mouth.

I wasn't the only one in the pool. My bulging, frantic eyes saw Ovir being dragged beneath the water too, his fingers scrabbling to loosen a vine garrotted around his throat. A garrotte held by a woman who was no woman, with reed muscle and a jumbled assortment of yellowed canine fangs. Bones peeked out from gouges in its unnatural flesh, patterned with markings as if they'd been chewed, lain on the forest floor for an age, and repurposed.

My feet dropped into the pool and water closed over my head. With the last of my strength I clawed for the face and head of my attacker. I found mossy flesh, teeth that ribboned the skin of fingers, then a rough throat.

I drove my torn fingers through a lattice of moss and mud and reed. I seized the first thing I could find—veins and sinew, or whatever equivalent this creature had. I ripped them out, pulling myself out of the water with the strength of my attack.

A hand closed over my ankle. I started to kick out, twisting to see what fresh horror assailed me. But I saw only Seera, her blood-splattered face wild in the gloom.

The arm around my throat loosened but did not let go. Water closed over my head again as my attacker and I sank in a tangle of reed and flesh limbs. I'd no air left to expel and instantly choked.

But Seera did not let go. She hauled at my leg, then grabbed my tunic and arm. I rolled out of the pool and half onto my cousin, who immediately extricated herself, snatched up an axe, and hacked.

A severed arm fell to the stone behind me. My attacker shrieked with a sound like moisture boiling in a damp log and collapsed back under the surface, its savaged throat yawning and skull ruptured.

The pool went quiet in its wake. Too quiet.

"Ovir!" I gasped to Seera. My voice was thin and my head spun from lack of air, but I forced it out in a painful thin wheeze. "In… the water…"

She left me. I heard her call for help and caught scattered responses as I crawled to my hands and knees. My cousin and Askir waded into the water, searching blindly with axes raised.

I lost sight of them as my need to breathe clawed to the forefront of my mind. I sunk back into a kneel and fought for breath, savoring every sliver of air in my crushed throat.

Someone grabbed my face. I was too dizzy to strike out this time. I stared into Berin's eyes instead, unable to fathom where he'd come from.

His lips moved and I heard the shape of words, but they meant nothing.

He searched my face, looked me over, then vanished again. His sword glinted—there was more light now, a wash of dawn in pale pink and violet. It spilled across the cave floor, scattered bedrolls, sprays of blood and the sight of Seera and Askir laboring over a limp body.

I lurched forward, my ears ringing and mind clouded, but my instinct strong.

"Move," I croaked, shoving Askir aside.

He complied, clambering back as I bent over Ovir's head. The garrotte was gone, hanging limply from Sedi's fingers, but the flesh of Ovir's throat was raw and bleeding. His face was swollen with blood and the veins around his fluttering eyes had burst. His chest did not move—though when I lowered an ear to his heart, I heard a few faint, fading beats.

"Ovir," I heard Berin rasp his friend's name, but couldn't look at him. I had no cure for this, no tonic or salve.

"You will not die," I hissed, and with those words a profound knowing overtook me. I was too rattled for coherent thought, half-drowned and shaking with adrenaline. But my knowing came with instinct, and I moved.

I straddled Ovir, taking his head between my bloody hands and putting my forehead to his, as if the closeness of my body could keep him in the world—my touch, my words, and the runes that followed.

I held my forehead to Ovir's and whispered the names of runes. My fingers itched to write them, but they were still shredded and shook too badly, and there was no time to calm myself. I felt that itch like I felt the cold water dripping from my hair and pooling around my bare toes.

Distantly, I heard Ittrid shouting that our attackers had fled. I heard Seera, insisting that we still needed to move, needed to run. Berin called back, ordering anyone able to pack our gear and keep watch.

I ignored them. I tasted something acrid on my tongue, dragging me back to the moment when Isik had given me Aita's gift. Threads of golden dust wafted from my pale skin onto Ovir's swollen cheeks, into his nose and mouth, eyes and ears.

Distantly, I became aware of Berin and Askir staring at me, their expressions blurred by dawn shadows. Outside, the rising sun broke through the forest. Golden sunlight crept through the air around us, illuminating the remnants of my new smoke-like magic on Ovir's skin. Magic that smelled of lavender and pine, and, when I looked closer, was colored with gold and pale, gentle purple. Like Aita's.

"Yske?" Berin murmured. His voice sounded too distant. "What are you doing?"

I couldn't answer. A wave of dizziness washed over me. My own wounds felt oddly better, even my tattered fingers, but I wasn't getting enough air. I mutely put out an arm for aid and Berin pulled it around his shoulders, helping me into a sitting position nearby.

"His throat…" Sedi's words were hushed with awe. I realized she was just behind me, a broken arm cradled to her chest and her face battered. "It's healed."

I closed my eyes. I felt no happiness at her words, only exhaustion and a lance of trepidation.

I felt a touch on my cheeks, then forehead—Berin, plucking locks of sodden hair from my face. I weakly pushed his hand away. "I'm all right. Check his breathing."

"Askir," Berin prompted, his hands still steadying me.

The priest crouched above Ovir's head and, hands braced on the wet stone, bent to put an ear to the injured man's mouth. A shadow passed over his brows. He pressed the fingers of one hand under Ovir's jaw and held still.

Thin breaths wheezed through my aching throat as I watched. With each exhale, a little of my hope faded. Dread crept in, skittering up my spine, tightening each muscle and making my head throb.

When he finally spoke, Askir's words fell like stones into my belly. "He's dead. Whatever you did was too late."

"We need to *move*," Seera cut in, her indignation filling the cave. She stood near a pile of hastily stuffed packs and bundled bedrolls at the mouth, axe in hand and Nui poised beside her, the dog's boar-bristle ruff standing out and her eyes still feral from the attack. Seera did not look at Ovir, but her voice cracked as she continued, "We can't help him now. Berin, carry your sister if she can't walk. We need to leave."

Berin looked at me, eyes round with shock. There was a horrible grief welling up in his expression, a dawning awareness and a coiling rage that both terrified me and broke me.

I hadn't been able to save him from this pain. I hadn't been able to save Ovir, who had been a fixture of my life since childhood. When—if—we returned to Albor, his children would run out to meet him... and he would not be there.

My own agony must have been plain on my face. Berin's expression closed as he fought for control and, with halting movements, slipped an arm under mine and pulled me upright. "Let's go."

FIFTEEN

We trekked for an hour before Askir decided we were far enough from the river to stop. "Rivermen can't leave the water for long," he told us. "They won't risk coming after us."

"That's a myth, and those weren't rivermen," I said, though my words sounded toneless to my own ears, edged with a new rasp. Whatever healing I'd enacted on Ovir had overflowed to me, but it hadn't been enough to completely heal me.

Or him.

"What else would they be?" Askir asked in a way that told me he'd already disregarded my observation. He said to the others, "We're safe to stop."

"We'll keep watch," Ittrid said of her and Bara, and the two of them slipped back into the trees.

I bit back another protest. I hadn't the strength to fight with the priest, and my conviction was weak. I wanted to believe him. I wanted to trust someone else, and rest here on the cool forest floor.

Any relief I'd found faded as Berin and Esan lowered Ovir's body to the ground nearby. Tears mingled with the sweat and blood on Berin's face. The sight of it was almost as painful as my injuries, and I pushed my concentration to that more constant physical pain.

I dragged my pack over, pulling out salves, bandages, and thread. If I couldn't convince the others to keep moving, I could patch them up and ready them for the next fight. Physical wounds, I could mend.

Memory welled like blood from a wound. I saw myself crouching over

Ovir, murmuring runes and feeling that, against all logic, they *would* heal him. And they had. But I'd been too late, or I simply hadn't used it properly. Now one of my brother's closest friends was the first casualty of his quest.

The thread in my hands blurred through unshed tears. I looked down, distantly noting a lattice of new scars on my fingers from the monster's fine teeth.

"Yske?" Sedi sank down beside me with her broken arm carefully held across her chest. She was gaunt with pain, her eyes haunted and pleading. "Can you…? Are you…?"

"Yes," I told her, not sure which half-question I was answering or even what it meant. But when I saw the other woman's need, my own grief and pain retreated. "Let me see."

Sedi shifted and gingerly held out her arm. "You won't do what you did with…"

It took me another moment to understand her question. "With Ovir? Oh… no. No. I don't even know if I can."

That surety that had compelled me to act with Ovir was gone. When I tried to recreate it, I felt only emptiness instead.

"What *did* you do?"

I ignored her question and began to feel, as gently as possible, down the limb. She flinched under my touch, but the break was not severe— no jagged ends or broken skin.

"I'll bind it and give you something for the pain," I told her, to which she nodded and set her jaw.

Still standing over Ovir's body, Berin, Askir, Seera, and Esan conferred in low voices. As I carefully applied a numbing salve to Sedi's arm, I turned my ear toward them.

Askir: "That cave was a trap."

Berin's posture was defeated, nearly uncaring. "I knew rivermen carried people off, but this…"

I inserted myself back into the conversation, perplexed. "I've seen rivermen before, and those were not them," I reasserted. "Close, but too different."

"There's nothing else they could be." Askir wouldn't quite look at me. Berin glanced at the priest briefly, but his own eyes were glassy.

"The moss and the bones," I clarified. "Rivermen are creatures purely of water and river and stone, not forest and moss. And the way those bones were visible... the tooth marks. They'd been reused, they—"

"Gods below, shut up," Esan snapped from where he slumped nearby, glaring at me from hollow eyes. "They killed Ovir. What else matters?"

His rebuke hit me like a slap. I licked my lips, looking from him to the others. They didn't care what I had to say, and really, what did it matter if I was right? The creatures were a threat, whatever we called them.

Ittrid spoke up, her voice gentle. "We should build a pyre."

Askir nodded. "Yes. We can't stay here, and we can't carry him any farther."

I glanced at Berin, expecting an outburst, but it did not come. His control was tremulous, though—his fingers shook as he jerked a woodsman's axe from the side of Seera's pack and stalked off into the trees.

Worry for him coiled through me—not to mention a constant, unyielding fear that the creatures would return—but there was little I could do. I finished wrapping Sedi's arm and looked for my next task. Esan had a gash down the back of one forearm, which he grudgingly let me stitch after a short standoff. His eyes had the same agonized, angry emptiness as Berin's. If he wondered what I'd done to heal Ovir, he did not ask.

We burned Ovir's body under the noonday sun and lingered until Seera, with growing urgency, insisted we move on. Berin and Esan did not rise, watching the body of their friend blacken and crumble, now nearly indiscernible from charred wood. Nui lay exhausted between them, her head in Berin's lap.

The rest of us went to work, redistributing Ovir's belongings between our packs. It felt callous, but we'd only brought what we needed to survive the journey and could leave nothing behind.

Before we left, Askir crouched and drew a series of runes in the earth beside the pyre. Ash wafted across his face as he offered a prayer to release Ovir's soul from the mound of charred wood and bone.

This was the way of things, a ritual I knew well. Once the soul was released, it would be drawn to the Shepherd of the Dead—my father, wherever he was. In Eangen or Algatt, anywhere the High Halls spread above the Waking World, that passage might be instantaneous. But as far east as we were, there was a chance the High Halls were already inaccessible. If so, Ovir's journey back to Eangen would be long and lonely—a journey made in a new body no longer bound to or visible in this world.

Touching my Sight, I saw Askir's runes ignite with a clean golden magic, much like my own. Then there was a whisper, a brush of a presence, and I saw Ovir standing in the ashes of his pyre—whole and clean, flesh and blood. Askir and I were the only ones to look at him. Berin's Sight was not strong enough, and the others had none at all.

Two blinks later, before Ovir could so much as look at us, he vanished, just as he should. An odd emptiness settled over the ashes, the clearing, and our battered company.

The High Halls were still within reach, I noted. Not bodily, not without doorways. But spiritually. That didn't mean the edges of the upper realm that Ovir had transitioned to were whole or safe, but it was comforting.

Askir let out a slow breath. "Thvynder," he murmured in relief, then unfolded his long limbs.

"Go on ahead," Berin's voice sounded dull. "Esan and I will bury the bones and catch up before dark."

I stiffened. "Berin—"

"Fine," Seera cut me off, shouldering her pack and picking up her wood axe, which Berin had left forgotten on the ground. "Follow the road."

"I'll stay too," I decided.

"No, you won't," Berin returned flatly. "Leave us in peace."

His refusal shocked me. "Berin—"

"Get as far up the road as you can and camp. Double watch, multiple fires," Berin told Seera without looking at me again. "We take no more chances. Now go."

I watched the sun set with growing trepidation. We had camped in the middle of the old road, erecting the tents against an evening downpour. The storm had eased now but the leaves and canvas still dripped, reminding me of the night I'd seen the foxfire and Isik.

I'd realized sometime over the course of the day that the figure I'd seen watching us outside the cave must have been one of the creatures, not my friend. If it had been him, he would have warned us. Helped us.

Instead, I'd seen an enemy and hadn't told anyone. Perhaps the others would have disregarded my warning, but it redoubled the weight of responsibility in my gut. I'd sworn to bring Berin and his companions home alive. I'd already failed.

I worried burrs from Nui's thick coat and watched the western road sink into a misty, damp twilight. Askir sat down beside me and folded his legs, resting his forearm across his knees. Nui glanced at him, then looked back to the road.

"Did Aita give you magic?" he asked, then added in a lower voice, "Or did your mother?"

"What?" I rasped. My throat still ached, and it had been hours since I'd spoken to anyone.

"I've been friends with your brother for some time," the priest said, "which means I've been closer to your mother than most other priests outside the inner circle. It hasn't slipped past me that most of that inner circle possess more power than the rest of us."

"They are the most powerful priests and priestesses," I pointed out. "That's why my mother keeps them close."

"See, that's not true." Askir followed Nui's gaze down the road now, but his eyes were focused beyond it. "You and Berin are not priestly, but you both have magic. Berin can Shadow Walk, and has the Sight, though mildly."

"It passed to us from our parents," I reminded him, voice still cool.

"In Berin's case, perhaps," Askir acknowledged. "But what you did today says otherwise. No, listen to me, I've more to say. The man your father has chosen to succeed him had minimal magic when he was initiated. Now he weaves shadows and speaks to the dead. Your mother's scion, Uspa, had no magic at all before she wandered into the Arpa High Halls *with* your mother. Now she heals with a touch." At the last, his eyes dragged to me. "Like you. Or rather, you seemed to need runes, but I see little difference."

"Thvynder blessed them. Us," I replied tightly.

Askir ignored me. "Your mother ages slowly and her power grows by the year. The last time I saw her, I thought she was half Miri, her aura was so bright."

Nui flinched and tugged away. I realized I'd been digging my fingers into her fur.

"Thvynder's doing," I insisted again.

"But Thvynder—" Now Askir lowered his voice even more, leaning to whisper in my ear, "—hasn't been in Eangen since before the Winterborn invaded, when you and I were both children."

"Pieces of them remain," I countered. I felt his eyes pinned on the side of my face, watching every flicker and twitch. "The Watchman and the Vestige. You shouldn't say things like this so loudly. This… That is a secret of the priesthood."

"A priesthood you're not part of. Still, you know everything. Likely because your parents let you live half your childhood in the High Halls with Aita." Askir glanced over at Nui. "Even Hessa's dog has a haze about her. Yes, I can see that too. My Sight is strong enough to see the subtleties of magics, and to know that the power that clings to this dog and Uspa looks different than mine. Your father's has a grayness— remnants of the days he worshiped the death goddess. And yours—it has a lavender taint. Why the differences? Do the magics, perhaps, have a different source? Various sources *in* the High Halls?"

My mind churned for a moment, trying to piece together a response. Askir was certainly observant, but I felt that his conclusions were too much of a leap—even if they were true. There had to be more behind his assumptions, a conversation overheard or a secret stolen.

I knew much about stolen secrets.

I took my time replying, letting the tension ease out of me, and letting Askir see it.

"My family is favored," I acknowledged eventually. "So are those close to them. But their sacrifices merit their rewards."

Askir's gaze pinned me. "What did you sacrifice?"

I lifted my eyes to the darkened leaves above our heads and watched the shadows shift in the black. As irritated as I was by him, it was a fair question. Magic given by a Miri always had a cost—usually blood sacrifice, as evidenced by the old scars that covered my parents' hands and arms.

Aita's voice slipped through my thoughts. *There is a cost to such magic—a cost to claim it, a cost to wield it, and a cost to replenish it.*

Was that why I felt so empty now? Did I need to make a sacrifice to replenish the magic Aita had given me?

I suppressed a shiver and a flush of resentment. I wanted to question Aita, to know why she'd done this to me with so little instruction or explanation. But I'd asked for a healing gift, twice, and she'd warned me of the price. I couldn't blame her entirely.

"It was a gift, Askir," I said, hiding my thoughts behind tired eyes. "Nothing more."

"A priestess's gift," he corrected, unswayed. "Except Aita is no longer a goddess, so you are not her priestess. Thvynder alone dispenses magic to humans. She had no right. Did you give her your blood?"

I glared back at him, irritated by the truth in his assessment. There was still much Askir didn't know, but pointing that out would put sacred secrets in jeopardy.

Thvynder alone could condone gifts of magic, but it was my parents who gathered it from the High Halls and dispensed it to the priesthood. I didn't think it honest that they hid the source of their power, but I understood why. They did it because of the way Askir looked at me now—with indignation and a spark of jealousy. Power had to be controlled, given only to those who would use it for the good of all.

That, my mother did to a fault. Mostly.

"No, I did not give Aita my blood," I said. "And I had no part in this. She gave it to me without my knowing. It didn't even work, did it?"

"It worked," Askir muttered, but I could see him pondering my response. "Just too late. Yske, you realize there is always a cost to magic like that. If you haven't paid it yet…"

I shifted in discomfort. "The payment is still coming."

"Could you heal again, now? Is the power still there?"

As I'd done earlier with Sedi, I reached for the feeling that had let me heal Ovir. I found the edges of it, but the well was empty.

"No."

Tension ebbed from Askir's body and concern shadowed his eyes. He didn't need to speak for me to know what he was thinking.

I thought of my mother's hands, covered with sacrificial scars. I looked down at my own fingers, knit with fine new marks from the teeth of the monster. With a start, I recalled the blood I'd smeared across Ovir's cheeks. My blood *had* been shed around the healing. I'd let it flow, done nothing to stop it. Did that count as a blood sacrifice? Or had the leaf I'd ingested been enough for that first act?

Did Aita expect me to bleed myself every time I needed to heal?

Grim quiet stretched between Askir and me, filled with the hum of insects and the occasional drip of water from a bowing fern. I heard wolves howl in the distance, so far away that Nui barely lifted her head. But she barked soon after, and I saw a light among the trees.

Nui got to her feet, head lowered. Askir stood too, but I remained where I was. Thin veins of foxfire appeared throughout the forest, tracing the cracks of tree trunks and deadfall like the veins of a single living creature. Blue and green, white and cream, it punctuated the night like stars, filling Askir's pale-skinned Algatt face with an eerie glow.

In this new illumination, Berin and Esan appeared from the darkness. Nui barked and leapt forward, half wary, half overjoyed— then came to a growling halt.

A stranger parted from the night behind them.

Sixteen

"I am Ursk."

The newcomer was older than any of us by perhaps ten years but his eyes were distinctly round, nearly childlike. He wore no beard and was clad in a linen undertunic, with a road-worn kaftan unbelted on top. His smile was warm and his posture polite. He might have been any traveler seeking shelter in the Morning Hall instead of a stranger in the wilds.

"You're Duamel," I observed. The man's large eyes and pale skin made his heritage undeniable, though I couldn't fathom how one of the northerners had wandered so far east, let alone happened upon us. He also looked ill, I noted—dark circles shadowed his eyes and his cheeks were too flushed. "What are you doing here?"

"He's a guest." Berin's voice was impatient. I glanced at him, startled, and he seemed to collect himself. His manner toward the Duamel was almost proprietary, while Esan simply looked tired. He shouldered through the group and dropped his pack in the outer circle of bedrolls, barely under the shelter of the tent.

"He's a Priest of Fate," Berin clarified, "sent by his goddess."

Askir shoved forward. "You would have had to leave Duamel months ago."

Ursk gave a small bow. I noticed a pack on his back, but he had no bedroll and no tent. "I left Atmeltan last year. Eirine—" the Duamel name for Fate, I recalled "—sent me to Algatt, where I wintered and learned more of your language. I set out from there when the snow melted."

"Why?" The question came from Sedi, blunt and perplexed.

Ursk shrugged and looked around at us. His manner of speaking was low, slow in the Duamel way, but his accent was Algatt, like my father's. "To guide you, I believe."

"You came to find us?" Seera asked. She had edged slightly in front of us, her hand conspicuously close to the axe at her belt. "Last year?"

"I obey my goddess," Ursk said. I eyed him, searching for a lie at the same time as I tried to identify his ailment. "I saw a vision of a road east, and a great tree, and two men beside a pyre." At this, he looked at Berin and Esan. "So here I am."

Nui prowled the edge of the firelight, head still low and eyes wary. I felt much the same, though I found my unease was directed less toward Ursk than to his mission overall. It was no great stretch to imagine Fate had foreseen our journey and sent one of her new order of priests to join us. But *why*? What did that mean for the magnitude of Berin's foolish quest?

Ittrid, evidently realizing no one else was going to step up, transformed into hostess. She ushered the stranger to the fire and pressed a cup of water into his hands.

"Do you heed Hearth Law?" she asked.

"As Fate upholds it," the stranger returned, giving her a shy smile. His childlike eyes were disarming and genuine.

I caught Berin's arm as he passed. "He found you in the forest?" I asked in a low voice. "Did he tell you anything else?"

My brother looked archly from my hand to my face. "Yes, and no. I wasn't about to leave him. He serves one of the Four Pillars, just like we do."

"His people also invaded when we were children." Seera shuffled in, arms laced across her chest, voice low. "My father nearly died because of them."

"They invaded because the Winterborn forced them to," Berin reminded her. "But they're our allies now, and good people. If you'd been to Duamel, you wouldn't speak like that."

"Forgive me, far traveler," Seera said dryly. "But after what just happened, I can't believe you'd trust a stranger wandering out of the forest. He could rob us. Kill us in our sleep."

For once, I agreed with Seera. This must have been plain in my face, because Berin leveled his gaze at me. "A Priest of *Fate* turning up is far less strange, in my opinion, than my twin sister hiding a divine gift."

I tensed. I wished Seera wasn't part of this conversation, but there would be no barring her out now. My best defense was honesty, and confidence.

"I haven't hidden anything," I said, low enough that the others were unlikely to overhear. "Aita gave me a gift for this journey. I didn't know what it was until Ovir… until that moment. I didn't know. I swear."

Berin still surveyed me, but his eyes once again took on a guarded, glassy quality at the reminder of Ovir's death.

"How could you not know?" Seera pushed.

"I didn't." My temper frayed. My thoughts snared on a memory of Ovir—the water dripping from my hair, the feel of his shuddering chest beneath my hands. The raw flesh of his throat and his bulging, bloodshot eyes. "Aita gave me no warning and no instruction. I don't know how to use it."

"That's obvious," Seera murmured.

I started to reply, but the sight of her face half turned away, tears brimming in her eyes, stayed my tongue.

Berin put an arm around her. She didn't fold into him as I might have done, but she blinked the tears from her eyes and cleared her throat.

I drew a deep breath and looked over my shoulder to the fire. Bara sat with Ursk now too, talking steadily.

"I'll do what I can to heal him," I said, turning my gaze back to my brother and ignoring Seera, still wrapped in his arm. "But we should be cautious."

"Of course," Berin said, squeezing Seera one last time before he let her go. "We'll have plenty of time to learn about our guest."

A warning horn blared in my mind. "You sound as if…"

"He's offered to guide us to the Hask."

"The Hask," I repeated flatly. "Do they worship the Bear?"

"Yes. They are the people who live beneath the great tree—" My brother gestured outward, encompassing the land ahead. "—at the edge of the world."

The next morning I fell into step beside Seera as we set off east. The day was gray, the air cool with whispers of autumn and the threat of rain. But according to our new guide, we would reach shelter before the storm hit.

"I don't like this," I murmured to my cousin as we walked. I eyed Berin and Ursk up ahead, conversing in quiet voices as they picked their way over tangled roots and ducked low branches. Seera and I were at the very rear of the party, with only Nui further behind. "He seems harmless, and I trust Fate, if he's speaking the truth. But why would she send us a guide?"

Seera made a noncommittal noise. She wore a light cloak under her pack with the hood down, and the tufts of her braids snagged in its folds as she glanced down at me. "What's wrong with him? His health."

"I'm not sure," I replied honestly. I'd listened to Ursk describe his symptoms to me last night, but the combination of them had been baffling. "It doesn't sound like anything that can spread. It's a poisoning, perhaps from something he's been eating. There're any number of dangerous mushrooms and berries out here, some of which have perfectly safe twins. I've given him something to clean his blood, but it will be days before I know if it's working."

Seera took this with consideration. "Then he's lucky Berin took him in."

I'd already heard Askir mutter that the decision should have been a communal one, but he, Seera, and I seemed to be the only ones concerned by the man's appearance.

"Berin does seem taken with him," I murmured.

"Ovir's dead," Seera said bluntly. She paused before she went on, and I saw her fight back emotion. "Berin isn't thinking clearly. He snatched up the closest thing he could save."

"I'm the one that failed Ovir." The words struck me as they came out of my mouth, and I quietened. Focusing on the path, I noted the edge of an ancient paving stone—an unnaturally smooth line in the pattern of moss and deadfall.

I thought of the same moss on the arm of the creature, locked around my throat, and resisted the urge to touch my neck.

Seera didn't correct me or taunt me. I thought she wouldn't speak at all, and I began to slow my pace to fall out of step with her.

Then she said, "Ovir tried to save you. When he went to protect you, the rivermen took him. You didn't just fail him. Your helplessness is the reason he died."

The sudden ice in her voice jarred me. "I fought," I bit out, desperate to shirk this new burden. "I tore out its throat."

"And you still would have drowned without one of us to save you. Me. I saved you. But I won't lose my life for you, Yske. You say you're here to keep us safe, to bring us home? Such a great sacrifice for you, Berin's poor meek sister, giving up her quiet life. But you won't pick up a sword when we need you to. You'll stand by and let us die for *you*."

I stopped in my tracks. "That's not what—"

My cousin spoke over me. "Next time you fail, I'll leave you to die." She spared me one more short, heavy look before turning her back on me and lengthening her strides.

I couldn't speak. Couldn't move, pinned in place by her cruelty. Maybe that was all it was—cruelty, born of grief and the need to blame.

Or perhaps she was right. Perhaps I was more of a burden than I was worth. Perhaps my passivity, my refusal to train and channel my potential for violence, *was* selfishness. Perhaps the responsibility of Ovir's death was mine and mine alone to carry.

The rest of the group continued on, all of them save Seera oblivious to the fact that they were leaving me behind.

The hurt and indignation burned, so deep I felt dizzy. I had fought. I'd done my best to take care of myself, but it hadn't been enough. I'd done my best to heal, and that hadn't been enough either.

Was this the price of my ideals? The lives of my friends?

A crack made me jump. I spun to see Nui land on the forest floor with a newly broken branch between her teeth. She caught up to me in self-satisfied trot and flopped unceremoniously at my feet, gnawing on the end of the branch in a flash of sharp white teeth.

I crouched, wavering under the weight of my pack, and scratched at the hound's pointed ears. She pliantly turned her head into my hand, still chewing, eyes soft and only a little distracted. Her tail thumped on the moss.

Grateful tears burned behind my eyes. My mother might have sent me to care for Berin—faulty as I was—but she'd sent Nui to comfort me.

"Come," I murmured, unfolding with a muscle-aching wince and starting off after the group. "We have to catch up."

Rain struck at noon, mere moments before Ursk led us into the shelter of a conifer grove. The trees were enormous, their trunks as thick as houses and their boughs so dense no light reached the cushion of needles beneath our feet. The only reminder of the storm berating the outside world was rain darkening the trunks and a steady dripping sound.

A dozen paces in, Ursk pushed back his hood and turned to smile at us. "See? Shelter. We can continue this way."

Grateful as I was to be out of the rain, I looked behind us. The more varied forest we'd emerged from was still in sight, green leaves and tall ferns shuddering under the assault of the storm. I could just make out a pair of waystones marking the road east.

"We shouldn't leave the road," I cautioned.

Ursk's haggard eyes found me, the rings under them especially pronounced in the dim light. "That's barely a road, and it will become impassable soon. If you want to reach the Hask before winter, you'll have to go around."

"Around what?" Askir asked.

Ursk looked at my brother, seeming discomfited for the first time. "Berin and I spoke of this last night. You must know of my priesthood's… abilities. We have a touch of Fate's foresight—sometimes in visions, sometimes simply knowledge. If we do not go south now, we will lose too much time."

I looked at my brother. His black curls stuck to his face and droplets of rain clung to his beard. A little of the grief that had haunted him since Ovir's death had ebbed, but I wasn't sure I liked what had replaced it any better—a distracted shallowness that didn't belong to my brother at all.

"Ursk knows the way," Berin reminded us. "If he says we need to veer south, we'll try it."

I looked, of all places, to Askir, wondering if I'd see any trace of my own unease in his face. Would he sense something amiss?

But the pale Algatt only eyed the forest around us, his thoughts hidden behind passive vigilance.

No one else spoke up in protest, so we began to walk. I fell behind as I usually did, keeping company with Nui as she ran before and behind us, sniffed under deadfall and dragged fallen branches. Eventually she tired of exploring and settled in at my side at a stately lope.

I'd just about convinced myself that my unease was unfounded when I saw the doe. She was far off through the trees, shielded by trunks, but from where I stood I had a clear line of sight.

The doe lifted her head, surrounded by the dripping hush of the forest. She was pale dun and speckled with white, her brown eyes large and innocent, even at this distance.

But from her mouth hung a young rabbit, little gray paws dangling limp and its head between her teeth. I halted and Nui looked up, letting out an instinctive warning huff.

As I watched, one hand resting protectively on Nui's back, the doe ate the rabbit. She did so politely, munching and crunching with her ears flicking and her eyes bright. Occasionally she shook the limp creature a little to adjust her hold. When the last limp paw vanished between blood-stained lips, the doe dropped her head to the forest floor, sniffing for remnants. Finding none, she flicked her tail and wandered out of sight.

Nui twitched beneath me and I realized I was crushing her to my hip. I crouched, hugging the hound instead, and tried to quell my racing heart.

Still, my stomach roiled. Nui squirmed again in my grasp and I reluctantly let her go, mourning the lost consolation of her smelly bulk. She started off in the direction the deer had gone, nose questing.

"Stay with me," I warned her, swallowing the gorge in my throat. The dog obeyed and I slowly unfolded, my stomach still clenched. "Gods below… What was that?"

There was no one to reply, but an answer already sat heavy in my gut. It felt like a warning. It felt like an omen.

SEVENTEEN

That night we camped by a burbling stream. It cut its way under the roots of one of the lording trees, its waters glistening like polished glass in the dim light. There was no sunset, no clear transition between overcast day and overcast night—just an inexorable descent into thick, impenetrable blackness.

I crouched by the stream, trailing my fingers in the cold water and letting my face dry from a half-hearted wash. What I truly needed was to strip and immerse myself, scrub away the sweat and dirt and the memory of the limp rabbit dangling from the mouth of an innocent-eyed doe.

"Yske," Berin called.

I looked up to find Berin and Ursk nearby, the newcomer standing a little behind my brother. The departure of daylight and the long day of walking had left the man looking more sickly, and my conscience twinged.

"Ursk is feeling worse. Will you see to him?" Berin said in a way that wasn't really a question. Despite the fact that we were all settling down for the night, he still wore his weapons and I could clearly see his lynx-painted shield, resting at the ready atop his pack nearby. The horn Father had given him was beside it, its silver edging glistening in the firelight.

I nodded and unfolded, pushing the sleeves of my undertunic back down to my wrists. The sweat-caked fabric immediately chafed my clean skin, but I ignored it.

"Of course," I said, conjuring a small, practiced smile.

We sat by the fire as the rest of our companions went through their nightly routines, cleaning clothes and gear, checking weapons, and adjusting their bedrolls and boots within their claimed spaces. Bara bent over the cookpot, where a stew of smoked meat and foraged vegetables simmered. Ittrid set grains to soak for morning. Nui had her head in Esan's lap, where he sat staring into the trees. Every so often his fingers scratched behind her ears, and she pressed her head into the touch with half-lidded eyes.

I brought my pack over to the fire. Ursk sat patiently on a blanket I recognized as Berin's and offered me a small, almost nervous smile.

"I appreciate this," he told me in his low voice. "I never thought to meet a healer out here, but perhaps I should not be surprised." He smiled wryly.

"I suppose so." I regarded him with what I hoped was professional detachment. "You truly came all this way because of a vision?"

He nodded, his smile becoming more knowing. "I understand why you are cautious, Yske. Even some of my own people still distrust my priesthood. But I promise you, I am only here to help, and I will prove myself however I can."

I simply nodded and moved on. "How are you feeling tonight?"

"Weary," he admitted. "I feel as though my blood is too thick in my veins, and I've no appetite. My head aches."

"How badly?"

He seemed unsure how to answer. "Not as bad as some days."

A flutter of compassion moved in my chest and my unease loosened another knot. It probably wasn't his fault he'd come into our company under the worst of circumstances or that I'd happened to see a carnivorous doe earlier that day. He was sick, and had been for some time.

I smiled again, and this time it felt genuine. "I can make you a tea to help you sleep and ease your headache. As to the lack of hunger, I'd encourage you to eat, regardless, but not so much that you strain your stomach."

The man smiled in gratitude.

I set about choosing my herbs and grinding them as Bara and Ittrid distributed supper. Nui watched Esan eat with doleful eyes, her chin still firmly planted on his thigh. I ate as I worked, and Ursk slowly made his way through his portion of meat, mushroom, and wild carrot stew.

Finally, the company settled down to sleep. Ursk drank his tea and curled up with his borrowed blanket near the periphery of the camp. Soft breathing turned to snores, and Berin met my gaze.

"Thank you," he said. "I know you don't like him."

"That's not it." I sighed and looked at my herbs and jars, laid out on a piece of leather before me. I was running low on many things, and would need to forage more consistently as we traveled—no matter how weary and footsore I was. "I just worry why Fate might have sent him. And I think of Ovir. And the creatures. I can't forget how the High Halls above us are… thinning, the further east we go. Then there's Aita's gift, whatever it's done to me. And today I saw…"

His brows twitched together in sudden interest. "Saw what?"

I described the unsettling scene, and he cringed.

"I'd agree, it feels like an omen," he admitted, blowing out his cheeks and squinting at the night, reminded that we were sitting watch. "But perhaps the deer in the east simply have a taste for blood. Perhaps the doe was a bit… off. Diseased."

"It seems too much, in combination with the river creatures."

"You still won't call them rivermen."

"They weren't rivermen."

"You know better than Askir?"

My pride rose. "In this, yes. He had never physically been to the High Halls before Mother took us through, do you realize that? Standard priests only travel in spirit, and even then only rarely."

Berin, to my increasing irritation, rolled his eyes. "Yske, you're the greatest human healer in generations, but you're not a priestess. Don't assume you know better simply because you spent a few years clinging to Aita's skirts."

Protests clotted my throat. To push back would not only be childish but risk my secrets. Still, I couldn't keep the bitterness from my tone as I said, "Of course. I'm just your sister, here to bandage your wounds, do your bidding and try not to get in the way."

Berin snorted, unyielding. "Everyone has their role."

I blinked at him, taken aback. "So my opinion on everything other than cuts and bruises is irrelevant?"

My brother appeared to consider this for a moment. I could see his guard coming up, the shadows that had haunted him since Ovir's death chasing away any restfulness or good humor. "Not irrelevant, just unnecessary."

Anger sparked in my belly. I knew I should quell it, but my will was slow to comply. "Isa complained about this, you know. The way you disregard others. That's not leadership, Berin. That's arrogance."

Mention of his wife made Berin's whole body stiffen. He glared at me, and as familiar as the planes of his face were, at that moment he looked a stranger. Shadows carved his handsome features in angles of callousness and resentment, and brooding, jagged hurt.

Without a word he rose to his feet and went over to Esan, whom he nudged with a boot. His friend evidently hadn't been asleep, because he sat up without a hint of startlement and listened to something Berin said in a low voice, then he came back to the fire with my brother.

"Esan will sit watch with me," Berin said. He added without kindness, "Get some rest."

"Berin," I started, looking from him to Esan.

Esan didn't look at either of us, too tired to be discomfited by the conflict.

"Sleep, Yske," Berin said with a flat, humorless smile. "Goodnight."

Sleep refused to come, or rather, I refused to let it. I lay on my back on my bedroll, pack beneath my head, and glared up at the blackness of the forest canopy high above. All around me my companions breathed softly. Nui slept at my feet and by the fire Esan and Berin murmured in low voices. I could hear the frustration in Berin's tone and Esan's answers were short, little more than agreements between my brother's rantings.

I waved away a buzzing mosquito and stretched my jaw, trying not to clench it. Berin was mourning. Dealing with mourners was one aspect of my occupation, and I'd seen grief come in all forms. I shouldn't begrudge Berin the way he was dealing with Ovir's death, but I did. It hurt. I hurt.

I shifted down in my blanket, more to keep the mosquitoes off my skin than to keep warm, and buried my toes in Nui's back. She let out a sleepy breath.

The attack in the cave came back to me, some details stark and clear, others blurred. For the first time since, I let my mind linger on it, stretching and exploring the memory.

I caught at the moment I'd poured Aita's strange magic into Ovir, the way his wound had knit and the feeling of intense surety I'd had when I enacted it. The blood on my fingers. What were the parameters of this magic, and could I replenish it?

I ran a thumb over the fingers of my opposite hand. It would be simple to find out. Just one cut, one marking. A test.

But that action meant so much more than a knife on skin. It would be blood intentionally shed for a Miri, payment for a magic I shouldn't have.

No. As much as I respected Aita, even cared for her, I could not do that. Aita was no goddess. I was no priestess. My blood was my own, my allegiance to Thvynder.

My resolve felt strong then, hard and solid. Then my imagination churned up an image of Berin dying beneath my hands, and I wavered. If Aita's magic could save him, would I truly turn my back on it?

Was there anything I wouldn't do for him?

I touched the ends of my fingers together, imagining I could feel the whorls of my fingerprints. I wished I could speak with Aita, sort out her motives and what I should do. My runework was strong, but an inquiry—a prayer—from this distance would not be received. If I was able to reach the High Halls, though…

I stared at the dark canopy. There might not be any doors to the High Halls in the east, but as I'd seen with Ovir, the upper realm was still accessible in spirit. For now.

By the time dawn came, creeping under the trees on a golden mist, I'd collected myself. I smiled when Sedi handed me my portion of breakfast. I readied my pack early and used the spare moments to forage by the creek for widow root, wandering back up its length and eyeing the canopy, looking for places where water met sunlight and more undergrowth appeared. Mist hung about me as I went, fine and tinted with captured gold that had nothing to do with my Sight.

The beauty of it cleansed and calmed me.

Then, as I stood and watched the mist drift between the trees, I saw the skull.

Eighteen

I thought it was a boulder at first. Taller than I was and twice as long, it lay on its side beneath the towering trees. I might not have identified it as a skull at all had a lynx not slipped out from an empty eye socket with a rodent in its jaws and sauntered off into the trees.

I watched the lynx go, then inched closer to the mound of bone. My mind worked, trying to identify what kind of beast the skull might have belonged to. It was larger than anything I'd seen in the Waking World or the High Halls. Sea serpents grew to near this size, and I'd seen their skulls, trophies from the war with the Winterborn, suspended from the rafters of halls along the coast. But we were far, far from the sea.

Furthermore, this skull was not… whole. Yes, it was intact, with eye sockets and arching browbone and a jaw with many teeth, thick with moss. But there were odd seams beneath a patchy skin of lichen and a cap of clinging, spindly wildflowers. Sections of bone did not quite meet up, and showed varying degrees of degradation and discoloration—as if it had been pieced back together.

A crash in the bushes announced Nui, who skittered around the skull, sniffing earnestly. But her tail also wagged, and I forced my breath out in a calming rush. The skull was disquieting, but no threat.

Seera came after the hound, followed by Ittrid. The other two women slowed when they saw my find.

"Gods below," Seera muttered, coming closer. "What left *that* behind?"

The rest of the company emerged from the mist after the women, staring and muttering. I spied Berin carrying my pack, and gave him a distracted look as he set it down.

Ursk reached out and felt a patch of exposed, weather-worn bone. I touched my Sight and saw a flare of power ripple down his outstretched arm—the palest gold, twined with a powdery, winter-sky blue.

The Duamel priest turned to look at us, his brows furrowed. "This is old. Too old to lie like this. It should be buried beneath rock and stone. It *was* buried, and then it was not."

No one asked how he knew, even though most of them couldn't have seen the flare of his magic like I had.

"What did it belong to?" Seera muttered, peering into the skull's empty eye socket.

"A monster," Esan replied.

Berin looked at Ursk. "How did it get here?"

The Duamel pulled his fingers from the bone and gave us all a tight, uncertain smile. "It walked."

He could offer no more explanation. But as we left, spurred by unease and the shadow of that ancient beast, I couldn't help but fixate on how the moss clung to the bone... just as it had clothed the creatures who had attacked at the river.

Time passed. I bled, my time corresponding with Sedi's, and Berin called a halt. For three days we camped in a rare meadow, where sunlight broke through the trees and wildflowers bloomed. I rested when my pains were too great and hobbled about when I could, restocking my stores. I made a salve to rub on my lower stomach and ease the pain, which Sedi shared. Her arm was also healing well, and my aid combined with the comradery of mutual trial dulled the edge between us—or so I felt.

Ursk's health had been improving, and his progress redoubled during those days of rest. He and the others hunted and foraged, repaired gear, and smoked meat, whiling away the hours as productively as they could.

It was during this time that I finally found widow root. It grew beside a stream, frail yellow flowers rustling in the breeze. I cut off the leaves and set them to dry for soap, then knelt eyeing the mound of leftover roots and flowers for some time.

I could make yifr with this and try to reach the High Halls in spirit. But I could not do so openly, not with Askir watching me.

Most of the company left early the next morning to hunt, before the first blush of dawn seeped through the canopy. Nui bounded after them, eager to run and chase. Bara and Sedi wandered off together, arm in arm, and Ittrid went to a nearby stream to bathe. That left me with Ursk, fast asleep on a bedroll of donated blankets and a pallet of woven grasses.

I eyed him for a time, watching him breathe as I pulled out the ingredients for yifr. I withdrew another pouch as well, one marked with red string. Covering my face with a lavender-scented cloth, I opened the pouch and held it just under Ursk's nose. His breathing immediately became deeper, longer, and the flicker of dreams behind his eyelids faded. Now, there was no chance of him intruding upon my ritual.

I made the yifr quickly, grinding and heating and mixing with quiet efficiency. I put away my tools and herbs as I went so that by the time a steaming cup of yifr rested before me, there was no sign of what I'd done. If anyone returned early, they'd find Ursk and I both fast asleep— he in true slumber, I in another world entirely.

I raised the concoction to my mouth and paused, the smooth wood of my cup brushing my bottom lip. The forest was full of dawn light now, warm and gold. I rooted myself in the moment, just for a breath, then I drank.

I took time to rinse the cup, dumping the dregs into the side of the fire, where the coals hissed and spat. Then I lay down, folded my hands over my fluttering belly and closed my eyes.

Sound began to blur. I felt momentarily as though I lay in a boat, tilting and rolling on gentle waves, then I lost physical sensation entirely.

I pried my eyes open. Instead of the lush canopy, I saw a night sky of pure and unadulterated black, smooth and vast. From where I lay, my view was hedged by waving, parched reeds.

I sat up, blinking through a wave of dizziness. The reeds swayed in a breeze I couldn't feel, and the textureless sky left me feeling disoriented.

Sensation slowly returned to my limbs, though muted and dull. Fingers braced in the cool, muddy earth, I slowly climbed to my feet. Waves of reeds spread in every direction except what I supposed must be west. There, faint on the horizon, I saw a variance—a mingling of vague colors and light, like a distant forest fire under a belly of cloud. The Eangen High Halls?

The only other illumination came from vague, pale curls of light among the reeds. Foxfire? No, there was no forest here, no wood for it to grow on. Perhaps they were some other form of fungus, or even dormant fireflies, clinging to the thick, dry blades. They were beautiful, in their way—stars cast across this divine earth, instead of the featureless sky above.

Everywhere else was a thick and impenetrable darkness. It was the essence of both potential and lack, and reminded me distantly of how the Miri described the Unmade itself.

I was tempted to walk further east, deeper into the speckled blackness, but fifteen years of experience in this realm kept my feet firmly rooted in place. Instead, I sketched runes in the air. They stood out boldly, glowing lines imprinted over the colorless landscape with my new lavender taint at their core.

My stomach turned in unease as I sketched the runes for prayer and travel, and Aita's name. I overlaid them, tangling them together in the artful way my parents had taught me. When I finished, I kept my fingers splayed, holding them open like a net to catch my words.

"Aita, hear me if you can," I said. Meanwhile, in the quiet of my heart I whispered, *This is not a prayer.* "Come to me. Tell me what this magic is, and how to use it."

With that, I pulled my fingers together. The runes vanished in a burst of fine, lavender-gold sparks and the wind swept it toward the faint glow in the west.

I waited. The reeds waved and rasped. My shoes soaked and dampness seeped into my clothes. I began to shiver, though I knew that my body lay in the comfort of my bedroll, beside a fire on a gentle morning. A morning that was swiftly passing by, its passage marked by the increasing clarity of my mind as the yifr's effects wore off. Already, the horizon was beginning to fade, and soon my soul would retreat through the fabric of the worlds.

Finally, a voice came. It was thin and distant, a murmur in a long tunnel, but I knew it was Aita. The power in my blood surged at the sound and my grip on the High Halls hardened again.

"...change nothing now," she said, her voice fragmented and thin, but waxing with each word. She did not sound pleased and I sensed I'd missed a longer tirade, but I had no time to ask her to repeat it.

Aita continued, coming to me in ebbs and flows—clear one moment, faint the next. "Have you forgotten all I taught you? ...old ways, Yske, for this power to succeed. My priestesses..."

Anxiety fluttered through my chest. "Have you marked me as a priestess?"

"Goddesses have priestesses. We are neither," Aita stated, harsh and clipped, then her voice faded for a breath. "...pay the price for this magic, at each turn of the moon. Use it sparingly. Blood will replenish it. Blood will stay the hand of death."

Something touched my face. Water? Droplets of water, like rain? I flinched back, hands flying to my cheeks, but there was nothing there. Again it came, a drop of wetness and... another voice. An urgent voice, coming not from the world around me but from inside my own skull.

The blackness closed in around me, then faded. I blinked. Ittrid leaned over me in the Waking World, black hair dangling between us in dripping braids. Her eyes were wide and, as I stared up at her, she made a relieved sound.

"We have to move," she said, pulling me to a sitting position. Belatedly, I saw the axe in her hand. "Yske, now!"

NINETEEN

A wolf that was not a wolf meandered toward the fire. Mossy patches of skin. Tendons of vines, visible beneath muscle of mud and reeds. Glimpses of greenish bones and elongated claws, sharp and dirty.

The creature glanced at us and cocked its head, seemingly unfazed by our presence. Ursk slept on, on the other side of the low-burning fire. No one else was in sight. Ittrid, the unconscious Ursk and I faced the beast alone.

The creature's head swiveled, ignoring Ursk. Its movements were unnaturally smooth, its posture unhurried, unthreatened. But as it focused on Ittrid and me, that changed. In the space of a blink it contorted into a true, hulking predator.

I launched myself to my feet at the same time as the beast leapt. Ittrid threw out an arm to ward me back, shouting words I didn't bother to understand. Off in the forest I heard crashing—the others? Nui? More monsters?

Horror and guilt coursed through me. Ursk was helpless because of me. The creature was already upon us because I'd been slow to wake. If we died, it would be my fault entirely.

Fear came, cold and blanching. Then hot, frustrated courage.

I avoided Ittrid's arm and stooped, seizing the horn my father had given me. I blasted it.

The creature charged. Ittrid seized a flaming log from the fire and threw it into the face of our attacker, following it with a downward snap of her axe.

"Berin!" I shouted into the forest, dropping the horn and snatching up a hefty stick. "Esan!"

My voice cut off as the creature barreled past us and I nearly fell into the fire.

Ittrid's axe came again. It impacted with the beast's side with a crack of bone. The creature staggered, then leapt at her.

Ittrid fell. I heard another crack, saw her head turn limply on the brim of Berin's shield, then the beast rounded on me. It snarled, low and feral and blood-curdling.

Nui barked. She pelted out of the forest and I glimpsed Sedi, Bara, and Askir following her before the dog launched herself through the air and took our attacker to the ground.

"Nui, no!" I cried out. Images of teeth shredding furry flesh roared through my head. I slammed a foot down on one of the monster's paws and stabbed the end of my branch into its side.

Nui leapt free. The beast twisted after her, impossibly lithe despite being pinned to the earth, and locked its jaws around my ankle. I screamed—not in pain, but horror—and toppled backward, dragging the thing with me.

I hit the ground with a thud at the same time as an axe came down on the creature's neck. It still bucked and slashed, but my companions were efficient in their killing—they pinned its limbs, stabbed at eyes and throat and stomach. Then there was a hush that was not really a hush—just a lack of screaming and the creature's rattling, screeching howls. I scrambled backward, helped by hands I identified as Askir's.

My companions separated again, easing back from the carnage with slow, cautious steps. Askir and Sedi turned to face the forest, wary for more attackers, while Bara remained over the body and made sure it was dead. Nui paced behind him, head low, panting. There was no blood on her, to my immeasurable relief.

I started to push myself upright so I could go to Ittrid, but my body wouldn't respond. I paused, a spike of hot anxiety shooting through me, and looked down at myself. My ankle was mangled and there was a huge claw in my side, embedded between my ribs behind one arm, like a knife. I stared at both wounds, blinking hard. That couldn't be right. I couldn't feel any pain. The claw grated between my ribs, but I felt nothing else.

The yifr. The yifr lingering in my blood wasn't enough to keep me in the Halls, but it was enough to dull my pain. I gave a huffing, shaky laugh.

Bara looked over at me and furrowed his brows. "What— Oh, gods below."

He brought me my pack. I murmured semi-coherent instructions and pacifications, trying to soothe the worry in his eyes. Then his face became Berin's and the camp was full of my companions again, questions flying, bodies moving and Nui darting anxiously between them all.

I made sure someone went to Ittrid and checked on Ursk, and pressed herbs and cloths for cleaning wounds into waiting hands. Berin hovered the whole time, face pale with concern.

"Tell me what to do," he said, holding my pack for me while I rummaged. I squinted at him, unable to remember what I'd been looking for, and his worried face grew even more concerned. "Yske?"

"Pull it out," I decided, looking down at the claw. "My ankle can wait. This thing didn't pierce my lung. Just pull it out, and ignore me if I try to stop you."

My brother looked from the claw to his hands and flexed his fingers, dispelling a brief quaver. Then he did as I asked, one hand braced on my arm to stop me from striking out, the other wrapping around the end of the claw. More figures hovered, clustering in, ready to help, but I saw only Berin's face, his Eangen-dark eyes fixed on mine. They looked so, so like our mother's.

The claw came free in a burst of blood. As it poured, someone pulled my tunic over my head, and then I leaned into Berin's shoulder as my wound was washed and stitched.

A minute or an age later, I lay on my side by the fire. A wool blanket was rough against the bare skin of my upper body, except where a bandage had been wound beneath my breasts.

"How did I sleep through that?"

I turned my weary eyes to Ursk, who sat across the fire from me, wrapped in a blanket of his own. It was the dead of night but the fire burned high, and I saw the shapes of my companions on watch. But he spoke low enough not to disturb them.

My lips felt heavy. I licked them, hoping he didn't actually expect an answer, and rested my head on the bundled clothes. They stank of sweat, but they were better than the ground.

"I am sorry I could not help."

I glanced at our guide again, guilt mixing with surprise at the sincerity in his voice. "Don't be. The medicine I've been giving you helps you sleep—and in this case it protected you."

Ursk pulled his blanket a little higher. He kept it loose over one bandaged shoulder, as shirtless as I was. My healer's eyes noticed the thinness of him, the lean muscle carved around visible ribs.

Ursk followed my gaze. "I could use more butter with my bread, I know."

I smiled dizzily. "Some would say I've had too much."

He stifled a laugh but didn't reply, which I was grateful for.

I twisted my head to look up at the canopy and listened to the crackle of the fire for a time, and the pattern of my own shallow breaths. There was pain now, but it was a clean pain, a natural one, and I was glad for it.

I'd spoken to Aita. The cost had been high and could have been much higher, but I had my answer.

The only question I had to wrestle with now was whether or not I would use Aita's gift—if I would shed my blood like a priestess of old, in return for the power of a Miri.

TWENTY

Between my injuries and Ittrid's, there was no question of breaking camp that day, but neither could anyone rest—save the Soulderni woman, who didn't awaken for several hours. We kept constant watch and no one left sight of the main camp alone or unarmed.

I tried to heal myself, once. But the well of power remained empty, the blood I'd shed the day before apparently ineffective. When I took my knife in hand, I could not bring myself to intentionally cut my skin. So I lay in disorientation and pain, battling with myself and watching Ittrid sleep.

By the time night fell, the mood among my companions was strained and terse. We shared a quiet meal, speaking little, every ear turned to the night and the possible dangers it concealed.

Finally, after a particularly eerie series of cracks off in the darkness, Berin shook himself and surveyed the company, finally setting his gaze on me. "Yske, will you sing? If you're well enough."

I looked up from the patch I was carefully sewing into my torn tunic, covering the blood-stained puncture in the brown fabric with a piece of fireweed green from my legwraps.

Askir lifted his head, glancing from my brother to the forest. "Is that wise?"

"A quiet tale will put us in no greater danger," Berin tempered. "Everything out there knows we're here. Yske?"

I pulled a stitch into place. My wound wasn't sore at the moment, newly dulled by a painkilling tea. "I could, if everyone's agreed."

Bara made an appreciative sound and Ittrid lifted her bruised face to the firelight, expectant. Even Esan glanced my way.

"Any requests?" I asked.

"'Oulden at the River,'" Ittrid said. "Do you know it?"

I hesitated, but nodded. The story came from Souldern, Ittrid's homeland, and had become common among the Eangen around the collapse of the Arpa Empire, when so many Soulderni had taken refuge in the north. It was one of the stories I'd liked as a child—there was no violent death, which was refreshing—but when Isik and I had come together, the story had taken on new meaning.

"I don't know that one," Bara said, sounding interested.

I cleared my throat and composed myself. Then, beginning with a low, melodic chanting common to the Soulderni, I started the tale.

The story followed Oulden, the Miri who had once been god of the Soulderni. He'd seen a herd of magnificent horses at the river and thought to take one for himself, only to find the herd watched over by an—unsurprisingly—beautiful woman.

The chanting pattern of the song changed here, becoming softer. These were the days when Oulden was young and, struck with longing, he posed as a mortal man and spoke with her on the riverbank, in the sun by the glistening water, and her skin was bronze, and her black hair blew long in the breeze, and other poetic details. After many such meetings, they lay together and fell asleep in one another's arms. But when he slept Oulden's guise fell away, and the woman sensed his divine aura, and knew she'd been lied to.

Again the song shifted, a sweet melody harkening back to that original, chanted pattern.

The woman, however, pretended not to know her lover's true identity. The years passed, and when her hair turned gray but Oulden's did not, he realized he must leave, or else watch her die.

This was the pattern of all stories of love between humans and Miri. But this one ended a little differently—with Oulden begging his love to linger in the High Halls after her death, and spend her spirit-life by his side instead of making the pilgrimage to the Hidden Hearth and eternal sleep.

The last verse was particularly hushed, delivered with the tone of a tragic secret, and it was no stretch for me to lend true emotion to my voice. Isik had asked me the same thing long ago, and I, like Oulden's lover, had refused. Human souls might linger in the High Halls for generations after their deaths, but not forever. A soul's passage to the rest of the Hidden Hearth was inexorable. Instinctual. A drive as natural as hunger and thirst and sleep itself.

So Oulden's lover had traveled to the Hidden Hearth, and there passed into the Long Sleep beside her ancestors. Desolate, Oulden made it his task to watch over horses when they came down to the river, in memory of her.

The final notes of the tale were soft, a little rough, mimicking grief. Ittrid's expression was distant and nostalgic, and Bara reached out to take Sedi's hand, which made her look vaguely embarrassed.

Ursk, for his part, watched me closely. "That was beautiful, Yske."

I nodded my thanks and took a sip of tea from my wooden mug. My mind was full of Isik, and an imagining of him and I in the High Halls after my own death. If we'd remained lovers, how long could I manage to linger with him in my spirit-flesh before following my kin to the Hidden Hearth?

"Do any of the Soulderni still worship Oulden?" Ursk was asking Ittrid. "As the Iskiri Devoted still worship Eang?"

"No, we accepted his death," Ittrid answered, leaning back on both palms. "It was near the beginning of the Upheaval."

"After he and our mother bound Ashaklon, a God of the Old World," Berin added, not even trying to sound humble about it.

Ursk twisted to look at Berin. "Is there a song about that?"

I laughed. "There is, but I've never been allowed to sing it."

"Our mother does not enjoy being a fireside tale." Berin grinned too, and when our eyes met, there was a shared warmth and memory that made my heart swell. "She says we can sing of her after she's dead."

"Well, she is not here," Ursk waved his hands at the forest. "She is Hessa, you said? The High Priestess?"

Berin nodded. "High Priestess of the Eangen, Curse-breaker, wife of the Shepherd of the Dead."

Seera perked up, and I sensed an insult coming. "Mother of Berin Sharp-Axe," she added, grinning wickedly. "And Yske No-Spine. Or was it Yske the Squishy?"

Berin scratched his beard, looking mildly disapproving. "You alternated."

I drew breath to voice my offense. The childish names didn't have the edge they once did, but Seera's tongue was a whetstone.

"Squishy isn't a bad thing." Lying flat on his back on his bedroll, Esan rolled his head to the side and met my gaze. It was the first time he'd shown anything other than closed, grim grief since Ovir's death, and I didn't begrudge him the distraction. His interest, I knew, was passive, the rare kind I could appreciate without concern.

I smirked back at him.

"Es," Berin frowned. "I'm right here."

Esan looked back up at the trees and yawned broadly. "Yske has a spine, we all know that."

"Thank you." I inclined my head with satisfaction.

"The story?" Ursk prompted, though his eyes danced. "About the binding?"

"All right." I composed myself. "The tale of the Black Binding Tree. Now, hush. I'll not be your story-singer if I'm constantly interrupted."

The company quieted, and I began.

Another two weeks passed, my wounds healed, and the signs of summer's end grew more numerous. The nights grew colder, the days more moderate, and what little undergrowth populated the lofty forest ignited with color or began to die back. Mushrooms burst from the bed of needles by the hundreds, mottling the forest floor, and the sky always seemed on the brink of rain.

The world grew quieter as songbirds began to leave and the frogs turned their minds to mud and sleep. Other, more sporadic sounds took their place—the bay of a rutting stag and the strident calls of geese fleeing the impending cold, though by then the canopy of the conifers was too thick to see them pass.

When we at last emerged at the top of a great cliff and saw the sky again, relief and awe washed over me. Here the land broke away into an erratic series of canyons, shattered like ice in a winter trough. Swaths of rain and low cloud blew in like carded wool, smothering clefts of sheer rock, stretches of clinging forest and a network of rivers and lakes. The whole of it was cast in somber storm light—rich deep greens, rain-darkened rock, fringes of scarlet brush and white-frothed channels of black water.

"That is what remains of the eastern road." Ursk pointed north but I could see no road, no bridges, not even unnatural lines or variances. There was no road at all, only canyons, peninsulas, and rivers under the fine, blowing rain.

Berin gave an impressed grunt. "Now where do we go?"

Ursk pondered the south-east for a long moment. When he spoke again, he directed our eyes across the landscape ahead. "We follow the rim here, then that peninsula. We can descend there."

"You saw this in a vision?" Askir asked.

Ursk did not look offended, though the other priest's voice had an edge. "Yes."

"How long will it take?" I pressed.

"I do not know," Ursk admitted. "The path will be treacherous. Weeks?"

"And there's no other way?" Ittrid stood close to me, I noted, and the anxiety in her eyes felt a lot like my own. I caught the other woman's gaze, her skin still mottled with bruises, and saw solidarity there.

Ursk pointed again, first north, then south. "There's another path north and one south. Both will see us trekking through winter snow."

Berin looked at the company, but there was really no choice to be made. We followed the Priest of Fate.

We reached the beginning of the peninsula two days later and set up camp on the mainland, still in the shelter of the lording conifers. The trees grew right to the cliff's edge and crept out onto the peninsula itself, though many had fallen off the edge, dragging huge chunks of forest floor with them. Exposed roots stood out like swollen veins and the rotting remnants of stumps dangled. But their passing had made room for new growth, a younger forest more adapted to its landscape—clinging, twisted and windblown, its leaves beginning to turn scarlet and yellow.

Daylight faded from the shattered land as ribbons of rain snaked in the distance, as our supper cooked and Nui laid her head on her paws, watching fat drip from crisping grouse. Overhead the treetops, rather than capture the setting sun, cut harshly into it. Broken beams of sunlight channeled down into the ravines, highlighting a lonely tree here, a rain-slick cliff there. I watched carrion birds circle on the wind and a trail of goats navigate a seemingly sheer rockface. Halfway down, they vanished into a streak of burgundy shrubs.

Berin came to sit next to me, crossing his legs and scratching at his beard. His fastidious grooming had begun to give way to the rigors of travel and he smelled of damp wool, sweat, pine sap and smoke. But his hair was still neatly brushed, the sides freshly shaved, and now he pulled a carved comb from his pocket to untangle his beard.

"The goats seem to think the forest is more dangerous than the cliffs at night," I observed, eyeing where the animals had vanished.

My brother gave a half-nod, half-shrug, and smoothed his beard after the comb. "They don't have axes."

I glanced behind us at the camp: Bara and Sedi combing and braiding one another's hair, Seera chopping wood with a violent intensity, and Ittrid stacking it to one side, watching the woman with bemused caution. The rest were by the fire, including Ursk.

"You don't seem to mind our guide so much now," Berin commented, sounding too off-handed not to be calculated.

I let out a long breath. "I just thought it strange that we found a stranger and decided to trust him with our lives."

Berin looked at me with eyebrows raised and comb poised. "And *that*, little sister, is why you have no friends."

It was the lightest expression I'd seen on his face in days, and I couldn't help but laugh. "Oh, stop. I have friends."

He leaned close and bumped his shoulder against mine. "Sure you do. Alone on that mountain. The fieldmice and bears make great conversation."

"You'd be surprised," I quipped. I thought of Isik and suppressed a smile.

Berin didn't appear to notice. "Truthfully, Yske, at the pyre, after you and the others went ahead... I prayed."

My smile faded, and I watched him with slightly rounded eyes. "We're too far away from Eangen for Thvynder to hear," I pointed out. *Even if they were still in Eangen.*

"I didn't pray to Thvynder," Berin said mildly. "I prayed to Fate."

"Oh," I frowned, considering. I took a moment to stare out at the fading beams of sunlight and distant, ribboning rain, and tried to cobble an appropriate response. "She can't directly interfere with current events."

"She didn't have to, because she already had." Berin shook his head wryly. "It twists my mind to think about. But I prayed and Ursk walked out of the forest—the only man we'd met in weeks, a Duamel who left his country a year ago looking for *us*. Someone who knows the way to the edge of the world and how to navigate this." My brother gestured at the darkening landscape. "What am I supposed to do? Turn away the answer I prayed for?"

I blew out a long breath. "Have you considered what this means? Fate's intervention?"

Berin nodded and I saw sparks of excitement in his eyes, though his overall demeanor was subdued. He set his comb down and reached to take my arm, his touch warm and gentle.

"I have," he said with a sobriety that reminded me of our father, and gave me hope for the man he might one day become. "This expedition is more than a simple journey. The gods are at work, and Fate has always had her thumb upon our family. Why would she disregard you and me?"

I tugged my forearm free and slipped my hand into his. I squeezed. "The attention of the gods is not always a good thing."

The corner of Berin's mouth curved up. "You're so serious."

"For good reason—hey!"

My protest cut off as he reached out and bundled me into a one-armed hug.

I squawked and twisted. "I don't bend that way!"

"Stop worrying," he chided, loosening his hold so I could settle into a more comfortable lean. "Start pondering how you want the story-singers to remember you."

"Maybe I don't want the story-singers to remember me," I murmured, resting my head back on his shoulder. "I understand why Mother doesn't want us to sing of her until she's gone. It's… It feels dishonest."

Berin scoffed. "Then do something so glorious, so magnificent, the singers have no need to exaggerate."

"Are you saying Mother's stories need exaggeration?"

I felt the rumble of his laughter against my ear. "The way she tells her stories certainly does. She's too practical."

"Perhaps practical is best?" I suggested. "We're just people doing what we believe is right."

"We're the children of god-slayers, with magic in our blood. We were bred for stories and songs," Berin said, but his voice held none of the vainglory I expected. Rather, he sounded burdened. "I suppose our children will be, too."

The hush that settled over us was shallow, and I sensed he had more to say.

He watched the sunset for another long instant, then said, "Isa will have had the baby by now, won't she?"

Sobering, I silently tracked back through the weeks. "Yes."

"Then I'm a father," he said, his eyes taking on an unsettled, aching note. "Or perhaps I am not. Perhaps I am even a widower."

I wrapped both arms around him and held him tight. "Whichever it is, Mother will be there to care for her… or them." I did not mention the third possibility, that when we returned home, our mother would lead him to a pair of rune-marked trees and a scattering of ashes.

My brother rested his chin atop my head and did not speak again.

Twenty-One

The next morning, the sun rose in the south. From the edge of a cliff, blanket wrapped around me against the chill, I watched its orange light spill out from under a bank of dark storm cloud.

Hidden in the forest or beset by clouds, I had not noticed the sunrise drift from east to south. The light of dawn had been ambivalent each day, usually muted and stifled by the trees. But now I saw it, whole and clear above the canyons.

We were now north of the sun, bound for the true east. Bound for the Unmade.

A path laced the peninsula before us, little more than a goat trail over uneven rock, occasionally sheltered by patches of forest. Rain came and went, leaving the rocks perpetually slick. Askir roamed ahead, warning us of particularly treacherous reaches and startling birds from their roosts. Nui brought up the rear, stopping to sniff mounds of goat scat and drink from puddles.

"Yske."

I looked up from where I was attempting to wedge my boots in the narrow strip of earth between two sheets of rock. To my right and left, the peninsula fell away entirely into the abyss, and the closeness of the edge made my stomach knot.

"Here, take this." Ursk stood just behind me, holding out a freshly cut length of sapling. "A walking staff," he clarified. He had a similar one in his other hand, already braced to help him balance on the rain-dark rock. "I offered them to your companions, but they seemed rather offended."

I reached out with a grateful nod. He looked healthier today, I noted, the hollows around his eyes lighter and his flesh less gaunt. My treatment was working.

I planted the staff between the rocks, immediately feeling steadier. "Thank you."

The Duamel smiled. "My pleasure."

Near nightfall, the winds came. We sheltered in a small forest and endured a long, frigid night, berated by the gale and doused with intermittent rain. I curled up with Nui for warmth on a patch of loam, and was startled in the morning when I found Berin sleeping on the hound's other side.

He cracked an eye and squinted at me over a mound of canine fur. "She stinks, you know," he grumbled sleepily.

I nearly smiled, but my body ached so much from the ground and the cold that it turned into a wince. "Ach. I need a night in a real bed, Berin. And a proper hearth."

"We'll have it as soon as we reach a Hask village," he promised, still stretched on the ground. Reaching out, he scratched at Nui's spine. She let her head flop over to look at him, and began to sleepily lick his ear. "Ugh. Not long now."

Days crawled by, each night more uncomfortable than the last. By the time we reached the path down into the ravine, I was almost grateful. No more wind or blowing rain beating us from all sides. Just a jagged path, switchbacking toward a swift-flowing river.

One by one, my companions stepped down onto the path. Nui stayed close to me, picking her way with a surety rivaled only by the goats I glimpsed on the other side of the ravine, watching us blithely through a veil of drifting mist.

Berin went just ahead of me, shield slung on one shoulder. I eyed its stylized lynx design when I paused to catch my breath, walking stick braced and cool mist prickling across my cheeks.

The shield made me think of my mother and home and the vast space between this world and that. My heart contorted, longing for the quiet safety of my little house on the mountain, the simplicity of my days, and… Isik. He stepped out from the quiet corner of my mind where he always lingered, and I found myself combing through memories of our days—and nights—together.

Berin offered me a hand at a particularly narrow part of the path and I took it, feeling the damp and grit between his warm skin and mine. Thoughts of Isik retreated, and I smiled at my brother.

"Thank you."

He ruffled my hair, which immediately stole my smile. I *tsk*ed and tried to bat his hand away.

Between lifting my hand and opening my mouth to rebuke him, I teetered backward over the foggy abyss.

Someone shouted. I planted my walking stick and balanced out at the same time as Berin grabbed my belt, pulling me into his arms. On the path below us Bara looked up through a veil of mist, mouth crooked in a breathless laugh.

The ground below him gave way. Sedi screamed. She lunged, reaching futilely over the edge after her husband. Ittrid and Askir closed on her from opposite sides, hauling her back to the ravine wall and pinning her there as she shrieked. I heard a crash off in the miasma, half-drowned by the shouts and Nui's startled barks.

The hound took off, baying and scrambling. She nearly knocked Ursk into the ravine after Bara as she leapt from one switchback to another and vanished from sight.

I did not breathe. Did not move. Berin too was frozen, one hand iron on my belt.

Sedi quietened her cries with the back of one hand. Silence swirled around us in the thickening mist. Then, from just below in the fog, I heard Bara laugh—hysterical and relieved.

Sedi shrugged off Askir, desperation and hope written in her eyes.

She shoved the priest aside and darted down the next switchback, then she too vanished.

We hastened after her. The trail switched one more time before the path abruptly leveled out. There, not three paces below the ledge he'd toppled from, Bara lay belly-up on his pack like an overturned beetle. Sedi was draped over him, scolding him while he laughed.

"I'm all right!" Bara flailed, and with Sedi and Askir's help he sat up and disentangled from his pack. He put a hand on his chest, still battling to breathe between his laughs. "Gods below, I think I pissed myself."

Sedi cursed and pushed her hair back from her face with pale, trembling hands. "You terrified me!"

"I'm sorry," Bara returned. "I'll never fall off a cliff again, I promise."

She kicked him, and I closed in. "Let me look at you."

Bara submitted to inspection, but proved to have no worse injuries than a bruised hand and winded lungs. "Still, we should rest for a time," I told the company. "To make sure no new pains come, once the shock has passed."

No one complained, and we dropped our packs.

We'd reached the bottom of the ravine. Leaving Bara under Sedi's watchful eye, I picked my way down shifting scree to the water's edge. The fog closed in behind me, but I saw Ittrid follow and could still hear the voices of our companions.

The river was deep and swift, sluicing through the canyon far too quietly for its obvious power. Its current disturbed the mist, causing it to billow back in eddies from the opposite bank—here revealing a jutting boulder, there a water-darkened ledge.

Ittrid elbowed me. Her eyes were wide and she looked upriver, toward the opposite shore.

There, across six paces of roaring, raging water, stood a… figure. Swaths of mist curled tightly about them, obscuring all features save pale, windblown hair, gathered back at the temples, and a strong frame. They perched on the top of a huge boulder, darkened by moisture and frothed with spray.

For an instant I thought they were Isik, but though the figure was tall, they were not distinctly male or female. No beard. No broad shoulders. No curve of the hip or rise of breasts.

I heard a choking noise and realized it had come from my own throat. I reached for the horn at my belt.

Before I could put it to my lips, the wind gusted and the mist cleared. We were left staring not at a person but an odd outcropping of rock, tall and vaguely human-shaped.

Ittrid let out a gasping laugh and pushed her hair back from her face. "Gods, I thought… I don't know what I thought. It didn't look like one of those creatures."

Mist wafted back in, shrouding the scene once more. I shook my head, looking sheepishly at the Soulderni. "Maybe we're a little skittish."

Ittrid grinned wryly.

"Yske!" Berin's voice called. "Where are you?"

We regrouped and, half an hour later, set off along the river. Ursk led the way down a discernible path, though whoever had built the way left no waymarkers. That was, until the road ended at a triangular doorway in the rock. The path turned into it and mist trailed across its darkened maw. At our backs, the river rushed under a lip of rock and vanished underground, this arm of the canyon at an end.

"Do you recognize these?" Askir asked me. I made out a series of runes in the stone, set in a row across the top of the triangle. "There's magic in them."

I paused. Since our conflict over the supposed rivermen and his questions about my newfound magic, we'd rarely spoken. Perhaps this deference was his way of apologizing. Or testing me.

I glanced at Ursk. "Has Fate shown you this?"

The Duamel examined the doorway without recognition. "No. But I knew there would be a tunnel."

"You never mentioned that," Askir said.

Ursk shrugged. "I thought nothing of it. It's… simply the way."

I wasn't sure I shared Ursk's blind trust of his visions. I raised my eyes to the doorway and glanced over the runes, inching closer. They were not easy to see—lichen grew on the stone and years of rain and floodwaters had smoothed and shallowed the markings.

I touched my Sight. Power sparked to life upon the stone, golden with a forest-green taint, dark as autumn pines. It outlined shapes that time and weather had obscured, bringing the characters into sharp relief.

They were a mixture of soft lines and gentle curves, natural shapes that made me think more of the forested world above than the harsh, rocky terrain of the ravines.

It took another moment, a few seconds of tracing my fingers along the lines, but I recognized them.

"These are woodmaiden runes," I said to Askir. "I've seen them before."

"Where?"

"Woodmaidens paint them on protected trees, or use them to mark paths through their forests," I said. "Aita once took me to such a wood, in the High Halls. Thvynder allows some to live in the Upper Realms."

"Woodmaidens?" Ursk looked curious. He glanced around, but the mist still obscured our surroundings. "There are woodmaidens here?"

"Were, I'd say," Askir interjected. "This looks very old. What do the runes say, Yske?"

"They mark a way." I shrugged. "That's all I can recognize. But woodmaidens are not like rivermen. They only do harm when harm is given, and like you said, these are very old."

Askir eyed the doorway for another long moment, then looked back to Berin.

"Into the tunnel it is," Berin said and waved us ahead. "Does anyone have a torch?"

Ursk and Berin went first, the guide holding a Duamel oil lamp while my twin loomed behind him, one hand on the wall and the other on his sword.

After the triangular doorway, the shape of the passage changed. It became natural, though still high with angled sides—a divide in the rock, pried apart by time and water. It was silent but for the retreating rush of the river, the crunch of our feet on the stone, and the tap of Nui's claws as she wove between us.

"This must flood... perhaps in spring?" Askir murmured, half to me, half to himself. He lingered at my shoulder, though whether that was out of convenience or comradery, I couldn't be sure. He ran the tips of his fingers across the smooth stone as he walked. "Why would woodmaidens be down here?"

"They must have needed to cross the chasms, like anyone else," I reasoned.

Askir was quiet for a moment, deep in thought. "Then they built this after the Miri road collapsed? I've been wondering how long ago that was. Aita gave you no clue?"

I shook my head. "She didn't know about the collapse. The Miri have ignored the east for a very long time. Perhaps the Hask will be able to tell us more, once we arrive?"

"I'm not convinced we *will* arrive," Askir murmured, so low I barely heard it, despite the confined space. "Not with rivermen and woodmaidens loose upon the world."

I glanced over my shoulder at him, but the shadows were too thick to make out his expression. We'd discussed the creatures who killed Ovir enough for me to know there was no point in trying to convince him they hadn't been rivermen. "You think they're both still here?"

He shrugged. "We saw the rivermen. It would be foolish to assume the woodmaidens are gone too."

The priest's words settled on me like stones. "Aita should have warned me of all this," I protested, only realizing I'd spoken when the words left my mouth.

Askir gave a soft huff, between laughter and disbelief. "If she didn't know the road had collapsed, how would she know what's living in these forests?"

The tunnel ended in another ravine, this one broader and brighter. A scattering of trees stretched toward a band of late-afternoon sky, and creeks and waterfalls wove their way through moss-thick rubble. Streams of birds poured in and out of the cliffs beyond the treetops and there was a gentle breeze, still cool and damp but not so invasive as the cold in the tunnel.

Deep in the night, I awoke to light on my cheeks, pale and soft. I cracked open an eye to see the light of a full moon shining down upon my bed of moss, oilskin, and blankets between Berin and the fire. Nui lay near Bara some way away, her shaggy chest rising and falling in steady time.

Slowly, my eyes adjusted. I stared up at the moon, round and whole. The gap between the sides of the canyon wasn't broad from down here—soon, the moonlight would be blocked again.

Pain struck me like a wall of water from the dark, smashing the breath from my lungs and the thoughts from my mind. I felt a garrotte around my throat, hands raking my body, claws piercing my flesh.

Aita's voice whispered on the wind, thin and distant in memory.

You will pay the price for your magic, at each turn of the moon. Blood will replenish it. Blood will stay the hand of death.

Still thoughtless, blind in agony, I pawed for my belt knife. There was no hesitation, no awareness of what this act meant—only the desperate need to save myself.

I slit my palm. Blood welled, but I was already in too much pain to feel it. I squeezed my hand, letting red droplets drain into the moss as I rattled out the name of a single rune. Healing.

My blood welled and the well of power within me refilled in a rush. No longer could I only feel its edges, hollow and empty. Now it brimmed, amber and warm and suffused with the scent of lavender and the taste of pine. My heart hammered, and my senses swam with the headiness of it.

With the barest effort of will, the magic overflowed. I felt it rush through my veins, gathering every source of phantom pain, and extinguishing them.

Slowly, the pain retreated—and with it, the well of power emptied again, every scrap given to the effort of keeping me alive. Blinking tears from my eyes, I stared listlessly at the half of the moon as it disappeared over the other canyon wall. Those on guard hadn't noticed my distress—they prowled the edge of the firelight, and Berin was fast asleep.

Blood will stay the hand of death.

Ovir's healing had truly come at a cost, one that had wracked my own body. Would it have killed me, if I hadn't bled myself?

Carefully, I reached into my pack, pulled out a clean cloth, and started to wrap my hand. But it had healed too. In its place I had a new scar, fine and thin and terribly familiar. It looked like the scars on my parents' hands and forearms. Symbols of a forgotten time. The scars from the river creature's teeth on my fingertips faded in comparison.

The reality of what I'd done crashed over me. I'd just shed my blood for Aita, gained her power, and used it to save myself. In my panic to live, I'd done what none but the Iskiri Devoted had dared to do for decades. I'd acted as a priestess of the days before Thvynder, when my mother had bled herself for Eang and my father for Frir.

It was all terribly clear to me now. If I shed my blood, Aita's magic would return to me. I could heal myself. I could heal others and snatch them from the jaws of death.

But I could never, ever use it again. If I did, come the next moon, I'd have to relive every wound I healed. To survive it I would bleed myself again, and the cycle would continue. I would willingly place myself back into the shackles the old Miri had forged and Thvynder had broken.

It did not matter that Aita had been reluctant to give me this power. It didn't matter that she refused the title of my goddess, and I her priestess.

I could not use her power again.

But I knew I would.

TWENTY-TWO

Time skewed in the damp and cool of the ravines. We found a trail heading east down a long arm of the canyon, and though it was old and scattered with debris from rockfalls, it showed signs of recent tending. Smaller boulders and rocks were rolled to the sides, and we found the remnants of fire pits, seasons out of use.

"The Hask?" Berin ventured, toeing the rocks lining the edge of one fire pit.

Ursk only shrugged. We kept our guard up and continued on.

Soon, however, the way became more treacherous. We scrambled through crevices and topped boulders the height of Albor's Morning Hall. Our progress was painstaking and slow, punctuated by slips and falls that kept me on edge. I fell into a sleep of pure exhaustion the first night, but by the second my muscles were too sore and the rock too hard. I dozed fitfully, and was so tired the next day that I almost cried when we faced clambering over another enormous boulder. But I grabbed the rope Esan tossed down, the same as everyone else, and made the climb. I descended the other side with equal grudging determination, clattering down onto loose rubble to join Berin, Esan, and Sedi. Nui emerged smeared with damp and lichen from her own more subterranean route, and flopped down at my side to pant.

"Look!"

I cast my gaze back up to the top of the boulder, some ten paces above where Seera was partially silhouetted against the gray sky. She pointed down the canyon as the others still on the rock gathered round, their voices distorted with the distance. But whatever they saw clearly encouraged them.

Seera looked down at us, smiled a rare, bright smile, and cupped her hands around her mouth. "We're almost out!"

An arrow tore past her head. She jerked back just in time, nearly sending Ittrid toppling. Someone shouted a warning, I grabbed Berin's arm, and an arrow slammed into my thigh.

I gasped and staggered, but was otherwise too stunned to make a sound. More arrows flew, clattering off rock and sinking into flesh. Nui bolted, barking wildly. Berin dropped his pack and jerked his shield free, its boss glinting dully in the meager light.

The shield came over our heads and Berin's arm slipped around my waist, holding me up—though I couldn't think why. I was wavering, my left leg threatening to buckle. Why? It was just an arrow, just a short span of wood pinning my tunic to my leg. Surely I could still move. Surely…

Another arrow clipped the rocks at our feet, and my haze broke.

"Berin," I wheezed, mind filled with blistering awareness. I couldn't run. I still felt no pain, at least not in the stabbing, screaming sense I expected—but waves of heat began to build inside me, a brooding, pulsing agony that, once it broke, would consume me.

Voices shouted, echoing and bouncing off the rocks—Esan and Seera, trying to coordinate. Bara, screaming Sedi's name. The savage, roaring bark Nui reserved for rivals and predators.

"I know." Berin's arm was a vice around my waist, his other hand keeping the shield between us and the arrows. He tried to shift in front of me, but another arrow clattered off the stone at our feet. "Get behind me."

"Where are they?" I could barely find my footing on the rubble and with each small movement, the wave of pain reared closer.

"I don't know," Berin said. "Stay behind me!"

Two more arrows thunked into the wood. I shifted as much as I could, placing my lower body in front of Berin's unprotected legs.

"No," I panted. My breath was coming short now, and my wounded leg trembled. But one thought was clear, simple and unyielding—I'd rather take a dozen more arrows than see Berin take one.

Berin hefted the shield higher over our heads. Light angled over my face and I squinted, taking in our surroundings in that brief moment— Bara and Sedi struggling through a narrow cleft, Ittrid streaking across the top of a massive boulder, Ursk scrambling down the side of another.

Berin's shield cracked and a spearhead stopped a breath from my brother's face—close enough to graze my hair. We both cried out in shock, the shield suddenly wavered down, and in that space an arrow thudded into Berin's chest.

My brother staggered. I twisted away, seeing every detail in terrible clarity: his pale face, the shock and dread dawning in his eyes, the way the shield slipped from his fingers. His hand hovered over the fletching, just below his heart.

I seized the falling shield and threw it up. The spear hinged free, leaving a splintered crack in the wood. Through the gap I glimpsed a blur of descending enemies and rocky outcroppings, figures weaving from shelter to shelter as they closed in.

Then I clamped the shield at my right shoulder and prodded Berin backward.

"Berin!" A new voice battered through my skull. I glanced back to see Esan grab my brother under the arms. Berin sagged into his friend, but stared at me.

"Yske," he said, his breath a thin gust.

I met Esan's eyes over his head, the communication between us silent and rapid. *Go.*

My vision narrowed, ignoring pain and fear and choosing only two things: the men's progress, and the shield I held aloft. There was no arrow in my leg. There was no me, no self. Just Berin and keeping him alive.

Five, seven, ten agonizing steps and we edged into the shelter of a boulder, nearly a cave. Esan eased Berin to the ground and turned, his eyes sweeping me. He seemed to see the arrow in my leg for the first time and cursed, grabbing the shield.

"I've got you." He crouched in the cave mouth and hefted the barrier. Several arrows clattered at his feet, but he didn't flinch. He just braced the shield and became immovable.

Berin fumbled for my arm and tugged me deeper into shelter. He had his lips pinned shut, but blood bubbled and dripped into his beard.

"Yske," he labored. As soon as his lips parted blood overflowed, and I fought the urge to scream. "Yske, please."

I put a hand on his shoulder and pulled him forward, away from the rock wall. The arrowhead had punched through his back, a good handspan clear. Whoever had shot him had been very close, or very strong.

That didn't matter. There was already blood in his lungs, and soon he would drown.

I jerked the knife from my belt and stripped the fletching from the arrow, then painstakingly shifted behind Berin to where the arrowhead gleamed a bloody red.

I slit my thumb on its edge. Fresh blood welled as I let my heart rise in a wordless plea to Aita and grasped the blood-darkened shaft.

"Brace," I warned.

He planted his hands on the opposite side of the crevice, and I pulled.

Berin cried out. The sound was a scream of agony, a bellow of rage and an unfettered sob, all of it clotted with blood. His body convulsed and he buckled forward. The arrow slid free.

I felt Esan shift, saw the change of light as the shield wavered, but he stayed in place.

Curled into himself, Berin began to choke. I grabbed him by the collar and turned him with more strength than I possessed, pushing him upright against the rock with one hand and holding his chin up with the other. His wild eyes pinned mine, the lower half of his face slick with blood.

The runes came to me, silent in my own mind, and slipped from my lips in a droning hiss. I blinked sweat and tears from my eyes as gold-laced magic burst into the air around us. It plunged through Berin's shuddering lips. It invaded his nose and eyes, his ears and wounds and skin itself. And then, the world slowed. The rush of blood gentled. Berin's spasming eased.

I became aware of a vice-like grip on my arm. Esan. But instead of stopping me, he'd gone still, gaping at Berin. Another arrow clattered outside, but every other sound had faded.

Abruptly Berin coughed and spat blood, splattering me as he did. I released his chin and he twisted, vomiting onto the rocks. A few gargling breaths later his gasping turned into a wheeze, then cleared into a full, rasping breath.

"Esan," he said, eyes flicking back to the cave mouth. "The others?"

Esan blinked, eyes glistening. He patted Berin's cheek in gruff, fraternal affection and moved back to the entrance, hefting the shield again.

Outside, the canyon had gone silent. That silence did not bode well—even I knew it. There was no more conflict out there in the gorge, and little chance that we'd been the victors. Even Nui had stopped barking—somehow the worst realization of all.

Our enemies would be closing in.

Still holding Berin upright, I parted the fabric of his tunic where the arrow had pierced. There was a knot of scar tissue now, soft and pink, but complete.

"It worked," I panted, elated and stunned and more than a little lightheaded. "It worked."

Berin grabbed the side of my face and kissed my forehead. It was curt thanks, but powerful and heartfelt, his grip on my jaw tight and just barely trembling, thick with the stink of blood and bile. Then he pulled back and grabbed his sword from the ground.

"Berin!" Seera's voice echoed through the strange hush out in the gorge. She sounded more angry than hurt, but I caught her desperation. "Berin!"

"Stay here," my brother panted, edging up beside Esan, who gave him a harrowed, feral grin. My brother's eyes flicked to my own forgotten wound, worry clouding his expression. "Promise me. Stay hidden."

Spent and reeling, I sagged back against the cave wall, wiping blood from my cheeks with shaking hands and trying to find my strength again. But I found only a heavy, bone-deep weariness and a surge of pain.

I fingered my knife as Esan led the way out of the cave. Berin wavered after him, found his balance and vanished behind another boulder in the direction of Seera's voice. Two arrows clattered off the rocks in his wake.

I glanced at Berin's blood on the floor, then at my thigh. My pain edged toward blinding now, a red mist smothering my vision. I wanted to throw up as Berin had, but my stomach wouldn't comply. I wanted to run after him, but my leg was becoming heavier by the second.

I had to get the arrow out. I had to heal myself, or I'd be no use to anyone.

I pushed and prodded at my wound, making more blood well. I noted, distantly, that blood shed without direct intent seemed to do nothing for my magic.

The red haze thickened and my vision skewed. The arrowhead was deep. I put my knife to a torn edge of flesh, willing myself to cut down, assuring myself that my magic would return as soon as the knife slit, but my hands refused to move. My breath came in quick, shuddering gasps and my vision blurred even more.

I wanted to call Berin and Esan back. I wanted to shout for Isik, a world away. But I bit my tongue.

I heard a clatter outside and caught a flicker of movement. Twisting blearily, I peered out of the cave.

Our attackers had reached the floor of the ravine and now sprinted through the rockfall. They wore light armor, gambesons and vests of boiled leather scales with sweat-soaked high collars of padded wool. Most had traded their bows for axes and thick knives, but archers still prowled what parts of the slopes I could see.

My silence did not save me. An enemy approached my hiding place, keeping close to the shelter of a boulder.

I had no more time to remove the arrow. I had to run. I forced my leg around, scrabbling at the rock with a scream of shredded muscle.

There was nowhere to go. Broad shoulders blocked the mouth of the crevice and a spear leveled at my shuddering throat. I couldn't see my attacker's face, not with the sunlight behind him. Nor could I understand his words, delivered in a language I'd never heard before. But his voice was commanding and even—a warning.

Switching the spear to one hand, the stranger reached for my forearm. His hair was sun-darkened and undergirded with copper, and there was a distinct broadness to his cheekbones.

His touch was almost gentle, fingers easing around my wrist. His voice lowered, cajoling. Obviously, he considered me no great threat.

I felt the knife in my hand, warm with blood and gritty with dirt. In my mind's eye, I saw myself stab it toward his face. But there was no rage in me to fuel my violence. There was only pain and a profound, crippling awareness of the solidarity, the humanity, in this stranger's eyes.

Instinct warred with knowledge, with my mother's voice in my mind urging me to act. Then my pain crested, my vision smeared and my head lolled with sudden, jarring force. When awareness returned I saw a man standing over me, shouting to someone unseen beneath a sky thick with brooding black cloud. I was outside of the cave.

The sky roiled and thunder cracked, making my captor look up in surprise. On the thunder's heels, wind blasted through the boulders. Shouts erupted only to be snatched away, then drowned under a barrage of rain.

I gasped as cold drops hammered my cheeks, and some sense returned to me. I made myself move, made my body twist and my hands push me to my feet. Rain drummed down so thickly I could barely see and I looked around dazedly, expecting my attacker to come at me again.

Instead, I turned and looked up into Isik's face. Lightning lanced across the sky behind him, throwing his face into silhouette, but I knew every rain-soaked lash, every worried crease around his lips.

I laughed, breathless and shallow. His being here was so ludicrous, so impossible. I grinned at him with rain in my eyes, sure I was losing my mind, that blood loss and shock had stripped my sanity.

Then the world lurched and I swayed back into blackness.

It was still raining when I came to. Hands gently lowered me to the ground and I forced my eyes to open, though that small act required all my strength.

I was out of the ravine and in a forest blurred into greens, grays, and browns by rainfall. Isik collapsed at my side, hands on his knees and head thrown back as he struggled for breath.

"Am I that heavy?" I whispered and tried to smile. I couldn't manage it. Murky thoughts swam around my pain-addled mind, fish hidden in muddy waters. Berin. Arrows. Berin. The way rain ran down Isik's flushed throat beneath the tangle of his beard.

Isik looked back down at me and gave a rattling, breathless laugh. "You are perfect. But drawing that storm… it took more energy than it gave."

I reached out and found his hand. No more words came to me, no thoughts or awareness—even of Berin, and Esan and the others, Nui or our attackers.

His fingers cinched around mine and for a time we lingered there—I with an arrow in my thigh on a bed of sodden moss and jutting roots, he fighting for breath as the wind tossed the glistening autumnal canopy over his head.

I must have slipped into unconsciousness again, for when I next blinked, the rain was gone. Isik lay curled around me, my face tucked into his chest, under the shelter of his arm.

The intimacy of the moment might have unsettled me if I hadn't cherished the contact so much. I pressed my nose into the damp of his tunic and gave a soft, oblivious sigh.

It was only as the sound faded, swallowed back into the silence of the forest, that I realized what had woken me. Berin's horn. It bayed in the distance, so far away I barely registered it.

I fumbled for my own, still clinging to my belt. But before I could unfasten it, I heard feet shuffling in the forest.

I turned slowly, twisting out from under Isik's heavy arm. He did not stir, even when I gasped and let his arm fall, too suddenly, to the ground.

Creatures of moss and bone stood to all sides beneath drooping leaves of red and gold and umber, two dozen or more watching us without sound, without movement, save for the drip of rain from claws and a few mismatched racks of flaking, half-skinned antlers.

A creature stepped forward. This one was no construct of forgotten bones and forest growth—the way he moved was too human, too intelligent, too self-aware. His skin was woven reed, his eyes polished stones. And his smile, when he unsheathed it, was horribly familiar.

"I know you," said the riverman I'd once watched Aita banish from the High Halls. He spoke in the Divine Tongue and his voice was sonorous, undergirded by delight and the rushing hush of water. "Aita's little shadow."

TWENTY-THREE

The following hours etched into my memory in bursts of pain and disbelief. I welcomed intervals of unconsciousness when they came, and endured the stretches of disorientation when I awoke to find myself dangling over the shoulder of a monstrous human construct, my leg possessed by unyielding agony.

I did not know where Berin was. Isik, I glimpsed here and there. The creatures dragged him on a makeshift litter like a fresh kill, and he showed no signs of waking. The side of his head was crusted with gold-tinted blood in my Sight. Ichor.

My blood ran gold, too. I saw it on my hands, dangling below me, and watched it smear across my captor's moss-and-wood flesh. Though tinted with lavender, it was nearly as bright as Isik's. Berin's blood too, dried and caked beneath my nails, glistened a duller amber.

Eventually, we came to a village. I didn't have the strength to raise my head, so I saw the settlement upside down. The homes were rudimentary but tidy, constructed of unhewn logs, chinked with moss and clay, and overhung with eaves of moss and small, hearty ferns. Scrawny forest chickens watched me from one roof, while under the eaves of another a cluster of cautious children stared, lorded over by a protective father. This man looked similar to the one who'd pulled me from the cave in the ravine—broad cheekbones, hair in varying shades of brown, and warm skin seemed to be features of the people of the East.

Children. Humans, watching the riverman and monsters—*his* monsters—pass them by with cautious familiarity.

Isik and I were deposited in a low empty building, dug into the earth and capped in moss. I pretended to be unconscious, and only moved once I heard a bar wedged into place across the door. I caught retreating voices, heavily muffled by the walls—questioning but not demanding, overridden by one whose tones I immediately recognized.

The riverman.

You and all your kind will be driven out of the High Halls, Aita had once said to this same riverman. *Go back to whatever den you've been hiding in, and never return.*

Was this village, here in the east, the den the riverman had been driven back to?

I shivered and forced myself to sit upright, taking stock of my surroundings. The cellar was small and dark, smelling of earth and straw, but not damp. The floor was layered with fresh cuttings and as my eyes adjusted, I made out deep shelves and racks for wintering food. They were empty, despite the season, and the scent of apples, carrots, and whatever other sundries that might have been here were absent.

There was only one door, heavy and at the top of a short stairway. There was another small opening for ventilation, but it was too small to crawl through, and covered with sturdy wooden grating.

I turned my focus to Isik. I bent over him in the weak light, brushing hair back from his face and gently touching his beard, looking for the source of the blood. I couldn't help but wonder why he'd come back to me, but my questions would have to wait.

I found a deep gash under one of Isik's ears, surrounded by swollen flesh and caked dirt. I *tsk*ed worriedly and paused, trying to collect myself. The urge to heal him was overpowering, to end his suffering and make sure my friend was whole and well.

Healing Isik would require another sacrifice. I was willing to do it—healing Berin had dulled the edges of guilt and obligation I felt at the thought of shedding my blood. I needed to heal myself too, if we were to have any chance of escape and finding out where the rest of our company had been taken. It was practical. Necessary.

But the riverman didn't know of my magic—though, as he was likely Sighted, he would suspect I had power of some kind. Perhaps it was best to wait, assess the situation, and keep my healing as a knife up my sleeve.

My horn was still at my belt, bizarrely. I stared at it for a long moment, then looked up to the grating. I could call for help, but surely the riverman knew that. Either we were too far from aid to be heard, or our captor wanted us to be found. Neither thought was comforting.

My eyes dragged to the shadowy arrow protruding from my thigh. The sight and the rush of pain that came with it made my stomach contort, but I swallowed it down.

I needed to bide my time, hide my magic, and try to learn what I could. My pack was lost, as was my knife. I had nothing but my horn, my worries and these few, quiet moments with my unconscious friend.

So, I took one of Isik's heavy hands, held it to my chest, and waited. He did not move, but his steady breathing, the weight of his arm, and the warmth of his skin consoled me.

Light from the setting sun had just begun to filter through the grating when the door opened and four humans flooded the cellar. Two spearmen prodded me back against the wall, away from Isik. Then the others took me by the arms and hauled me toward the stairs.

Pain clapped over me, and my next clear understanding was lying on the floor of a hut. My disoriented mind detected the scents of musky sage and earthy camphor and stale valerian before my eyes found their desiccated bundles hanging from the beams, and an old man squatting at my side with a shallow bowl.

He spoke to me, face surrounded by carefully combed white hair, and pointed to the arrow in my leg. Then he held out the bowl and motioned for me to drink.

Panic seized me, quick and violent. If this man was a healer, I could guess what was in that bowl, and I doubted it would clear my mind. The thought of being unconscious, helpless while a stranger cut into me—

I started to sit up, but the hands of two other people came down upon me. My breath was thin and fast, but I slowly regained control of myself.

This was a good thing. It meant they wanted to keep me alive. It meant they didn't know my secret.

I looked at the hovering locals, letting them see the submission in my eyes, and took the bowl.

I sat in a corner of the healer's hut as darkness fell over the forest. I was still groggy, but my pain was distant and the lack of an arrow in my thigh was reassuring.

"What did she name you?"

I looked up as the riverman filled the open door. The hair rose on the back of my neck and I resisted the urge to flatten myself into the wall.

"Yske." My name passed over my lips before I could consider lying. I blinked forcefully, shocked at my honesty.

"Your tongue will be loose for a time." The riverman stepped inside and stood over me, the watery rasp of his voice filling the small, close space.

I glanced at the healer's bowl, set on a nearby low table, and pressed my lips closed. There were multiple things the healer could have added to loosen my tongue, including several that were tasteless or easy to mask. In my pain, I hadn't identified them.

"So, why are there two young Miri in my lands?" the riverman inquired. "And who are the humans who travel with you? My Revenants have been reporting you for some time."

My lips started to open, almost spilling the truth before I diverted. "We came to see... By Revenants, you mean the monsters. The constructs." I was careful to speak in statements, not questions—a lifetime of warnings held fast, even through the drugs in my blood.

The creature nodded. "You came to see what?"

"The tree in the East," my traitorous tongue supplied.

"How did you learn of it?"

"The Arpa."

"Arpa." The riverman's tongue moved over the inside of his woven lips, a nearly reptilian gesture. "So, they did make it home?"

"You did not intend them to."

His river-stone eyes glistened in the dim light. "I had nothing to do with them. But the Guardians of the Tree are diligent in keeping its existence hidden from the outside world. Other explorers have come, but either they stay or they die."

He unfurled his grin, revealing a forest of fish teeth. "You should be grateful I found you before the Guardians. You would not have lasted long with the Hask."

"Your people are not the Hask."

He shook his head slowly and cast his gaze toward the hut and the village as a whole. "No. The Hask live by the lake and worship the Bear; the Fith inhabit the deep forest and look to me and my Revenants for their protection. These clans are not allies."

Ursk hadn't known this, and it raised a host of questions about the politics and relationships of the peoples whose land we had so blindly entered.

"Where are my friends—" I cut my question off too late, and my captor leveled a cold gaze.

"They are not here. You were attacked by Fith, yes, but outliers, worshipers of a foreign god. They call themselves the Aruth. They captured some of your companions, while others escaped into Hask territory."

I kept silent, mind scrambling. This riverman could be lying, but for the moment, I could not fathom what he'd gain by that. He was dangerous, but apparently so was everyone else in the East—to us and to one another.

The riverman's depthless river-stone eyes watched my face with unsettling intent. "Your company is sundered, Yske, and your people obviously unequipped to navigate my realm. You need allies."

Outside, the sounds of a village settling in for the night drifted to us—chattering children, a mother's lullaby, the clinking of pots and slosh of water. It sounded so similar to home—from east to west, from a mossy village ruled by a riverman to one watched over by my black-haired mother, her smile warm and her eyes like flint.

Make allies of your enemies, Yske, murmured my mother's voice, repeating one of her favored proverbs. *Or put them in the ground.*

Wind trickled through the open door beyond the riverman, tugging me back to the moment. I swore the wind tasted of winter, clean and sharp, layered with the promise of snow and icy nights.

Perhaps the strife between the peoples of the east was something I could use.

"We need not be enemies," I stated, even though my skin crawled. I imagined the constructs this being had created, their human and animal bones cobbled into a grotesque semblance of life. "Let me and my friend go. Let us rescue our companions from the Aruth, and we'll go home."

The riverman considered me for so long, I questioned whether I'd spoken at all. Then he crouched before me with a creak and rasp. "All right. But first, do something for me."

Here was my opportunity. I met his inhuman eyes.

He held out a hand. "Come."

I didn't protest. I took his hand, startled to find the woven reed of his skin warm with life, and wavered to my feet.

My world spun, sparked, and settled. The riverman put a worn staff in my hand and led me into the village.

People stared as we passed, the riverman pausing every so often to wait for me while I hobbled painstakingly behind. I met the eyes of a few locals, trying to gauge if I might find allies among them, but their gazes glossed over me and rooted on the riverman, or looked back on the ground.

They all fell away as we left the village, heading north. Dusky light purpled among half-stripped autumn branches and the cold prickled at my skin, making me shiver. I inhaled deeply, trying to calm myself, and choked.

The scent of decay hit me like a fist. I shied back, covering my mouth with one arm.

The riverman kept walking, striding through the trees with the roaming, diligent gaze of a gardener among the furrows.

I saw a body in a tree first, vines suspending it by the wrists. It had no legs save for one dangling femur, stained dark with old blood, attached to the rotting torso with a single shriveled tendon. Its skull had no skin but tufts of mossy spoors spilled from every orifice, including a slack jaw full of canine teeth.

Next, a half-constructed animal twitched from the shadow of a huge oak. It raised the sightless head of a fox, though it had a dead serpent for a spine and tail, and its ribs were mismatched, woven with strips of rough leather like a grisly basket.

Everywhere I looked, more and more half-formed—half-grown— constructs looked back. Some stared blankly, eyeless and inanimate. Others watched me hungrily, still others pitifully. Most were human. Some were not. Larger shadows off in the woods foretold even more terrifying beasts, and as the riverman neared, the trees wavered as if nudged by a massive body.

The riverman stopped in the center of the terrible grove, his face obscured by blossoming shadows. All eyes moved to him, including mine.

I gripped my staff fiercely and battled the urge to shrink into myself, seeking the embers of my anger and stoking them instead. The riverman wanted something from me. He'd simply brought me here to frighten me.

Light sparked, thin in the dark. Foxfire lit along exposed roots and up the trunks of several dead trees, but unlike the foxfire I'd seen along our journey, this was only blue and not so bright. Weaker somehow, here in the riverman's domain.

My captor glanced at the foxfire too, then back at me. I saw consideration pass through his eyes, then decision—as if he'd intended to say one thing and decided on another.

"What do you want from me?" The question leaked from my lips.

The riverman let out a soft hiss of displeasure. "Question me again and I will kill you. I have two prisoners; I need only one."

I closed my lips.

"Who sired you?" the riverman demanded.

I held my tongue, turning over my options. Back when I'd met this creature in the High Halls, he'd speculated that either Gadr or Estavius were my father—which made sense, they being the only male Miri left, other than Isik and half-blood Winterborn.

But I was no Miri at all. My blood might look like ichor to the Sighted, but I was still a human. That, however, seemed unwise to confess. Rivermen might hate the Miri, but they still feared them. That might protect me.

"Gadr," I lied, with effort. "My companion is my brother, Isik."

"Mmm," the riverman made a considering sound. "Did your parents tell you of our history? The rivermen and the Miri? And the woodmaidens?"

I hesitated, but the silence stretched, demanding an answer. I spoke carefully, choosing the version of events that he would want to hear.

"I know you—we—were all made equal, in the beginning," I said, earning a wry smile from the riverman. He knew I was pandering. "The Miri took the High Halls, and the rivermen were driven away. Some of the woodmaidens were permitted into the Halls, but many of them vanished instead, to the far corners of the world."

"To the edge of creation," the riverman added in an affirming murmur. "Go on."

I changed my grip on my staff to ease the weight on my bad leg. I felt pinned by the empty stares of the Revenants, grotesque and pitiful. "That's all I know."

He picked up the tale. "Some of us outcasts were driven east, to the edge of the world. And here, we made a home. This is our realm. The Fith are my people. I am their god and protector."

The cool of the night seemed to double. I glanced up at the canopy, half expecting to see snow beginning to fall, but dry leaves just rattled in the breeze.

"But," the riverman dropped his voice, "we found more here in the east than forests and the Unmade, and the tribes that became the Hask and Fith. There was a door to the High Halls here, once." He smiled when surprise flickered over my face. "Forgotten and neglected. So we used it. And gleaned the power of the Halls, for a time."

I gripped my new staff with both hands.

"That doorway was closed through… unforeseen events. Long have I sought a way to reopen it." The riverman stepped closer, the structure of his neck creaking as he stared down at me. I shifted my grip, ready to turn the staff into a weapon, but he did not touch me. "I saw your golden blood on the moss, daughter of Aita. I saw your brother on the wind, and I thought… these children, these young Miri. They can help me."

I met his gaze, refusing to shrink. "How?" I asked, consciously questioning him this time. A small test of power. A tiny rebellion, charring the edges of my insidious fear.

He grimaced in a flash of needle teeth. "All Miri can open doorways to the High Halls. Your holy grounds. Do you have one? Can you forge one?"

My life hung on my answer, even if I hadn't the faintest idea how to accomplish such a task—even if I would consider doing it. I knew Thvynder's Watchman Omaskat had made a door at the White Lake, but he was a part of the god. How the Miri forged doors was a secret I'd never learned.

"Of course," I lied, infusing my tone with a restrained imperiousness, as if I'd been holding it back this entire time.

"Do you know the cost?" he asked, clearly testing me.

"Of course," I lied again, and took a chance. I was claiming to be a Miri—I might as well act like one. "Release my brother and me, safe and unharmed, and I will make a new door for you."

The riverman considered me for a breath, giving me ample time to consider that I'd no idea if he truly believed me, no guarantee he would keep his word, no notion of how to fulfil my promise, and no intention of doing so. I was buying time, pure and simple.

Finally, he nodded, his eyes glittering in the dark. "We have a deal."

TWENTY-FOUR

"Isik." I hobbled back to the man-shaped mound on the floor of the cellar, nestled and unmoving in the straw. I leaned heavily on my staff, dragged down both by pain and my conversation with the riverman. I needed to speak to my friend. I needed his reassurance. I needed him healed, well and capable so we could leave this horrific village behind.

Isik lay in a more comfortable position than when I'd left, more at ease. Consoled, I touched the horn at my belt, half hoping to find a chip or edge I could cut myself on, but there was nothing. I reached for the shelves next, searching for a rough patch of wood. I pawed and staggered for a moment, feet rustling in the straw and breaths thin with pain.

The figure that should have been Isik sat up, languid and slow, a wolf stretching after a nap in the sun. There was no discomfort to his movements, no hesitation or fatigue. In the vague starlight from the grating, the figure's hair was white, his skin pale, and the outline of him leaner, too graceful.

This was not my friend.

"I was beginning to think he had realized you're a fraud and fed you to the Revenants," the stranger said, rising to his feet. Like the riverman, his voice rang with the distinct power of the Divine Tongue.

The air grew markedly colder, rife with the clean, brisk scent of winter. Dread prickled up my spine and I glanced to the grating, then back to the intruder.

"Who are you? Where's Isik?"

"Isik is safe." He flapped a dismissive hand. "Consider that my gift to you."

"You rescued him?" I pressed, though I wasn't sure "rescued" was the right word to use. I'd no idea who this stranger was, though if the cold and his white hair were any indication… But no. What would a Winterborn be doing here, in the east?

"He rescued himself when I told him you'd already escaped into the forest. Handy, turning to wind like that; very convenient if you don't have a mortal holding you back," the stranger replied. "He won't get far in his condition though, so you'd best go after him. Use those healing hands of yours before the Revenants catch his scent."

I grasped the shelf and put my staff between us, ignoring the sting of splinters in my other hand. My leg quivered, sore and beyond spent. I prayed the dark would hide it.

"What do you want from me?" I asked. "Obviously there's something."

"I want a favor, when the time comes." He stepped closer, and I sensed that the darkness was no barrier to him—he could see me clearly, while I was left straining. "Heal yourself."

I grasped the shelf tighter. I could feel my skin threatening to break on the splinters now, blood surging to the surface, ready to well.

"Why?"

"My people said they saw you heal one of your companions in the canyons," the stranger answered. "If it's true, I have a use for you. If it's not, I'll leave you here. Watching you try to open a door to the High Halls for Logur would be entertaining."

"That's the riverman's name? Logur?"

The Winterborn nodded. "Go on, heal yourself. You should obey me more willingly, Eangen. Your people killed my siblings, and my patience with you will not last."

"You *are* Winterborn," I breathed. The truth came with another knife to my throat. My mother had overseen the slaughter of multiple Winterborn during the invasion when I was a child. My own cousin, Thray, had betrayed them.

My kin and connections might damn me in this Winterborn's eyes, whatever my potential uses.

"Of course I am," the stranger laughed, a soft, low sound, so pleasant that it turned my stomach. "But I am also your only ally—or potential one. Or do you not understand what's happening here? Logur will toy with you for a while before it becomes obvious you can't help him. Then he'll open a door the traditional way."

I didn't know what that way was, but I didn't want to admit my ignorance either.

"I can do it," I returned coolly.

"No, you can't," he crowded closer, backing me into the shelves. I nearly dropped the staff, but managed to keep it between us, my knuckles to his chest, holding him inches away. "Your companions already told me of you, Eangen. No one and nothing. No family—other than a brother fleeing, right now, for the eastern lake. Leaving you behind. No connections, except the pity of a fallen goddess. Aita blessed you with power, yes—that much is obvious—but you're no Miri. Your blood *might* have enough magic to break, but it cannot forge."

Multiple revelations hit me, one after the other. Berin was still free? The rest of my companions—the Winterborn must know where they were. And they had been wise enough not to reveal who I was, which I was immeasurably grateful for.

But the Winterborn's last revelation shoved to the forefront, ominous and deadly. "What do you mean, my blood can break?"

"It can break the barrier between worlds. Miri usually open doors to the High Halls with the heart blood, the last life blood, of other Miri," the Winterborn said, his voice losing its humor. He was grim now, grim and cold like the winter nights soon to blanket this forest. "Which is why I ensured your friend's escape. His blood would certainly do the trick, so it's in everyone's best interest to keep him from Logur. Your blood… is more questionable. Mine he's already tried, and that did not go well, as I cannot die."

What little strength I had left fled my body. I felt my leg give way and I wavered, barely keeping grip on the staff and shelf. I gripped the latter so tightly that splinters punctured my skin, and blood began to trickle down my wrist.

I squeezed tighter.

The Winterborn took my arms in a mockery of a supportive embrace. "Heal yourself. Prove you've value, and I'll help you escape tonight. You can find your Miri friend, and I'll ensure your tracks are covered."

I closed my eyes for an instant, trying to quell a roaring in my head. Too much had happened; there were too many parties at play and too much to consider. I needed sleep, food, safety—I needed time to process and make the right decisions.

But Winterborn were from my world, from the west. This man was a threat I understood, while the riverman was new and surrounded by horrific living dead.

I slowly lifted my bloody hand, ready to sketch the first healing rune in the air. Gathering myself, I asked dully, "What are you called?"

"Arune," he said.

The name meant nothing to me, but I nodded and forged my second deal of the evening—albeit the only one I intended to keep.

"I hope you keep your promises, Arune," I said and began to sketch.

The door of the cellar creaked in the quiet, cold night. My breath billowed in the air as I slipped out on steady, newly healed legs. Arune was already out in the village, having vanished through the wooden grating as a breath of wind—a skill many of his siblings possessed, though my cousin Thray had not.

She lingered in my mind, vague and edged with sadness, as I surveyed the village. The wood of my new staff was warm in my hand, my horn heavy at my belt and determination hot in my belly. I waited. Watching. Sensing.

As Arune had promised, no one was in sight. Premature snowflakes gathered on my bare head, gradually melting into cold trickles across my scalp. A dog barked on the other side of the settlement, reminding me of Nui. Someone shouted at it and the hound quietened, leaving me with only the wind in the dry leaves and the soundless fall of snow.

Satisfied, I crept around the cellar, between two houses, and behind a third. I found an axe in a chopping block and took it with a soft crack. My head remained clear, the last of the inebriating drug burned off by Aita's magic.

I didn't breathe freely until I'd passed through the concealing wall of evergreens outside the village. I sagged for an instant, glancing back toward the huts, then retightened my grip on my staff and axe.

"Isik is this way," a tendril of winter wind whispered, tugging me right. "Stay alive, and I will find you soon."

I hastened away, relishing each painless step and the flame of hope that came with them. A dozen paces. Two dozen. The forest closed in and the scents of the village—smoke, animals, mud and rot—faded away.

I found Isik sitting against a tree. He rose when I came into sight, steadying himself on the trunk. His face was still crusted with blood, and slack with pain and relief.

"Yske," he breathed. I saw the questions in his eyes, multiplying as I stopped just out of his reach and set my staff aside, hefting the woodcutter's axe high on the shaft.

I didn't speak. My relief at seeing him made my throat thick and my heart ache, but every word risked giving us away. Besides, I didn't know what to say, and I didn't want to risk him talking me out of what I would do next.

I laid one palm over the blade of the axe and squeezed until blood welled. A muffled cry hit the back of my clenched teeth. Isik flinched forward, hissing a startled rebuke, but stopped short of grabbing me. His fingers spread wide instead, warding me off as I turned my gaze back up to him.

"This is the cost of Aita's gift," I explained compulsively, hating the horror in his eyes. "Do not try and stop me."

TWENTY-FIVE

I awoke to the rush of wind through leaves. My eyes were closed, but my senses stretched out—I lay on the frigid ground, rocks and roots digging into me and snow damp in my hair.

The forest floor spread before me, moss-covered stumps and fallen branches topped with half-thawed blankets of white. Nui lay nearby, her head on her front paws. I stared at her, sure that I must be imagining the dog's presence. Her paws twitched in a dream, and the leaves beneath her shifted ever so slightly.

Slowly, I began to piece my memories together. Berin, screaming as I tore an arrow from his back. The riverman, surrounded by monsters. A Winterborn, laughing. My bloody fingers drawing runes in the air between myself and Isik. Then a hasty, endless flight through darkened woods, until dawn broke and we stopped to rest, panting in the snowy, pastel light.

"Where's Isik?" I croaked. Nui looked up at me, eyes exhausted and melancholy, but her tail thumped. "How did you find me?"

She bellied a little closer and rested her head on my hip. I scratched her instinctively, and she closed her eyes in pleasure. Her trust, her warmth and realness, made my throat clog. I'd never been more grateful that my mother sent her along.

I raised my voice a little more, daring to break the forest hush. "Isik? Are you here?"

Wind rustled the leaves around me and, in a heartbeat, my friend appeared. Nui glanced his way, the whites of her eyes large, but she did not get up.

Isik noted the dog without surprise. His cheeks were flush with color and he'd washed the blood from his skin. His expression was worried but cold, reserved in a forceful way that I couldn't analyze just yet, but likely had to do with my blood sacrifice. Still, he looked healthy, and I tried to smile.

To my horror, the smile immediately quavered into tears as my exhaustion reared, and his cool regard failed to soften.

I swallowed and sniffled for a breath. I expected him to comfort me, to pull me into the embrace I desperately needed, but he didn't. Instead, he stepped back into the forest and reappeared a moment later with two packs.

"Once Nui came, I went back and found these," he said. I noticed he was wearing a cloak now too, not his but Askir's, from the blue and yellow Algatt embroidery at the collar. One of the packs was mine, while the other was Seera's—plain and unadorned.

I was relieved to see my pack, but Isik's demeanor unsettled me. "Isik... about the healing..."

"Aita is no goddess," he cut in, dropping my pack beside me with a weighty thunk. "Don't give her your blood. Don't let her treat you like a priestess."

I rankled. "I'm not. She gave me a gift and it saved Berin's life. It saved mine, and yours. I can't ignore power like that, not... not right now."

"It's wrong."

"What in this world is right?" I threw out a hand—my bloodied one, unfortunately. As cold as I was, I hadn't realized that the wound was still partially open. I'd given every scrap of my healing to Isik, and hadn't had enough left to finish my own.

He looked at the cut, crusted with dried blood and dirt. "You should clean that."

I fought the urge to snap at him, and instead fumbled with the fastenings on my pack. Nearly everything was intact, though I had to shoo a large spider from the clutch of leather-wrapped packets.

Isik watched me struggle for longer than I thought he would. When I dropped a bundle of clean bandages into the snow, he finally let out a frustrated hiss and shifted Nui out of the way so he could kneel beside me.

"Let me help."

"Why would you help?" I shot back. "I've betrayed Thvynder. Isn't that what you think?"

He unrolled a section of bandage and held it out to me. "Yske, I'm a Miri. I think you forget that too often. I think we both forget that."

I poured vinegar from a small flask onto the bandage, releasing the tart, sour scent into the winter air, and tried to tug the fabric from his grip. He didn't let go, but instead took my bad hand and began to clean away the blood. The sting caught me off guard and I bit my tongue.

"I've never had worshipers," Isik continued, cleaning with gentle precision. "But I feel the lure of it. Aita, my parents, those who remember what it was to be worshiped—I can't imagine how much greater their struggle is. They remember the power. The love. Fear."

I watched his face now, trusting his hands to do their work. He'd never spoken of his nature like this before, and I did not want to stop him.

"If Aita falls back into old ways, perhaps we all will," Isik murmured. "Thvynder is still away. The Winterborn gain power and influence across the world, and not all of them are allies. My siblings and I... we are the new Miri. Perhaps we're all that will ever be, the last pure-blooded of our kind. Perhaps that's for the best. But for now we stand in the middle, born in a new age, but with millennia of crimes and mistakes and... needs... on our shoulders."

He paused cleaning my hand and met my eyes. There was prompting there, and for a moment I thought he wanted me to speak, to say something.

"What should I put on this?" he asked.

"Oh. That." I pointed to a jar and he set my hand back on my knee. My fingers felt cold without his touch and my wound ached.

"I will never worship Aita," I said lowly. "You know that. Thvynder is a true god. And I've... I've as much Miri power in my blood as a human can have. You and I are not so dissimilar, aside from how we'll age."

"We're still different." He took my hand again and carefully applied the salve, both bitter and sweet with honey and herbs. "That is what I'm trying to say. Aita has power and strength you do not."

"It's a simple exchange. Blood for magic."

"For *her* magic." Isik, ever transparent, looked pained and pitying, almost guilty. "She still gains from it."

My doubt over Aita's motives was only momentary—she cared for me, I knew that, and she would not abuse me in the way Isik suggested.

"Aita did what she could for me." My voice felt hot now, indignant. "And if that benefits her in some way, I do not care. Everything comes with a cost, and this is the cost of keeping us alive. What's the blood of one human, anyway? What could I give—"

"Even if she intends nothing by it," Isik cut me off in a tone that suggested he was humoring me, "it opens a door that should be closed. A temptation."

"A temptation for *you*," I shot back, unsettled and indignant. "Don't assume Aita is as weak as you. You're young. And don't be so arrogant as to think you'd be worshiped by anyone. Let alone by me, if that's in your head."

Isik sat back, blank-faced, resting his forearms on his knees. Nui raised her head, watching the two of us with a new alertness.

"What are you even doing here?" I demanded, lowering my voice. "You're accusing me of being too close to Aita, but you followed me across the world. What does *that* mean, Son of Esach?"

Isik bristled. "I came to keep you alive. Your priest didn't sense a Binding Tree right next to your camp, or that I was close. You spoke with me for... how long? Yet your own brother slept unaware and your watchman didn't even think to check on you. You would all have died a dozen times if I didn't follow you."

"Follow me? You've been here all along?" I ran back over the miles, the weeks that had passed since that night by the Binding Tree. I searched for hints of his presence, but found none—save the night Ovir had died. "Did I see you the night the Revenants attacked us? Listening to me sing?"

He shook his head. "That night I left before dark to scout ahead."

"How helpful," I said. I knew I was being childish, but I was exhausted, my brother was missing, a riverman was out for my blood, and my best friend was pushing me away. "Ovir is grateful, I'm sure."

Isik's eyebrows rose in the casual, collected shock of a parent insulted by a child. "I was scouting ahead, as I did every night. I chased off wolves and bears and worse, Yske. I pushed back storms that would have made the rivers impassable and your journey impossible. I did what I could."

"Why?" I demanded, needing to hear his answer. "Because we used to be lovers? Because we were friends? Because you want us to be grateful?"

"Because I should," he answered. "Because I can."

"Because you're a Miri, and we're humans, weak and helpless," I clarified.

"If that's how you want to describe it, yes."

I stared at him. I'd seen inklings of this mentality in him before, but where previously I'd seen a self-imposed purpose, charming and useful, now I saw it as superiority and pity. And perhaps, hidden there around his eyes as he watched me now, threads of old ties between us, twisted and cheapened.

"You came to keep Berin alive," Isik said finally, his voice softer. "Because you have a skill and power he does not. I came to do the same for you. We serve the ones we love, as best we can."

Love. A winter wind chased his words around the clearing, icy and tasting of snow and frost-rimmed deadfall. Was Arune here now, listening in amusement as we bickered?

I didn't sense or glimpse the Winterborn, but the thought of him—and the weight of Isik's words—sobered me.

"Do we still love one another?" I asked quietly.

The corner of his lip curved in a melancholy half-smile. His gaze was fixed, wholly centered upon me. "Growing up beside you has taught me there are many kinds of love, Yske. Many shades of it. Many seasons and verses."

I stared at him, simultaneously longing for him to go on and wishing he'd never spoken at all. There was too much possibility in his confession. Too much unsaid.

I released a long-held breath. "Thank you for watching over us," I said, hiding in the steady voice my mother used as ruler and priestess. "But you needn't any longer. You can go home."

"I'm not leaving you." Isik brushed the thought away, his voice still quiet. Slowly, the intensity in his gaze retreated, and he stood and glanced out at the trees. "Not with a riverman in the woods and your companions missing. Berin might be an ass, but you're better off with him now."

I ground my jaw, even as my throat clotted with unsorted emotion. I didn't want him to go, but I also couldn't face this new complexity between us, the memories and the possibility.

I looked down at my hand, the wound now clean and the salve thick. Distantly I acknowledged that I could simply make another sacrifice and heal it, but the weight of Isik's judgement was too heavy.

"Do you know how your kind open doorways to the High Halls?" I asked.

Isik looked back down at me, caution in his eyes. I took that for affirmation.

"The riverman intends to open one," I told him. "He'll use your blood to do it. That's why he took us. He'll kill you, and likely use us against each other. You should go back west. Tell your mother and father what's happening here. That is the best thing you can do for me."

Isik's eyes moved back to the trees again, suddenly alert, and I watched the thoughts pass over his face. Calculating. Weighing. Burdened?

"I will not leave you," he said at last. He met my gaze again and I saw a flicker there, a care and softness so profoundly Isik that my heart swelled uncomfortably.

"Then go find Berin for me," I said, tossing him a useful distraction. "I have Nui."

"Arune will be back."

"He has a use for me, and he doesn't know who my parents are. He won't harm me."

"What use?" Isik demanded, going cold again.

"I assume it's someone he wants to be healed. He wanted to see my power." I gestured to my leg. "He also knows where some of my companions are."

Isik clearly wasn't comforted by that, but nodded. "All right. I will go find your brother, after I make sure Logur hasn't found our trail."

I nodded, closing the matter, and began to dig in my pack for more bandages. I didn't look at him again, but I felt his eyes on me as I wrapped my hand instead of healing it.

It wasn't a concession to him, my choice to let the wound finish healing naturally. But it was something small I could do to restore peace between us.

He made a soft sound, a relieved, resigned exhalation, and vanished to the wind.

After their failed invasion when I was eleven years old, the Winterborn—half-Miri children of Ogam, grandchildren of Eang and the elemental spirit Winter—scattered to the winds. Some chose to remain in their homeland of Duamel in the far north, though few found forgiveness among the people they'd deceived into fighting their war. Most Winterborn simply left, becoming errant adventurers. Tales of them began to crop up across the world, in Algatt, Eangen, and every reach of the Arpa Empire.

Thus when I pondered Arune's presence here in the East, I felt little real surprise. If the tales and rumors of this land had been enough to tempt Berin and his company, it seemed fitting that they should also have drawn one of Ogam's reckless children. Though, immortal as the Winterborn were, there was considerably less risk for them in exploration—particularly as this one was a Windwalker, capable of shirking flesh and blood and moving with the elements, as Isik and his mother did.

Isik was gone all evening and into the night. I hated to remain in one spot, my mind full of images of hunting Revenants and the riverman's watching eyes, but I also wanted Isik to be able to find me again quickly. So I remained where I was, trusting Arune had properly concealed our trail.

I wove firescreens and made a small blaze to chase back the cold and damp. The snow had melted but the air was still frigid and frost rimed my blankets when I awoke the next morning. Leaves crackled as I searched for firewood, the snap of sticks was overloud in the waning forest.

At some point Nui appeared with a blood-smeared mouth and a limp rabbit, which I wrestled from her and turned into a stew before the day began to darken toward dusk again. The hound, deprived of her kill, watched me sullenly for a time, then vanished back into the woods.

As the shadows grew, I ate quickly, glancing up at every curl of wind and hoping it would bring Isik back. I was still unsure what to feel when I thought of my old friend, but I knew I wanted him here, by me as night drew in.

Stranger.

I stiffened and twisted, staring at the night with wide, sharp eyes.

Stranger.

I stood. The voice came from the forest, but it didn't drift on the air between the trees—it thrummed up through the earth beneath my feet. Who, or what, would speak in such a way?

I turned full circle, looking for any variance in the night. I found too many, too many shapes of darkness beyond the light of my fire.

I picked up my staff, steeled myself, and edged out of the circle of firelight. Back to the fire, I waited for my eyes to adjust, toes curling in my shoes. Silence. Shadows. Then, glistening trails of white foxfire came into focus on the trees. It was brighter than it had been in the riverman's village and pulsed ever so slightly—like a heartbeat.

Free me.

The whisper came with a creak of limbs and a rustle of leaves. I hastily stepped back into the firelight, but the warmth at my back did nothing to soothe me. The light cast my shadow starkly across the ground, where roots contracted like spasming serpents and shriveled autumn ferns shuddered in an unseen breeze.

"Thvynder." My god's name burst from my lips in a prayer. I didn't care that there was almost no chance they would hear. Something was alive in the forest. "Thvynder, what is this?"

No answer came, though I could swear I felt a distant touch of power, a hint of the deity's presence. But perhaps that was wishful thinking. I was alone in the night, and my imagination was very, very alive.

The foxfire faded to a dull, persistent glow and the ferns ceased to rustle. Roots settled back into the earth and in the distance, an owl hooted mournfully, at ease in the night.

Still, I didn't move. I stood alert by the fire as time stretched and the forest returned to slumber.

So alert was I that when the creature came, I heard it from far, far away. It started as a lack in the gathering night, a gradual shushing of the owl and rodents in the brush. Then came the steady, shuffling thumps of great paws on the earth. Steaming water in my clay pot, nestled among the coals of the fire, rippled. A dead tree crackled as something nudged it, and my heart stopped beating in my chest.

When the creature was close enough that the ground shook and I hopelessly considered fleeing the frail safety of my fire, a deeper hush fell. The footsteps ceased and for a breath absolute silence reigned.

I heard a huff, the brush trembled, and two huge eyes blinked at me from mere paces away. I reached for the horn at my belt, but had no breath to blow it. I could only tilt my head back, slowly looking up to meet the creature's eyes.

They glistened gold in the firelight and as the beast breathed, the stink of mushroom, must, and damp fur gusted over me. It made the fire dance and flare, and in the sudden light, I made out the face of an enormous, scarred bear.

"Aegr," I breathed.

The Bear regarded me for a long, long moment, then he advanced. One great paw thudded down on the other side of my firescreens and I felt all blood drain from my face in a slap of cold. I was struck dumb, but not out of fear—at least, not purely. Unreality and awe overwhelmed me.

I tore my eyes from the Bear's and ducked my head in reverence. My hair, half-bound in braids, fell over my face and I fixed my gaze on Aegr's enormous brown paw. It was, I suspected, the very same that had shaken the ground next to me on the shores of the Headwaters.

Something brushed my scalp and moist breath gusted around me again, stirring stray hairs and turning my stomach. A second brush turned into a nudge, and my head tipped back.

Aegr stared down into my face, so close our noses met. His broad head and immense shoulders filled my vision, and I could see my own reflection in the black depths of his eyes, silhouetted by firelight.

"I honor you." When I spoke my words were soft, but I was grateful they didn't waver. A little voice in the back of my mind wondered if the Bear was connected to the whispering I'd heard, but Aegr felt entirely different. He had a presence, like an unveiled Miri, and it was not what I'd felt when the pale foxfire blazed.

"You saved my mother once, on the shores of the Pasidon," I continued. "Our family has not forgotten your kindness."

Aegr continued to watch me, breath rushing over my skin.

"We came to see the tree," I added, feeling as though I should explain my presence. "And to meet those who worship you."

It seemed to me that the Great Bear became even more still at that. I'd no doubt he could understand my words, but replying was another matter entirely. For all the magic he'd absorbed over the centuries in the High Halls, he was still a bear.

Aegr lowered his nose to my healed thigh and sniffed carefully, without touching my clothing. Then he eased back, stepping over the firescreen with the tips of huge claws just clearing the top. The boughs of the trees and the undergrowth shifted around him, jostled by fur and muscle, and the foxfire faded as he passed.

The Bear turned and wandered off, out of sight.

I sat frozen by the fire until the last of his footsteps faded. The owl hooted again, low in the night, and Isik peeled from the shadows.

My friend didn't need to speak—I could tell from the shock, awe, and soul-deep relief in his expression that he'd seen my encounter with the Bear. Still facing the direction Aegr had gone, I reached out a hand to him, our conflict and uncertainties forgotten in the power of the moment. He took my fingers in his, neither of us speaking a word.

Beneath my grip, his blood thrummed as fast as my own.

TWENTY-SIX

I sik and I stood together until the pounding of our hearts slowed, then I stepped away.

He ran his hands over his beard, letting out a short breath. "So he *is* here."

I nodded, still too awestruck to speak, and touched my hair where the Bear had breathed on me. It was warm, and a little damp. I shivered. "I think he has been from the beginning. I saw him, on the shores of the Headwaters."

Isik shook his head, overcome. "I thought I saw him too, once, perhaps twice. But I was never sure. He seems... content, to leave us in peace?"

I nodded. The memory of the Bear's eyes still saturated me, but other concerns began to resurface.

"Did you hear the voice?" I asked. "Before the Bear came."

"When I arrived, he was already here. What voice?"

I told him, explaining how the sound had seemed to come from the earth itself, how the roots had spasmed and the foxfire had awoken.

"This foxfire isn't... normal," I added, gesturing at the night. Tendrils of illumination remained among the trees, but I could barely see them now in the firelight. "It dimmed when Aegr was near, and I've seen it during the day. It burns even when the forest is dry. And the colors, they're not right. And," I added with growing realization, "I've seen it before. In the High Halls, that night we spoke in the forest."

Isik's brows drew together. "Have you noticed there's more of it, the further east we go?"

I suppressed a shiver. "Yes. It seems a great coincidence, the foxfire waking when the voice came. Whoever spoke asked me to free them, Isik. And if I'm right, Aegr chased them away. Or at least, they fled his coming. The foxfire dimmed where he passed, too."

Isik surveyed the night for a somber, contemplative moment. The fire crackled at our backs and the forest slowly regained its sleepy chorus—the repetitive call of a nightbird and the occasional dance of dry leaves in the wind.

"I have no answers, though I suspect Aegr might, if he could speak. Perhaps he came *because* of the voice," the Miri suggested. "Or perhaps they were both drawn to you for the same reason. Did you use your magic again?"

I searched for the rebuke in his voice. But there wasn't one. Just a question. In fact, the hard edges he'd worn when he left seemed to have faded and his gaze was concerned, but not accusatory. Perhaps he'd reconciled himself to my sacrifices?

"No," I answered simply and pushed the topic aside. We could do nothing more than stew in our own questions, and my brother was still missing. "Did you find Berin?"

"I didn't. But I found a village. Arune rules there, if what I saw was any indication. The people speak Fith, but they do not seem to be allies with the riverman's folk."

"The riverman spoke of another clan of Fith who had a foreign 'god,'" I shared, though the mention of gods and worship felt heavy on my tongue, charged with more potential conflict. "He called them the Aruth."

Isik gave a thin laugh. "Aruth. Arune. Gods below, he's conceited. Your companions are there, except for Berin and Ursk. I saw no sign of them."

"They're all right? Seera and the rest?"

"They're alive and looked as though they were being cared for."

Relief and unease sifted through me. "So Berin and Ursk escaped and carried on to the coast."

Or they're dead, I thought. I'd heard Berin's horn, but that didn't mean he had been the one to blow it, or that he had lived long after that.

I dropped a hand to the horn at my own belt, anchoring myself to the smooth, cool feel of it.

Isik nodded. More tension ebbed from his frame and he glanced back at the fire and the pot of stew. He looked so human in that moment, so tired and hungry.

I crouched and started to reach for the pot, shielding my hand with a fold of skirt, but he beat me to it.

"Let me," he said mildly, his mind clearly elsewhere. He sat by the fire and edged the stew out of the coals with a stick. I offered him a spoon from my pack, and he began to eat with obvious hunger. His shoulders slumped as he chewed and he smiled in satisfaction. "I forgot what a good cook you are."

"Don't tell the others." I waved a finger at him, though the humor felt forced. It seemed we were both going to ignore our earlier conversation, and I was glad for it. Perhaps we need never speak again of love and worship and obligation. We could return to being friends. "Then I'll be cook *and* story-singer and healer."

"Our secret," he said through another mouthful. "Tomorrow I'll go to the lake and see these Hask. That's the direction Berin and Ursk went, last sign I saw of them. That man Ursk is very good at hiding his passage."

Another day of waiting. Displeased, I prodded at the fire with a stick, nudging a charred chunk of wood deeper into the flames. "Do you think—"

Arune stepped from the shadows, glancing around with overdone curiosity. Isik was up in a flash, woodcutting axe raised, and I snatched up my staff.

In the firelight I saw Arune clearly for the first time. His face was beautiful, almost feminine, white hair wild and wind-tousled, except for where it was bound back at the temples in thin braids, twined with black threads and hung with fine animal teeth. A long tunic slit at the hips clothed a narrow-hipped, athletic frame with long, trouser-clad legs and well-kept wrapped leather boots, embossed and braided with intricate depictions of snow and wind.

The Winterborn eyed Isik. "Greetings, Son of Esach. Yske."

"I hear you have my people captive," I stated, pleased when my voice came out cool and devoid of emotion. "Release them."

Arune appraised me momentarily. "They're not prisoners, just… surprise houseguests. You're welcome to fetch them, whenever you please. I've just come to arrange the payment of your debt."

The ease with which he agreed made me suspicious. "Who do you want me to heal?"

"My sister. A desire I'm sure you can understand."

My apprehension began to retreat into the clear, analytical purpose Aita had taught me. "What is wrong with her?"

"As I told you, Logur tried to use my blood to open a door to the High Halls, some seven years ago. That blood was, in fact, my sister's. My kin's." Arune delivered his words with a deadly lightness. "But she is immortal as I, and had no death blood to spill. Yet her wounds were grave, so now she sleeps in a tomb of ice. Heal her and I will consider your debt paid in full."

I came to stand next to Isik. "You'll free my people and swear to do us no harm?"

"Yes." Arune nodded with overdone graciousness. "I'll even lead you to your brother. I know where he is now, he and the other that escaped with him. And I'll allow your people to winter with mine— largely to keep you from causing trouble, but I could also use a healer and more good warriors within my walls. Trust me when I say you will not survive alone in this land, and the other clans in this region are prone to butchery. The Hask may throw you to their bears. The Fith to the riverman's monsters." His eyes moved to Isik. "You really should leave though, and take your blood with you."

Isik let out a gust of breath and glanced at me. "So everyone tells me."

"Regardless, come to my hall in the morning," the Winterborn concluded, with a vulpine smile. "You already know where it is."

Isik scowled. "You followed me back."

"You're a child, young Miri," Arune said, a doting uncle despite the fact that they, deceptively, looked no more than a year or two apart in age. "I may be a half-blood but I've walked this world longer than you. So believe me when I tell you that I do not simply ride the winter wind. I am the wind. It is I. And it whispered of your presence for many days before you trespassed here."

I saw a flush creep up Isik's neck and his fingers tighten on the axe, knuckles white.

"We will be there," I promised, brushing Isik's arm with one hand to keep him quiet. He stilled beneath my touch. "Thank you, Arune."

Arune seemed delighted by my politeness. He offered a bow, white hair falling forward and the fine animal teeth in his braids tinkling.

"Until tomorrow," he said, and vanished to the wind.

Thunder rolled, rain drenched the forest, and Isik let his human façade fall away. In my Sight his Miri aura saturated the gloom, drifts of dust the color of soaked slate, edged with gold. It swirled and gusted without heed to raindrops or shuddering leaves. His shoulders were level, his chin high and his pace determined but smooth, a king in his court. The son of a once-goddess, surrounded by her power. Fueled by it.

My breath was shallow as I followed in his wake, staff in hand and Nui at my side. I'd rarely seen my friend in this state, and it impacted me more than I wanted to admit, fanning the embers of thoughts and truths best left untouched.

The pull of him was... intoxicating. I told myself this reaction was purely physical, a natural response to seeing someone who was objectively beautiful, soaked with rain and at the height of their power. There was nothing spiritual about his draw, no soul-deep tug of worship, nor the inexplicable bindings of romantic love.

Still, when he looked back to check on my progress and I saw the familiar lines of his face, the coolness in his eyes, his words came back to me.

I've never had worshipers... but I feel the lure of it.

I coaxed my expression into impassivity and looked away. This show was for the Aruth and Arune. Not me.

The forest ended and the walls of Arune's settlement came into sight. Rain battered a network of fenced, dying gardens and shelters for animals, running right up to the palisade. Throughout, chickens and rugged goats watched us through the downpour with the same steady silence as the guards at the high, narrow gate.

Arune waited, framed by open, iron-banded oak doors and half a dozen warriors with spears and helmets. The rain did not touch the Winterborn, though his hair stirred in the breeze. When lightning laced across the sky, light flooded his pale-skinned face and made his white hair glisten like silver.

The eyes of the guards—boasting the distinctive eastern cheekbones and rain-soaked brown hair—fixed on the two Miri-blooded men, awe leaking through their stalwart exteriors. I felt it too. The power of the moment was undeniable, but I kept my composure.

Arune cocked his head to one side, blue eyes flicking from Isik to the sky above. "Remind me never to fight you in the rain," the Winterborn commented dryly, then stepped aside and threw out an arm, welcoming us to the settlement. "Come."

We passed through the muddy, rain-splattered streets. Despite the weather, locals clustered in small windows and open doorways, or lingered under the dripping eaves of wood-tiled roofs. Nui pranced past a few growling dogs, unbothered by their hostility, and I laid one hand on her sodden back.

Arune's hall was built in the style of the far north, circular with an outer tier and a lower central pit, where a fire burned away the chill and damp. Carved animal totems sat atop the ceiling's spoke-like beams, each one watching us enter. A few villagers passed to and fro, stoking the fire and tending three cooking tripods which filled the air with the scent of baking flatbreads, roasting venison, and a pot of earthy mushroom stew. Smoke trailed up toward a broad chimney, where sparks danced in the shadows.

Not far from the flames, I saw my companions. Askir, Bara, Sedi, Ittrid, Esan, and Seera hovered as if they'd only just entered the hall themselves, their hair and clothing wet from rain.

They perked up as one as I stepped inside, though Askir's eyes immediately jumped to Isik at my shoulder. Bara and Ittrid sprinted across the wooden floor, outpacing the priest.

Bara pulled me into a firm, relieved embrace. Ittrid took his place a moment later, enfolding me in warm arms and the scent of smoke and a sweet medicinal herb that made me take her arm as she pulled back. The smell came from a paste, crusted beneath a bandage at her collar.

"I'm fine," she told me. Her smile was warm but I saw the strain behind it, the days of anxiety and frustration. "Their healers have been good to us."

"You're alive." Bara squeezed my shoulder. "The Winterborn told us, but I hardly believed him."

Arune tsked. "You're so distrustful."

"Why are you with a Miri?" Askir cut in, still eyeing Isik. "A full-blooded one, at that."

Bara glanced at the tall form of Isik behind me and kept his hand on my shoulder.

Before I could reply, Sedi, Esan, and Seera closed in. All sported a mosaic of minor injuries and several more serious ones, Seera's arm in a sling and the fabric of Esan's tunic showing layers of bandages beneath.

Esan nodded and smiled in a rare display of affection, though he gave none of that smile to Isik. Sedi smiled and Seera looked almost relieved to see me, though her eyes roamed, noting the distance Isik and I kept from one another.

"This is the son of Esach," I explained. "Sent by Aita."

"Fathered by Gadr," Askir concluded.

"The priest knows his business," Arune commented, fluffing his hair out with his fingers to dislodge the rain.

"I'm Algatt," Askir replied to the Winterborn. "Gadr is still our ruler, under Thvynder, and he is not quiet about his relationship with Esach. But why is a Miri here?"

"Aita sent me," Isik said, repeating my earlier assertion. "I assure you, I've only come to help. There have been rumors of strange sights in the Unmade. I came both to investigate and protect Yske."

"And Yske and I have struck a deal," Arune cut in, usurping the conversation.

"Let's sit," I suggested to the Winterborn. "Perhaps drink something warm while we dry off and I explain the situation to my companions?"

Arune nodded and called to the villagers at the hearth. A few moments later, we clustered in a corner of the hall, steaming cups in hand. Arune left us with a half-bow, and my companions and I were alone with Isik and the servants, the latter of whom studiously ignored us.

"Have you been treated well?" I asked in a low voice.

"Yes," Ittrid admitted, grudgingly.

"We're captives," Sedi growled.

"We're fine, for now." Bara glanced across the hall as if he feared we'd be overheard. "Where are Berin and Ursk?"

"According to Arune, they went east toward the Hask. We'll follow them soon." I sniffed at my tea, which no one had touched yet, and sipped it. The flavor was sweet, pine touched with honey. *Not so different from home*, I thought with a pang of longing. "I've agreed to heal Arune's sister, in return for your freedom and finding Berin."

"Where is this sister?" Ittrid asked. "We've seen no other Winterborn."

"I'm not sure. But Arune will tell me where, I'll heal her, and you'll be free. We'll find Berin and figure out what to do."

"What can we do?" Seera asked. "Winter's coming. We can't turn back now."

"We'll survive," I promised, running my gaze over each of my companions in turn and conjuring a soft, courageous smile. I didn't think of Berin then, lost and alone with Ursk. I didn't think of Isik's pending departure, Arune's offer of shelter, or the riverman out for my blood. I just took in the faces of my companions, alive and near, and smiled. "We will get home."

Twenty-Seven

I awoke to silence and warmth, the crackle of a fire, and the even breathing of my companions sleeping around me. The air was close and smelled of beeswax, smoke, leather and sweat—familiar, yet edged with something foreign. The wheel of the ceiling beams spread above me in the firelight, topped by the sightless wooden totems. A little gray owl watched me too, its eyes as round and golden as autumn moons.

A messenger, my half-awake mind decided. "Mother, is that you?" I whispered.

The owl ruffled its feathers and looked away. I followed its gaze to a throne on the upper tier of the hall. There Arune sat, one leg crooked over an armrest, the other stretched lazily out before him. His hair was fully loose in the firelight, his icy eyes colorless and considering.

"Your brother has reached the Hask," his voice said in my ear, though he remained on the throne. His words came with a prickle of wind, so soft and light that it barely stirred my hair and didn't rouse my companions—Isik to one side, Seera to the other. "I think it would be profitable for you to go directly to him, on your way to heal my sister."

"Is he safe?" The wind took my words, carrying them away.

Arune nodded. "He and the Priest of Fate have been welcomed. For now."

I took a moment to digest that, stilling a sudden tremble in my hands. Safe. Berin was safe.

"I see. So where is your sister?" I asked.

Arune sat forward, putting both feet flat on the ground and bracing his elbows on his knees, fingers laced between them. His eyes took on a hard, distant look. "She lies in her barrow of ice on the edge of the world. Where the riverman slew her. On the Hask's sacred island, at the foot of the great tree."

"Why there?" I asked, sensing this was important.

"That's where the original door was, long ago. Before the tree consumed it."

"Did the tree grow out of the High Halls?"

Arune shrugged languorously. "I do not know or care. All I want is my sister healed."

"Do the Hask allow just anyone onto their sacred island?" I asked, though I already suspected the answer.

"No. You will have to go unseen. Run to the Hask, allow them to take you in like they did your brother, then steal a boat. Do not get caught."

"What if I am?"

Arune leaned further forward and the distance between us suddenly felt like a single breath. "If you're very unlucky, they'll butcher you and feed you to their sacred bears. They'll be fattening for their winter sleep right now. It's excellent timing."

I considered that for a moment. "I saw Aegr. Perhaps I could... use that?"

Arune tilted his head to one side. "Maybe, if you had a common tongue. The Bear hasn't been seen for several years, though. If the Hask realize he's back..." The Winterborn trailed off, staring through me, calculating. "It could either be a useful distraction or cause unnecessary turmoil. The Fith and the Hask are always out for one another's blood, Eangen. Keep that in mind when you go to the lake."

"I will. Arune..." I hesitated, mulling over another confession. "I didn't just see Aegr. I heard a voice in the forest. It came with white foxfire I've never seen before this year, and it asked me to free it. Do you know who it is?"

Arune shrugged. "There are many things in this land I can't begin to understand, nor do I care to. The sun rises in the south. A riverman rules as a god, a giant tree grows at the edge of the world and, yes, white foxfire flares at noon. Once, I even saw a flock of starlings peck one another to death in absolute silence. This place… is what it is."

I suppressed the urge to shiver. "So you have no answers for me."

"No. The east is full of mysteries." Arune lounged back in his throne. "Take my advice: dwell on only what touches you. Get to the island and heal my sister. Winter with me if you choose—and then go home before the forest devours you."

The lake stretched toward an empty horizon, a vast lack that I might have called the sky if it hadn't been so devoid of depth, movement, and hue.

The Unmade. It was the space between the stars, the belly of an endless sea and the pause after exhale. It was everything and nothing, both the potential of life and the impossibility of it. It stretched unbroken to the north and south, fading into the distance and reaching up into the clouds.

The magnitude and impossibility of the sight left me speechless, crushed by my own fragility and temporality. Glancing at Isik, where he crouched next to me in the forest above the lakeshore, I saw the same depth of wonderment in his handsome face.

The Unmade, however, was not all that loomed before us. Just before the edge of the world grew a great spreading tree. It was an ash, as tall and broad as a mountain, its trunk burdened by ten thousand branches and its heights lost in the clouds. But not a single branch was in leaf. Now, in the height of autumn, when it should have bathed the sky in scarlet and purple, every branch was barren, and there was no sign that the leaves had already fallen. It made the tree's magnificence desolate and heightened my sense of mortal fragility.

"It's completely dead," Isik murmured. Nui and the rest of my companions remained back in the Fith village, their cautions and solemn eyes still heavy in my mind.

Arune, on my other side, appeared unaffected by the tree or the nearness of the world's edge.

"That is the Hask's main settlement." He directed my gaze toward the lakeshore, where marshy peninsulas of dead trees reached gnarled fingers into the water around a walled town. "There are others, but this is the largest. It's where your brother went."

The Hask settlement was indeed large, jumbled in behind well-settled palisade walls. Fishing boats anchored at docks on the lakeside and storehouses on stilts straddled the edge of the water. Gulls alighted on sod roofs and soared on lazy currents of air. Smoke drifted from the chimneys and Hask moved everywhere, throughout the settlement and the surrounding forest and fields. Other villages hazed in the distance, two or three—some on the shore, others closer to the forest.

Arune continued, reminding me, "Berin is no prisoner to the Hask. They have taken him in, and they've no reason to suspect our alliance, so give them none. Play the victim. A few tears on a pretty face go a long way in any place, regardless of the fact that they won't understand a word you say. Let them play the heroes."

Isik murmured on my other side, "I still think it's best not to tell Berin our plans. Your brother is—"

"I'll judge what's best when I see him," I interjected. I reached to squeeze his hand before I unfolded from the ferns. "Just be at the island when I arrive. Both of you."

"Yske!" Berin shoved through the crowd gathered around the gate of the Hask village. He pushed past the guards I'd been waiting with and enfolded me in his arms, squeezing so tight I lost my breath.

I couldn't speak, couldn't see beyond the burn of relieved tears. I dropped my staff, leaning all my weight into him and burying my face in his beard. His clothes were clean, his hair freshly braided and he smelled of oil and cedar—healthy and alive.

"Where are the others?" Berin asked, finally pulling back. Around us, Hask villagers—indistinguishable from the Fith—stared and murmured, but made no move to interfere. Some even smiled fondly, charmed by our reunion.

"What happened?" my brother pressed. "How did you escape?"

"The others are all alive and well, for now," I said, grasping his forearm like an anchor. "They're with the Fith tribe that captured us. Can we speak somewhere more private?"

"Yes. In the headman's hall," Berin said, glancing over his shoulder. "Ursk is there. We've been trying to convince the Hask to rescue you."

I was taken aback. "How are you communicating?"

"We're not." Berin pushed stray hair back from his face with his free hand and gave a wan half-smile. "But there's been a lot of gesturing, and Ursk has picked up more of the language than I can believe. Fate is at work. Gods know where we'd be without him."

I twisted my lips in response. "We wouldn't be here at all. But, Berin, we shouldn't involve the Hask in any of this. We're foreigners here. We shouldn't cause conflict."

"We may not have a choice. But we can discuss that later." Berin bent to pick up my staff and handed it back to me. "You need to rest. Do you need a healer? They have wonderful baths."

Ursk appeared with a woman in heavily embroidered burgundy skirts. She wore a scarf over her coiled gray hair—a style I saw among the rest of the crowd, now that I looked closer. She had broad cheekbones, lovely, intelligent eyes and unbowed lips—a combination that seemed, at once, to echo every Easterner I had yet seen. As if she were a carving they had made to summarize themselves.

I smiled in relief, an expression which Ursk returned.

"You escaped!" His eyes ran over me, noting my dirty, battered clothing. "Well come. This is Feen, member of the ruling council of the Hask and leader of this settlement."

The headwoman laid an open palm over her stomach and inclined her head in a gesture of respect. I nodded in reply as Ursk spoke to the woman in her own language. His speech was careful and halting, but not so much that I couldn't tell the language sounded similar to the Fith's, with slurred clusters of consonants and a jostling tempo.

"Come," Ursk said when he'd finished. "We'll return to the hall and you can regale us with the tale of how you escaped. Then, I suspect, we must turn to plans." His eyes shifted to Berin. "Plans of rescue, without starting a war."

I sat at a table in the Hask's meeting hall. The building was broad and long but low, lower than a Eangen hall would be, though in other ways it looked much the same—smoke-darkened beams, small slit windows that allowed glimpses of light and the village beyond, and a large central hearth. The Hask, it seemed, were a people of forest and water, as the Eangen were.

The Eangen, however, did not worship bears. Everywhere around me I saw evidence of the Hask's venerations, from the heavy bearskin mantles on the cloaks of local leaders to the ursine skulls tucked into alcoves on every side. A young girl went from skull to skull, lighting smoky tallow candles inside their propped-open jaws. The flames made their eyes glow in the dimness of the hall, and their discolored teeth glistened.

Feen, the headwoman, took a high-backed chair at the hearth. The chair was modestly adorned save for a drape of bearskin, brown and reddish in the firelight. Folding wooden stools, their seats made of fine, dense cloth, were set out for Berin and me, while Ursk took position beside Feen and offered us a bracing smile.

Feen began to speak, and Ursk translated her words slowly and thoughtfully. "Do you need to rest or bathe, or see a healer? Before we speak?"

I was sorely tempted to say yes, but Ursk followed his translation with a slight warning shake of the head.

"No, thank you," I replied to Feen. "I'm simply grateful to be safely inside your walls."

Ursk related this with a mixture of gestures and carefully chosen words. The corner of Feen's mouth twitched at his efforts and she replied with slow, articulate patience.

"You will be able to go soon, then. To the baths," Ursk related, looking embarrassed by his own fumbling. "She wants to know how you came here, so I assume she means how you escaped the Fith."

I glanced at Berin and found him watching me closely. His expression was grim, braced for whatever horrors I was about to share.

Arune and I had discussed the lies I was to give the Hask, but now that I was here and the Hask were real, warm-eyed strangers who'd accepted me with little suspicion, guilt reared up inside me.

"I was separated after the attack in the gorge," I began, nodding toward my brother. "I found a tunnel leading into the forest and ran, but the Aruth caught me."

As Ursk painstakingly labored to translate this, silence crept over the hall. Even the girl who'd been lighting the lamps paused, a waning wick in one hand and her other cupped to catch the ash. Beside her, the eyes of a bear skull glowed with captive flame.

"I was brought to a settlement ruled by a white-haired man, an immortal from the north." I looked at Berin as I said this, knowing it would be a shock to him. Sure enough, his eyes widened.

"Arune," Feen named him, her smile flat and bracing. Through Ursk she communicated, "We're familiar with him."

"The rest of our people are with him. As guests." I hesitated over the word, unsure of how it would translate. "They're all alive and cared for. They weren't harmed, other than in that initial attack, and I was able to escape when the others caused a distraction."

Feen watched me closely as Ursk translated my words. She questioned him a great deal before her narrowed eyes relaxed in understanding.

"I do not think there is a need for violence," I ventured, holding Feen's gaze and waiting for Ursk to translate.

Feen straightened in her chair and spoke a little more quickly.

"She also does not want violence," Ursk said, his expression grave and thoughtful as he worked through the leader's words. "She speaks much of the Divine Bear and his... protection? I am sorry, I cannot understand."

The Hask in the hall, however, had no such difficulties. A murmur rippled through the assembly. A paler-haired woman spoke, stepping in from the side. She had the slightly rounded belly and full breasts of a recent mother, and I'd seen her pass a tiny, red-faced baby to a young boy not long ago. Protective indignation etched her posture.

Ursk's eyes flicked between Berin and me as he tried to parse this new woman's words.

"I think she's saying that we owe them for taking us in," Ursk related to us in a low voice. He met Berin's gaze. "They want our help to fight the Fith and someone called Logur."

"He's the one who captured me. He's a riverman—Ursk, please do not translate that." I shot a worried look between the two men. I'd already feared becoming trapped in the conflict between the peoples of the East, but this went beyond that. "Why would they want our help? What do they know about us?"

Berin grimaced, while around us the Hask continued to debate among themselves. "They took us in because they saw me kill one of those bone monsters. I Shadow Walked to do it. They've gotten it into their heads that a priest of Fate would be useful. And I may have... told them of your skills."

I flinched. "Berin."

"I needed them to know how valuable you and the others are. I wanted them to help—"

Berin cut off as Ursk raised a hand, his eyes fixed on the pale-haired woman. "She's proposing... She wants to help rescue the others if we kill the riverman. And lend the Hask Yske's healing power."

The Hask now fully descended into their heated discussion, and our increasingly baffled translator stood in the middle of the fray, lips closed and one eye half-slitted, as if he had a headache coming on.

"There will be a council in one day… two days," Ursk said, rubbing his forehead with two fingers and a thumb. "I don't think they will do anything before then. But I do not like this, any of it."

I didn't either, and from the tic in Berin's jaw he shared our feelings. He'd made us more valuable than we wanted to be, as strangers in a foreign land rife with conflict—and swiftly being pinned down by an approaching winter.

We were at the Hask's mercy.

Twenty-Eight

The Hask bathed in common bathhouses, one for men and one for women. They were just outside the settlement gate, built of stone and mounded with earth. Sheep grazed around their thick chimneys, impassive to the drifts of smoke that eddied in the breeze off the lake.

"Where is this Winterborn woman?" Berin sat in the open door of the women's bathhouse, facing the water and ignoring the stares of Hask as they flowed in and out of the settlement.

"On the island," I replied. The light filtering around Berin cast a misshapen pool of illumination on the damp stone floor. Shadows swallowed the rest of the chamber, but my eyes had adjusted enough to see the water draining into a stone basin in the center. Shallow channels in the floor carried away the dirt that I scraped from my shivering, naked skin. The stone of the basin was warm but the water tepid, the elevated fire beneath the bowl left to cool after the Hask finished their morning ablutions.

I took up a shaving of strange gritty soap and scrubbed myself. "Once I get there, Arune will meet me and take me to the tomb."

Isik would too, but I hadn't found the right way to tell my brother about him yet. He knew me too well, and I feared he'd see through my promises of simple friendship.

"A tomb of ice…" Berin mulled over the words and shifted, stretching his legs out long before him. "How long has she been in there?"

"Seven years, he said."

"Who is she?"

219

Water splashed onto the stones as I upended a bucket over my head, spluttered, and shook out my hair. "He didn't say her name."

Berin flinched from a spattering of droplets, giving me an annoyed half-glance. But he was preoccupied; I could see it in the lines of his silhouette, and tucked around his eyes where the light fell across his face. He looked older than when we'd left Albor, more like the father he perhaps was. A world away.

"How can we trust a Winterborn?" He spoke quietly, though there were no Hask in sight and Ursk, the only person who would understand us, was back in the hall cajoling language lessons out of anyone who cast him a second glance.

"How can we trust the Hask?" I replied, wringing out my hair and drying myself with a cloth provided by Feen—along with fresh clothing, a comb, and a head covering I likely wouldn't wear. "Arune is from our world, at least. And his interests are selfish, which makes him predictable. The Hask and Fith have centuries of history and conflict we don't understand. We can't even communicate with them directly. We have to trust Ursk."

"I do trust Ursk," Berin murmured absently. "Yske… I still don't understand how you escaped. That storm felt so unnatural, and then you were gone."

I pulled a loaned linen undergown over my head. "The Miri have taken an interest in your expedition," I admitted. The undergown was too snug across the breasts and hips, but it was clean. I shrugged a sleeveless overgown atop it, one that fastened from chest to knees with bone buttons. "Isik, the son of Esach and Gadr, followed us. Apparently, he has been protecting us along the way, as much as he could. He intervened in the gorge and we escaped together."

"Oh? What do the Miri want?"

"They're curious," I said, slipping my own belt around my waist and gathering up my soiled clothes. My trousers were still stiff with blood and dirt, and the sight of the hole where the arrow had been made my stomach twist with remembered pain. "The rumors the Arpa brought north reached them too. The whispers of movement in the Unmade, in particular."

"So this Isik came to see if the rumors were true?" Berin shifted to make space as I joined him in the doorway. "And he saved you? Why did you lie to Feen?"

I dug stubborn dirt out from beneath my nails. "Because he and I were captured by Logur. Summoning the storm was too much for him. He passed out, and I was injured—there was nothing we could do when the Revenants came."

"Revenants?"

"The monsters. Logur makes them."

Berin didn't speak for a long moment, then he murmured a pained, "Yske... If I'd known what would happen..."

"I survived," I said, offering him a soft smile. "Don't look at me like that. And don't be self-pitying, my capture wasn't your fault. We would have found one another if we could. I heard your horn, but I couldn't come to you either."

He put a hand on my forearm. "Still. I should have kept looking. There were just so many Fith, and you'd vanished. Ursk said the Hask might help... It was the only thing that kept me from losing my mind. What else happened?"

I told him everything, from Isik's and my capture to the garden of growing Revenants, to the deal I'd made with the riverman and the second deal I'd forged with Arune.

"We've struck deals with nearly every power in the East," Berin commented once I'd finished. "But we're still surrounded by enemies."

We both looked out at the island and the lording branches of the tree overhead, from the island to the shore on which we sat.

I saw the weariness in Berin's face, and the edge of something worse—regret. I thought he'd say sorry, then. I thought he'd admit the foolishness of this entire journey and apologize for dragging me into it.

Instead he straightened his shoulders and asked, "What should we do?"

My hair hung heavy over one shoulder, half-dry and tangled. I began to comb it, unraveling my thoughts with each knot. "I'll heal Arune's sister. If he betrays us, we still try to negotiate for our companions' freedom. If that goes nowhere, we…"

I'd been about to say that we should let the Hask use us, that we should fight for them and do anything necessary to get our friends back. But that would mean taking part in the dissolution of an apparent peace between the eastern peoples. It would mean bloodshed and war. I might not wield a weapon in that conflict, but I'd still be endorsing it. That went against all I wanted to be.

Logur was a menace though, a monster and a creator of monsters. Would it not be righteous to help the Hask bring him down? My mother would say it was.

Her voice twined through my head, a hundred rebukes and instructions swirling into an increasing, wordless pressure. Yes, I was here to heal and protect, not encourage violence. But how could I claim to protect my friends, to sacrifice for them, when the greatest barrier to their survival was my conscience?

"We do what we have to," I relented, vague and unhappy.

"The riverman may come for you before we reach that point," Berin reminded me, apparently unaware of my inner turmoil, "if he thinks your blood will help him. The Hask may have to fight the Fith, regardless."

I turned my face into the wind. Berin was right. The riverman would be searching for Isik and me, and there were only two places for us to hide for long—with Arune, or the Hask. I might not trust the Hask, but I hardly wanted to bring the Revenants down on their heads. And as for Arune? Our people—and Nui—were in his little walled village. Could they withstand a full assault if Logur decided to search there?

"We go find Arune's sister tonight, while the village sleeps," I decided, squeezing Berin's hand and meeting his gaze. "You and I. Alone. We can ask Ursk to cover for us."

Berin nodded and cleared his throat. Standing up, he offered me a hand and produced a wan smile. "Right. Have you ever stolen a boat before?"

The reeds parted in a rustling shush. Our boat was a small, narrow craft, meant for speed and forging rivers instead of fishing. We plied our oars as silently as we could, pushing off submerged logs and mounds of mossy, sodden earth. The air was cool and charged, thick with misty rain, but that consoled me—Isik would be at his full strength tonight, wherever he was. And in the meantime, Berin and I were shrouded.

Ursk had remained behind in the village, to cover our trail and ensure Feen was preoccupied.

"We'll be back before dawn," Berin had said as we'd clustered in the privacy of the empty house we foreigners had been given.

Ursk had nodded, his smile assured save a slight tightening around his eyes. But if his god-given premonitions gave him any sense of what lay ahead of any of us that night, he'd said nothing of it.

"Go," he'd urged. "I will do what I can."

Now, our little boat entered open water. We wavered side to side in the wash, but soon steadied under our measured strokes, and in the cold I was grateful for the burn of my muscles.

Eventually, the island materialized from the downpour. I could see little of it, just a dark hillock in the rain-shrouded lake. The branches of the tree above were obscured, but I felt their presence like eyes on the back of my neck.

With one last thrust of our paddles, we slipped into a stand of reeds and ran aground. I started to rise, using my paddle to balance myself.

I froze. A thin light moved on shore and voices drifted to me— one, two? More? Other than the vague suggestion of a lantern bearer, I couldn't see their owners in the gloom. I could barely see Berin, leaning close to me in the boat, his oar braced across his knees.

But he could see. My brother laid four fingers on my arm, tapping each one to catch my attention. Four Hask warriors, presumably Guardians of the Tree. I touched his hand in acknowledgement and we waited in silence for the voices to pass on.

The night quietened into a patter of rain once more. I gathered my damp skirts around my thighs and stepped from the boat into the shallows, not bothering to take off my shoes; they were already soaked. Berin passed me my staff and shouldered his battered shield, then we tucked our oars into the belly of the boat, wedged it more firmly into the reeds and headed for shore.

"Where's Arune?" Berin whispered, squinting through the rain in his eyes. "And Isik?"

I surveyed the sky, but there was no glint of gold or silver in the mist.

"Isik," I called to the breeze, daring to raise my voice a fraction. Moisture saturated my hair and clothes, trickling down my scalp and making my skin crawl. I gripped my staff tightly. "Arune?"

Silence stretched. No answer came.

"We can't wait," I whispered to Berin. "We'll have to go without them."

Berin shrugged, barely a shift in the gloom. He unshouldered his shield and drew his sword.

We made our way along the shore, heading for the side of the island that faced the Unmade. I couldn't see the void and I had no sense of it—that was no surprise, I supposed. There was nothing to feel.

Once we left the smooth mud and reeds of the lakeshore, the terrain became increasingly uneven and interrupted by huge roots, which bulged from the earth like burial mounds. Some were exposed, others covered with earth here and there. Goat paths latticed their sides and the grass was close-cropped, though there were no animals to be seen.

We slipped between the mounds, avoiding rivulets of water and alert for any variance in the patter of rain and swish of wind.

Not alert enough. Berin grabbed my arm at the same time as light spilled over the wet grass. The unveiled lantern revealed a tall, slim woman and three warriors with spears leveled toward our chests. Hask spears were shorter than Eangen, but no less deadly. They also had a crossguard of heavy, piercing beaks just below their spearheads, deadly and pointed and ready to swing.

So Revenants can't crawl up the shaft, a grim corner of my mind speculated.

Berin and I froze. The woman with the lantern stared at us, her face creased with confusion, then recognition and blossoming, righteous fury.

It was Feen. Her hair was covered and her rich clothing exchanged for more practical garb, but this was the Hask's headwoman. She demanded something of Berin in Hask, her anger boiling over into a fruitless series of rebukes and questions.

My stomach dropped. Berin pulled me behind him, readying his shield, and I bumped back into a curling root. I looked up, startled, and saw that it arched high over my head like a rain-slick boulder. We were trapped.

Berin drew his sword, slowly and measuredly. Indecision assailed me, then I relinquished myself to the shelter of his back and slit my palm with the knife Feen herself had gifted me earlier that day.

Hask words flew as Feen and her warriors conferred. At the same time the wind picked up and the rain thickened, driving down upon us in a way that left me blinking and half-drowned. But I felt Aita's power swell inside me, warming my blood and tasting like honey and lavender on my tongue. I sketched a subtle rune in the air, and rested my open palm on Berin's back.

I did not consider what I might have to do tonight—to strike and kill and defend. I stifled my dread and guilt with magic, and promised, just loud enough for Berin to hear over the rain and the Hask, "I have you. I won't let you fall."

I saw him nod, though he kept his eyes on the enemy. "I'm going to Shadow Walk, and destroy that lantern. Keep low. I'll find you again."

"All right," I whispered.

The shape of him became indistinct, eluding the eye and impossible to follow. My fingers on his back slipped into shadow, cool and immaterial. I had to touch my Sight to find the edges of him once again, gold and gray and liquid in the night.

My twin surged and twisted, spinning his shield out to catch all three spearheads. Then he was inside the gap he'd made, sword stabbing and flicking out. Once. Twice.

Two Hask fell with agonized shrieks. Feen shouted, the lantern hit the ground and a spear clattered to the mud. Burning oil flowed around it, spreading rather than extinguishing.

More warriors appeared in its flickering light. I saw them materialize atop mounds of roots and begin to fill the gaps between, spears leveled, clothes drenched with rain. Blocking every possible escape.

Berin vanished entirely, and in that instant, the last warrior thrust his spear toward my belly. I acted in a thoughtless blur—I met it with my staff and twisted, grabbing the shaft of his weapon and jerking it forward. The spearman was too experienced to be pulled off balance, but his grip slipped and the spear embedded into the root at my back.

He released the spear and grabbed for me.

I darted away. His hand grasped the air, then hit the mud as Berin hacked it off at the wrist. The man's howl split the night, crackling with anguish, and I experienced a spasm of guilt.

The light of Feen's spilled lantern finally extinguished. Darkness stuttered over us.

"Up," Berin grunted and I felt hands on my waist. I scrabbled up the slick side of a root, anchored my staff over the crest, and found his shoulder with my heel. I vaulted over the top, and my brother followed a moment later.

Soon I'd no sense of the Guardians or if we'd lost them, but I couldn't shake a growing sense that the roots were funneling us, leading us into a trap. To make matters worse, Berin kept slipping back into the shadows when I least expected it, leaving me in stretches of terrifying solitude.

"Arune!" I dared to hiss in one lonely stretch. "Isik! Where are you?"

I walked into someone and stifled a shriek.

"Ouch!" Berin hissed, disentangling. "Some of the Guardians are Sighted. They could see me, once they realized what I was doing. Arune and Isik may have been discovered before they could get into place."

I cursed under my breath, blinking furiously—as if that could help me see in the darkness and rain. "How? Where would the Hask's Sight come from? Surely not Aegr."

"I don't know."

We both stilled as shouts drifted through the night. Another light pricked into existence and drew closer. Closer.

"There's a path under the tree," Berin finished, his voice so low I almost didn't hear it. "You won't be able to see but—"

The light came still closer.

"I already can't see!" I hissed, grabbing his hand and prodding his back with my staff. "Go!"

His fingers tightened on mine and we plunged underground. The rain ceased and the sweet scent of earth and forest rot assaulted me, as did a trickle of loosened dirt. I shivered as it tumbled down my collar and into my hair, but made no noise of protest.

We broke through into an open space in a chorus of wheezing gasps.

"We're under the tree." I couldn't make out my brother, but his voice was close.

I took my staff in the crook of an elbow and reached out for the wall. I found a barrier of raw wood, crumbling slightly beneath my touch. But though these roots were dead, I felt a tingle of power. Presence.

"Do you feel that?" I whispered.

Berin stilled, maintaining his grip on my other hand, and I wondered how much he held on for comfort. "Faintly. The Guardians will know this tunnel. We should keep moving."

I agreed. Facing the darkness beneath a dead tree seemed wiser than facing the raging Feen and her spears.

"We can't go back to the village now," I murmured as we began to push deeper. "The Hask will likely kill us, and Ursk will be in danger."

He cursed softly. "Of all the things for a Priest of Fate *not* to see…"

I felt his hand atop my head and obligingly crouched to avoid a low root. "Hopefully he'll see enough to get himself to safety. If not, Isik can get him out."

Berin's grunt of affirmation didn't sound as confident as I would have liked.

The way was not easy, now. We had to squeeze and crawl, and though I appreciated my generous figure, now I cursed every curve that had survived the journey east. Berin struggled more, bone and muscle even less forgiving. But at least he could see the roots threatening to poke out his eyes or squish him into the tunnel floor.

Any moment I expected to find a dead end. But we did not. The density of the roots began to lessen and my panting breath echoed around me. When I reached out and found nothing in my way, I fumbled for the pouch at my belt and pulled out a striker, a patch of oiled fabric, and tinder.

Berin waited as I crouched and struck. A fall of sparks momentarily illuminated our surroundings in cool orange light—moist earth, a ceiling of roots, Berin with shanks of wet hair scraped back from his face. The blood rimming his nails.

"You lost your shield," I said as darkness fell over us again. My heart ached a little at the realization, the loss of connection to our mother.

"It can be replaced," he replied, but his voice was rough.

Three more strikes and a spark caught, nestling in the tinder. I gently cupped it between my hands and blew, coaxing the spark into life. A flame bloomed, washing my twin and me in steady, welcome light.

"It'll only last a few minutes," I admitted as I found a stick and wrapped the oiled fabric about the end, then lit it. I let the tinder fall back to the ground, where it quickly turned to ash. "But I'll go mad without it."

Berin nodded and squinted around the chamber. "What is this?"

We stood in a space walled by roots and earth—no surprise there. But there was a consistency to the shape of it that suggested intentionality. Had someone shaped this tree, as it grew? Or had the tree naturally averted itself from this area for a reason?

In the center of the chamber was a flat stone. I edged closer, noting the worn surface and more half-buried stones around it, together with another, longer slab.

"A fallen doorway?" I murmured, glancing at Berin.

He shrugged, as perplexed as I was, and crossed the chamber to where another tunnel branched off. He peered down it, alert for danger with sword in hand.

Left alone with the slab, I touched my Sight. There, over the worn rock, I saw a thread of power in the air—like a door to the High Halls, but thinner, fainter. Sapped of strength.

It was not the only one. More threads spread through the chamber, passing through roots and away in every direction like a spectral spider's web.

My breath caught in my throat. This tree had grown over a doorway between the High Halls and the Waking World. But now that portal was closed and sapped of strength, and the tree had died.

"This is the door the riverman wants to open," I said to Berin. My voice was barely above a whisper, but overloud in the silence of the earthen tomb.

"Then where's Arune's sister?"

I turned, straining to see into every shadow. My torch was already dimming, pieces of fabric turning to ash and drifting to the earth. "He said she was in a tomb of ice."

"There's no ice here."

"We'll have to keep searching. If we can't go back to the Hask, Arune is our best hope."

Berin conjured a humorless smile. "Just our luck."

The sound of rain guided us out the other passage and to an exit between the roots—that and the water that trickled down the tunnel. My torch flickered in a fresh breeze and the last singed fabric fell away in flame-glazed chunks. I dropped the stick into the water, took up my knife, and slipped with Berin back into the storm.

Someone immediately barreled me to the ground. I screamed and lashed out with my staff first, but it was tangled in something I couldn't see. My assailant tore it away and tried to flip me over.

I resisted, screaming in frustration. I beat with my free hand, but it was quickly pinned to the ground. I tried to bite—an elbow mashed my cheek into the mud.

I still had the knife in my other hand. It was half trapped under my body, threatening to stab me as we tussled.

Its grip was warm with sweat and cool with rain. The urge to use it was a wordless thing, accompanied by the impression of memories—of a feral child protecting her mother on another rainy, desperate day.

Then I heard Berin cry out in pain. No more thought. No more memories, not even a distant, guilt-ridden twinge. I drove the knife upward. There was an instant of resistance—a push of leather, a parting of flesh. Then my knuckles hit the Guardian's stomach and I twisted the blade.

He shrieked and spasmed. I jerked the blade back out and squirmed away, avoiding limbs and gushes of hot blood.

I stumbled free and staggered upright. Dizziness came. Cold fluttered across my cheeks and my own blood felt too light in my veins, stuttering instead of thundering.

At my feet, the man I'd stabbed screamed, and screamed, and screamed. I couldn't see him, but I could hear him—every crack and hiss and plead and shriek as the pain overcame him.

"Berin!" I called, terrified to move. Surely this moment was not real. I hadn't just maimed another human, wasn't hearing his horrific cries in my ears. He was a Revenant, I told myself—not real, not living. This wasn't happening, and I needed my brother here to prove that. I needed his arms and his voice and his strength to bring me back to reality.

But Berin didn't come. So I took one step. I tripped over my staff. Using it as a lever I climbed back to my feet, knife numb in the other hand, and stumbled on.

I skidded, and slid, and ran. I did not stop until the ground beneath me turned to ice, a lantern was unveiled, and I came to a clumsy halt.

The cold, slick surface glistened in the rain-dulled light. But I didn't look up to see who held it. I couldn't.

There, beneath my feet through a distorting layer of ice, I saw a woman. Her eyes were closed, her head tilted to one side, lips parted. A mass of white braids floated around her in the ice, as if she were sleeping at the bottom of a pond. But there was little peace to this rest. Her head was fully separated from her body by a handspan of ice and great gouging wounds mottled her chest and limbs.

It was Thray.

TWENTY-NINE

My world narrowed, filled by my exiled cousin's face. I barely noticed the Guardians closing in, barely heard their shouts or the wind, or felt the rain. I saw Berin part from the night nearby, a stolen spear in one hand and his axe in the other, but I couldn't go to him.

Thray, my cousin, was here. Thray was Arune's sister—half-sister. Thray was the one I'd come to heal.

I dropped my staff and raised my knife again. Part of me was shocked I still held it—the other part of me was appalled. But the need to heal, to make well, to erase what I'd just done was overwhelming.

I slit my palm without a moment's hesitation. The cut was too deep. Pain made me reel and sway, earning a frantic glance from Berin, but I immediately regrouped. I pressed my shaking hand onto the ice and began to sketch runes in the air with the other, voicing their names in low, raw sounds. Each syllable vibrated in my chest, and every beat of my heart brought a torrent of blood and pain.

Magic burst around my splayed fingers. Blinded, I clenched my eyes shut and kept humming, kept willing Thray to heal and wake, the ice to break, for something in this terrible night to be good and right.

Fighting broke out around me and the wind turned arctic, thick with the threat of snow. Rain began to freeze, coating the world—and my clothes, my hair—with flurries of ice.

Hands hauled me back. I cried out in frustration and willed the last scraps of my magic into the tomb, but I was hefted bodily from the ground. A Guardian locked his arms over my chest, pinning my own arms to my sides.

I saw Feen, her face smooth with contained rage, and a dozen more Guardians. I saw Berin, on his knees with his own sword at his throat. And I saw the vestiges of my lavender-gold magic, trailing with my skin into the earth. It felt like lightning, but it looked like the long, slow pulse of a firefly on a summer night. Time seemed to slow in the swell and crest of its gentle light.

Soon, that light was not alone. A newer, eerier illumination awoke. Feen spun and half a dozen other Guardians looked in shock—up at the ash tree.

Foxfire flared on the roots closest to Thray's icy tomb and spread, tracing symbols upon the dead, barkless trunk. At first I thought the shapes random, twists and turns of knots, the paths of burrowing insects and small cracks. But as I looked closer, I saw runes. Hundreds, thousands—countless symbols, covering not only the roots and the trunk, but stretching up into the branches far, far above our heads. There the lights blurred in the rain.

The Great Tree, the Hask's sacred ash at the edge of the world, was a Binding Tree.

Feen stared at the glowing trunk, obviously trying to gather herself. Then she advanced, ignoring the panting, kneeling Berin and stopping before me—standing right over Thray's grave. Beneath the ice, I noticed, my cousin's neck had knit together.

Feen spoke in Hask, and though I didn't know the words, I understood their meaning. A promise. A warning. A threat.

They dragged us off into the night. The last thing I saw before a cloth was bound across my eyes was the gleaming tree, brightest where I had stood and Thray still slumbered.

Then I saw no more. But I felt the brush of wind on my cheeks, thick with the scent of summer storms, and the rain began to turn to snow.

My arms hurt. I shifted, trying to ease the strain, and felt something bite into my wrists. Vines. No, what a strange thought. Ropes, of course. Ropes, because I'd been captured.

My first thought was for Berin, and by extension Isik and Arune—summer storms and swirling snow. If both Miri-blooded men had arrived, why was I a prisoner? And where was Berin?

My mind jumped to Thray's face, locked beneath the ice. Had my healing worked? Was that why Arune hadn't helped me—he'd gotten what he wanted and fled?

I was alone in a stone chamber, windowless and close, but not lacking in comforts. Pallets and bedrolls lined the walls and a table was pushed off to one side, chairs scattered back with apparent haste. I was in the middle of it all, sagging on my knees. A Guardian outpost, perhaps?

A high triangular fireplace was built into the wall in front of me, along with two equally triangular doorways—one to my left, the other to my right. The impression of them was familiar, significant somehow, but my jumbled mind couldn't settle on why.

My wrists were bound with a rough rope tied to a sturdy lantern hook, embedded in a thick, rune-etched root. Foxfire pulsed in the carvings, and I blinked in recognition.

I was still on the island, likely back under the tree in an area Berin and I hadn't found before.

Stranger.

The voice came to me as eerily as it had the night in the forest, humming up through the ground and radiating from the root above my head. But this time, I felt a stronger presence—the same one I'd felt beneath the tree. And this time, I knew with certainty where the voice originated from.

Whoever was trapped in the Binding Tree was speaking to me.

"Hello?" I replied, voice just above a whisper.

The sound of footsteps came from outside and Feen appeared, framed in one of the doorways. Her simple dress was unbelted, loose around her lean frame in a way that made her look like any common woman, but her expression set her apart. Calculating, self-possessed, and oddly... resigned?

Her eyes flicked to the glowing runes on the root above my head. The foxfire dimmed, but only slightly.

Satisfied, Feen stepped into the room. "You're awake," she observed.

"Who is in the tree?" I asked. "Where is my brother?"

"If you promise to listen to me without interruption, I will tell you. We've much to discuss."

I blinked, realizing that I'd understood Feen's words. She spoke in the Divine Tongue, like Arune and Isik. Like the Miri.

Intuition stirred, linking together fragments of information and memory. The shape of the doorways. The roots. The tree. The history Logur had spoken of. The Divine Tongue, and the way Feen looked at me now.

"You're a woodmaiden," I guessed.

To my surprise, Feen cracked a smile. She shook her head—not in negation, but pleasure. "I'm honored you've seen through this face... I've worn it for so long, sometimes I fear even I forget what I am."

She stretched out her arms to either side and let out a long breath. As the air left her lips, she changed, just for a moment. I saw a woman with skin of smooth, pale birch, eyes like knots with polished amber hearts, and fingers as graceful and delicate as willow wands.

With the next intake of breath, she was Feen again, plain and dignified.

Silence filled the room. Feen watched me for a reaction and I kept my expression as closed as I could, contemplating why she would reveal herself to me. And what fresh dangers this knowledge might unleash.

Slowly, I found my way to my feet, battling cramped muscles. The tension of the rope eased, though not enough to gain ground on the woodmaiden.

As much as I wanted to escape, I sensed how critical this meeting was. I needed to know what this creature was doing here, masquerading as a woman, guarding a Binding Tree at the edge of the world. I needed to know who was in the tree, calling to me. I needed to finish healing Thray, and learn where Berin, Arune, and Isik were.

"Did you make this tree?" I asked, holding on to the rope to steady myself as my muscles shuddered. "Or do you just guard it?"

"Again, I'm flattered," Feen said, unfolding one of the Hask's fabric stools nearby and perching upon it. "I haven't the power to make something like this. Not alone, at least. But I had a hand in its creation, yes, and now I watch over it. You should know that your companions have fled—both the Winterborn and the… other. They found my nature rather surprising, it seems, and did not expect my Guardians to be able to see them. So, Yske, know that I wholly control you and your brother's fate."

I imagined Berin wounded and unconscious, bleeding somewhere beyond my sight.

But I wasn't afraid. There was no space for fear now, not with Berin and Thray under threat. Not when I'd broken my promise to myself and stabbed a Guardian. I felt as though I were only half of myself—shallow and cold.

I lifted my bound wrists to show the woodmaiden my swollen and reddened skin. "I'm not going anywhere."

Feen accepted this and began to speak. "I'll tell the story as simply as I can. Given your power and the company you keep, I assume you've some familiarity with the history of the world, of how those you call the Miri were given stewardship of the High Halls, and the Four Pillars—Thvynder, Eiohe, Imilidese, and Fate—left. But there is more—more that I suspect you do know, though your brother does not. Not all kinds of Miri went to the High Halls after its creation. We cherished our places in the rivers and forests—until, too late, we realized the blessing we had been excluded from. The sustenance, and power, of the High Halls could be taken. Used. That power took the natural affinities of the Miri in the Halls and turned them into gods. They changed, and we did not."

A chill swept over me. Were Logur and Feen allies, somehow? Or had they been, long ago?

"You know that the Miri rose against the Four Pillars, the true gods," Feen went on. "They bound Thvynder. They wounded Eiohe before he fled. Fate wove herself into time to escape them and maintain some control over the world. But Imilidese? She never returned at all. She was not there on that day. She was absent from creation and could not be found."

Feen stepped closer, lowering her voice to a rich, sonorous murmur. "Imilidese was in the Unmade," the woodmaiden confessed. "She returned too late to help her siblings and emerged here, at our lake on the edge of the world. Here, she found us."

"Us?" I repeated.

"Us. Woodmaidens and rivermen the Miri had rejected and driven away after their rise to divinity. We came east looking for peace and our own source of power, and we found it. We found a door to the High Halls."

"Logur was one of you," I surmised.

"Yes. But Imilidese threatened to take our newfound power from us." Feen glanced toward the fire as it popped. "Not only that, she threatened to destroy the world altogether—to unmake and remake what she and the other Pillars had forged. To bring about the end of ages, in fire and ash. So my sisters and I, together with the rivermen, used the power we had found to bind her."

I took in her every word, my mind working quickly. Binding a god. The threads of power beneath the tree. The foxfire, igniting countless runes on dead, starved wood—both here and in the High Halls, as I'd seen that night with Isik. The presence I'd felt when I pressed a hand to the roots.

"Imilidese is the one in the tree, and her influence has spread," I murmured. Every other thought fled my mind. The whispers I'd heard in the forest had been a goddess, a Pillar. All this time Thvynder had been absent from creation searching for his sister, she had been here in the east, bound like a common demon.

Feen nodded somberly. "Yes. Many of us died in the struggle—burned up by the very power we tried to harness. It stripped the rest of us, parching us and leaving us little more than humans. Few lived to see the tree forged and the runes carved. And only two—myself and Logur—remained here once the deed was done."

The magnitude of what I'd learned threatened to overwhelm me. Feen and her kin had stopped Imilidese and saved the world from Unmaking. Should I be grateful? Terrified? The being before me had thwarted the will of a true god.

"What happened with Logur?" I asked. "You're enemies now."

"We had a disagreement." Feen rested her hands in her lap. Her words were careful, her tone neutral, but even that piqued my curiosity. A disagreement yet to be resolved?

The woodmaiden went on. "The doorway to the High Halls was sealed in the binding of Imilidese—an unforeseen repercussion. Logur was obsessed with finding a way to reopen it, but if that were to happen, the power that holds the tree together would flow back into the High Halls, and Imilidese would be free. So I drove him out. He found his own people, time passed. Now the tree weakens and Imilidese's influence spreads with the foxfire, but the binding holds, and will for centuries to come. Unless Logur can break it. He serves Imilidese now. I don't know what she has promised him, her whispers in the dark... but he is deceived. If Imilidese is freed, we will all die."

The thought of Imilidese unbound was terrifying, too huge to be reckoned with. I teased out smaller details first, the details that might free Berin, Thray and me, and find us allies.

"Do the Hask realize what you are?" I asked.

"No," Feen said. "But they know I am more than they can see—a priestess, blessed with long life by the Bear. But my true power was stripped by forging the tree. I am a shadow of what I was." Her voice was thick with bitterness, raw with perceived injustice. "I have given everything for this cause."

"Your cause is protecting the tree from Logur," I clarified. "How can he not see what would happen if the rift was remade?"

"His mind is closed to me. Perhaps Imilidese has promised him a place in her new world..." As she spoke, Feen looked at the roots spreading overhead. "Perhaps he simply doesn't believe she would destroy creation. But he is wrong. Her rage will be unquenchable, after so long imprisoned."

"Then you and I are not at odds," I stated, holding on to that hope. "If I'd known—"

"None of this can be known," Feen cut me off. "There will always be misled beings, human and otherwise—those hungry for power and willing to do anything to achieve it. Imilidese may be bound, but she is not silent. You've seen the foxfire in the forests, spreading west. It has even spread into the Unmade itself, stirring shadows where there can be none."

I couldn't keep a shiver from creeping up my spine. So that was what the Arpa had seen. "It has begun to touch the Eangen High Halls too."

Feen frowned grimly and went on, "I have done what I could. I battled for years to keep her presence a secret from the broader world, but now... The Arpa came. You have come. And everywhere the foxfire spreads, so does her voice."

I thought of the stories I had grown up with, both in the human world and the High Halls—tales of the end of the age, when the world would be reforged in fire and ash and born anew. I'd no desire to live to see that day, see the forests I loved burn or the people suffocate, lungs clotted with ash.

Would Thvynder condone the actions of Feen and her counterparts, or shatter the binding and release their sister? I trusted my god, but no matter what the outcome was, if the truth of Imilidese's presence in the East was discovered, our world would change.

"My question now is—" Feen looked to me, head cocked to one side "—can you heal the Binding Tree, and repair Imilidese's bonds? Or will your power heal the doorway to the High Halls and release her instead?"

I stared. "Heal the tree? I can't do something so—"

"True, you can't do any of it," Arune affirmed, sauntering into the room. Behind him came Isik, who supported a beaten and bloody Berin. "Hello, Feen. I really am impressed—you hid your nature so very well."

Feen stood up quickly, but not quickly enough. In a blink and a burst of bitter winter wind, Arune was at her side, Berin's sword leveled at her throat.

"I assume you can still die," he said to the woodmaiden, scratching his cheek with his free hand. "Right? Or else—" He waved the tip of the sword. "—I'd feel silly doing this."

Feen's expression shuddered into a rage-filled sneer. "I curse the day you came out of the west."

"Regrets are useless things." Arune eyed her for another moment, then lowered the sword and made for me. "Go away. Revenants have taken the lakeshore and are about to land on the island."

Feen did not move for a stunned moment, then she spun for the door. She eyed Isik and the bloodied Berin as she approached, but neither moved against her.

"Stay out of the way and get off the island," she spat, slipping past the both of them. She stabbed a finger at Isik. "Especially you, Son of Esach. You foolish child."

Isik looked after her incredulously, but she'd already vanished.

The rope suspending me went slack. My shoulders and back screamed as my arms finally lowered, but I focused on the Winterborn, and my brother and friend in the doorway. My relief at the sight of them was potent, threatening to weaken my already trembling knees. I found a watery smile and steadied myself.

"I trust you'll keep your word, Eangen?" Arune slit my bonds efficiently. He nodded toward Berin, his expression becoming unreadable. "Your brother tells me you know Thray."

"Yes." As soon as the ropes fell away, I held out my hand for the sword. "Give me that."

The Winterborn put the hilt in my hand with a shallow bow and watched as I slit my palm for the third time that night. My stomach turned and my head spun, the myriad aches and pains of the last hours meeting with sleeplessness and anxiety in a sordid rush. Again, I strengthened myself. Again, I let the blood fall, coating my fingers and dripping onto the hard-packed floor with barely audible drips.

My brother met my gaze as I approached, heavy with pain and promise. Isik watched me too, expression inscrutable, as I sketched runes in the air and breathed them into Berin's flesh. His wounds immediately began to knit. I healed my own aches too, though I let my open palm continue to drip, refilling the well of my power.

"Wonderful," Arune said, following us with a light step and a broad grin. "Let's go wake up Thray."

THIRTY

The snow fell thick, muffling the island and covering the roots in an ankle-deep layer of white. I could see no further than a few paces to either side and hear nothing beyond my companions' breaths as we made our way back to Thray's tomb. Around us, the tree and its roots glowed with foxfire runes, their illumination diffused by the snow.

Arune and Isik vanished to the wind along the way, Isik giving me a long, promising look before he disappeared.

Berin strode just ahead of me, his footsteps silent and his frame edged with the bruised amber aura of his magic, sword in hand. I strode after him through the snow, a knife at my belt once more, and relished the bite of the cold. It numbed the pain of my still-bleeding hand and I could almost pretend that he and I were home again, in a snowstorm outside Albor. But I did not indulge that fantasy, not with Berin's sword bared and blood in the snow.

We approached a crouching figure with windblown hair, the bones at the end of his fine braids rattling in the wind. Arune looked up, blinking white flakes from his long, pale lashes. Beneath him lay the tomb of ice, its surface freshly cleaned of snow.

"She's nearly healed, but hasn't awoken," Arune unfolded back to his feet. He glanced up as the wind turned—Isik, keeping watch—and fixed his eyes on me. "Hurry."

I knelt at the Winterborn's feet, hiding my face beneath the veil of my tangled, wind-ravaged hair. Briefly, I wondered what price I would pay for this healing, how much pain I would endure. How deadly it might be to my mortal frame.

But when I saw Thray, still lying beneath the ice with her eyelashes pale against freckled cheeks, that fear lost its potency.

I gathered my power around me, pulling the scent of winter, water, pine, and lavender into my lungs. Arune's eyes remained pinned on his half-sister's face. And for all that he was a Winterborn, a half-Miri and an immortal, I saw humanity in the longing in his eyes.

Compassion lent me strength. I drew bloody runes on the ice, gathered my magic into my lungs, and breathed out. Golden light ignited my runes in a brief pulse, then seeped into the ice like smoke into a frozen sky.

That golden light gathered around Thray, then flared and overflowed. It seeped into the ice, earth, and roots that protruded into the Winterborn's frozen cairn. I felt it trace through the ground beneath my feet, even seeping back into my own wounded hand and knitting it closed with glimmer of sunset gold. My posture strengthened.

"Her eyes are opening," Arune breathed.

Before I could see that for myself, a crack shattered the snowy stillness. I twisted, sure that a horde of Revenants were coming upon us, but we were still alone. Instead, foxfire runes blazed above us in a riot of blues, greens, and whites as power billowed from the Binding Tree. Snow swirled with unseen impact, curling in waves before it resumed its placid, drifting descent.

Berin looked slowly up at the tree, but Arune remained focused on the ice. No, no longer ice. It had begun to melt, turning to warm liquid beneath my hands. I drew back, daring to hope that Thray would sit up, that she'd reach for me. But all I saw was water and snow, and the shadowed blur that was my cousin's motionless body.

The ground beneath our feet moaned. Foreboding coiled in my stomach and I followed Berin's gaze up. Foxfire runes continued to strengthen on the Binding Tree, and now I saw the colors begin to change—blue being replaced by gold, and green by amber. The colors of the High Halls.

My question now is… Feen's voice drifted back to me. *Can you heal the Binding Tree, and restrengthen Imilidese's bonds? Or will your power heal the doorway to the High Halls and release her instead?*

Slowly, I stood and faced the tree. Berin shifted closer to my side, his watchful gaze now divided between the trunk and the snow. Behind us, Arune's hovered at the edge of the former ice cairn, as if he held himself back from reaching in and physically pulling his sister out.

"What did Feen say about the Binding Tree?" Berin murmured. "And your power?"

"Creating it accidentally sealed the door to the High Halls." I found it hard to breathe, my thoughts racing through possibilities too staggering to comprehend. "That reopening the rift between worlds would likely release Imilidese, and she'll destroy creation. She… Feen thought I might be able to heal the tree instead and fix the binding. But I can't have enough power for any of that."

Blowing snowflakes caught in Berin's beard and his eyes were darker than I'd ever seen before. "I seems you do, little sister."

A gasp came from behind us, followed by a fit of coughing. I spun to find Arune beside the pit with a sodden Thray crumpled next to him, one arm around her half-brother's shoulders as she wheezed, eyes glassy with shock.

A low, drawn-out creak of timber reverberated across the island. Foxfire runes sparked and flared and began a slow firefly pulse.

"Thray," Arune whispered, his smile watery and his cheeks streaked with tears. He stroked her cheek and nodded to the glowing tree as the ground rumbled a third time. Far above our heads, I heard another ominous crack of splintering wood. "Welcome to the end of the world."

Thray's glossy eyes dragged from her brother to the snow and the tree. "How long?"

"Seven years. But we have to go now."

Thray's breaths began to come more quickly, her expression clearly overwhelmed. "The tree? What's happening to the tree?"

Arune shrugged. "Can you stand?"

Thray nodded. As her brother helped her upright, her eyes slipped to Berin and me. She was focused, curious and wary, but clearly didn't recognize us.

Why would she? Last time she'd seen us we were eleven years old and a world away, and my face had been swollen with tears as she left to battle her siblings on the coast of Eangen.

"I'm Yske." My voice came out stronger than I thought it would. I rounded her former tomb, little more than a pool of water between the roots now, and stood behind Arune.

Berin came behind me, moving more slowly.

"Hessa's Yske," I clarified. "This is Berin."

Thray stared, her expression slack. "This isn't real," she croaked, looking from us to Arune. "You're not real."

"Oh, I assure you, all of this is very real." Arune glanced out at the snow, impatient now. "We need to go. I wasn't lying to Feen—the Revenants were almost to shore."

Another crack rang out and foxfire flared through the thinning snow, rays of light condensing into tangling, knotting threads. The threads looked like the ones I'd seen beneath the tree, but these lanced into the air over the island in a chaotic spiderweb of renewing, humming power. There were more cracks, followed by a moan and a crash that shook the ground.

"Branches are falling," Isik's voice warned on the wind. "The Revenants are almost upon you. Run. Run!"

We started to move, Arune supporting Thray until she steadied into a wolfish lope. She drew a bone-handled knife from her belt and flicked it into a long white spear.

The sight filled me with courage—then all was replaced with the chattering, nattering screech of Revenants on the hunt. A wind came with them, swirling with the scent of summer storms and a blast of freezing rain.

Isik materialized at my side in mid-sprint, dark hair tousled by the wind and a stolen Hask spear in hand. My staff was in the other, and he handed it to me without a word. I was so preoccupied by his face, his flash of a grim smile and his windblown hair, that it took me a moment to register the figures over his shoulder. Revenants, shambling, striding, and crawling out of the storm after us.

"The island is overrun," Isik panted, keeping pace with me but following my gaze. "The mainland too. Winterborn! Can either of you freeze the lake?"

Thray didn't ask who he was, but shook her head.

"We're no Icecarvers," Arune said. "Your only hope is the boat."

"It's not far," I cut in. "Keep—"

I broke off into a startled shout as the first Revenant came into range—a leaping, snarling thing that might once have been a mountain cat. I spun my staff in two hands to fight it off, but Thray was already in motion. She charged in front of me and snapped out her spear, opening the construct's throat with the first slash and stabbing into its belly with the second. The sound of its shrieking cut off into a whistling gargle and it dropped, pawing at the snow.

"Glad your nap didn't slow you down," Arune commented, ducking to his sister's side and pulling the axe from his belt. He unfastened the hood with apparent nonchalance and tossed the boiled leather aside.

Another Revenant charged straight for me. I brought one end of my staff down on its head just as Isik turned and Arune vanished. The Winterborn reappeared just long enough to split the stunned creature's skull and throw it to the ground, hacking its face and throat twice more before he looked up at Isik, who hadn't had a chance to intervene.

"You're not very helpful, are you?" Arune asked, lips peeled back in a vulpine smile.

Isik, to my surprise, laughed. It was bizarre in the tension of the moment, Isik's limbs loosening and his grin broad, his eyes alight. "Do you know how many of these I've already killed?"

"No, but do tell me. We've plenty of time for bragging."

A nearby Revenant howled, so close and so loud my bones trembled.

Instinct took over. I grabbed Berin's sleeve and bolted for the shoreline. Isik shouted directions, but the Revenants were everywhere, circling in. I avoided them where I could and trusted my companions to cut them down where I couldn't, all the while searching for a path through our enemies.

Steadily, though, we were driven east. I didn't notice until I saw the snow fade into an emptiness—colorless, devoid of light or shape. As snowflakes struck its edges they disappeared, as if they had never been.

The Unmade. I shouted a warning and diverted along the precipice, gripped by a terror deeper than ever before—a terror of the unknown, of unmaking, and what might happen if I stumbled over that divide.

Multiple Revenants parted from the snow, mantled with white, river-stone eyes glistening with frozen moisture. I battered aside a reaching hand and stepped neatly out of Berin's way. He smashed the back of his axe into the head of my attacker and Thray darted in, dispatching the next with quick, precise movements. Arune was a blur, further out in the snow, slicing and turning, obscured in the white. Isik brought up the rear, but I didn't dare risk looking back at him.

The ground beneath my feet softened, mud eating up the snow and turning the shore into a patchwork of snow-topped rocks and stands of reeds with white-laden heads. The lake lay beyond.

A gust of wind cleared the snow from the shoreline as Berin plunged into the reeds, searching for the boat. The light of the tree swelled into the open air, now bright as dawn.

It also brought the black abyss of the Unmade into stark clarity. And there, in its unyielding blackness, I saw... foxfire. It moved the same way as the runes on the tree, pulsing and flaring, yet it had no light. It was the opposite of light, a deeper darkness in the shapes of ancient binding symbols.

A body hit me. Cold water punched the air from my lungs and poured into my open mouth. I struck out, eyes wide—but the water was thick and blurry. I saw nothing more than a distortion of wood and moss, then six rows of fine fish teeth snapped at my throat.

I shoved the end of my staff into the mouth, and reached for the beast's neck. I was distantly aware of claws tearing at my arms, my face and torso. But I let them. I accepted them, a sacrifice I made as sinew and flesh tore beneath my grasp. Brackish blood bloomed in the water. Claws wrapped around my ribs and shook me like a child's toy.

This was the pool in Aegr's cave all over again. This was Ovir dying. This was the edge of life, the edge of the creation itself.

I grabbed the creature's shuddering jaw as it tried to clamp onto my shoulder. My fingers shredded on razor teeth but I barely felt it, my awareness of the Unmade growing. We'd drifted toward it, the creature and I, until it was no farther than a few accidental kicks away. Water rippled at its edges and disappeared with each wave and churn.

The Revenant followed my gaze and stilled. Lungs burning, blood drumming against the inside of my skull, I tore the creature's claws from my flesh, twisted in the water, and thrust myself off the lakebed with my staff.

The Revenant drifted the other way, blurred by water and the mingling of our blood—mine pink, its rotted and discolored. Light from the blazing Binding Tree cut through the waves above us in a swaying placid blur.

Then the monster reached the barrier between Made and Unmade, its jaw open in a silent, stunned shriek. I saw something human in its face then, something haunted and forgotten, the echo of the true life that had once inhabited its bones. Then it vanished as if it had never been.

I floated, suspended in the bloodied, rune-lit lake. Between two heartbeats, I thought of the spark of humanity in the Revenant's eyes. I thought of the Hask Guardian I'd stabbed. I thought of the man I'd butchered as a child, while my mother lay helpless. I thought of healing and peace, and how badly I wanted to vanish into the solitude of my home on the mountainside.

Then my head broke the surface. Blinking, I looked back toward the shore. I saw Thray running, partially silhouetted against a backdrop of rune-lit snow. Arune, materializing at her side. Berin, beheading a

Revenant and turning, searching for me as four more monsters peeled from the snow and charged him.

I stalked from the water with my staff in hand and a deep, inevitable peace in my chest. I felt no hesitation at the violence I was about to wreak, nor did I feel rage. There was only need and action, a cleanliness and an unyielding justice. My power burned—I knew that distantly, felt my wounds knitting, but I had no conscious control.

In this moment, to save, I had to destroy. To heal, I had to bleed.

So I would.

I began to run. One heartbeat, I raised my staff. Two, and I clubbed a Revenant off my brother's back. I pinned it to the mud on its belly and tore out the sinews of its throat like weeds from a garden. Again when its claws tore into me, I allowed them—let my flesh part and golden-scarlet blood fall. I needed no runes to corral it anymore. The magic sang. The worst of my wounds healed while others bled on and my power swelled once more.

Aita's power was completely leaving my control. I knew that even as I welcomed its healing and lunged back to my feet.

Berin threw the last Revenant off. Small and knotted with vines, it slammed into the blackness of the Unmade and vanished, just as the Revenant in the water had. There was no impact, no ripple or change. Just a cessation of being.

Berin staggered, chest heaving. Then he met my eyes, I clasped his hand, and we ran again.

The next moments were a haze of action and movement. More claws came, more blood fell, and more power moved through me. Berin's injuries healed. Our companions came and went, fighting back the dozens of Revenants that harried us, and their wounds, too, stitched back together.

Finally, I saw the boat. It remained wedged in the reeds, but a dozen figures were in the shallows between us and it. They were not Revenants—at least not all of them. They were Fith warriors, many armed with bows.

The five of us regrouped just out of bowshot, blood-splattered, bleeding and gasping. Around us Revenants screeched and circled, cautious and bloodthirsty—we had a moment of reprieve, no more.

No one had the breath for words, but Thray's gaze was a question and a prompt. Berin nodded, Arune drew a breath and vanished, and Isik looked at me, a hundred warnings in his eyes.

"I'm a fool," he said. "I followed you because I love you, Yske."

I smiled at him, sharp-edged and fragile and heady with the constant flow of magic. "Then I'm a fool, too."

Thray charged our enemies, loosing an Eangen war-cry as she went. Six of the Fith toppled, blood mist bursting around them and falling like snow. The horror of it passed over me, one ineffectual terror in the midst of a thousand.

The rest fled and our way was clear. Berin leapt to a reedy island and dragged the boat close. I tumbled inside. Thray followed, taking the tiller as Berin pushed us off and joined us in a sloshing leap.

I used my staff to shove us out onto the lake, then traded it for an oar and scanned the shoreline for Isik. He and Arune remained covering our retreat, cutting down Revenants and human worshipers on every side. Then a gust of wind and freezing rain swept the two Miri-blooded men away, leaving our remaining enemies to scream and shriek alone on the shore.

When we reached the open lake, I looked back at the tree. The snow around its base was mottled with fallen branches and foxfire light steadily pulsed, transforming into a lattice of golden threads that encased the island.

The trunk of the Binding Tree remained intact, but I sensed a straining, a captive against bonds. And through the water itself, undergirded by roots and lorded over by branches, a presence hummed.

THIRTY-ONE

Halfway across the lake, the glow of the tree was replaced by a lower, richer smolder of fire in the west. It seethed beneath a belly of low cloud and clotted in a fog across the water, thick with bitter smoke and the stink of wood and reed, flesh and oil.

I'd smelled that particular kind of smoke only once before, when a house had burned down with a family and their livestock trapped inside. But this was stronger and thicker, and it was no stretch for my sickened heart to realize what it meant.

The Hask settlements were burning.

We rowed north, hushed and grim. Berin and I didn't speak of Ursk, but I saw the burden on his shoulders, growing heavier and heavier the closer we came to shore.

"He would have run," I finally murmured to him, unable to keep silent any longer. I shivered in my wet clothes, and spent magic ached in my veins. "Fate would not send him this far only to let him die in the fire."

He continued to labor at his oar. "Maybe. This is bigger than any of us now."

At long last, our boat bumped into the lakeshore. Thray and Berin stepped out, hauling the boat further into the mud, and I joined them onshore.

There was a light in Berin's eyes as he gazed toward the nearest burning settlement. I knew that look from watching him spar—a thrill and a haze that flushed his cheeks and turned his squint a little feral. But there was preoccupation too, and calculation.

Thray, I noticed, was also watching him. How strange this must be for her, I thought. To her we were still the children she'd left in Albor, and her last waking memory was of being struck down by Logur seven years ago.

Her thoughts must have followed a similar path, because suddenly she came to us, her expression crumpling. She pulled me into her arms and reached for Berin, tugging him close. Through the press and the rush of emotion I heard Arune arrive with some half-hearted complaint, then yelp as Thray dragged him into the crush.

The embrace was momentary, our words few, but when the four of us disentangled, we remained close together.

Isik hovered, his eyes scanning the miasma around us, but I didn't miss the discomfort in his posture. And, perhaps, the loneliness in his eyes.

I stepped out and snagged his arm, turning him toward me. He opened his mouth to speak—some practical observation I didn't care to hear—but stopped short when I wrapped my arms around his chest and buried my face under his beard.

He held out for a moment, then wrapped his arms around me in return. I felt his breath in my damp hair, felt the tension ease from his muscles, and couldn't bring myself to care that the others saw.

Our journey to the forest was cautious, Arune keeping us concealed in a veil of snow. We heard Hask or Fith several times, screams and shouts and cautions, but they were always in the distance. We passed tracks, wide-spaced and interspersed with drag marks. Signs of flight. A few lifeless bodies. But we saw none living, and no one saw us.

Moments turned to hours. The light of the Binding Tree and burning village receded. The forest surrounded us, layered with white and pulsing with foxfire—not as strong as on the island, but present. The snow muffled all sound and softened our footsteps, shielding them from foxfire-laden roots. But it could not muffle a newer, stranger sound.

Every so often I heard a crack or a creak, and saw a tree shudder. At first, I thought it was the wind and the deepening cold, but as our march stretched long, I realized it was more than that.

"Imilidese is connected to the forest," I murmured to Berin, striding at my side as much as the thick forest allowed. "Whatever happened to the Binding Tree, its effect is spreading."

"The lake is between us," he replied, worry in his eyes. "How is that possible?"

I shrugged. "Its branches reach from shore to shore. Why not its roots?"

My brother touched the back of one hand to his lower lip, split and bleeding—one final wound I hadn't managed to heal before we made our getaway.

I considered healing it now, but the thought passed without rooting.

You will pay the price for your magic, at each turn of the moon. Use it sparingly.

Dread awoke inside me, compounding as I tried and failed to count the injuries I'd healed—not least of which had overflowed into the tree and awoken its light.

I could not say what my price would be. But I knew in a distant, hushed way that when the next moon came, I would be lucky to survive it.

When we could go no further, we rested. Arune disappeared to the wind, and when he returned we clustered in to hear his report, our breaths misting in the cold.

"The Revenants attacked my hold as well. It's surrounded," Arune said without preamble. "But I've already spoken to the elders. We will break through the line and make for the gate. It will open for us."

He spoke so casually, I was ashamed at my hesitation. "But then we'll be trapped inside."

Arune snorted. "Trapped within safe walls with food, shelter and the rest of your companions. This storm is only going to worsen, and neither I nor Isik can stop that."

Isik nodded grudgingly. He stood close to me, and his nearness softened the edges of my anxiety.

Berin nodded. "Shelter, rest, and fight another day."

"We'll have to run for it," Thray warned, the head of her spear glistening sharp, her eyelashes speckled with snow. "Are we ready?"

When no one protested, she gave us a bracing smile. "Then let's move."

My world became one of simple images, shallow feelings. Snow, ceasing to melt on my cold skin. My knife, warm in my hand. The forest parting and shapes appearing—Revenants watching, startling, moving, converging.

We ran. The hold came into sight, heralded by abandoned outbuildings, churned snow, and buried paths. Enemies gave chase. Some were cut down, others fell behind. Arrows flew through the air and blood mist burst at Thray's command.

Then the stockade wall rose above us and its doors cracked open. Berin slid through, I sprinted after him and Thray came last, the other two immaterial.

The gates slammed closed behind us. I dropped my knife and doubled over, breathing raggedly, muscles trembling and vision sparking red. I heard Aruth voices on all sides, saw blurs of archers on the walls and people rushing to welcome Arune and Thray with shouts of joy and shock and hope.

Then, through my sweat-blurred vision, I saw Seera. She shouldered through the crowd with Esan in her wake. Askir and the others came from another direction, fighting their way through the massing Aruth.

Seera threw herself at Berin, tears streaming down her face. He enfolded her in his arms and hefted her off the ground, laughing and crushing her until she squawked. Esan came next, the two men barreling one another into laughing, back-thumping embraces and a brush of foreheads, tears in Esan's eyes.

Seera turned to me and pressed her lips together for a moment, as if preparing what to say. I didn't give her time to decide. I threw my arms around her neck, nearly losing my footing. She laughed and hugged me in return.

"Welcome back, cousins," she said, parting from me and looking at Berin, eyes glossy with tears and gratitude. "Welcome back."

THIRTY-TWO

The atmosphere in Arune's hall was a tumultuous mix of celebration and tension, hope and anxiety. Half the village was crammed between the walls, everyone from bent elders to fussing babies. Food was distributed by children while clan leaders and warriors clustered around Arune, Thray, Berin, Seera, and Askir. The rest of our companions were outside, taking their turn at watch. Isik and I sat near the council, Nui draped heavily across my lap as I dug my fingers into her fur and tried to forget the horde of Revenants in the forest. It was easier when the Aruth chattered in their own language, less so when Thray or Arune translated their words.

"We cannot hold out forever," Thray related the words of Aruth's spokesman. The Winterborn woman was clothed in a fresh kaftan now, her broad, muscular shoulders accentuated by a fur-trimmed cloak and a waist cinched by two weapons belts—one with an axe ring and hooded short axe, and the other with the bone-handled knife that had once belonged to Frir, her aunt and Goddess of Death. "We—the Aruth—are discussing fleeing into the ravines."

"That's a long run," Arune muttered in the Divine Tongue, looking around the hall through his white lashes. His gaze lingered on the children and elders. "Too long for some."

The Aruth spoke again, falling into rapid conversation I couldn't understand and Thray ceased to translate.

Isik reached to scratch Nui's ears, and she obligingly flopped her massive head into his lap. He smiled fondly, his expression too soft, too gentle for this room and its talk of war. I enjoyed the expression, watching him until it occurred to me to wonder how he would look if I placed a child—our child—in his arms.

I slammed the door on that and forced my eyes back to the assembly.

"We must send word to Omaskat and the High Priesthood," Thray said. She sat back, surveying the rafters. "Where's Mawny?"

Arune turned to one of the Aruth leaders. "Where's my owl?" he asked in the Divine Tongue.

The Aruth replied in their own language and pointed to Askir.

"It's gone," Askir said, looking satisfied with himself. "I sent it to Eangen as soon as Berin and Yske disappeared."

Arune made a discontented sound, but I felt only relief. News that our expedition had gone awry was already on its way to my mother. She wouldn't know of Logur or Imilidese, but a warning had been sounded. When the owl returned, hopefully it would be with some measure of counsel, and we could send the whole terrible truth back to Eangen.

A wave of fatigue beset me. I felt the scars on my hand, knotted and smoothed, and looked down at them.

There would be many more wounds to heal in the coming days, and not all of them could be treated by salves and stitches. With each one, I would pile more pain upon my own head.

"When is the full moon?" I asked Isik quietly.

His brows furrowed in passing curiosity. "Soon. Within a few days. Why?"

I shrugged. "I've just lost track of the days."

He accepted that, taking Nui's face between his hands and muttering nonsense while her tail thumped. But my mind churned. Days. That was too soon. Perhaps I should bring someone into my confidence, someone who could help me if, when the full moon rose, I was in too much pain to make my sacrifice to Aita without help.

"Isik," Arune's voice called, dragging us both back into the conversation. "When will you leave for the west?"

Isik stilled then, giving Nui's ears one last scratch, and got to his feet. When he spoke, it was in the rolling, distant-thunder timbre of his Divine Tongue. "Soon. If we've any luck, the Eangen and Algatt will already have organized some response to the owl. But they have no idea how grave things have become."

Thray glanced at Arune, reluctance in her eyes. "You can move more quickly than him," she pointed out. "What if you went instead?"

"I've no desire to go," her half-brother replied smoothly. "And I've a responsibility to my people."

The Aruth murmured their agreement at that.

Arune went on, "It may be that Yske's power healed the rift, or the tree, or both. Maybe in the next few hours, the binding will shatter. Maybe it will grow stronger. Maybe nothing will change. But Logur's forces will not stop assaulting us here. He's out for blood." At this, his eyes sought out Isik and me, and my heart twisted as he included Berin in the glance. "He will do everything in his power to open that rift, however small the chance of success."

"Bindings on a being this powerful do not unravel quickly under the best of circumstances," Thray interjected thoughtfully. Her tone was plain and sure—speaking from the knowledge she'd gained during her years as a priestess, before her exile. "During the Upheaval, the Omaskat began the process of waking Thvynder years before the Vestige was born and the god awoke."

"Does Imilidese have a Vestige?" Askir asked. Vestiges, like my cousin Vistic, were pieces of a god—or Miri—which could be bonded with a human and used to pull their creator back from death or out of a binding.

When no one else replied, I shook my head and spoke. "Imilidese's goal was to remake creation. I doubt she had the inclination or chance to bind herself to it."

"My blood is the most dangerous in this company," Isik pointed out. There was no arrogance in his voice, only regret. He looked at me and switched back to Eangen. "I have to go. Though I hate to leave you."

I felt a flush creep across my cheeks. He had spoken loud enough for everyone to hear, even if only the Winterborn, Berin, and our companions could understand.

"I'm here," Thray said, whatever she thought of Isik's and my relationship obscure. She added without falter, "She'll come to no harm."

Berin glanced at her quizzically, then swept his gaze to Isik and me. I saw the moment his inevitable suspicion solidified into understanding. Wariness sparked in his eyes, but I saw no accusation or surge of proprietary instinct.

I offered him a small smile and a look that I hoped communicated, *I'll explain later.*

"Of course," Isik replied to Thray, nodding grudgingly. "I'll leave tonight."

I washed shaking hands in a bowl of steaming water out the back of the hall as night closed in. Archers patrolled the walls and Nui, who'd refused to leave my side since I arrived, sat nearby.

"Yske."

Isik stood nearby. He carried a small satchel and bedroll—even as the wind, it would take him days to reach home—along with an Aruth bow. Snow caught on the fur collar of his cloak as he looked down at me, his expression open and melancholic.

I finished washing and shook droplets of water from my fingers. I'd been thinking of him and I and this moment since the council, and when I spoke my words were calm. "Did you mean what you said back in the forest? About the lure of worship?"

Isik searched my face. His already thin façade weakened and his lips twisted unhappily beneath his freshly trimmed beard. "I always mean what I say."

"Isik. Everyone faces temptations, whether they're human or Miri. Those temptations don't define you. What you do in response to them does."

He held very still. I saw his eyes flick to my lips, but his focus remained on my words. "Why are you saying this?"

"Because we agreed we're fools," I said simply. "But we're not children anymore, Isik. And I've seen enough of the world, and myself, and you, to realize what I want from my days. And that you and I are not too different to be together, if we do so with awareness, and patience."

He was closer now, his head bowed, his fingers ghosting across my hips. "What do you want?"

I took hold of his forearm, and I wasn't sure if the tremble I felt came from him or me. Perhaps it was both of us. "To go home and live a quiet life. To heal and care for those I love. To have them close. And to have you with me."

His one hand lifted to clasp my arm in return, the other resting on the curve of my waist. His touch was familiar, full of youthful memories, but his hands were more calloused now, heavier and more intentional.

"We have our differences. I have my battles and so do you," I told him, wondering if he could hear the hammering of my heart. "But if you choose me instead of them, I'll be here."

"You'll die," he said, his voice rough with want.

I gave a short, soft laugh. "Swords and spears could kill either of us tomorrow. Imilidese could Unmake the world. And just because I'll age and die doesn't mean my death is the end."

He pulled back slightly, his grip tightening. "Are you saying… you'd linger in the High Halls?"

I resisted the urge to smile and pushed past the weight of his question. "As long as I could. There's much I can do for the world, in body and in spirit."

There was hope in him, then. "Yske… I—"

Nui barked, startling the both of us. We turned as she bolted after a small, long-tailed shadow and vanished off into the village.

I became aware of the night again, the cold and the snow-capped rooftops all around. I heard the voices of the Aruth, continuing daily life even when they were besieged by monsters.

"It may be months before I return with help," Isik said quietly. I suspected that wasn't what he'd intended to say. "You may have to flee into the ravines with the Aruth."

I nodded, but I couldn't think about myself just then. My thoughts were still full of him, us, and the glimmer of hope that we had kindled. It was a frail thing, crowded on all sides by challenges and fears.

"What were you going to say?" I pressed.

He raised an eyebrow. "What do you mean?"

I just stared at him, pinning him with my gaze.

"It's nothing, Yske," he placated, taking my shoulders in his hands.

A new thought surfaced in the back of my mind, like a whale from a darkened sea.

"Isik…" I began, slowly translating my thoughts. "The Binding Tree may be the only reason the eastern High Halls are inaccessible. I saw lights there, like the foxfire. If the rift reopens and the power of the binding returns to the Halls… the Halls may heal. They may become traversable again."

"If that's so…"

I nodded, encouraging his train of thought. "You could bring aid back through the High Halls. My parents. *Your* parents. The Watchman. The Vestige. The armies of the Eangen and the Algatt. Even the Duamel and the Arpa."

"That is a great deal to hope for," Isik cautioned, but his eyes were brighter. "Help could be here in a day. Even hours."

I nodded quickly. "But the timing would be difficult. If the rift does open, Imilidese will begin to break free."

"Vistic and Omaskat will know more," Isik decided. I felt him shift, easing his weight back as he began to step back. His fingers slipped away. "I'll send you an owl as soon as I reach them."

A second breath of silence passed, both of us skimming across the surface of what we wanted to say.

Leaning up, I cupped the side of his face with my free hand, feeling the warmth of his skin and the snow melting in the roughness of his beard, and I kissed him. The scent of him surrounded me—woodsmoke and sweat, damp wool and storms, the oil in his beard and the brush of warm breath.

He held still for a moment, then bent in, slow and deliberate. He kissed me back until, eventually, the gentle brush and part of our lips began to slow—thoughts and worries seeping back through the haze of warmth and want.

I pulled back, but his teeth nipped at my bottom lip, and I laughed in surprise. He laughed too, still close, hushed and relieved.

"We will find a way through this," I repeated to him. I held his eyes, and his smile was so honest and my heart so full that I ached. But he held something back, a truth unspoken.

I wouldn't press him. My mind had already begun to slip back to the island, and the tree, and the image of myself with my hands upon the stones of the fallen doorway. Healing. Opening. Breaking.

We will find a way.

Or I will make one.

Winter settled over the forests of the east. The nights became vengefully cold and the snow ceased to melt, even under the unrepentant sun. Other days, woodsmoke trailed into a snow-cloud sky. Livestock was packed into hutches attached to the Aruth's houses, or in some cases, brought right in to share the hearths of the forest people. Each morning was a chorus of animals, sleepy calling voices, and the crack of ice in barrels and troughs but all birdsong faded from the woods, leaving only the raucous rattle of ravens on the bodies of the dead.

There were many, many dead. I watched from the town wall as the black birds swarmed frozen corpses between us and the forest. Some were Revenants, slim pickings for the hungry birds, but others were human—Logur's living devotees, who now stalked the forests with short bows and quick, deadly arrows.

"They'll attack today," Berin said from beside me, cloak wrapped around his upper body and cheeks reddened with cold. He looked tired but hale, his eyes keen and his brows furrowed.

"How do you know?" I asked, watching a raven alight on a horizontal arrow, stuck in the head of a dead attacker. We were far enough away that I couldn't see the gruesome details of the corpse, but it was still obvious when the raven began to peck not at the body, but its own feathers. It plucked them out, one by one, twitching at the pain and heedless of the blood.

"That," my brother returned, prying his eyes from the raven. "Like the doe you saw. Another omen?"

I couldn't deny that, but affirming it felt too dangerous.

Below, wind caught at black feathers, scudding them across the white of the snow.

"And there's the stillness," Berin added. "It feels like the forest is holding its breath."

Behind him, down the wall, I glimpsed a few Aruth warriors clustered around a steaming pot. The pot was held by a pretty young woman with a baby strapped to her back. The infant slept, its cheek heavy on its mother's shoulder and tiny bowed lips squished to one side. One of the warriors leaned in to kiss the woman and gently brush the baby's cheek with the back of one finger. The child did not stir.

I missed Isik. The kiss I'd given him before his departure had been more than a meeting of lips—it was an admission, an acceptance of something that we'd denied for many long years.

Berin's expression twitched and his lips parted to speak, but it took him a while to get the words out. "I've been thinking of Isa."

I watched the little family and pondered the empty ache in my heart. "I'm sure they are both well. The women of Albor survived without me for centuries."

"That's not what you said before we left."

"I think too highly of myself," I admitted, slipping closer and leaning against his arm. "Apparently we're both known for that."

He grunted. "I suppose I shouldn't be surprised you've taken up with a Miri, then?"

"You might not realize it, Berin, but between your sunny disposition and our infamous parents, not many human men have approached me."

"So you're scraping the bottom of the barrel with the son of dethroned gods?"

"I have to take what I can get."

"What about Esan?" Berin gave a considering frown. "I know he tried to kiss you once."

I peered up at him, startled. "You knew about that?"

Berin pointed out one of the white scars on his knuckles. "Of course I did."

I tried to stifle a laugh and failed. "I wondered why he never tried again. I didn't stop him, you know."

Berin grinned nostalgically and looked out over the forest. "I wouldn't mind if you married him now."

"Isik and I have been friends since Father first brought me to Aita, and we were together, once we grew older. He's always been kind to me, and gentle."

It had begun to snow again—sparse, small flakes fluttering out of the gray sky above.

"He's a Miri," my twin repeated. "But considering the world might end before spring, perhaps it doesn't matter."

I smiled, a little sadly, and wrapped both my arms around his one, fully burrowing into his side as if we were children listening to our father sing stories.

"Happiness is worth having," I told him. "Even if it's brief."

"Some might call you short-sighted," Berin pointed out.

I snorted softly. "Says the man who gave a boar a bucket of ale and tried to saddle it."

I felt the rumble of his laughter, but when he spoke again, his voice was raw with honesty. "Love is difficult, Yske. If you choose to be with Isik, you are guaranteeing yourself pain."

"Every path in life has pain. I don't want to spend my days hiding from it," I murmured. "Or mourning a future that might not come."

The truth of the words sank into me as I said them, half-formed thoughts and emotion coalescing into truth.

I heard a soft laugh from behind us and turned to see Thray stepping up onto the wall, her hair bound in two thick, long braids. The last handspans of her braids were encased in delicately embossed leather in the style of the Aruth, and it suited her well.

"I spend seven years in the ice," she commented, "and awake to find my little cousin fifty years wiser than me."

I smiled, preening a little. "You were betrothed before your exile? I remember you speaking about a man."

She looked up at the sky as a cool breeze brushed past, perhaps searching for Arune. "I was. But I made my choices, and walked the path I chose to walk. It was not with him."

"Do you regret it?" I asked. I knew the question might cause her pain, but I needed to know.

The Winterborn smiled, crooked and a little sad. "I don't know. I'm not as wise as you yet," she quipped, still watching the sky. "Arune is coming."

I touched my Sight and followed her gaze. There was silver on the wind, shifting and turning as it surveyed the world below. Then it swept down to the wall and coalesced into a human shape.

I blinked away my Sight. It was not Arune who stood on the wall before us but someone else entirely. Tall and broad-shouldered, with white hair shaved here and there to reveal intricate tattoos in a looping, unfamiliar style. The rest of his thick white hair hung in a braid down his back, twined with simple leather strands, and his kaftan was a deep, rich blue. Legwraps cinched loose trousers at the knee and a sword hung at his belt, along with a pair of long, slightly curved knives.

Thray went pale and her hand dropped to her own knife. Berin immediately stepped in front of me and drew his sword as, all along the wall, Aruth archers noticed the confrontation and nocked arrows.

"Thray," the newcomer said, his voice low and rumbling like the first tremors of an avalanche.

"Kygga," she breathed.

Thirty-Three

The newcomer's smile was thin and self-assured. Thray had betrayed her siblings, and though nearly a decade had passed since that day, it seemed the remembrance had not faded.

Thray's fingers closed around her knife, but she didn't draw it. Berin stepped up beside her, shoulder to shoulder, while I held back and pulled my own knife. I wasn't sure what I could do against a Winterborn attack, but one nick of my thumb and I'd have the power to prevent Thray from returning to a tomb of ice.

"Where is Arune?" Kygga asked, impassive to the Aruth's waiting arrows and Thray's and Berin's naked weapons. "Esach's son said he was with you."

My friend had found help already? I pressed up onto my toes to see over Thray and Berin, snow melting beneath my hand as I steadied myself on the top of the wall. "You've seen Isik? Where?"

The man spared me a short, impatient glance. "We met him on the wind two days ago. The priests of Fate sent us."

"Us?" Thray breathed.

The wind picked up, cool and sharp and clear. With it came swirls and currents of silver, and where each settled, a Winterborn Windwalker took shape. They stepped into sight with fluid grace, alighting on the ramparts to all sides. They sauntered among the trees, eyeing corpses and shadows. They materialized on the pathways of the village, startling watching Aruth and facing down stumbling warriors. A belated warning horn blasted.

There were dozens of them. Scores. I turned and found one just behind me, a woman with a hundred fine braids in her white hair and skin the color of sun-bleached bone. She was slight and willowy, her cheekbones soft and her eyes large, almost childish. But she bore a long-headed spear in one hand.

She smiled at me, an ice-shard grin with bright, cheerful eyes.

"Daughter of Hessa," she said. "Don't be afraid. We're here to kill, but not you."

Arune materialized on the edge of the rampart. "Kygga! Effa. What—" He wavered slightly, too close to the edge of the ramparts in his haste.

Kygga grabbed him by the collar and hauled him further in. He didn't release him immediately but held him close, scrutinizing the smaller man.

Arune grinned into his brother's face. "Hello," he said, unfazed.

Kygga gave a huffing sigh and released Arune. Arune stepped back, brushing at his clothes and surveying all the Winterborn with a playful grin.

"Siblings!" Arune greeted, opening his hands graciously. "Welcome to our humble home. Are you here to punish Thray for destroying our lives, or would you rather help us kill a riverman who wants to unleash a very vengeful god and destroy the world?"

Kygga was squinting at Thray, waging some silent war of wills with her, but he spoke to Arune. "We're here to save you."

Arune made as if he might decide to be offended, then shrugged. "All right."

"And bring you news," the woman behind me added. Effa, Arune had called her.

"Let's us go to the hall to hear it," Thray said. I heard a guardedness to her voice that made the skin on the back of my neck prickle. She matched gazes with Kygga. "Then we can speak of war."

The Winterborn settled in, arranging themselves in circles out from the main central hearth. There was a familiarity to the way they moved, as if this had been done a hundred times in a hundred similar spaces.

Thray, Arune, Kygga, and Effa stood in the center, beside the blazing hearth. I lingered behind the outer ring with Berin and our companions and a scattering of important Aruth. No Winterborn invited us closer and I felt more than a few cool glances sweep our way. We were Eangen, Algatt, and Soulderni, after all—representatives of the people who'd slain their immortal siblings and defeated them ten years ago. Because of our people, their power over the land of Duamel had shattered and they had been forced to disperse.

"Beyond the ice fields, at the very edge of the north, we found shadows in the Unmade," Effa explained, her voiced raised to fill the hall. Speaking in the Divine Tongue as she did, every ear could understand her. "I was one of those sent. But we were not the first to arrive. At the border of the Unmade we met Dreamer Priests. They serve Eirine—called Fate, the Second Pillar of the World and sister to Thvynder."

I considered mentioning Ursk—the thought of the man accompanied by a pang of uncertainty and regret—but Effa's tone was one that didn't brook interruption.

"They gave us a vision," Effa continued. "One of a great dead tree, cracking and turning to ash. A glimpse of the end of the age."

Silence followed her words, then one of the Aruth hissed something in their own language. That opened a floodgate, and whispers and muffled exclamations traversed the hall.

"I saw the tree too," Thray said. She was straight-backed, her outer clothing shed and arms crossed over her chest, the muscles of her shoulders standing out against her tunic. "In a vision from Fate."

"We are all pieces on a board." Arune toed the end of a singed log deeper into the fire pit. He added to Thray, "We should have gone south. Wastelands of endless sand, I said. Big unnatural tree, you insisted."

A passing smile tugged at the corner of her lips, despite the gravity of the conversation. I eyed Arune, noting the change in him now that more of his siblings were here. He was lighter, more childish—but also more guarded. The Winterborn might all have the same father, but they clearly didn't trust one another.

"The tree holds Imilidese," Thray said. "She was bound by rivermen and woodmaidens through the power of a rift into the eastern High Halls. That rift was closed when the tree was made, but there are those intent on reopening it—the same forces that now surround this village. Imilidese intends to unmake and reforge the world, and her servants will do everything they can to set her free."

The simplicity of the statements did not detract from their weight. Even Kygga's expression hollowed as he surveyed his traitorous half-sister.

"Then we stop her," Effa said.

Murmurs and nods rippled around the hall, though many were still too shocked to respond. I saw heads lean together, spines straighten, eyes widen or narrow.

"We stop her," Kygga agreed. The central fire popped, and sparks illuminated his handsome face. "Our remaining siblings are gathering at the White Lake, as are the Eangen, Soulderni, Duamel, and Algatt."

Relief coursed through me.

"The earliest they could arrive is spring," Askir pointed out, speaking from his position near me. "We might all be dead by then. Those of us who can die, that is."

Impulsively, I stepped up to the edge of the hall's highest tier, moving in front of my companions. "I was at the council in the High Halls where Estavius spoke to the Miri about movement in the Unmade."

"And?" Kygga prompted, eyes fixing on me.

Another might have retreated or been cowed by his regard, but I'd grown up under the watchful eyes of Aita, Gadr, and Esach. "The Arpa knew something was amiss in the East long before we did, and I doubt Estavius has sat by since then. So where is the Empire?"

"Your Vestige of Thvynder said they set out north some time ago," Kygga replied, his disdain for the Vestige clear. The Eangen, Algatt, and Soulderni had fought the Winterborn, but it was Vistic's sword that had slain them. "If you haven't seen them yet, their journey likely failed."

"If the Arpa come, they come." Effa waved the topic aside. "Here are things as they stand. We are alone here, facing the threat of a riverman with an army of human worshipers and constructs. All the local tribes have been pulled into the conflict. The woodmaiden, Feen, could be an ally, but her people are overrun. And she told you most of her power was gone?"

I nodded.

Effa accepted this and went on. "As Kygga says, the western peoples and our Winterborn siblings gather at the White Lake. Isik, Son of Esach, has gone to them. But it will take months for them to reach us. Can we hold until then?"

"They could move faster," I spoke up again, drawing all eyes to me. "If the rift to the High Halls was opened."

Effa's pale blue eyes were glossed with amber in the firelight. "What do you mean?"

"When I healed Thray, my power overflowed into the Binding Tree," I explained. "I believe I began to heal the rift, accidentally. Imilidese's power immediately began to spread—did you see the foxfire, in the forest?"

"It's spread everywhere," Kygga replied. "We first saw it on the shores of the Headwaters."

"It did get brighter, though," a Windwalker who'd yet to be introduced added, a man with a braided white beard and a shaved head. "The further we came east."

"It even glows in the daylight," another put in, and agreement circulated the hall.

"I believe," I said, raising my voice again, "that if I heal the rift fully, the High Halls will open and our armies can come through."

"What good will that do?" Kygga cut in. "Imilidese will be free and the world will end."

"She may be free soon, regardless." This was Thray, her voice calm and steady. "I believe the dam has already been breached, and we have no idea when it will shatter. If Yske heals the rift herself, we take what little control we have and use it to our advantage."

"To do what?" Kygga asked his half-sister. "Fight a Pillar of Creation as the world ends in ash and fire?"

"Yes." Berin's voice filled the hall, deep and low and full of portent. "That's exactly what we'll do."

Shouts and protests broke out. I took a step back, letting others take my place. I'd said my part, and I found that my hands were shaking. I needed a moment to calm my nerves.

As I retreated against the wall, a glimmer of light caught my eye. I looked to the shadows where the wall met the floor and saw something glisten, low and gentle, like the last light fading from a burning coal.

I crouched, looking closer. A rune glowed at me from the wood, lines of foxfire forming each branch and curve of the symbol.

My breath lodged in my throat. I pulled my knife and scraped the rune away, but the little pile of wood shavings continued to pulse with unnatural light. A whisper came with it, the distant sound of a woman's voice, growing louder. Imilidese.

Heal me.

My blood ran cold. I began to prowl the circumference of the hall, ducking around agitated Aruth and Winterborn. I spied more lights here and there, the edges of runes taking shape, all low and close to the ground—as if they crept up from it.

Urgency drove me out of the hall. There were no Aruth in the darkened streets, though I saw guards on the walls. Everyone was either packed into the hall for the council, guarding the ramparts or hiding in their homes.

More runes glowed around the bases of houses, posts, doorframes and troughs—anything and everything made of wood. The closer to the edge of the settlement I came, the brighter they grew. At the ring wall, I saw glowing runes not just at the base of the bark-stripped logs but seeping up to the height of my hip.

I climbed one of the steep ladder-like stairs to the ramparts. A fresh layer of snow separated my boots from the wood, but when my feet touched the freshly cleared top of the wall, the foxfire flared in... recognition?

Heal me. The voice came louder, and I began to pick my way cautiously along a narrow ridge of snow. The foxfire dimmed, and the voice faded.

I found the Aruth archers on watch already clustered together, staring out at the trees and murmuring, wrapped in shadow and misted breath. Foxfire flared around their feet, but their eyes were on something far more unsettling.

Beyond the ring of empty fields and paddocks, the trees glowed bright enough to cast the corpse-strewn fields into unnatural twilight. Even as I watched, more foxfire runes appeared on their branches, gleaming beneath a thin layer of clinging snow.

In the gloaming, forms moved. Shambling, silent forms. Smooth, creeping forms.

I snatched the horn from my belt and blew a long, sonorous call. An Aruth horn picked up the cry, then another and another until the night reverberated with warning.

The first volley of arrows slammed into our attackers before the last horn faded. Down the wall, Aruth watchers dropped to their knees, return arrows whisking overhead. Shouts broke out in the village, but only one or two screams—children's, high and wailing. I darted back to the ladder and was down in a heartbeat, sprinting back through the village toward the hall.

Ittrid and Askir met me halfway.

"An attack?" the Soulderni woman asked.

"More than an attack." I pointed to the runes, though I could see from Askir's face that he'd already noticed them. "This is Imilidese. She's listening. She's here."

"What can she do?" Ittrid asked, looking at Askir.

As if in answer, we heard a crack. The three of us spun to look at the wall as more figures joined us in the dark—Berin, Esan, Sedi, Seera, and Bara. We clustered as Aruth swarmed and Winterborn flowed out of the hall, some immediately transitioning to wind and vanishing into the darkness.

In the light of an Aruth torch, dust began to fall from the palisade wall. It was subtle at first, but then I heard a more cracks, groans, and creaks. A visible divide appeared, not between segments of the wall but in the logs themselves. The wood was corroding, rotting as the runes blazed bright.

Thray appeared at our side, her bone-handled knife now a long, slim bone spear. "It's affecting all the wood in the settlement."

More cracks filled the air, rapid punches of sound, and a section of the wall crumpled at the end of the street. I saw right into the forest and the mass of oncoming figures.

"Flee!" Arune's voice roared through the encampment to his Aruth. "Make for the ravines!"

Screams came then, panicked shouts interspersed by wailing babies, bleating goats, and barking dogs. Aruth tore out of their homes with satchels on their shoulders and children in their arms, some of the buildings already crumbling around them.

"Go with them, guard their retreat," Thray said to us. "We'll be right behind you."

The next moments were a blur. I found Nui in the chaos and ducked back into the hall, seizing my pack as the dog paced and whined. Berin met me at the door and we joined the chaos of fleeing Aruth. Someone shoved a toddler at me and I took them without question, clutching the sobbing child to my chest as I ran. Faces flashed in torchlight—elders and Aruth warriors shouting encouragement, Winterborn coming and going in snatches of wind. Berin ran behind me, his sword and a commandeered square shield in hand.

We ducked through the western gate in a haze of rot and dust. Winterborn swarmed the forest ahead of us, hacking a path through a swath of enemies. I jumped over a gutted woman, not knowing if she was friend or foe. The child in my arms clung with an iron grip, nearly strangling me. The child's father sprinted beside me, shouting encouragements and pleading in Aruth with an older child in his own arms.

A Revenant slunk from the shadows, moving so calmly and smoothly I almost didn't react. But Nui did. She tore the throat from the creature and bowled it over, scrambling back as its claws spasmed after her.

"Yske!" a frantic voice shouted from just behind us. Bara, his voice cracking and panicked. "Yske, he can't move!"

I slowed, looking from the child in my arms to their father, just behind me. The man reached for the toddler, already overburdened, but Berin shook his head and grabbed another fleeing Aruth. He pried tiny hands from my face and hair with a gentleness at odds with the situation and placed the child into the stranger's arms. The child sobbed, and the Aruth ran on together.

Berin and I doubled back to find Bara kneeling beside Esan. The man's thigh was slashed, blood sluicing into the snow, black and glistening in the light of foxfire and sporadic, flickering torches. Seera stood with her back to us, an Aruth shield raised and an axe tucked behind it, her eyes on the forest.

I didn't hesitate. I slit the ends of two fingers, seized a billow of power, and thrust it into Esan's leg with a spoken rune. The wound knitted and Esan scrambled upright.

We moved off again as a unit, though I noted Ittrid and Askir were missing. The Aruth were thinning, and a new light bloomed through the trees. The hold was burning behind us.

"Ittrid!" I shouted into the night. A few figures darted past, an old woman dragging a round-faced girl who in turn led a goat on a string. An Aruth warrior loped alongside them, arrow nocked and head low. A Winterborn stabbed a spear down into a flailing enemy, then vanished into the wind.

Hush descended. My gaze dragged to foxfire in the trees above us, so bright now that I could see the blood clotting Seera's eyelashes and the marks of claws on Berin's shield.

In the tree, a weasel watched me with empty, fixed eyes. There was a calmness about it, eerie and placid—the same calm that had radiated from the doe I'd seen devour the rabbit on our journey, and from the wall of black in the east. From the Unmade.

But there was a permanence to this peace. The weasel sat slumped in the crook between branch and tree, its limbs overgrown with moss and scales of white mushrooms pouring out of its lockjawed maw.

I made to grab Berin's arm, but he was turning away, bellowing for Askir.

"Here!" Ittrid's voice echoed back, curt and distracted. She came into sight with Askir at her shoulder, the pair of them followed by a cluster of terrified Aruth and two more Winterborn. And, to my shock, Ursk.

I glanced back at the weasel. Unmoving. Dead. Bara followed my gaze and grimaced, but a dead animal was a lesser concern than burning holds and closing enemies.

"Greetings," the Priest of Fate panted as they caught up. He gave a short thud of a laugh as Berin clapped him on the shoulder, but he looked haggard. His clothing was stained with soot and he smelled strongly of smoke.

"You escaped!" Berin said. "Ursk, I'm so sorry."

"You had to go, and I knew you'd make for the canyons." He spoke without a hint of offense and glanced toward the burning hold. "I saw this too... but I am too late."

"Clearly. We need to go," Seera urged. Between us and the burning village, more Revenants reorganized themselves into a twitching mass.

I met Berin's eyes, half convinced the weasel had never been, a product of panic and strain. And what did it matter when we were fleeing, hunted?

But Ursk had returned—our company was whole once more, and our next step clear.

"To the ravines," Berin said.

THIRTY-FOUR

Voices reverberated through stone tunnels and melded with the bleat of animals, the crying of children, and the thump of packs dropped from aching shoulders. Fires began to spring up, one by one, and the darkness fled to reveal a small system of natural caves. Outside, where the eastern edge of the canyons cut into the forest in jagged slices, steadily falling snow muffled the morning light—and guarded our footsteps from watching, pulsing foxfire.

"The snow and rock should hide us from Imilidese," I murmured to Berin. I'd joined him beside the cave's large, triangular mouth, watching Aruth families shepherd one another into safety beneath woodmaidens' runes.

Though I was long past the edge of fatigue and shivering under my Hask cloak, I couldn't help marking the myriad wounded hobbling past us. I assessed them with tired eyes. I would need to begin my work soon.

"She'll know the direction we fled in, but…" I rubbed at my eyes with the back of one hand. "We've bought some time."

"Hopefully it's enough." Berin nudged me toward the cave mouth. "Yske, rest. You look spent."

I was too tired to comment on his own disheveled appearance, and simply joined the flow of Aruth. Firelight illuminated their drawn, haggard faces and cast a motif of shadows on the gray walls—the wounded leaning on one another, a father with no fewer than three children in his arms, an old man and woman holding one another. A young woman standing unmoving, staring down at her round, pregnant belly.

A head shoved under my arm and I looked down into Nui's earnest eyes. The strain and worry of the night ebbed at the sight of her, and I crouched to wrap my arms around her damp bulk. She endured the gesture patiently for a time, then began to chew industriously on my hood.

I dropped my pack and set out a wooden bowl for her, filling it from a flask. The dog immediately drank, the steady wag of her tail and the slosh of water consoling in the midst of so much upheaval.

I did rest, for sparse moments. Then I eased my aching body upright, picked my way to the neighboring hearth, and healed. I bled. I soothed, though the Aruth and I could not understand one another. I touched tear-streaked cheeks and gaping, bloody wounds. I assisted Aruth healers, anyone with any knowledge of medicine scrambling to do what they could. All the while Nui followed, lying at my feet or allowing red-eyed children to pet her.

The hound and the children's happy chatter were only temporary reliefs from the pain and uncertainty all around. At some point, as I traversed a darkened corridor between two caves, my head spun. I put a hand on the wall and closed my eyes, focusing on the cool damp of the stone. The clatter of voices and muffled sobs battered me, overwhelming until I picked out a grandmother's distant, lilting lullaby. I didn't know the words, but her tone and emotion were universal—consolation, rest, and comfort.

I sank into a crouch with my back against the wall and Nui nuzzled close. She was so large that her head loomed over me, and it made me feel like a child again. But I did not mind. Being a child, cared for and held and with only a dim understanding of the odds stacked against us seemed an enviable thing.

Berin found me sometime later, still scratching Nui's ears. The distant lullaby had faded but a spattering of new melodies drifted from various caves and hearths. The Aruth were settled in, the panic of the night abating.

"You need to sleep." My brother crouched, surveying me. His eyes found my hands, marked with small cuts and new scars. "And stop doing that."

He didn't know just how right he was. I considered telling him the truth. The full moon was days away, and I wouldn't be able to hide my payment in such close quarters.

But I was too tired to admit that now.

"I also need to eat and drink and go home to my mountain," I added with forced good humor. I pulled down my sleeves to cover my hands and stood up, bracing myself on the wall. When I found I couldn't push myself off the stone, my bravado faded. "Do you happen to have a bedroll?"

Berin steadied me, concern written across his face. "No, but you're welcome to my cloak."

"Then find me a fire, feed me and let me sleep," I requested, slipping my arm through his.

I did sleep soon after, drifting off as my companions murmured around me—Berin's deep rumble interjected with Seera's sharp words, Askir's corrections and Ittrid's observations. Nui curled at my back and one by one, my worries faded—yielding to a haze of warmth and the soothing presence of my own language.

When I jolted back awake, their voices were gone. The caves were full of the sound of crackling fires, the drip of water, the shift of animals, snores, and the occasional hushed conversation.

I held still, wondering what had awoken me. My immediate fear was that the moon was already full and the time for payment had come, but though my body ached there were no newer, sharper pains.

An owl fluttered through the air with a muted ripple of wings. It was small and gray, with black tufts around its beak and wide, searching eyes.

He alighted on my pack, next to me, and hooted softly. His eyes were full moons, harbingers of my impending fate.

I slowly sat up and released my breath in a long, steady exhale. "I'm listening."

The cave faded, the details obscuring and sounds retreating. My mother coalesced before me in smoke and shadow and plays of light. She wore her legendary axes in a brace upon her back, their heads framing her face with hooded blades angled out. Her gray-streaked hair was fastened into a single tight braid over one shoulder, its end bound with beaded leather. She wore a padded tunic, overlaid with a mail vest and multiple weapons belts, hung with knife and hatchets and pouch. Her Eangen-dark eyes, so like Berin's, were smudged with black paint.

"The High Halls east of the Headwaters have begun to open," Hessa said without preamble. Her lack of a greeting prodded a lonely place in my heart, but I couldn't truly be hurt by it. The connection the owl brought would not last long. There was no time. "Isik says you can open the Eastern Rift."

"I can." Despite my resolve, I discovered my voice was thick with emotion. Isik had reached the White Lake. He was safe, and with my mother. "Though I can't guarantee it will work."

"Vistic and Omaskat believe it will," my mother said. "But can you get to it?"

"Yes," I said with certainty. *If all else fails,* I thought, *Logur would gladly take me back to the island.*

"Timing will be key," my mother reminded me. "And it must be soon. Send the owl through as soon as the door is open, and we will come."

The little owl, still seated on my pack in a corner of the vision, blinked broadly.

"How much time do you need?" Hessa asked.

I thought of the forest between the lake and I, of the Revenants and human enemies between. I could reach the lake in two days under normal circumstances, but I was hunted and the world was at war. Imilidese's foxfire had spread everywhere, and despite the snow swept in by the Winterborn, it was only a matter of time before her servants found me—both here and in the forest above.

Understanding unfurled inside me, so grim I couldn't speak it aloud. So I didn't.

"I can be there in three days," I said. "Will you be ready to stop her?"

I didn't need to specify who "her" was. Hessa nodded and spoke quickly, sketching details. But though I heard her, my mind was filled not with her words, but the way her mask slipped from her face as she spoke. By the time her voice was spent, she looked at me plainly, with raw fear and determination and resignation in her eyes.

"I love you, child," she murmured as the edges of her began to blur and the owl, still perched on my pack, ruffled his feathers. "Stay strong, just a little longer. We're coming."

I'd forgotten how early dusk came in the canyons, and the onset of winter only made the darkness more premature. I slipped east past a stand of hearty pines, ignoring how the foxfire fluttered and flared as I passed. I was careful not to touch it, and to keep my footfalls from exposed roots. I didn't want to be found just yet.

Mawny, the owl, flew on ahead into the forest. I carried nothing but the knife at my belt, though I didn't expect to keep that for long. I'd left everything else in the cave, save the blue and yellow Algatt paints I'd found in the bottom of my pack and smudged at the temples of my carefully combed and braided hair. The paints reminded me of my father, of my connection to home, and I needed that now more than ever.

I'd left my horn behind too, lying on Berin's folded cloak. He'd know what it meant, but by the time he returned from scouting and saw it, I'd be long gone.

The sound of snow-muffled paws made me turn. Nui bounded along my trail, tail wagging, snow scattering.

I cursed. "What are you doing?" I scolded as she barreled into my legs, happily nipping at my cold hands. "You're supposed to be sleeping."

The hound put her paws on my shoulders and enthusiastically licked my face. I spluttered and pushed her back, wiping slobber and tears from my cheeks.

My determination lagged. No part of me wanted this—to trek off alone into the forest until the Revenants found me and Logur led me east. My will was weak, my heart quavering in my chest. And now that Nui was here, what would I do? She'd follow me and get herself killed.

I put the back of a hand to my eyes, finding them wet with yet more tears.

"Yske!"

Berin jogged up the path Nui and I had left, his face stricken with anger. More figures came behind him, parting from the growing night. Seera. Askir. Ursk, his eyes knowing and his mouth twisting into an apologetic smile.

My escape had had no chance of success.

"What are you doing?" Berin demanded. Both our horns hung from his belt and he was fully armed, an Aruth shield slung over one shoulder and his hair in a smooth topknot.

I closed my lips, watching the company surround me. Everyone had come, trailing out of the gloom with weapons at their belts and various expressions of annoyance, exasperation, or guardedness on their faces. Thray was there too. The most reserved of the group, she watched me with an inscrutable expression.

"You knew I'd leave?" I asked, directing my question mostly at Ursk, who looked more than a little blurry. Why were there more tears in my eyes? I wasn't crying.

Ursk gave a half-shrug. "I had a feeling."

"You weren't the only one to receive an owl from Hessa," Thray added. The others parted in front of her. "I asked the Windwalkers to keep an eye on you."

I looked up at the wind. Mawny circled high overhead, and silver sparked on currents of wind. I cursed myself. "I must get to the island. The rock and snow can only protect us for so long; Imilidese *will* realize where we're hiding, so I'll go to Logur willingly and let him take me to the rift. You can't stop me, and you can't come with me."

Seera looked at me blandly. "You know very well we can stop you."

Despite the threat in her words, my heart warmed—too full, too painful.

"Logur will kill you," Bara pointed out.

"There is a chance I can convince him to let me heal the tree instead," I replied, though I didn't bother infusing my tone with false optimism. "Either way, I can get there and open the rift."

"You're not going anywhere alone," Berin said with finality, and looked from Thray to Ursk. "Can we do it?"

"Do what?" I interjected.

"Get you to the island." Berin gestured impatiently at the company. "Together."

At my side, Nui snuffled through the snow distractedly, ears pricked.

"If we keep to snow, rock, and do not touch the foxfire directly," Ursk said, eyes taking on a distant, perceptive light. "It will not be easy, but it is possible."

Behind him, I saw Esan rub at his beard, hiding a flinch of tension behind the stretch of his hand and neck.

As useless as it was, I gave one final protest. "I don't want to risk you all. It would be easier alone…"

I trailed off as Berin moved closer, unhooking my horn from his belt and reaching to fix it to mine. Then he took my cheek with chiding affection and held my gaze. "You're my blood. My sister. My twin. Nothing in this world or any other will convince me to leave you."

I blinked back a rush of tears and gave a grimacing, choked laugh.

"Fine," I managed, squeezing his hand. "Fine."

THIRTY-FIVE

The full moon came on the second night of our journey east. Guided by Ursk, we camped in the shelter of a stand of boulders and huddled close, not daring to risk a fire. So it was that when the light of the moon spilled across me, I was nestled between Thray and Berin, and there was nowhere to hide.

The pain began slowly—memories of cuts and bruises, swelling and fading and chasing one another as my body began to seize. Then came the aching of my bones and the phantom taste of blood in my mouth. I felt the bite of arrowheads, crushing blows and lacerating claws.

I reached for my knife. My arm moved sluggishly, each stretch of my finger marked with absolute agony. I would have screamed, but all that left my lips was a thin, crackling exhalation.

The frigid handle of the knife brushed my palm. I closed my fingers, but could find no grip. My teeth ground, my lungs labored, and every muscle in my body began to quake.

A shadow fell over me, interrupting the light of the moon. Through a haze of pain, I saw Ursk. His face was hidden in silhouette but the white fur of his hood was full of moonlight. He wrapped his steady hand around mine and closed my fingers around the hilt of the knife. He—we—drew it.

"What are you doing?" I felt Berin sit up, but my eyes could no longer focus and my ears began to ring.

Ursk replied, his words lost to me. Other voices came too, and I felt Nui's paws briefly on my chest.

My secret was exposed, now. All my companions would see the price I paid for my magic, here, in the darkened woods.

It did not matter. It could not matter.

Blood will stay the hand of death.

Pain latticed my body in a fresh, writhing wave. I twisted, feeling earth and snow and rock beneath me. My knife jarred against rock, and someone tried to pry it from me—gently, worriedly, trying not to hurt me. Ursk spoke, and their grip retreated.

I felt the back of my other hand on the cool ground, open and twitching with the remnants of someone else's pain. Then my blade found the exposed palm, and I cut.

There was no new pain, only a sudden cessation of it—the breaking of a fever, the relief after birth, the departure of a smothering hand.

I opened my eyes and stared at my hand, pale and bloodied in a pool of moonlight. Beyond it was a haze of knees and feet and peering faces.

My dazed eyes traveled up Berin's form. Unconsciousness swelled close, but before the shadows took me, I saw the horror in his dark eyes.

When I awoke again my forehead was pressed to Berin's shoulder, my head cushioned on one of his arms. We lay mirroring one another—I with my bandaged hand tucked into my chest, he with my sheathed knife held to his, as if to keep it from me.

I looked upward, blinking to clear my eyes. The now moonless sky was latticed by bare branches and the night was hushed, punctuated by the forms of my friends as they dozed nearby. Nui's head was heavy on my waist and I saw Thray's white-haired form sitting watch at the mouth of the cleft.

"Ursk said you relive it all." Berin's voice was close to my head, low and devoid of sleep. "Everything you've healed?"

I nodded, not trusting myself to speak yet. There was no point asking how Ursk knew.

"The arrow that nearly killed me?"

I nodded again.

His arm under my head curled inward, pulling me more tightly into his embrace. "I didn't know."

I found my voice, though my throat felt thick with fatigue. "I didn't want you to."

He gave a humorless huff of a laugh. "Yske. I'm sorry. I'm… I don't have the words. Why do you still use it?"

"Because I will bring you home," I replied. His contrition soothed a resentful knot inside of me, but I still felt a tug of indignation. "I couldn't turn my back on a power like that."

"Even though it's blood magic." He spoke low, though this truth was certainly no secret anymore. "Even though it could kill you."

"Yes," I said, the word a shield.

"The priesthood will… I don't know what they'll do." I felt Berin shift, and wondered if he was looking at Askir. "Mother and Father will protect you. We all will. But blood magic is—"

"Old magic." My thoughts drifted back west, to the White Lake and the priesthood, my parents, and the Vestige and the Watchman of Thvynder. But as heavy and uncertain as my imaginings were, Aita was the figure who remained at the forefront of my mind. "But Aita is not my goddess, and I am not her priestess."

Berin was quiet for a long, weighty moment. Whatever he thought of my assurances, he only said, "I'm sorry. I'm sorry for bringing you here. I'm sorry for all of it."

The words were simple, his tone devoid of great emotion, but there was a depth of self-reflection that struck me.

"You can make it up to me," I said, burying my forehead into his shoulder.

"Oh?" There was a new waver in his voice now. "How's that?"

"Be nice to Isik."

He laughed, and murmured, "I'll do more than that. I'll make Mother be nice to him too."

The tension eased, and I pulled the cloak a little higher. Nui made a discontented huff and shifted position, lying with her back to mine.

"What will happen when you heal the tree?" my brother asked softly. "To you?"

"I don't know. I won't pay the price until the next full moon. If all goes to plan… we'll be home by then. Aita can help me."

"I can't ask you to heal me again. None of us can. Or will."

It was my turn to laugh. "Good thing you'll never have to ask."

The next morning Ursk watched the forest and Thray stood above our hiding place on a shoulder of rock, one ear cocked to the wind. The now perpetual light of foxfire glowed over her head from the treetops, lending her pale hair and lashes an eerie glow in the purple dawn. Beyond her, branches latticed the sky, dark and decorated with snow-laden autumn leaves.

"There are Revenants close by, but Kygga is leading them away," she told us as she dropped back into the cleft, snow muffling her footfalls. "We need to circle south."

We set off, eating dried meat and nuts as we went. My breath misted in tired gusts and I kept my eyes down. The company seemed to share my mood, even Nui trotting soberly in our midst.

Noon came and passed. The forest became rockier the further south we traveled and though I felt safer with my feet on solid stone, I couldn't help but fear we were adding too much time to our journey.

Midafternoon, Kygga materialized in a windblown, stalking stride. We immediately stopped, hands dropping to weapons—not against him, but whatever danger he brought word of. The Winterborn tapped the tips of two fingers over his lips in the Duamel signal for quiet and beckoned us.

I broke into a jog to keep up, avoiding roots and keeping to the thickest patches of snow and rock. A ridge appeared through the trees and Kygga waved us onwards, into the space between the stony rise and the sheltering bulk of a drift-laden rockfall.

We piled into the shelter like pups into a den, Berin grabbed Nui, and we went still. I glanced around for Mawny the owl, but I hadn't seen him in hours.

Pressed between Ittrid and Seera, I could just see over the drifts of snow. Foxfire continued to trace a steady glow across exposed wood and beneath the mantle of white, passive and unaware. The sky above was murky with cloud and the daylight muted.

"What are we hiding from?" Askir murmured to the Windwalker.

"Hush," was Kygga's only reply.

At first I heard nothing but the wind and the creak of frozen branches. Nui gave a plaintive whine, shushed as Berin scratched her ears.

Thud. Thud. Thud.

The frozen earth shivered beneath us. Branches rattled. The echoes of cracking, breaking trees chased snow from the canopy in trails of drifting white, the softness of its falling contrasting with the continued snap and rupture of old wood.

A ridge appeared in the forest, draped in moss and snow. But no— that couldn't be right. The hulking shape was *moving*. It was so huge the trees shuddered and snapped in its path and I struggled to find the end of it, but there was no denying that it was alive. A beast larger than Aegr, easily the size of the Hask's meeting hall.

I grabbed Ittrid's arm, and the other woman caught mine in return. Even Seera, on my other side, quivered closer.

A cluster of thick pines toppled with a squealing, cracking groan, and at last I caught a clear view of the beast.

It was a Revenant. The vague melding of a mountain lion and a boar, its powerful body was clad in flaking, mismatched furs, mosses, and vines. Its ribs jutted through here and there and its empty eye sockets oozed a constant, thick pus of white and yellow. Its teeth were a haphazard jumble, though its tusks—as long as I was tall—matched. Perhaps they were even original, still clinging in the skull of a beast that died long, long ago. And should have stayed dead.

At long last its swishing, molting tail flicked from sight.

"Tell me that wasn't hunting us," Bara breathed.

"It wasn't," Kygga said, unfolding from his own crouch beside Thray. "There are a dozen of them, all heading east to join Logur and his army at the lake. The island is already thick with Revenants, and there will be no getting to the tree without bloodshed. But theirs is not the only army massing."

I straightened slowly. "Who?"

"The Arpa have arrived," Kygga said, giving us a tight, satisfied smile. "Estavius awaits you on the southern shore."

THIRTY-SIX

E stavius had frightened me when I was a child. His copper eyes were
too inhuman, too cool and pragmatic. His stance was unyielding,
always alert and assured. His strange, layered tunics and sashes marked
him as foreign, as did his eerily pale skin. I knew from my mother's
stories that the man had once been a friend, kind and loyal. But the
culmination of that kindness and loyalty had been drinking the blood of
the Pillar Eiohe, Imilidese's brother, and accepting the rule of an empire.
And though Estavius's memories remained, their emotion was gone.

The soft fall of his dark blonde curls had done nothing to gentle his
searching expression back then, nor did they now.

The Ascended Emperor of the Arpa Empire, Bearer of the Blood of
Eiohe, held his plumed helmet beneath his arm as he met us at the edge
of the forest with a knot of twenty guards. Behind him, the southern
shore of the lake had been overtaken by a war camp, banners snapping
over sturdy tents, blazing cook fires, milling horses, and some two
thousand men. The sight was jarring, a piece of the south uprooted
and replanted against the backdrop of the Unmade.

The eeriness of the sight was only increased by the ring of fire that
surrounded the camp. Rows of watchful legionaries with their tall
shields were visible through the flames, and smoke drifted up toward
the glowing branches of the Binding Tree high above.

"Yske." Estavius ducked his head to me and surveyed our company,
his eyes lingering on Thray and Kygga, then Ursk. His Arpa armor
was elegant and functional, a cuirass of layered plate buckled over a

padded tunic and covered with a heavy fur-trimmed cloak of lavish but understated plum.

He looked back to Kygga. "Will the rest of the Windwalkers arrive before this evening?"

The Winterborn nodded gravely.

"You must have heard from my mother," I observed. The tree lorded in the corner of my vision, warning and beckoning. "I can still go alone. Logur wants me on that island. No one has to die to get me there."

"No one other than you," Estavius said. His voice was practical, his gaze one of quiet observation. Unnerving, and steady. "I do not take risks, not with the lives of my people, or the children of my allies. We take the island. We heal the tree. We will be there when the portal opens and your people come through." Estavius spoke of each step with impeccable finality and certainty. "Otherwise the western forces will step out into a sea of Revenants, surrounded on all sides."

As reluctant as I was to see anyone else's blood shed, the Emperor's tone brooked no debate.

"Nisien will be there," I commented, still watching his face. I'd grown up with my uncle's stories of his years with Estavius as he once was, hunting monsters in the wild. They had loved one another, and the depth of their affection had been one of the greatest sacrifices Estavius made when he took the throne and became a conduit for one of the Four Pillars.

Now a smile touched Estavius's eyes, though it lacked the depth it might once have had. "He will, and I will be there to meet him. For now, come with me."

The Miri beckoned toward a gap in the ring of fire and we fell to heel. Heat gusted over me with a roar as we passed through, to where the flames had pushed back the snow to expose swaths of withered, parched grasses and fallen leaves.

Beyond the ring was a broad no man's land, interspersed with roped corrals of horses. The camp was a hive of activity, neat rows of sturdy tents amidst the continuous churn of an army preparing for conflict.

Every soldier was beardless, armored and armed, and every knee—soldiers, aides, camp-followers—bowed as Estavius passed. Curious eyes followed our small group, and I caught several legionaries looking at me with more than passing appraisal. But there was no threat here, only the quiet dread of the hours before battle.

We rallied in a large tent at the center of the camp where servants stoked braziers and layered a makeshift table with food and plates and jugs of warmed wine. One skittered in fright as Nui bounded up to him, tail wagging, then surreptitiously scratched her ears.

Estavius came to stand at the head of the table, murmured something in the ear of a servant, then looked at us. "Eat and rest here, while you can. Yske, do what you need to do to prepare."

There was a gravity to his regard that I understood—he knew I was here to heal the tree, and he knew the cost.

I nodded, thumb brushing the knife at my belt.

"How do you intend to get to the island?" Berin asked.

"We walk." Estavius looked to Kygga and Thray, who stood quietly next to one another beside the door. The space between them, I noted, was smaller than it had been a few days before. "Bring me your Icecarvers as soon as they arrive."

I knelt in the snow outside the camp, facing the ring of fire, the shoreline, the lake, and the island beyond. The wind was cool and I was aware of two presences at my back—Thray and Berin—but neither interrupted me.

I laid my knife in the snow between my knees and pushed back my sleeves. Until now I'd marked most of my sacrifices on my hands, but the height, the breadth, and the magnitude of Imilidese's Binding Tree would require far more than that. To accomplish my task, I would need to be more powerful than ever before.

I sketched five runes in the snow around the knife. They were old runes, runes for power and strength, bravery, steadiness, and success.

I felt Berin shift behind me, heard Thray murmur to him.

I infused each rune with the power of the High Halls, the power given to me by its waters and its fruits, its rain and its earth, over so many years at Aita's side. To my Sight they began to glow a steady amber, threads of lavender twined into their hearts like blue in a blacksmith's forge.

I laid my closed fist on my knee, knuckles up, and surveyed the back of my forearm. In my other hand, I picked up the knife with cold-bitten fingers.

"Yske." Berin's voice was strained, pleading in a way that did not ask me to stop, but rather lamented the necessity of this.

"Just stay by me." I looked over my shoulder at him and Thray, the two of them of a height—her white hair blowing in a myriad of braids across her chest, his black hair carefully smoothed back and bound with leather.

Berin nodded and Thray smiled sadly.

I looked up at the tree again, the distant glow of its foxfire diffused by smoke and low cloud. I felt so small and fragile in its sight, one woman in the shadow of a god, facing the end of the world.

I cut. Line by bloody line, I traced runes in my skin. These ones also spoke of power and strength, but they were older than the Eangen markings in the snow at my feet. These were Aita's symbols, learned at her side. I carved my mistress's name rune too, just above my elbow, and traced one for Thvynder in the back of my hand.

I sang as I worked, a low, lilting song under my breath—a prayer to Thvynder I'd learned as a child, when the world was still healing from the fall of the Miri and the war in the south. My voice quavered and a part of my mind squirmed, terrified that in acknowledging my god as I worked old magic, I would invite wrath upon my head. But blood magic was mysterious, and its power vast—if there was a chance my god could hear me today, I would take the risk, and bear the repercussions.

By the time I'd finished there was so much blood on my skin and clothes that I swayed, ears roaring and stomach churning. But my power swelled. At last, I sent a thread of it across my skin and the runes turned to scars, fine pink lines against the parched white of my skin.

A crack like lightning echoed over the lake. I watched an enormous branch of the Binding Tree hit the water with a thunderous crash. Foxfire on the branch flared as waves rocked and beyond it, in the dark void of the Unmade, I saw shadows… roil.

I looked over my shoulder at Berin. He and Thray were not alone. The rest of the company had come, staring at the lake and the Unmade with the same mixture of unease and awe. The Windwalkers had come too, three score Winterborn now arrayed around us with their white hair and scent of snow.

I sheathed my knife, climbed to my feet, and flicked blood from my fingers into the snow.

THIRTY-SEVEN

Frigid wind blasted across the lake, sweeping flurries into my eyes as the surface began to lock in ice. It spread in a thickening fan from the toes of the Winterborn called Effa and one of her brothers, both of them doubly graced with their father's gifts—Windwalking and Icecarving.

The ice began to crackle beneath the snap of Arpa banners, the click and shift of armor, the stamp of feet and the whispers of waiting legionaries.

Beside me, Berin carried a tear-shaped Arpa cavalry shield, sword bared. Esan stood to his other side, with Seera beyond him. Ittrid, Bara, Sedi, and Askir arrayed themselves behind us, and Ursk stood beside me with his chin level and his attention focused on the island. He, like I, carried no weapon save a staff and belt knife.

Lastly Nui stalked the lakeshore under the eyes of the Winterborn and the first lines of stalwart legionaries.

I followed my twin's gaze toward the island, willing my heart to steady. I held my staff in both hands, its end firmly planted in the churned snow. Ahead, the island writhed with Revenants, and I saw more than one great hulking form like the giant from the forest. As I watched another lumbered out of the lake, sheeting water and stretching like a hound as smaller Revenants scattered.

The forming ice gave a deep, rippling boom. It had solidified into a broad bridge, crystal clear, reflecting the light and yawning with the darkness of the water below. It stretched nearly to the island, where a gap remained between the bridge and the far shore. Revenants swarmed and shrieked, climbing atop one another and tumbling into the water in their haste to jump the gap and charge us.

Kygga and Arune stepped forward, eyes set on the bridge. More wind rushed across the lake at their unspoken call, scattering snow onto the crystalline surface. It caught and froze, turning the slick surface into snowy, crunchy grit.

Then an Arpa horn blew, and another and another, and we stepped out onto the ice.

Those moments on the lake writ deep on my memory—the crunch of my boots, the bite of the bitter wind igniting my mind and stripping all tiredness, all reserve and hesitation. Driven snow was our vanguard and the wind was threaded with silver. The sound of the moving army was a susurration and a roar, the blending of two thousand footfalls, the grind of leather and chink of armor and rumble of hooves at our flanks.

Sheltered in the heart of our company, I held out my hand and crushed several snowflakes between my fingers. Some melted, cool and gentle. Others smeared, gray and dirty. Not snow, but ash.

I traced their fall to the branches of the Binding Tree, lording over us against a backdrop of gray sky. The light had taken on an ominous quality, a pulsing, roiling movement like wind-brushed coals. And where the branches burned, ash rained.

"All is as it should be," Ursk murmured at my side, his voice barely loud enough to hear. He spoke to himself—a consolation and a prayer. "The gods are coming."

Another horn blasted, clear and high. The Arpa lines ahead of us solidified, clapping their shields together, spears resting atop and short swords poised.

Ursk and I retreated behind our companions, giving way to their shields and ready weapons. Nui, beside Berin, scented the air with her ears pinned back and growled, low in her chest.

The wind continued to blow and the ash to fall. I couldn't see what was happening ahead of us, but thuds and screeches came to my ears—the first few Revenants, those brave enough to swim the gap from shore to ice. I heard movement down the line too, barked orders and shrills of inhuman pain. Then the horn blew again, and our advance resumed.

Soon I stepped over a butchered corpse, the body of what had once been a child sewn back together with fur and vine and vulpine teeth.

"Which gods are coming?" I asked Ursk as we went. I didn't dare hope he meant Thvynder, and at the same time, feared he did. But would Thvynder side with us and Eiohe to stop Imilidese? Or would they join her?

"The true gods," he replied, turning to me, his eyes glazed with fervor. "All of them. Do you hear the loom?"

All I heard was another horn, this one whining and oddly angular in sound—crooked and off-key, yet sonorous and billowing. Silver streamed overhead in response and forming ice once again stretched over the lake.

The last protective barrier between us and the shore sealed. The not-so-distant shrieks and howls and roars of the Revenant horde took on a harsher, greedier quality.

The hairs on the back of my neck rose.

"This is it," Berin said, hefting his shield. "We make for the caves beneath the tree. Yske, stop for nothing. We have you."

Trepidation and warmth washed through me at his words. I caught his eye and smiled as we stepped from ice to solid ground. His smile back was brief, at once deep and passing, full of meaning and portent.

He was ready. So was I.

Revenants leapt at the shield wall ahead of us, throwing themselves to certain death amid the unstoppable Arpa advance. I tasted the blood and putrefaction on the breeze, the mingling of moldering flesh and rotting mushrooms, of earth and damp and green and twisted life. More and more Revenants already lay dead in our path, and above us the trunk of the Binding Tree smoldered.

A bone-rattling roar shook the ground as not one but two of the massive Revenant beasts charged the lines. One reared on its powerful, boar-like haunches, the jaws of its lichen-crusted skull open and its rotting piecemeal lungs releasing a horrid, whistling shriek.

The monster crashed down on the first three rows of legionaries and swung its head, sweeping aside dozens of men—including the line right before my companions and me.

Only the screaming and dead now lay between us and the horde. The huge beast shook its head, dislodging a limp body from its tusks, and charged straight toward us. A hundred smaller Revenants churned around its feet, leaping and streaking and clawing.

Three Windwalkers materialized, two facing the monstrous Revenant down and one climbing its exposed ribs—Arune, lithe and fast and armed with a vicious spear and a bone-white bow across his back. A fourth Winterborn burst from the carnage to one side, her own spear lengthening as she came. Thray. I just had time to see her slash at the sinews of the Revenant's legs, her pale hair already slathered with black blood, then Berin blocked her from sight.

"This way!" My brother darted and we surged after him. Nui flitted alongside with a vengeful snarl. Smaller Revenants swarmed, legionaries stepped in to cut them down, and the roots of the great tree bubbled from the earth.

Berin's memory led us true. A narrow tunnel opened between the roots and we flowed through, one by one, as the presence of Imilidese swelled. Foxfire raced through the roots around us in serpentine welcome, tracing fresh cracks and igniting old runes. I wiped dirt from my sweaty brow and hurried faster through the eerie foxfire-lit shadows.

Gradually, the path lightened even more, blazing around the forms of Berin and Esan and Seera ahead of me. We entered the central chamber to the light of a dozen torches, laid out as if in preparation for a ritual.

My blood chilled. I glimpsed Logur standing beside the ancient rift, surrounded by a sea of living flesh. Not Revenants, but humans. His servile Fith—men and women with varied expressions of terror, determination, and zeal.

My presence of Imilidese tripled, now so thick the air itself seemed to have fled. I grasped my staff tighter and stood my ground.

My friends spread out by unspoken command, shields locking, and Ursk's arm brushed mine.

"The Gods are coming," he murmured again in my ear. When I looked at him, his eyes were glazed, edged with an ecstatic intensity I recognized from the Vynder priesthood. "All is as it should be."

The Fith formed a line on the other side of the cavern, staggered and twitching, and Logur spoke to them in a voice I couldn't hear.

"Ursk." I tried to catch the Duamel priest's attention, but his eyes would not focus. "Are you here? Are you with me?"

He smiled, and though his eyes did not clear, I sensed his attention return to the room. "I am present. As is Fate. Duck."

I dropped. An arrow sang over my head and embedded in a root. I had just enough time to gawk back at the Priest of Fate before the Fith charged with shrieks and howls.

A spear flashed toward Berin's face. He threw up his shield and spun it, tearing the embedded spear from the wide-eyed Fith woman. In the same movement he hunched, shielding himself as he stabbed out his sword.

The Fith woman fell back into the riot of her kin.

Over Berin's head, I glimpsed Logur on the far side of the cavern. He grinned as our eyes met, satisfaction thick in his obsidian eyes.

Someone jostled me forward. I braced my forearm on Berin's back, sheltering behind his bulk as another spear stabbed past my head. Behind me, Ursk calmly stepped back. The spear stopped a handsbreadth short of his glassy eyes.

Windwalkers laced around us on threads of winter wind and legionaries flowed out of the tunnel on the far side of the hollow. Instantly the cave was full to bursting, with Logur and his Fith surrounded. The smells of blood and viscera became stifling, screams of fear and vengeance battering my skull.

Something fluttered beside my ear. I flinched, turning just in time to see the owl Mawny alight on Ursk's shoulder and fix me with an impatient gaze. It was time.

"I'll open it!" I shouted to Logur, but my voice was drowned. Taken by sudden inspiration, I reached up and seized a root of the tree. Foxfire flared at my touch, and the presence of Imilidese drove into me like a spear.

I shuddered, gagging and breathless, and clasped the root harder.

I will heal you, I willed the god in the tree to hear. *I will free you. Let me through.*

"Stop!" Logur's voice reverberated through the chamber. His human servants skittered back to the walls, more terrified of his voice than our weapons. One dragged at the body of a fallen companion, but the rest of the dead and wounded were left strewn across the floor, dismembered and twitching.

"Yske." Logur remained behind his barrier of subservient flesh. It crossed my mind that there must be a reason for his hiding—a mortality he feared. "Do it."

I stepped between Berin and Esan, shoulder to shoulder before me. "Let me through."

Berin shot me a hard look but broke the line to precede me, advancing through the carnage with the rest of our company spread around us. Mawny fluttered ahead, alighting on the tumbled stone, trailed by Ursk. Logur eyed the bird sharply, but if he recognized it as a messenger, he had no time to intervene.

The Winterborn and legionaries formed into a circle around the ancient doorway, closing me off from the rest of the chamber. Seera pulled a dead Fith away, leaving the stone streaked with blood, and I came to stand over it.

I touched my Sight. The once lifeless network of threads still converged over the central slab, now half-awake and radiating a thin, luring light. I reached my hands into the web, brushing them like the strings of a tangled loom.

I closed my eyes, drawing in upon myself. I listened to the drum of my heart, the rush of my blood. I smelled the earthen damp, and the sour, vile stench of butchered flesh. I drew upon my magic, taking it in and exhaling it with steady, measured breaths.

I waited until my magic was thick enough to drift like mist through the cavern, then I sketched one last rune in the air and pushed it into the threads of awakening power.

Open.

Light burned on my closed eyelids. Power skittered across my skin like the charge before a storm, growing and rising and condensing. The runes on my arms burned like strained muscles and the swell of power... leveled.

It was not enough. My power drained and the rift flickered, still closed to me.

Without conscious thought, I knelt beside the stone slab and laid an open palm on the cool, blood-streaked stone. I stabbed my hand. I felt the pain, felt the jar of blade off bone and heard Berin's strangled protest.

As the pain reared and bile struck my teeth, I experienced a blistering moment of clarity. I saw myself from a distance, from another doorway—the door of my little house on the mountainside, where the wings of dragonflies captured the sunlight and the yarrow bowed under the weight of contented bees.

Then power blossomed in my blood like lust, demanding and insatiable. My head spun with the potency of it and the runes I'd carved in my flesh threaded with sparks of lavender-gold fire.

I whispered the name of the rune for opening again. Then there was no more sound, nothing more to see. The rift unlocked in a blaze of golden light and I toppled out of time and space.

I knelt in a world of hip-high, swaying meadow grasses. Above, the sky shifted from color to shadow, light to aura. The air itself seemed to flicker like a waterfall beneath the sun, and Mawny alighted on my shoulder with a soft flutter of wings.

In that odd, ever-changing light, I saw the island as it must have been, before the tree. The door itself was an archway, leading into a small, empty stone temple with a thatched, Hask-style roof. Soft grasses, flowers, and heavy-laden sumac spread in every direction toward the lakeshore and the Unmade, which yawned as broad and empty here as in the Waking World.

In the archway stretched a golden rift, its light becoming brighter and steadier with every moment that passed. And as it did, the reforging sky began to solidify and separate into the familiar quadrants of the High Halls, though they were skewed from my vantage. A clear horizon took on shape too, to the south and west and north. East, the vastness of the Unmade still yawned.

I raised my hand, still oozing blood, and sketched runes in the air for communication and speech. "Go," I breathed to Mawny. The little owl took off with a second rustle of wings, passed through my runes, and vanished west.

Time and space distorted again as I waited. I bled, not willing to risk the flow of power, and for a time I lost myself in the heady pain. I heard no sound save the swish and clack that I distantly marked as a loom. The loom of Fate, I supposed. Weaving. Weaving time, weaving our lives. Weaving the beginnings and ends of us all.

Finally, across the meadow, a sea of faces came into sight. But I saw only one—my mother, her lynx-painted shield at her shoulder and her eyes smeared with black paint.

She began to run as they drew near, her boots eating up the distance, grasses parting. The full force of the west followed with her—Eangen and Algatt, Soulderni and Duamel, Winterborn and Vynder.

I rose to my feet, slowly. I put a hand to the rift and it opened, golden power filling the archway to bursting.

I led my mother out into the Waking World.

THIRTY-EIGHT

I stepped out into absolute, unhindered chaos. The chamber was filled with a thunderous, fracturing moan, fading screams and furious shouts.

Berin threw an arm around me as soon as I appeared and braced his shield over our heads. Dirt and crumbling wood, still tainted with foxfire, drummed down like rain.

I blinked dust and disorientation from my eyes. The Fith had fled, leaving only the dead strewn on the ground. Logur too was gone and the chamber contained only our companions, Thray, Arune and some of the Windwalkers, a handful of legionaries and Estavius.

"They're coming!" I shouted to Estavius, his own shield held over his head. "Make room!"

His expression of calm determination did not change. He nodded and shouted in Arpa. His legionaries poured out of the chamber, leaving the blood-soaked dirt open for the army to come.

My mother stepped through the rift as the great Binding Tree crackled above us. Muffled light spilled through the roots and, outside, pieces of the tree fell away with earth-shuddering impacts.

Seera shrieked through gritted teeth and jerked Esan under the cover of her shield.

Hessa threw up her shield too, weathering the barrage. My father came after her, ducking under her shield and resting a protective arm across her back as more and more figures poured through the rift after them—Vynder priests and Winterborn, Nisien and Aita and Gadr and Esach.

As dazed by magic, pain and blood loss as I was, I found Isik's searching gaze. Then more dirt rained down between us, and the ground trembled.

"Effa!" Kygga bellowed.

With a ripple and a hiss, a great shield of ice formed over our heads. I felt all moisture leave the air and the barrage of debris ceased, contained by the silvered power of a dozen Winterborn Icecarvers.

"Clear the way!" Estavius commanded us, but his eyes were pinned on Nisien. My uncle met his gaze and smiled a warm, nostalgic smile as dust rained down between them. He unsheathed his curved sword and wove through the press to the Ascended Emperor's side.

Estavius issued orders and instructions, directing the newcomers out of the chamber, but when Nisien took up position at his side, their shoulders brushing, his posture eased.

We fled the shattering Binding Tree and burst outside in a cloud of dust, disintegrating wood, and falling ash.

I expected to find daylight, but it was gone. Ash smothered the sun and the only illumination now came from a rippling, pulsing network of golden threads across the sky, and the blaze of foxfire from pieces of the crumbling tree.

Revenants hit us in a screeching, clambering rush. There was no time or space to form up—the flow of westerners kept coming, the Revenants kept attacking, and Berin was torn away from me.

A blur of moss, fur and rot bowled me over. Claws pierced my shoulders, a jaw unhinged in my face and—

A wordless shout filled the air. The creature collapsed on top of me in a plume of black mist, revealing Thray running my way. Another figure joined her, dark-haired, lightly armored and armed with a long sword. Vistic, the Vestige of Thvynder, her half-brother by a mortal mother.

They were still half a dozen paces away, chaos between us. The creature's long claws pinned me to the earth, prying skin from muscle and muscle from bone. My breath thin with shock and horror, I fought to pull the claws from my flesh. Blood squelched and pain washed over me in hot, fevered waves, but even in death, the creature seemed intent on holding me down.

Another shadow fell over me, but it wasn't Thray. An unnaturally long mouth opened to reveal rows of mismatched teeth, set in a face that had once been a woman's. Now it looked as though it had been inhabited by beetles and termites, its skin pocked and putrefied and patched with mold.

With a flash, I remembered my staff. I fumbled for it through the frigid mud and swung at my new attacker. Another claw popped free of my shoulder in a wash of warm blood and I ground my teeth.

The new creature stumbled—right into the beheading arc of a sword. Its skull cleaved, and Vistic, the Vestige of Thvynder, bent to pull me free.

"Thank you," I gasped, panting on the snowy ground.

Vistic nodded and wordlessly vanished back into the fray. Thray was nowhere to be seen. Berin was still gone and my parents were out of sight. For a breath I was alone with my staff in the haze of running figures, falling ash and snow, and the reek of rot. Then the wind came.

Isik materialized on his knees before me. I folded into him, arms momentarily too weak to lift. He bundled me close, his chin atop my head, his chest a solid barrier between me and the turmoil.

In that moment, what remained of the Binding Tree exploded. Isik and I moved as one, scrambling into the shelter of the nearest root. I was crushed, nearly blinded and deafened by his shielding bulk—but what I did glimpse beyond him was a vision from a nightmare. The realization of a child's tale of the end of the world.

Over his shoulder, I watched two legionaries bring down a charging Revenant stag. The beast hit the earth but didn't cease to move, instead unleashing a dozen smaller monsters from its belly—weasels and snakes and rodents that burrowed under armor and leapt for exposed eyes. The legionaries fell screaming, writhing, until Thray dispatched the Revenants with a shout.

Someone joined her, pulling the legionaries to their feet and speaking to her, nodding away into the chaos. The Windwalker, Kygga.

Then a huge branch crashed down between us in a thunderhead of ash and dust, shards of wood and scattering combatants.

The dustwave hit us. Isik buried my face in his chest, his face in my neck. Dust and splinters assailed us, choking me even through the press of fabric and the nest of his beard. His body was wracked with a suppressed cough.

Without thought, I grabbed the back of his neck and let magic flow from my body to his. Our wounds knitted and his coughing eased.

When the barrage of debris passed, we peeled apart. But dust lingered in the air, so thick I could barely see more than a few meters—dirty, blood-churned snow, walls of roots and swirling ash on my tongue.

It took me a moment to realize that the pressure against my ears was no longer sound, but silence. Only a few shrieks and calls trailed through the clouds, each bizarrely muffled. All I truly heard was the rustle of the ash's fall, the rattle of Isik's and my breaths, and the creak of settling wood.

A once-human Revenant stumbled by, tearing off and discarding its own jaw with talon-like claws. Then they were gone, and Isik and I stood alone at the end of the world, a mountain of bodies at our feet.

For the end of the world was surely what this was. The rampant death. The presence of the Unmade, so close beyond the veil of ash. The joining of armies from across our world. Imilidese, freed, somewhere out in the murk.

The Gods are coming. All is as it should be. Ursk's words slipped through my mind, devoid of comfort in the midst of so much destruction. For all I knew, the gods wanted the world to end today.

A dead legionnaire lay nearby, eyes half-lidded and chest speared by a long shard. Silently, I stole the cloth that protected the man's throat from his armor, tore it and pressed half into Isik's hands.

We bound the rags over our faces, then I slipped my hand into Isik's. There was a trembling deep in my core, making my teeth chatter and my body shiver, but my mind was clear. I was not afraid—not for myself. My thoughts flicked through all the faces, all the loved ones I could not see. My family. My friends. Nui. I hoped they were alive, but that hope felt too fragile, so small and lacking in the face of this. A pebble dropped into a sea of dread.

Isik's fingers cinched around mine. As we anchored one another, the ash began to move. Its steady billowing changed direction and seeped back in upon itself, revealing a golden light at the heart of it— the healed rift, surrounded by the silhouettes of hundreds of moving figures. The army of the west, still flowing out of the High Halls.

The fragile hope in me strengthened.

"They're still coming through," I whispered to Isik.

Wind came with sudden, staggering force. No, not a wind. An inhalation. Ash rushed inward from all directions, reforming into a swirling pillar near where the Binding Tree had been—a pillar that stretched from the sullied snow to the crest of the sky. At its feet, the rift flickered but held strong, continuing to funnel westerners onto the island's devastated ground.

The rush of ash was over in an instant. The rest of the world became clear in its wake: ruptured roots, fallen branches, scattered bodies and the huddled forms of survivors. Revenants began to flee north, south, and west, scrambling and clawing and leaping back toward the shores of the island. Their number was punctuated by knots of Fith. The humans shouted to one another, coordinating, and the Revenants followed their lead—or responded to the same, unseen directive.

"What are they doing?" I whispered to Isik. "Can you understand?"

"They're hemming us in, along the shore," he replied, his tone far too light, far too distracted for the information it communicated. "Yske, look."

I followed his gaze not toward the pillar of ash, but toward the Unmade. The abyss snaked out above us in tendrils, as if it were wool and the pillar a distaff. Its progress was slow, so slow my watering eyes could barely perceive its movement. But it *was* thickening. Advancing. Swallowing the eastern edges of the island.

The golden light of the rift, still pulsing at the foot of the pillar, suddenly dimmed and closed. I looked back, fearful that my magic had failed, but the doorway to the High Halls was simply no longer in use. Our army had arrived.

Several figures lingered at the rift. They were caked with dust and ash, just as Isik and I were, but there was no mistaking the woman with axes framing her head, or the men at her side. Both their bodies held a deep inner light to my Sight. Omaskat, the Watchman of Thvynder, and Vistic—together Thvynder's representation in creation, all that remained of our absent god.

My mother raised a warhorn to her lips and let out three sharp blasts, followed by one long one.

"A rally," I said to Isik. "Hurry."

We started off at a careful run, picking our way across bodies and joining a flow of survivors. I caught sight of Arune and Thray in a knot of Winterborn. Seera sprinted beside the woman I recognized as her mother, Uspa. Three dogs ran with them, and one of those darted toward me with a frantic, happy whine.

My heart felt as though it would rupture at the sight of Nui's ash-clotted fur and desperately wagging tail, but all I could do was breathe her name and urge her on.

"Where are the others?" I called to Seera. "Berin?"

She looked behind her, her eyes grim but not grieving. "Coming!"

They outpaced us as Isik and I skirted a great mound of root so thick with ash I could barely see the wood. The tendrils of the Unmade spooled out at our backs and over our heads, and where they reached the pillar, they began to ignite in a fiery, crackling light. It washed over us in an eerie, oscillating illumination—burned red and bloody brown.

I was so focused on the Unmade that I barely noticed a mound beside me shift. A jaw opened, right next to my running feet, and teeth snapped toward me.

An enormous paw slammed into the Revenant's head. Aegr roared and lunged, bowling the massive Revenant over as if it were a cub, even though it was bigger than he. He tore out the undead beast's throat with a savage shake of his head.

Isik and I bolted but I couldn't help staring backward, transfixed by the awesome sight of the god-bear planting his paws atop his kill and roaring again across the battlefield.

We scrambled over a rise and there, in the shallow hollow where the base of the Binding Tree had been, the remnants of the army of the west gathered by the thousands. Eyes raked us as we joined, hope flaring and dying in the faces of strangers as we too searched for loved ones.

I did not see Berin.

Eiohe.

The word was a physical force in the air, prying into my mind. Every single person reacted, flinching and covering their ears, and staring up at the pillar of ash that was Imilidese.

Up ahead, I saw Estavius take up position beside the rift, at the very foot of the pillar. His eyes blazed the bloody copper light of his aforementioned god in his veins.

Eirine.

A second name scoured our minds, this the Duamel title for Fate. A smaller form I recognized as Ursk settled himself near Estavius, his body radiating the softest blue light, powdery and threaded with amber.

Thvynder.

The third name came as a hiss. Something inside my body tugged toward it, but I held myself back.

Vistic and Omaskat joined Ursk—Eirine—and Estavius—Eiohe. Everyone else withdrew from the rift, leaving the four of them alone, framed by shattered roots and lorded over by the swirling, darkening pillar.

A new pressure began against my ribs. The tug I'd felt when Imilidese spoke Thvynder's name came again, but this time it was stronger and pulled me not toward Omaskat and Vistic, but upward.

I tilted back my head. The sky was still a haze of smoke, punctuated by swirling tendrils of the Unmade. But beneath the arch of the sky, a blinding new light began. Opalescent and milky, it seeped down toward Vistic and Omaskat, and when it touched them, my heart ceased to beat of its own accord. Something else compelled it—a rush of life-force not my own, accompanied by a presence I hadn't felt since childhood.

"Thvynder returned." I couldn't move, my feet pinned to the grit-darkened snow by my god's presence. I should have felt fear, I knew. Fear of the scars on my arms and the magic in my blood, and the accounting I must make. But I felt only relief, and an understanding that in the face of current events, I was blissfully irrelevant.

This will not be. Thvynder's voice made my blood surge, light and fast. They sounded like Vistic and I sensed the voice came from him, the man who, as a child, had instigated the downfall of the Miri and the release of Thvynder themself.

It will be. Imilidese's response made the shattered roots of the trees shudder and dead Revenants twitch. Distantly, I could see the circle of living Revenants and Fith warriors hemming us in along the shorelines, silent and shuffling and careless of their tattered limbs.

"Form up!" The unmistakable voice of Gadr cracked out over the island, inhumanly loud in its own right and carried to every ear by threads of Winterborn wind. "They will try to kill the vessels of Thvynder, Eiohe, and Eirine. Do not let them!"

Legionaries and western warriors alike began to fan out, raising battered shields into a wall around the pit where the rift glistened and the gods manifested through their mortal vessels. I glimpsed Seera again, and Esan and Askir and Ittrid, but Berin, Sedi, and Bara were still out of sight.

My heart churned. I bent to whisper in Nui's ear, "Find Berin."

The dog cocked her head, huffed deep in her chest, and took off through the crowd. I set off in the opposite direction and Isik followed behind, his eyes straying to the gods.

As we searched, the Four Pillars of the World continued to speak.

All will be as it should have been, Imilidese said, still disembodied in her churning pillar of ash. *Scoured and made new, these poisoned bloodlines ended.*

You have no right. This voice was Estavius's, and when he spoke I tasted copper on the air. *We are the ones who remained and suffered their rebellion. I bled. Thvynder was bound. Eirine gave herself up. But you left us and did not return. We will decide the fate of this creation. Not you.*

I did return, Imilidese raged. There was a direction to her voice now, outside the swirling pillar and near the ground. I sensed it drawing closer. Had she taken a vessel, like the others?

I returned to find my siblings bound and vanished. I would have reforged the world then and saved you, and returned all to the way it should have been. I could not do it then. But I will now.

I stopped walking, transfixed by the power and reality of Imilidese's threat. Would Thvynder concede, as I'd feared before? They all had the power to do as they pleased, these gods who had woven life and creation long ago. That truth chilled me to the bone.

I picked up my pace, desperately seeking Berin with Isik on my tail. Still he was nowhere to be found.

Very little in this world is as it should be, Thvynder replied. Vistic stepped aside and a fifth figure joined them beside the rift. *But that does not make it worthless.*

The newcomer was Feen. Reverted to her true woodmaiden form with its birch skin, she appeared listless, her head sagging slightly and her hands limp at her sides. If Vistic, Omaskat, Estavius, and Ursk willingly acted as conduits to their gods, Feen certainly did not. Imilidese puppeted the woodmaiden, whose skin glowed with twining, insidious foxfire.

The woman hadn't precisely been an ally, but the sight shook me. Beside me, Isik made a pitying sound.

A new sound began with the arrival of Feen. It was a chattering, yelping chorus, and the coordinating shouts of Fith warriors preparing for attack.

The protective circle of Arpa and westerners thickened, shields locking and weapons leveling. Arpa cavalry milled behind, horses stomping and snorting around the snow- and ash-dusted monstrosity that was Aegr. The Great Bear roared. The sound had no words, but I felt its alarm like the rumble of distant thunder.

Beyond our lines, the regathering horde of Revenants and Fith began to advance.

"How are so many of them still alive?" I breathed to Isik.

"They're already dead," he replied, stepping back and drawing his short sword. He glanced up at a swirl of silver as Windwalkers streaked overhead. "I must help. I'll keep watch over you, and if I see Berin, I'll bring him to you."

I swallowed the selfish urge to stop him and nodded instead.

A dull determination overtook me as Isik disappeared into the wind and I joined the flow of warriors and legionaries to the shield circle. I grabbed the arm of a man I thought was Berin, and was rewarded by a blank stare from a stranger. I didn't dare call for my brother, or raise the horn at my belt—not when the gods still spoke, their voices filling the entire island. But I wove my way to the spot where I'd last glimpsed Seera and Esan, and prayed he would be there.

I came face to face with my mother instead. One eye still on the gods in their human hosts, she took my arm.

"Where is your brother?" she asked, her shield and one of her axes clenched in her other hand.

"I'm looking for him."

That wasn't the answer she wanted. After a momentary pause she released me, pulled her second axe from her back with a swift tug, and offered the weighty weapon to me.

I stared at the axe, from its hooded head to its iron-wrapped haft replete with runes. Its name glistened there—Galger, the weapon of Eang's right hand. The weapon my mother had slain her false goddess with, when she was barely more than a girl.

Beyond the lines, the Revenants and Fith continued their approach.

"I know you don't want this," Hessa said, her voice low, gentle without being soft. "None of us do. But our world is broken—that is the simple, unavoidable truth. And if we do not act, if we do not use every tool available to us and sacrifice our own desires, there will be no one left to heal."

Slowly, I laid my staff down and took the axe instead. I untied the hood and clipped it to my belt, leaving the long, bearded blade exposed to the muted light.

There was power in peace and a gentle hand. I knew that with the same surety that I knew my mother loved me, that Berin was alive and that, today, the price of peace would be blood.

My mother passed me her shield, painted with a leaping lynx, and I took it without question. Then she reached out, cupped the back of my head, and kissed my forehead.

I closed my eyes, bowed to her touch, and grasped my weapons with hands that did not shake.

THIRTY-NINE

I left my mother as a Fith horn blared and Revenants charged the circle of shields. The ever-advancing wall of the Unmade was just outside of bowshot now—the Unmade was closing in, driving the Revenants toward us, and the gods had fallen silent. The crash of wood and flesh and steel and bone filled the gap, along with battle cries and screams.

I lifted my horn to my lips and blew. My call was weak, shuddering with each fall of my feet, but it drifted over the shrinking island.

An answering bay sounded from across the battlefield, to the north. I diverted, streaking across the lines of retreating Arpa, Duamel, Eangen, Algatt, and Soulderni.

Seera materialized, then Esan and Ittrid. We didn't have the breath to greet one another, but fell in together as we topped a rise of roots and looked down into a hollow.

There, Berin struggled to one knee, braced on his wavering shield. Nui crouched before him, facing down Logur. Behind him, Bara lay limp in Sedi's arms. Sedi herself slumped over her husband, her face so sheeted with blood I couldn't see if her eyes were open.

Logur looked up as we crested the lip of the hollow. He sneered. It was a sneer of victory and malice, utterly unconcerned by the warriors at my side or the axe in my hand, or even the relentless approach of the Unmade. Twenty Revenants and Fith surrounded him, gore-caked and wild-eyed.

Berin caught sight of us and found new strength, staggering to his feet and hefting his shield. Neither Sedi nor Bara stirred.

Nui released a howling, snarling bark at the riverman. He flicked his hand toward her, and Revenants scattered—half toward the hound, Berin, Sedi, and Bara, and half toward us.

I started down the slope, leaping and scrambling with the others on my heels. We met the enemy with an eerie silence—no shouts or war-cries, just grim, jaded intent.

When a Fith charged, I hacked. When my companions stumbled, I healed them. When a clawed hand nearly tore my stomach open, Seera cut the creature down. When a Revenant pinned Nui to the ground, I took off its limbs with brutal, efficient cuts, and greeted the hound with a bloody, ruffling hand.

There was no fury in my actions, no hunger to give pain or drive for vengeance. Every movement I made was a sacrifice, an act of love and loyalty, grim and bloody though it was. And when I thought of my mother's face as I'd left her, streaked with blood and speckled with ash, I thought that I perhaps understood her for the first time.

When I met Logur, I did not hesitate to swing. The riverman snarled. He dodged my axe and twisted lithely, slipping through my guard, but my shield was there. I threw my weight forward and barreled into the riverman, knocking him backward. Esan and Ittrid surged into the opening, slashing.

Logur fled behind a cluster of Fith—more easterners appeared from over the ridge, answering some unspoken call. They surged to protect him with their fragile bodies and war-cries of determination and dread.

I hesitated, then, as I met the eyes of the young woman throwing herself toward me, spear angled for a gutting stab.

Then Askir was there, thrusting into the gap between me and my assailant. He knocked the spear aside and brought a hatchet down on the woman's shoulder, the movements so fast I could barely follow.

Another Fith tackled him. My axe stuck in their back. I wrenched and twisted the blade, dragging the man off Askir as I did. Distantly, I was aware of the horror of that action—cracking bone, raw lips of flesh and the convulsing of my enemy.

Before I could free my axe, Askir stumbled into me. His hand grasped my arm, fingers digging painfully into my skin. His face was too close, his blue eyes stark and clean amid a face streaked with ash and blood. The Algatt paints in his hairline were nearly wiped away, yellows and blues faded. He'd dropped his weapon, and he pawed at an arrow embedded in his ribs—pawed with the stump where his right hand had been.

He began to collapse. I fumbled to catch him, already trying to pour healing power into his broken body, but he was too heavy and the chaos too thick. My knees threatened to buckle. Another Fith stabbed at me with a commandeered Arpa sword, and I barely raised my shield in time.

The sword slammed into the other side, tactless and untrained. Desperate. I dropped Askir and braced, standing over the prone priest. I caught the Fith's next thrust with my shield and slammed the weapon forward, smashing the rim into his jaw.

The Fith's head snapped back and he dropped like a stone. I dropped my shield too, arm aching, knuckles raw from impacting the inside of the boss. I shook out my hand and reclaimed my axe, then grabbed Askir's tunic to pull him—where? There were enemies on every side. Except for where Berin now knelt, Ittrid and Seera holding back the tide of attackers.

Hands joined mine and Esan heaved Askir toward our friends. "Here! I have him. Go to Berin!"

I left them with one more push of healing power, grabbed my shield again, and bolted for Berin. Ittrid wove past me going the other way, Berin's sword in her hand, and a flood of new warriors joined the melee—a mixture of legionaries, Algatt and Soulderni and Eangen, and the white-haired maelstrom that was Kygga.

The remaining Revenants fled the hollow. If Logur went with them, I did not see. All I saw was Berin. He held his Arpa shield at chest height, but as I approached, he let it drop and sagged back into a wall of the hollow.

I saw the gashes across his stomach before I registered the glassiness of his eyes, and the unhealthy paleness of his usually tawny cheeks. I dropped my shield and grabbed the blade of my axe, ignoring a flash of pain.

"Yske," he said, the word greeting and thanks and love all at once.

"I'm here," I reassured him, and pressed my palm into his chest.

Magic flared and flowed. Berin clasped his hand over mine and held my gaze as I worked, his dark eyes holding my green ones, the skin of his palm gritty with blood and dirt.

"We need to go," Esan panted, rejoining us. His eyes lingered on the approaching Unmade, stretching far above us and too close for comfort. It was a stone's throw away now, and I glimpsed westerners and legionaries chasing fleeing Revenants west around the lip of our hollow, followed by a thunder of Arpa cavalry. Horns sounded, calling a rally.

Esan said, "Seera, take Sedi."

"She's gone."

My cousin's voice tore my eyes from Berin. There she knelt beside Sedi and Bara, her face stricken and her hands clasping Sedi's limp fingers. "Bara…"

She didn't have to say. I could tell by looking at Bara now, this close, that his life had ended—half his face was buried in Sedi's side, but I saw the distant emptiness of his eyes.

I felt the color drain from my face. Berin shuddered beneath my grip and the tears in his eyes had nothing to do with the dust. His one hand tightened on mine, on his chest, and he climbed slowly to his feet, taking me with him. Then he went to Seera, pulled her to her feet and into his embrace, wordless and watery-eyed.

"We have to go," he rasped, his eyes sweeping us and fixing on Askir.

"I have him," Esan said.

"Run!" Arune's voice bellowed from the western edge of the hollow. He was already jogging out of sight, surrounded by a flood of obedient warriors. In moments, we would be alone—alone with the bodies of our friends, Revenants and Fith, and the wall of the oncoming void.

"Can we… Can we go through the rift? Is there any escaping this?" Ittrid's voice was raw and her dark skin crusted with blood. She kept looking back at Bara and Sedi as we left the hollow, ignoring how the Unmade reared in tatters above our heads.

"It's not over yet." It was all I could do not to look back, too, but one last glimpse of our friends, crumpled forms again would help no one. I squeezed Berin's hand one more time and nodded back toward the door to the High Halls. "Our god is here. Come."

The fight to the rift was the bloodiest and closest yet. I moved by instinct alone, all immediate thought silenced, my head an echo of distant observations—a knot of Duamel, harrying and butchering a pack of Revenant wolves. Seera's mother, Uspa, joining us with her running hounds, her hand gentle on her daughter's back as she cried and ran. Nui, racing ahead over mounds of bodies.

In the midst of the destruction, Gadr, former god of the Algatt, lay dead upon one of the tree's ruptured roots, his ribs torn open and his blood ceased in its flow. Esach stood over him against the carded sky, her eyes dull, her gray hair windblown about her head. Isik stood beside her, disheveled and unmoving, his shoulders hunched forward in cresting grief and anger. The Unmade inched closer to them, but the former Goddess of Storms and her son lingered.

I hesitated. My first thought was to run to Gadr, to try to save him, but I'd seen enough death to recognize there was nothing to be done.

Isik must have sensed my gaze. He looked up, reached to touch his mother's arm, and whispered to her. The exchange took only a breath, then Isik descended toward me, taking each laborious step in anguished, human form.

I took him into my arms for one brief crush. I did not bother asking if he was all right; he did not bother placating me. We simply knit our hands together and rejoined the flow toward the rift.

There is a wonderment and terror, I learned that day, in being a human at the mercy of the gods—the created at the feet of one's creator. I thought I knew that feeling already. I thought I had felt it a hundred times as I stood in temples and holy places, as I prayed and sacrificed and sang the songs of our history.

But as we rejoined the survivors at the golden rift, I realized I had never truly known what it meant to be a creation. The worship

I'd experienced before was a shadow of this yawning, crippling, exhilarating knowledge.

The vessels of the Four Pillars still stood beside the doorway to the High Halls. They were silent now, their bodies still and their heads upturned, but I had a sense of conflict, of communication, and the ominous, pressing build of a gathering wave. Light radiated from each of them, and three pillars of light—golden, copper, and palest blue—began to emanate from their bodies. They stretched up into the sky to join Imilidese. The Four Pillars of Creation.

Berin, our companions and I fell in beside our parents, Hessa and Imnir, well but bloodied. My father kissed my forehead, and Nui laced between our legs. The Unmade loomed, its tendrils thick and spiraling, but no one ran. The survivors clustered instead, rank upon rank, a solid mass of flesh that even the last, most devoted Revenants and Fith could not break—no matter how viciously they tried.

In a breath of petrichor, Esach reformed beside us. She did not meet my eyes, her gaze fixed on the Pillars. When I glanced back over my shoulder, I saw the root where Gadr had lain had been swallowed by the Unmade. The former god of the Miri, enemy of Eang and child of the Gods of the Old World, was gone. Hundreds, thousands of bodies vanished with him, and the world shrank. I could only think in passing of their souls, of Bara's and Sedi's, and what would become of them.

All at once the void closed around us, swallowing everything and throwing us into unnatural night. Screams and shouts burst from the assembly, survivors crushing closer, holding one another and praying in half a dozen tongues.

But we did not fade. The ground beneath us did not disappear. The light of Thvynder, Eiohe, and Imilidese remained—blazing brighter and brighter, holding the darkness back until I could look at it no longer. I bowed my head into Isik's chest.

The pressure broke. The gathering darkness shattered and rushed back into the east, back to where the border of the Unmade had stood since the beginning of time. But instead of reforming, it continued on and began to change. It knit into itself and laced with shadows, taking on light and depth and form.

Not unmaking, but making.

Imilidese yielded not with a scream, but a whisper. Feen crumpled to the earth, followed moments later by Ursk, Estavius, Omaskat, and Vistic. All four Pillars vanished from the sky, wrapping us in sudden gloom, and the eastern horizon rolled aside like storm clouds from the sea.

I stared at a new world, its far horizon crested with the light of a distant blooming sun. Light fell across us in bold golden streams and stars ignited in the sky, brighter and clearer and thicker than I'd ever seen before. Mountains rose in the distance, belching fire into a young sky, and the water of the lake began to spill over the boundary into new rivers, new creeks and tributaries between shoulders of barren rock. Steam hissed up through beams of light, and my heart thundered against my ribs.

"How? How are we still here?" Berin asked, hovering close to Isik and me with our mother's shield at his feet. He stared at the newly forged east. "How is that... Where did that come from?"

"They turned her power to creation instead of destruction," Esach explained softly, standing tall and pale-faced next to her son.

"A world beyond the Unmade," I breathed. "A new creation."

FORTY

I watched the pyres cool as midnight drew close. Beyond their low, flickering glow, charred bones and drifts of smoke, the newly made eastern land roiled in restless sleep. Rivers of fire traced the horizon, carving and shaping the new land under a blanket of night.

"Where is Imilidese now?" I asked Aita. She'd drawn up to my side some time ago, her fur-tufted boots silent on a clean blanket of snow. The air was chilled, despite the fires, and I held the sides of my cloak closed—my father's cloak, wrapped around my shoulders by his gentle hands as I watched Sedi's and Bara's pyres burn. My tears had long dried, and my companions had slipped away to nurse their grief together.

"In the land itself." Aita nodded to the fiery horizon. She had spent the battle healing, keeping the vessels of Thvynder, Eiohe, and Eirine alive during the assault. "She poured herself into unmaking this world. Thvynder and the others pushed her power back into the Unmade, and she… went with it. Along with the souls of so many dead." The Miri crossed her arms beneath the fall of her own lavender cloak.

I looked down at my feet. Sedi and Bara's souls, Gadr's soul—they could not be found. The soul of every person who had died on the island was gone, seemingly into the new creation. What that meant, no one could begin to guess.

"I could not save Feen," Aita went on. "Even I could not repair the damage Imilidese's possession did to her… The foxfire was… unstoppable. But Ursk, Estavius, Vistic and Thvynder live."

I nodded slowly. The latter news was a balm to my aching heart, but I had more questions. "Logur?" I asked.

"Some of the Winterborn have gone after him, but it seems he headed further east." Aita's eyes narrowed at the new world. When I looked up at her, she shook her head, anticipating my question. "No, not Thray. She remained. They may not find Logur. That land is too young, too raw. It will settle someday, and will become a land like any other. But for now, it rages."

I let my eyes fall to the pyres, most of which held no bones, bodies lost to the sweep of the Unmade. Beyond them, hulking in the night, Aegr wandered, the profile of his great ursine head silhouetted here and there against the fires. The arch of his powerful shoulders. The claws of his plodding feet.

"I wish I could have saved them all," I said quietly. My grief was an understated thing, hard-edged and waiting for a lonely moment to crumble. "But without your gift... none of us would have survived."

Aita looked at me, cool surprise in her features. "He hasn't told you."

I furrowed my brows. "What?"

"Isik stole the adris leaf from me," she said. "Just as Liv did, long ago. I did not send it. And he did not realize what it would do to you. He thought only to ensure you came home alive. Instead, he bound you to magic I would never have burdened you with."

My overtaxed emotions barely stirred. I thought of the way Isik had reacted the first time he saw me bleed. I thought of the anger and dismay in his eyes, and realized that it hadn't been directed toward me at all.

"Can you... take it away?" I asked. "My magic?"

"No." Aita's response was factual and calm. "It's as much part of you now as your own blood."

I drew a deep breath. "What price will I pay for healing the tree?"

The former goddess shook her head. "I cannot say. But I will be there, by your side."

The promise made my throat thick. "Thank you."

She nodded and the silence stretched. Wind whisked over the coals and I saw a foxfire rune outlined on a half-burned branch, its light extinguished but its form remaining.

"I should never use my magic again," I murmured. "Now that this is over. But I know I will."

Aita's laugh was soft and she looked at me knowingly. "You have power you never should have gained, yes, but that does not erase the good that you can do with it. So do good with what you have. Heal and protect, with whatever tools you are given."

She offered me her hand, smooth and pale. "Now, come. There are wounded to be healed, and I would like my apprentice at my side."

I let her fold my hand in hers and she led me away from the pyres.

The next day, the sun rose in the east. The sky above the new-forged land of Imilidese was scarlet, the orb of the sun golden orange. In the twilight of the island, the door to the High Halls maintained a steady amber glow. Already, warriors were beginning to leave, traversing the High Halls under the vigilant escort of Isik and Esach, and Vynder and Duamel priests. In the face of the end of the world, concessions regarding travel through the High Halls had already been made. It seemed, perhaps, some would continue.

A large company remained behind, mostly Arpa, who, under Estavius's direction and partnered with Arune and Thray, had already begun to help the Hask rebuild and ensure conflict with the Fith was at an end. In the coming years, trade would bloom between the Arpa, the peoples of the east and the west—but for now, homes needed to be rebuilt and bodies healed. The sounds of life soon filled the shores of the lake once more.

Berin and the remainder of our company departed before me, all save Nui—and, to my surprise, Seera. She stayed with me and her mother as I spent four days by Aita's side healing, speaking with my parents and Thray over our campfire at night, and walking the edge of the new world.

I saw Isik little during those days—he gave himself wholly to his role of guarding human travelers through the Halls, and in the moments of quiet we stole together, his grief over his father's death was all-encompassing. We did not speak of the stolen adris leaf. We did not speak of the future, not yet. But we took solace from one another's presence and moved through one day after the next.

When I finally returned to Albor with my mother and the last of our people, our departure was quiet. I embraced Thray tightly and gave Arune a genuine smile, and bowed to Estavius. Nisien would remain here with him, for a time, and his embrace when I said goodbye was warm and tight and familiar.

"Will you come visit?" I asked Thray as I lingered beside the flickering rift.

"I've ten more years to my exile," my cousin admitted, squeezing my hand and letting it fall. "I will finish it, as I swore I would. Though I will miss you, and I hope you will visit me?"

I nodded, smiling for her. I would likely return to see her soon, but for now I longed for home, so deeply and compulsively my bones ached.

Arune caught Thray's eye and cocked his head toward the newly made east. "Oh come now, don't look so grim. Ten more years with me, exploring *that*?"

"And guarding the Aruth," Thray reminded him, but her tone was mild.

"And hunting down Logur," Arune countered, pointing to the new east with a suggestive grin.

"Go on, Yske," Nisien interrupted, pointing me toward the rift. I'd nearly been left behind, I realized, all my fellow travelers having passed through. "And give your brother my love. I'll be home soon."

The journey back to Albor was quiet. The endless reeds of the eastern High Halls had turned into a lush and fertile land of forest and meadows and plains, running right up to the former Unmade. There, the High Halls of the new east were as raw as their counterpart in the Waking World, rocky and barren and riddled with molten rock.

We passed back into the Eangen High Halls through a haze of runelight. I glimpsed the Hall of the Gods on the horizon, once, above the layered, mist-tangled pines. The air sat easy in my lungs, sweet and heady. From the fog, the dead watched us come and go, and I swore I saw Ovir among them, leading his second life in this gentler, stranger realm. My eyes burned at the thought of him and Bara and Sedi, and when I blinked my tears away, Ovir was gone.

Berin stood at the head of the Morning Hall with Isa at his side. The young woman had gained weight since we'd left, the thinness of her frame replaced with a plump, healthy glow. She had her arm around Berin's back and her head on his shoulder while he held their son before the gathered assembly.

"Headwaters of Life, Weaver of the Stars. Pillar of the Four, Eternal, Unfaltering." My mother's voice carried throughout the hall. She stood next to Berin in a tunic of pale fireweed green, her gray-streaked hair braided over one shoulder and knotted with a beaded leather thong. Ursk stood beside her, Eirine's new representation among the Eangen, and a temporary resident of the Morning Hall.

"We dedicate this child," Hessa went on. "A son, born through pain and suffering, beloved and cherished."

Isa began the dedication song, her voice high and sweet. Berin joined in a moment later than he should have, his deep voice thick with emotion. The rest of the hall picked up the words, carrying our hopes, our prayers and solidarity, up into the smoke-darkened rafters of the hall.

Berin's eyes found mine through the crowd, heavy with gratitude. I smiled and, as distracted as I was with Berin and memories, I did not miss the way Ursk looked at the child—his eyes kind and knowing. Did he see little Ovir's future, now? I willed that it be a kind one, though Fate had never been gentle to our bloodline.

I began to sing, too, as Berin looked down to his child. Isik stood nearby but the distance between us was marked, inches that felt like oceans, opened when I'd told him I knew the truth about Aita's supposed gift on the shores of the island, the night before we left.

Isik's lips were closed, the song unfamiliar to him, but the longing and regret I saw in his open, honest eyes made my heart ache.

Slipping my hand into his, I pulled him toward the back of the hall and out the door, into the cold hush of the winter night.

"Where are we going?" he asked.

"Home," I said, making for the gate and the trail up the mountain to where my little house slept, burdened with snow. "I'm taking you home."

EPILOGUE

Warm light filtered through the trees as I shook dirt from my apron and picked up my basket. The earth was cool beneath my bare feet and the air gentle, not warm but not cold. The raining snow and ash, the bitter winds, and the welling fire of Imilidese's new creation were distant memories, now.

The door of the house opened and Isik wandered out, pushing sleep-mussed hair back from his forehead. He smiled at the sight of me, softness touching each line of his face, and shifted the sleepy toddler on his hip. Eela's mass of dark brown hair was as ruffled as his own and she leaned her forehead against his chest, looking at me through sleepy eyes, a half-smile on her lips.

"Walk me to the rift?" Isik asked.

I joined him as he passed through the garden, leaving my basket hooked over a fence post. I followed him barefoot down the familiar forest trail, doubly worn now that Isik spent most nights at my side.

Eela began to chatter, her arms around her father's throat as she called over his shoulder, "Nui! Faster, Nui!"

The dog appeared from the trees, content to trail us with her tail absently waving. I tugged at Eela's tunic as we walked, marking how small it had already become. I'd have to make new ones soon and tuck this one away for the next time my belly swelled.

The shrine sat pale in the sunlit meadow, all weather-worn beams and tiles and stark angles. Isik passed me the child and I trailed him through bowing poppies, black hearts shrouded in red petals.

At the rift between worlds, Isik stopped and looked down at us. He prodded Eela's cheek until she looked up at him, and he bent his face down for a kiss, which she gave wholeheartedly.

Then Isik surveyed me, moving my braids back from one shoulder and trailing a thumb down my neck. We said our goodbyes, the rift flashed and he vanished.

Just as I turned away, the rift opened again. My mother appeared, her pack and shield at her back and one axe at her belt.

"Mama," I greeted, surprised.

"Your father sends his love," she said, leaning over to kiss my cheek, then ruffled Eela's hair. She lowered her pack and glanced around the meadow, her eyes soft and touched with nostalgia. "It's such a beautiful day, child. Sit with me for a time?"

I nodded. With Eela in my arms, we wandered past the shrine with its empty offering bowl. Windblown deadfall and leaves gathered inside but otherwise the bowl was clean, and there were no scuffs on the floor. No one had knelt here in decades.

"Down, down!" Eela protested, and I lowered her to her feet. She darted for Nui, who had lain down in the poppies nearby. In moments my daughter was on her knees beside the hound, tugging up grass and throwing it onto the dog's back. Nui's tail thumped. The girl shrilled in delight and my mother caught my eye, sharing a moment of amused affection.

I settled in, warm and content, and Hessa plucked a poppy. She twirled the stem between her callused, scarred fingers as we spoke of ordinary things, of family and home and summertime.

All the while the poppy spun, black-hearted and blood-red, beneath the sun.

GLOSSARY OF NAMES

A

Addack—A coastal tribe of the Eangen peoples and the name of their former Miri god.

Aegr (*Ahy-ger*)—An immortal bear demi-god, healed by the woodmaiden Liv, and thereafter protector of young women. Also called the Great Bear, or simply the Bear.

Aita (*Ahy-tah*)—A Miri, former goddess. The Great Healer who resides in the High Halls of the Dead.

Albor—The seat of the Eangen High Priesthood.

Algatt—The mountain peoples residing between Eangen and the Hinterlands.

Aliastros—The Miri who became the Ascended Emperor of the Arpa Empire and vessel of Eiohe. Also called Estavius.

Arpa—The empire to the south of Eangen.

Arune (*Ah-rune*)—A Windwalker, son of Ogam. Thray's half-brother.

Aruth (*Ah-rooth*)—One of the three peoples of the east, those that split off from the Fith and are protected by a Winterborn.

Askir—One of Berin's companions, a Vynder priest. Algatt.

B–D

Bara—One of Berin's companions, husband of Sedi. Eangen.

Berin—Son of Hessa and Imnir, twin to Yske and named after Hessa's late father.

Diviners, the—Adherents to the primary religion of the Duamel, which worships the sons and daughters of Ogam.

Duamel (*Dh-wah-mel*)—The people once called the Erene, dwellers of the far north and worshipers of Ogam.

E

Eangen (*Een-gehn*)—The peoples called after the fallen Miri Eang, who live between the Algatt Mountains and the Arpa Empire. Comprised of multiple smaller tribes, including the Addack, the Iskiri, the Meadan, and the Dur.

Eela (*Ee-lah*)—Yske's daughter.

Effa (*Ee-fah*)—A Winterborn Icecarver and Windwalker, half-sister to Thray.

Eiohe—One of the Four Pillars, who interacts with the world through Estavius, the Ascended Emperor of the Arpa Empire.

Eirine (*Eye-rin-ee*)—A god of destiny and time, worshiped by the Duamel cult of the Sleepers.

Erene (*Air-een*)—An old Miri name for the people that became the Duamel.

Esach (*Ee-sack*)—A Miri, former Goddess of Storms and Harvest. Mother of Isik and numerous other children.

Esan—One of Berin's companions. Eangen.

Estavius—The Ascended Emperor of the Arpa Empire. Also called Aliastros.

F–H

Fate—One of the Four Pillars, creator of the High Halls. Now bound within time itself, she governs and guides the destinies of all.

Feen—A woodmaiden.

Fith—One of the three peoples of the east, those that live in the forests and are enemies of the Hask.

Four Pillars, the—The four original deities of the Hall of Smoke world: Thvynder, Imilidese, Fate and Eiohe.

Frir (*Fur-eer*)—A Miri, former Goddess of the Dead, and patron goddess of Imnir, husband to Hessa and father of Yske and Berin.

Gadr (*Gad*, or *Gad-er*)—A Miri, former god who rules the Algatt as king.

Great Tree, the—The ash tree that stands at the eastern edge of the world, in the center of a lake.

Hask—One of the three peoples of the east, those that live on the shores of the Eastern Lake.

Hessa—Warrior and High Priestess of Thvynder among the Eangen, wife of Imnir, aunt to Thray, mother of Berin and Yske.

Hidden Hearth, the—The place within the High Halls where dead mortals are inexorably drawn to lie down for the Long Sleep, where they will rest until the end of the age. Formerly ruled by Frir.

High Halls, the (plural)—The Realm of the Dead.

High Hall, the (singular)—Eang's former hall in the Realm of the Dead, the gathering place of the Miri and home of the Eangen Pantheon.

I–M

Icecarvers—Winterborn who can manipulate water and ice.

Imilidese—One of the Four Pillars.

Imnir (*Ihm-neer*)—High Priest of the Algatt and Shepherd of the Dead, husband to Hessa and father to Berin, Yske, and Uspa.

Inheritor, the—Chief ruler of the Duamel, a descendant of Ogam who inherits the right to rule, as ordained by Ogam himself.

Isa (*Ee-sah)*—Berin's wife.

Isik (*Iss-ick*)—Son of Gadr and Esach. A Miri.

Iskiri—The northernmost Eangen tribe.

Iskiri Devoted—Members of the northern Eangen tribe who remain devoted to the Miri Eang. Enemies of the Vynder priesthood.

Ittrid—One of Berin's companions. Soulderni.

Kygga (*K-eye-geh*)—A Windwalker, son of Ogam. Thray and Arune's half-brother.

Logur (*Low-gurr*)—A riverman.

Miri (*Meer-ee*)—A powerful being possessed of semi-immortality, once worshiped as divinities. They reside, for the most part, in the High Halls.

N–R

Nisien—A horseman of the Soulderni plains, former Arpa legionary, protector of the north, and uncle to Thray.

Nui—Faithful hound and beloved god-dog, offspring of Ayo. Known for stealing hats. Mother of many pups.

Ogam (*Oh-gam*)—Son of the Miri Goddess of War Eang and her consort, the Elemental Winter. Killed by Eang during the Upheaval for his crime of releasing the Gods of the Old World from their tombs.

Omaskat (*Om-ah-skat*)—The Watchman of Thvynder.

Ovir—One of Berin's companions. Eangen.

Revenants—Creatures made of moss and bone.

Rivermen—Male beings of reed and water, related to the Miri.

S–U

Savn—Monsters originating from the High Halls that merge wolves and bears.

Sedi—One of Berin's companions, wife of Bara. Eangen.

Seera—One of Berin's companions. Daughter of Uspa and Sillo, niece of Hessa, cousin to Yske and Berin. Eangen.

Sillo—Hessa's cousin. Warchief of the Eangen, husband to Uspa, and father of Seera, Ulmen, and others.

Siru (*See-rue*)—Daughter of Ogam and a devotee of Aita. Thray's half-sister.

Sixnit—Mother of Thray and Vistic, an Eangen woman of Albor. Died sixteen years after the Upheaval.

Sleepers, the—A cult of the Duamel that worships the goddess Eirine.

Souldern—Once the northernmost territory of the Arpa Empire, now free. Homeland of Nisien and Ittrid.

Stormbringers—Those among the Winterborn who can manipulate the weather.

Thray—Daughter of Sixnit and Ogam, niece to Hessa, Imnir, and Nisien. Cousin to Yske, Berin, and Uspa. Half-sister of Vistic on her mother's side. Half-sister to the Winterborn on her father's side.

Thvynder (*Th-vin-der*)—One of the Four Pillars of the World, an ancient and original deity of creation and order, represented to the Eangen, Algatt, and Arpa peoples by the Watchman Omaskat and the Vestige Vistic.

Upheaval, the—The series of events that brought about the end of Miri worship in Algatt, Eangen, and Arpa, and led to the reawakening of Thvynder.

Ulmen—Seera's young brother, son of Uspa and Sillo. Cousin to Yske and Berin.

Ursk—A Duamel Priest of Fate, a Dreamer Priest.

Uspa (*Oos-pah*)—Heir to the High Priesthood of the Eangen, wife of Sillo, mother of Seera, Ulmen, and others. Adopted daughter of Imnir and Hessa.

V–Z

Vist—First husband of Sixnit, mother of Vistic. An Eangi in service to Eang prior to his death during the Upheaval.

Vistic—Son of Sixnit and her first husband, Vist. Vestige of Thvynder and bearer of a piece of the God's immortal soul, though he himself is mortal.

Vynder (*Vin-der*)—Priests and priestesses of the god Thvynder.

Widow root—An ingredient in yifr.

Windwalkers—Those of Ogam's children who possess his ability to move with and control the winter wind.

Winter (person)—An Elemental spirit, counterpart to Summer, capable of taking human form. Father to Ogam, lover of Eang, and grandfather to Thray and the Winterborn.

Winterborn, the—Ogam's children.

Woodmaidens—Female beings of the forest and trees, related to Miri.

Yifr—A drink that the Eangen and Algatt High Priesthood use to travel spiritually to the High Halls of the Dead.

Yske (*Yih-sk-ah*)—Daughter of Hessa and Imnir, twin to Berin, and named after Hessa's cousin who perished during the Upheaval.

ACKNOWLEDGEMENTS

It's hard for me to believe that, with *Pillar of Ash*, the *Hall of Smoke* world has come to a close. It's been something of an unexpected journey—from the original short story that was *Hall of Smoke* to a quartet of novels. I never imagined I'd first be published with a Norse-inspired fantasy series! But I love that this is the path my author journey has taken, and I'm grateful for everyone who helped me, every step of the way.

My wonderful agent Naomi Davis, thank you for believing in *Hall of Smoke* and my work, for guiding me and for fighting for me. Thank you to George Sandison and Elora Hartway, my genius editors. I probably sound like a broken record, but without you two my books would be a shadow of what they are today. Thank you.

Thank you so much to Katharine Carroll, Kabriya Coghlan and the entire Titan team for getting my books into the sights and hands of readers across the world. A huge thank you also to Julia Lloyd for designing the covers for all my books, including this beautiful final face for *Pillar of Ash*—it's so perfect.

To all my writer friends, those who listen to my woes and slog their way through my early drafts, who help me brainstorm and cheer me on, thank you. May we tackle many more challenges, celebrate many more victories, and write many, many more books together. A special thanks Kritika H Rao, for your unending emotional support during the writing and editing of *Pillar of Ash* and what was one of the most tumultuous and difficult seasons of my personal life.

To my friends, my parents and brother, my husband, my grandparents and extended family, thank you for your tireless support and excitement!

An immense thank you to the reviewers, bloggers and creators who have supported this series and my work as a whole. You are absolute heroes, and please know that your work is seen and appreciated, and truly makes a difference.

Finally, thank you so much to all my readers, especially YOU, reading these words right now—you who have stuck with this series from beginning to end, who saw young and desperate Hessa through to her final, indomitable form, who have followed the generations of the *Hall of Smoke* world and filled my inbox with excitement about each cover reveal and publication day. Thank you! From here, I hope you'll continue to journey with me to many more new worlds, with new characters and new adventures.

About the author

H.M. Long is a Canadian author who inhabits a ramshackle cabin in Ontario, Canada, with her husband and dog. However, she can often be spotted snooping about museums or wandering the Alps. She is the author of *Hall of Smoke*, *Temple of No God*, *Barrow of Winter* and *Pillar of Ash*, along with *Dark Water Daughter* and *Black Tide Son*.

For more fantastic fiction, author events,
exclusive excerpts, competitions, limited editions and more

VISIT OUR WEBSITE
titanbooks.com

LIKE US ON FACEBOOK
facebook.com/titanbooks

FOLLOW US ON TWITTER AND INSTAGRAM
@TitanBooks

EMAIL US
readerfeedback@titanemail.com